W9-AUX-101

STARSIGHT

VOLUME 2

MINNETTE MEADOR

Minnette Meador

Stonegarden.net Publishing
http://www.stonegarden.net

Reading from a different angle.

Starsight Volume 2 Copyright © 2008 Minnette Meador

ISBN: 1-60076-074-0

This is a work of fiction. Names, characters, places and incidents are products of the author's imagination or are used fictitiously and are not to be construed as real. Any resemblance to actual events, locales organizations or persons, living or dead, is entirely coincidental.

StoneGarden.net Publishing
3851 Cottonwood Dr.
Danville, CA   94506

All rights reserved. Printed in the United States of America. No part of this book may be used or reproduced in any manner whatsoever without written permission, except in the case of brief quotations embodied in critical articles and reviews. For information address StoneGarden.net Publishing.

First StoneGarden.net Publishing paperback printing:
November 2008

Visit StoneGarden.net Publishing on the web at
http://www.stonegarden.net.

Cover art and design by Derrick Freeland

The courageous are those who do what is right...
despite their better judgment.

To Piers for his inspiration and support
To Spider for the days of joy and laughter
To Roland for believing in his little sister
To Shirley for her guidance and faith

STARSIGHT, VOLUME II

(For a synopsis of Volume I, please refer to Appendix E at the end of this book)

TABLE OF CONTENTS

BOOK III - THE SIGHT

BOOK IV - THE GODS

APPENDICES

ACKNOWLEDGEMENTS

As always, creativity does not happen without support from loving family, good friends, or kind strangers. There are simply too many people who have encouraged, inspired, and helped over the years it has taken to complete this story to name them all here. Below are but a few brave souls who listened patiently, made suggestions, held me when I cried, or kicked me in the butt. I could not have done this without them.

Matt Meador
Paul Powell
Derrick Freeland
Devon Freeland
Gina Freeland
Jared Meador
Patrick Smith
Roland Smith
Shirley Ann Howard
Dawn Hummel
Steph Bremner
Kris Stamp
Jenny Caress
Piers Anthony
Spider Robinson

CAST OF CHARACTERS

BOUGHMAN - A Master of the Trillone

CAPTAIN ELTS - Sasaran Ships' Captain

CONIFERE - The Trillone Founder

DEINOS - A reptilian creature serving Sirdar

DONNELLY - Sark's first lieutenant

DOTTIE - Saldorian's lady

ENA - Trenara's aide

ERAZE - God of the Earth

ETHOS - Goddess of Ethics, Rule & Government - Leader of the Gods

GANAFIRA - The Trillone name for Joshan

GRANDOR - Keeper of the Books, Mathisma, Third Trial Starguider

HAIDEN BAILS - Captain of the Guard - Joshan's Companion

JENHADA THORINGALE EVENSON - Joshan's Father – Emperor

JONA - Lieutenant of the Elite

JOSHAN JENHADA THORINGALE - Emperor of Eight Provinces – Starsight

KERILLIAN - The Prophet

LEAFLIGHT - A Tyro of the Trillone

LIMBSHADE - A Tyro of the Trillone

MASTER GREEN - Master of the Trillone, The Tyro Trainer

MEIRE - A Master of the Trillone

MOLLY - Madame of The House

NISSA - The Last Mourna

PORPHONT - Master of the Trillone – A deaf mute

PRENTICE ILENA - Chief Engineer, Master of the Ship Builders

RICILYN - Third Trial Starguider

SALDORIAN - Jenhada's Consort - Joshan's mother

SAREH - Sark's Daughter - Master of the Trillone

SARK DEMONTAIRE - General of The Imperial Army

SHADEDALE - Leader of the Trillone Tribe

SIRDAR - Lord of Badain

TAM - Vanderlinden's First Mate

THE DALIGON - Sirdar's Champion

THE OBET - Oracle of the Trillone

THIELS - Commander of the Elite

THORINGALE - Joshan's grandfather

TIGE - One of Sark's lieutenants, a woman

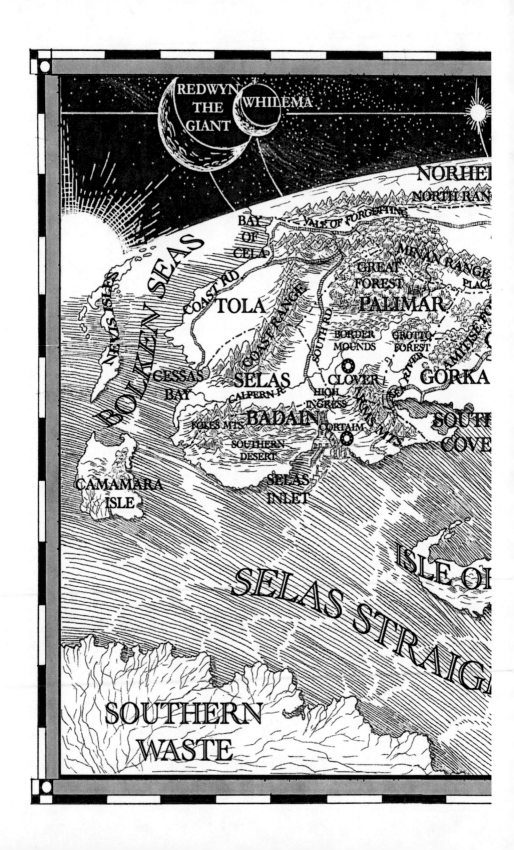

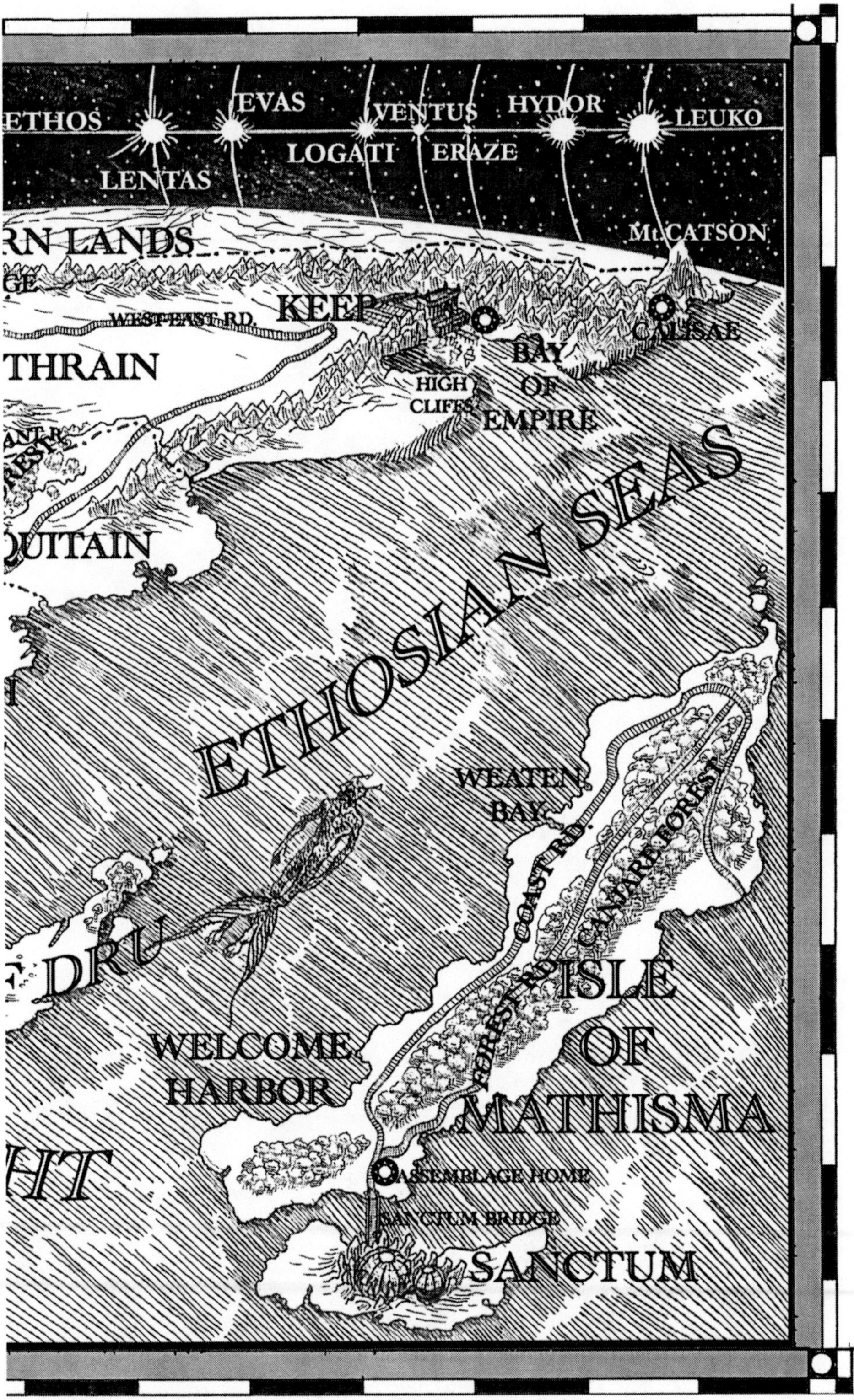
EVAS
VENTUS
HYDOR
LEUKO
LENTAS
LOGATI
ERAZE
Mt. CATSON
WEST-EAST RD.
KEEP
CALISAE
BAY
OF
EMPIRE
HIGH
CLIFFS
ETHOSIAN SEAS
WEATEN
BAY
COAST RD.
FOREST RD.
ISLE
OF
MATHISMA
WELCOME
HARBOR
ASSEMBLAGE HOME
SANCTUM BRIDGE
SANCTUM

Starsight Volume II
Book III – The Sight

CHAPTER ONE
THE ENEMY'S MOVE

The Mourna stretched her wings in the dead night and honed her beak against the ancient stones for what must have been the hundredth time. Nissa stood on the central tower and craned her neck to see beyond the horizon. Initially all that greeted her almost human eyes was the black night in a clear eastern sky and faint icy stars. Had there been anything left of her heart, it would have broken. Crippling loneliness had turned her emotions to stone long ago, so that now all she could feel was a kind of soft pain and a thud of emptiness.

Where is Dornarth? Why has he not returned? She scanned the horizon with those odd eyes and took a deep breath. If Dornarth dies, there will be only one of us left—me. The thought sparked something deep within her like satisfaction. Perhaps it is better that way.

The Mourna had flown to the tower because of the starling dreams. She had dreamt she was a child again, a human child. Dewy grass had cooled her tiny pink feet and a garland of wild korfra had crowned her golden hair like jewels. It was a happy time, a time of innocence, a springtide of youth.

How did it happen? How did I become this monster? Oh, yes, now I remember. It was an attack by night, the screams of her mother and father, the sudden silence— the blood. Then he came. Sirdar, the madman, surrounded by his servants, the giant ebony sasarans with their shining black horns, the laminia with their hideous mouths, and a shadow of fear, the daligon.

How old had she been? Six? Seven? Nissa did not know or care anymore. All she had known then was fear, then later pain, and still later complete degradation when she woke one morning forever encased in the body of a grim and deadly bird.

Nissa looked at the wings where hands and arms had been and the taloned claws that were once running feet—human feet.

How she hated him. How she loathed him for the creature he had made her—and yet, how faithfully the Mourna had served him, as they all had. Her mother and father who died early, her brother who went mad and threw himself from this very ledge, the villagers and royalty of Cortaim, each tortured, broken, and then enslaved by the touch of the catalyst and Sirdar's compelling persuasion.

Sirdar said only the most worthy would receive the gift: a nightmarish existence as the black Mourna. That honor went to twenty-five of them. Sirdar created the horrors in the far north and then waited until he could force a human spirit into the feathered monsters. He tortured them into submission, so they could release the deadly cry of the creature's voice, fill the blank eyes with human fire, and bring to life the lump of ice that served as a heart.

Yes, they had all served him—and hated him.

Then he had fallen, had died under the mountain. They were free from his corrupt touch. Their joy was short-lived. People hunted them like the atrocities they had become. They knew no better. One by one, the Mournas fell to the blades of revenge, until deep beneath the blackened waste of Mt. Cortaim, starved, weak, and beaten, the final six hid from sight.

Season after season passed, and over the long torment, four more died. When the master returned, only two remained—Dornarth the Warrior, and his mate Nissa, the Weaver of Enchantment. Sirdar came before them with renewed strength and demands. They tried to rail against him—tried to fight the words, the voice, the compelling command of the red fire—but they could no longer resist his will. Again, they served him.

Nissa could not decide, even now, whom she hated more—Sirdar or herself. She had wanted to live, even if it meant a half-life in the shell of a perversion. No, she thought again, I hate him more. It was the only thing that kept her alive.

"Do you despise me so much, my pet? Have I not been kind to you?"

Nissa bowed her head low and closed her eyes to the shadow that had appeared at her back, terror seizing her heart. "Forgive me, master. I did not hear you approach. What is your command?" It was everything she could do to keep the spite from her voice.

"You can answer my question, Mourna." The finely manipulated tones of Sirdar's voice made Nissa cry out in pain. "Do you hate me so much?"

The Mourna cursed herself for not guarding her thoughts. "Hate you, sire?" She did not lift her eyes for fear they would betray her. "You are my lord, my master. How could I hate you?"

"It is well to remember that, my pet." Sirdar then chuckled. "Keep your hate, Nissa. It will serve me, as all things do, in the end." He crossed to the stone railing and leaned toward the east. "You seek news of Dornarth, yes?"

The bird lifted her head and regarded the demon's back. "I was wondering when he would return, my lord."

Sirdar folded his hands and the crimson hood tilted. "He will not return. But you already knew that."

The Mourna stared at the dark sea, her voice as fragile as spring ice. "Yes, sire. I suppose I have always known."

There was a sadistic glower in the eyes that sparkled from beneath the cowl. "Does it bother you?"

Nissa twisted her neck and blinked at the sky, trying desperately to dig up some emotion from deep within her numbed existence. There should be sadness, loss, or even hopelessness, but those feelings were as foreign to her now as dewy grass on naked human feet. There was nothing left in her—only hate.

"No," she answered flatly. Sirdar's cruel chuckle rolled harshly on the air. "Has he failed in his mission, lord?"

"No, my pet, he has succeeded; he and Balinar both. They will fall as planned. Joshan will come to me now. Sanctum will also fall. Assemblage will be helpless without their power. It will be your turn soon."

Nissa's eyes sparked with hope. Would the master release her from life as well? Had she dared, she would have begged it.

"Will I be expended like Dornarth, sire?" She could not keep her voice from breaking.

"No, Nissa. I have something entirely different planned for you." The hood pivoted back to her and those soulless eyes cut into her hatred like hot knives. "How would you like to have your human form back?"

A faint light akin to interest flashed in her eyes for the first time in many seasons, quickly replaced by suspicion. "The lord teases me," she replied dryly, ruffling her feathers.

"No, Mourna, I do not tease you." His voice was suddenly smooth and kind, making Nissa cringe at its sweetness. She had learned long ago not to trust that voice, although she would obey it without hesitation. "Come, if you do not believe me. I will show you." There was a murmur of soft sound followed by a tinge of red power and the air became black around them. "Watch."

A faint luminosity irised slowly from within the darkness. Like a midnight flower opening, the light took on form, hazy at first, then suddenly very clear. An elongated bed of crystal appeared in the middle of the darkness. A transparent dome covered it. Within the glass, shrouded by mist from head to foot, reclined a naked human. The woman had long golden tresses that cascaded over her shoulders and around her breasts to end in fine silky curls at her hips. Her lifeless eyes were radiant blue-green. She stared up without blinking. Her form was slight, but flawless. Nissa stepped back from the vision in shock, and Sirdar brought up a gloved hand to touch it. It passed through the illusion like a cloud.

"Yes, Nissa, it is you, if you had been allowed to keep the human body." He let a faint lusty breath escape his teeth. "Beautiful, isn't she? She is almost my greatest achievement. The body has life and breath; she grows and matures. However, her life is small. You could give it more, Nissa. You could give it passion and fire again. All you have to do…"

His voice chocked to a stop abruptly and he staggered back. It was the first time she had ever seen fear in those blazing red eyes and it terrified her. "Quickly, Nissa, take me to the Tower," he said harshly. He jumped to her back and clung to the feathers until her eyes watered. She leapt into the air and took him high above the castle.

When they settled on the landing before the tall tower, he stumbled to the railing like a drunkard and stared out at the sea. Uncertainty trembled in his hands as they rested on the ancient stone. The daligon appeared as a shadow behind them and rushed to Sirdar.

"Master!" the shadow hissed urgently. "I felt…"

"Silence!"

Sirdar leaned against the railing and intently watched the horizon. He spoke fiercely under his breath in a language Nissa did not know. Then, for a long time he stood very still. A small breeze lifted from the east. As it picked up speed, Sirdar swayed to its rhythm. In a startling movement, he brought a black-gloved fist hard against the stone railing that shattered the ancient granite.

"No! I am not ready!" Sirdar cried at the stars. He put a finger to his lips and thought for a long time. He finally whirled on the shadow at his back. "What strength have we left in reserve?" he said to the daligon.

"Nearly three-quarters, my lord," the shadow whispered. "They prepare for the final attack."

"How is our progress on the field?"

The daligon moved closer to Sirdar. "Would you have me speak truthfully, lord?"

Sirdar's eyes flashed brightly and the cloud surrounding his head swirled in violent eddies. "Do you imply the reports are false, demon?"

The shadow lowered before the hooded Sirdar. "Not false, sire. However, your generals are perhaps more optimistic than the facts warrant. The troops move the humans back, yes, though slowly, mere inches in days rather than leagues, as they should. There is a captain among them, a westerner named Sark DeMontaire. He drives his people with hope and fills them with such strength of will, everywhere he appears the humans sing as they fight. The idiot laminia flee from his bright eyes and many southern humans have deserted our ranks to join the Thrain scum. Wherever he rides, he cries the emperor's name and his soldiers take up the challenge until the field rings with the noise.

"Lord," he continued urgently in that dark whisper. "If I could have your leave, I would take half of those that yet remain and march them against this cur from the west. We will trample him under our beasts' hooves to capture Thrain. I would deem it a personal honor, my lord, to rid the Palimar Plains of this menace Sark, whom I am certain would flee like a frightened mongrel at my approach."

"You think so, daligon?" Sirdar said quietly. "Then you do not know this mercenary or the master he serves so well."

"You know him, my lord?"

"It is the breed I know; the hero who fights for what he thinks is right, then finds in the end it is all for nothing, save the vile taste of honor." Sirdar's bitter words robbed the air of substance for a moment, and both creatures gasped for breath until his rage passed. "We have little time, watchman. I will give you what you wish… indeed, more. Release all that remain tonight and smash them down!"

"All, lord?" the daligon hissed. "That would leave Cortaim without protection."

"It will matter little, daligon. You will do as I say."

The shadow bowed low. "Immediately, my lord."

"Now," Sirdar said to the shadow, but regarded Nissa, "that boy, the one Balinar said the deinos captured. Where is he?"

"We still have not been able to locate him," the daligon replied. "We suspect he must be somewhere east of Dru. I can send the tarsian out again to search if you wish, sire."

"No," Sirdar replied thoughtfully. "I will attend to it personally. How long will it take the soldiers to reach the Palimar Plains?"

The daligon remained silent as he calculated. "From here, lord, a fortnight, perhaps a day or two longer."

There was no passion in Sirdar's smoldering eyes. "You have fifteen days, no more, watchman. Do you understand?"

Again, the daligon bowed. "Yes, my lord, fifteen days. With your permission, I must make haste to the camps." Sirdar nodded and the daligon rushed down the wide ramp, disappearing into the night.

Nissa returned her master's gaze and lowered her head. "What is your command, lord?"

Sirdar ran a gloved hand seductively along her neck, sending a repugnant chill through her spine. "A special task for you, my sweet, to prove your loyalty." She looked down at him and those crimson eyes narrowed. "No, I do not trust you, but I do not need to. After you take me on a small errand, you will fly to the Isle of Dru. If you succeed, we will reunite you with your lost humanity. What would you do for that?"

Desire flickered unguarded through her mind. "Anything, my lord," she whispered.

Sirdar pointed to the east. "You are about to witness the end of many things. After you have watched, then give me your answer."

On the horizon, looking like the rosy haze of sunrise, a faint light began to shine. The hour was too soon for dawn. She suddenly realized what it was, a pillar of fire rising in the sky.

"You witness the fall of Sanctum, Nissa, the fall of wisdom, knowledge, and the last hope of peace for these people. You also witness the destruction of Dornarth your lover, Balinar the Heretic, and Palarine the old fool. An era has passed, my pet, and a new world is about to emerge. The Sight is born tonight." The unbridled fervor in his voice startled Nissa. "Watch well. For a force has awoken in the world you will never see again. Trenara will be mine—all of creation will be mine—and Joshan will fall to darkness, as the island has. Light will be gone from the universe forever. Such is my revenge.

"I now ask you again, Mourna. What would you do to become human, faced with only eternal darkness?"

Great tears formed in her cold, almost-human eyes for the first time in twenty seasons, but she did not speak. "What will you do, Nissa?" he breathed into her ear.

"Anything, my master," she whispered.

Sirdar's voice was as cold as death. "Then this is what I command…"

As the light faded, a great rolling thunder of drums echoed across the valley floor beyond Cortaim, heralding the troops that would march to crush the empire.

CHAPTER TWO
ENA

"You! Work!"

The deinos brought the strap across her hunched shoulders and Ena grimaced against the sharp agony that coursed through her body. She bit her tongue to keep the scream inside and scrubbed harder at the wooden planks at her knees. The creature shuffled off to the other side of the ship, his horny head bent as he snuffled at the air, and slobbered faint grumblings at the hot weather. The ship stank of the slimy carcass of the reptilian creature as he shot Ena a hungry glance and went down into the hold to feast on un-named delicacies.

When the deinos disappeared, Ena lowered her head. Tears rolled down her cheeks as she shuddered in pain from the whip cuts on her back. She set the brush on the blackened deck and cupped seawater into her hands. Gritting her teeth, she threw it on her back. The sting was almost unbearable and twisted her face into a silent scream, but it was better than dying of infection. When the pain diminished, she sat on the deck and again tried to calculate where they were.

How long had it been? A week? A month? She did not know any longer. All she knew was torture and tedium. Ena almost begged for the sight of land, even if it meant death... or worse.

All she could see through the crude wooden railings was blue, immeasurable sea in all directions. Ena tried to piece together all that had happened since she had been on this small, blackened ship.

There was the day Ena had seen the symbols on Trenara's brow. That was still clear. Other memories seemed hazy and vague. The days with Trenara, training on the ship was nothing now, only strange words and a feeling Ena had called happiness. She could not remember the guider's face and that frightened her. Closing her eyes in the blazing afternoon sun, she tried to conjure it up. Trenara's eyes were blue—clear, bright blue, like transparent lakes at high season. Trenara had a mane of flowing gray hair; she was tall and slim. Ah, Ena could see her now.

Then there was the emperor, Joshan Jenhada Thoringale, Emperor of the Eight Provinces, and... Ena concentrated on Joshan. He was tall, dark haired, black eyed— there, she had him. Ena's chest heaved in relief. The small crush she had had on him was now nothing more than a fleeting wisp.

Ena could feel her sanity and youth slipping away into obscurity at the snap of the whip and the hours of useless labor. The innocence of her eighteen seasons had succumbed to the abuse; Ena felt ancient.

She wondered if there was anything beyond pain. The blisters on her back stung, and her joints were a continuous ache. Badly bruised when the deinos first captured her, her head throbbed every time she moved it. Her reddened hands were cracked and broken almost beyond anything like relief.

Ena looked at the hands—strange hands that belonged to a full-grown man. Just like the rest of her body—the body that did not belong to her. It was male, tall, and dark, unlike the pale body she had before the monster had whisked her from the Morning Star. Ena buried her face in those hands and thought again that she must be going mad. It was Joshan's body and she did not understand. Why would she have the emperor's body?

An echoing sound came from the hold and she immediately went back to her scrubbing.

After the deinos captured her, she remembered being startled awake by icy seawater when they plunged overboard. She almost drowned with the sack over her head. Then there was the solid deck of this bizarre ship—black with tall, naked masts, and an odd whirling whistle that radiated from somewhere deep in its bowels. The ship moved with the speed of a storm without sails.

Then there had been the day after day of endless toil with nothing more to eat than a sliver of stale bread and a sip or two of brackish water.

The deinos was no companion. He had said less than ten words in the common speech. He needed few words. The language of the whip had proven to be universal. The monster had communicated his wants with the strike of the lash.

From before sunrise to well after sunset he ordered Ena to do mindless chores repeatedly until she would become delirious with tedium. Each day was more dreadful than the last until Ena wondered how much longer she could withstand it.

The only break in the routine came in the early sky of the second day. Lights erupted on the eastern horizon, faint at first and then glowing brightly.

Sputtering in broken hisses, the deinos beat Ena more than usual that day. Ena felt a constricting loss that morning and she could not stop crying. It was as if something terrible had happened. The feeling left her vacant inside.

Ena knew by the fourth day that the ship was heading straight for Badain.

What will Sirdar do to me? What will he do when he discovers the creature's error?

Then, with sudden clarity, it came to her. That was why she had Joshan's body. The emperor had given her the disguise so the deinos would not kill her. They were coming to rescue her. A faint hope echoed behind her ears and made her dizzy. They have not deserted me.

Ena smiled at the thought but the deinos snuck up behind her and brought the strap hard against her tender back. Pain shot through her. Suppressing the tears, she scrubbed at the wooden planks with renewed vigor. I have to delay this ship. I have to stop it. She allowed hope to crawl back into her awareness. Although she did not know how, Ena would find a way—some way to keep them from Badain.

That night, exhausted beyond cure, she forced her eyes open when she heard the hiss of the deinos's sleep. He was on a cot of rotten straw some feet away from the hard floor where she lay tense in the darkness. A cord wound around her ankle, connected to the monster's wrist. Ena knew how lightly the deinos slept. She had often tried to sneak away from the beast in search of food, but he always woke to beat her for her efforts. Even now, his eyes, as always in sleep, were only half-closed, showing glistening slits of green beneath the brown, wrinkled lids.

Ena had to escape, if only for a few minutes so she could get to the hold. If she could manage to undermine whatever was propelling this ship, the Morning Star could catch them. It was her only chance… the only hope that kept her alive. It meant a beating or even death, but she did not care anymore.

Ena spent hours untying the cord. Thread by thread it unraveled. The deinos woke once, but Ena had only to close her eyes to convince him she was asleep. The cord hid between her curled up legs. The deinos closed his eyes and slept.

Just before dawn, the rope was loose from her leg. She allowed herself to sink into the wooden planks to regain her strength.

Ena looked at the section of deck where she had earlier mixed seawater with grease she had taken from the riggings when the deinos had gone below for his dinner. She hoped it would be enough. There had been precious little time to set the trap.

She scanned the hatchway that led to the source of the sound. It was unlocked. The deinos had gone down it often by simply lifting it on its rusty hinges. Ena hoped she would be strong enough to open it.

Saying a silent prayer to Ethos, Ena uncurled her legs, all the time watching the deinos, turned onto her stomach, and got to her hands and knees. In a flowing leap, she jumped and ran for the hatch. She heard his growl and the click of his long nails against the deck as he stumbled after her a split second later.

She jumped over the slippery puddle and ran for the hatch. The hissing curses were getting closer, but with a shout of surprise and a resounding crack, the monster slipped and thudded against the deck. Ena was at the hatch and allowed herself a quick glance at the creature. The deinos was sprawled on the deck, stunned to stillness. Ena knew it would not last. She hauled up on the heavy hatch. Pulling against it with the last of her strength, it finally gave with a creaking squeak of un-oiled hinges.

The air inside was black and offensive. Nearly retching at the stench, she slid into the gloom and scurried down the long ladder, letting the hatch slam shut behind her.

Once at the bottom, she followed the murky corridor as quickly as she could. The machinery hummed and whistled so loudly, the sound made her ears ache. All she could see was a distant outline of red somewhere in front of her.

Ena stumbled against a bin and fell forward. The smell of bread was so overwhelming she nearly gave up to gorge herself. Instead, she snatched a small piece and held it to her chest as she staggered to the heavy door at the end of the corridor. Gobbling the precious food in two bites, she frowned up at the massive door and then pushed it with her shoulder. The door snapped open and Ena stumbled inside. She could hear the deinos stir on the deck above her head.

At the heart of the ship was a strange device. It consisted of many circular metal flats with dull teeth and straps made of a material Ena had never seen before. The chamber was illuminated by a bloody glow that radiated from somewhere within the contraption. When Ena squinted, she could make out a piece of glowing rock at the machine's center that pulsated with light. Ena did not approach it at once. Instead, she stepped away.

The rock radiated darkly, the nearly invisible fumes falling off it like poured oil that flowed up instead of down, making the air unnaturally heavy and hot. She searched the walls, but there was only one porthole on the other side of the whirling, whistling machinery. Over her head, she heard the deinos run across the deck. There was little time.

Ena swallowed the lump rising in her throat. Her feet hung like leaden balls under her ankles as she approached the machine. All she wanted to do was open the port to smell the clean air, to escape the hot, greasy odor. She edged against the wall until she was nearly behind the giant machine and reached up for the port. Sealed tight by corroded metal, the glass was cloudy with salt and decay.

She could hear the deinos struggling with the hatch.

Ena had to do something. That stone. If she could rid the monstrous machinery of its heart, she thought it would stop. Was she brave enough to touch it? Even that small piece of the stone sent shivers through her spine. It was—wrong somehow. Ena took a lumbering step toward it and bit her lip. Her foot kicked something metal. She could barely see the long metal tongs covered with seasons of filth when she stooped to pick them up. They gave her little comfort.

The whirling gears and slapping whistle of the rotating straps loomed up before her when she rose. Her only fear now was touching that stone. Ena laced the tongs through the intricate machinery and opened them wide. A gear bit into her arm taking a piece of mangled flesh with it, but she grimaced without stopping. Sweat poured into her eyes temporarily blinding her. Ena wrapped the tongs around the stone.

Pain shot through her arms. Blisters blossomed on her hands, searing bubbles of fire. Quaking, her scream muted by the metallic babble of the machine, she lifted the stone from it small shelf and pulled it through the spinning belts.

Stumbling and half-blind with pain, she held the stone before her and ran to the porthole. Ena smashed the porthole with the rock and the window shattered into a million pieces of fiery glass. When she released the rock into the sea, an explosion of steam and smoke threw her into the machinery. It ate at her back hungrily as it slowed its ceaseless beat, just as the deinos burst through the door.

Ena's last conscious sight was confusion painted on the scaled face of the creature as he glared at the gaping hole where the porthole had been. Her last awareness was complete stillness.

Ena woke up sputtering to the taste of a bitter liquid forced down her throat. She smelled the rotting carcass of the deinos. Around Ena's ankles were well shod manacles that bit into her flesh and around her neck was a collar made of hammered copper with a chain that dangled to iron bands around her wrists.

She was naked except for the chains and her skin stank of some green ichorous slime the creature had smeared over her wounds. There was no pain. A numb tingling made her skin itch and crawl. Though the skin was numb, her head throbbed until she thought an explosion had burst inside her skull. The liquid worked its way swiftly through her aching muscles, replacing the pain with a hot rush of nauseating fire.

Whether it was the same evening or the next she did not know. The night was black with scattered southern stars and the two moons misty on the horizon to the west. The deinos took the flask away and re-corked it.

"You not die," he hissed in his slithering treatment of the common speech. "You get well. I not kill you." A slow hideous grin spread over the scaled cheeks. "Master kill you when he see you—as truly be."

Ena gave him an unsteady stare, but then saw her own hands and the rest of her body. The disguise was gone, the magic broken by the touch of fire in the hold. She was again the girl. Terror flushed through her neck and crashed into her ears until they rang with its sound.

"Master make you pay, girl. Me make you strong for master." The deinos pounded on his chest proudly. "Strong and ready for master's touch." He caressed her face almost tenderly, the gnarled hand ice cold against her flushed cheeks. Ena buried her face in her hands and wept. The chains rattled and moved in the tie buried deeply in the deck. The deinos lumbered back to his straw pallet on the other side of the ship.

How many hours Ena sat there, she did not know. She was barely able to move in the constriction of the chains, her head pounding when the liquid wore away leaving her stomach cramped and nauseous. Hours passed like days before the sun finally broke the horizon and crawled into the sky.

The ship did not move. The wind had died to a fitful breeze that did not have the strength to fill the tattered sails. It was a sliver of hope that kept her heart from breaking. The sea churned sluggishly beneath them.

Ena watched the eastern horizon in this dead, water-filled world until her eyes burned to see a mast on the skyline. It was a naked dawn. At length, when she could keep them open no longer, she slumped into the deck to sleep.

Day after day went by with no sight of mast or land in all directions. Where before Ena had spent hours of useless toil with little food, now she spent in desperation with no toil, no movement beyond the few scant inches her bonds allowed her. She could not even stand. Where there had been little food, now there was an abundance. At first, this was a blessing. She thanked the gods for relief from famine. Now it was toil more engrossing than the earlier labor had been.

The deinos made her eat and watched as each morsel went from hand to mouth until he was satisfied Ena had eaten it all. The food was stale or dried, and each mouthful became a torment as her shrunken stomach bloated from the effort. If she looked as if she would retch, the deinos poured more of the disgusting liquid down her throat. It would course through her veins and renew her appetite.

Living had become a nightmare of eating, sleeping, and watching the endless sea. The smallest consolation came when she realized her wounds were healing quickly and she was becoming stronger as the days passed.

The deinos had managed to unfurl the sails enough to catch sluggish breezes. By the tenth day, the winds had increased and now the ship sailed at a great clip to the southeast.

Ena sat on her spot of deck and stared at the westering sun as it sank beyond the limitless horizon. As the sun's last ray painted the sky, she thought she saw something to her right. It seemed like a giant cloud of white mist on the horizon. She rubbed her eyes and looked again. There was no mistaking it. Something was there, something of hope and deliverance. Her heart labored in her chest.

Her joy was short lived. The deinos came up behind her with another plate of food and set it before her.

"Eat!" he said hoarsely.

Ena looked at the plate and pushed it away. "I do not want to eat, you slobbering bastard!"

The deinos grabbed the chain and pulled her viciously to the extent of her bonds, causing the collar to dig into her neck.

"You eat!" His breath was foul in Ena's face. She tried to pull away, but the chains held her tight. "You eat, or me push food in throat 'til choke. I make you strong for master!" With that, he threw Ena down until her face hit the platter and spilled much of the food.

With ultimate disgust, Ena stuffed the food into her mouth and the deinos watched until all of it was gone.

When she was through, the creature took the platter and threw it in a pile where others had landed earlier to putrefy in the hot high season weather.

He pointed to the foggy bank of clouds that grew slowly to their right. "Dru— but you not see. Deinos go once. Long season ago. Evil humans with bright eyes. You not see."

But Ena did see it now and longed for those 'evil humans.' Whomever this abomination hated could only mean salvation for her. It was too far away to hear a feeble cry and too near to save her tortured heart.

For hours, she watched the island, each minute a hope that a ship would appear from the strange shroud around it, each second a devastating loss then it did not appear. By dusk they had nearly sailed passed it.

Finally, when she could see no more in the darkness, she once again turned her attention to the eastern horizon. Why, she did not know, for one more sight of an empty sea would tip her over the brink of sanity.

Ena's eyes widened as she looked and her mouth fell open.

Silhouetted against the brilliance of Whilema, rising from the Ethosian Sea, were the tall masts and proud stern of the imperial Morning Star. Ena's heart leapt in her throat and pounded against her ears, as her eyes brimmed with tears. She could almost see the golden serpent shining in the white moonlight, could almost hear Trenara's voice saying, 'Well, my girl, it seems you have had quite an adventure.' She longed for that voice or even the harsh bass of Admiral Vanderlinden as he ordered his crew and shouted for obedience.

The ship was gaining on the smaller vessel. Even now, they may have the ship in sight and were rushing to rescue her. Her heart suddenly sank. They would not be able to see the ship—this black, small ship, shadowed by night.

Ena got to her knees and tried to wave, but the chains held her. She pulled at them as if once loosed she could run across the water and climb on board that ship.

Heedless of her peril she cupped her mouth and cried, "Hoy! Over here! Can't you see me?" Her throat ached with grief.

A hand grabbed the collar around her neck and fitted a key into the latch. The deinos pushed her face in the direction of the ship and unlocked the chains. They slid away and the deinos wrapped his claws around her throat.

"They not hear you, girl." His voice was a vicious hiss in Ena's ear. "Too far. Look good. Last time see mighty ship and friends. Last time!"

The creature grabbed her shoulders in his scaly hands and whirled her around to face the dark foredeck. Ena fell to her knees in despair and tried to scream, but her voice failed her.

On a giant black bird, a robed figure sat. His eyes were a red fire beneath a crimson cowl, his long fingered hands gloved in black and around his shoulder, a ruby mist undulated in the darkness. Ena was numb with terror and could not move.

The deinos whispered his derision. "The master comes for you, girl."

Ena's heart and mind caved in. She folded into a constricted ball of surrender on the deck.

"This is the child?" Sirdar asked.

The deinos went to his knees beside Ena and bowed his head low. "Yes, master, but not him. We were deceived by magicians."

"I know, you idiot. I came for this one."

As graceful as water Sirdar slid from the back of the Mourna and crossed to Ena, his black boots scraping the wooden planks, the sound echoing like a nightmare behind her ears. At a touch, Ena rose. Almost tenderly, Sirdar threw a cloak around her trembling shoulders.

He put a gloved finger to her chin and lifted it to search her face.

"Such pretty eyes," he whispered. "They see much, do they not, Ena? Has my sweet Trenara taught you well, little girl? Has she shared with you her gift? I certainly hope so. The lessons you will learn with me will free you, Ena. You are going to help me change the future." His chuckle grated against the quiet night. "Such pretty eyes."

Although Ena was screaming hysterically inside, outside she was silent and obedient. Sirdar returned to his mount.

"Come." The robes around him flowed like honey as he mounted the quiet Mourna. Completely devoid of self-will, Ena stumbled to the bird. The deinos lifted her to sit behind Sirdar, and then positioned himself behind the girl crushing her between them.

Sirdar pulled on the bird's reins and the giant wings opened to rise into the sky. Nissa hovered above the black ship as Sirdar stared at the Morning Star. He remained silent for many minutes.

"Come to me, Joshan. Come to Cortaim and rescue this child where my gift waits for you. Your transformation must begin."

The Mourna turned on the air and flew toward Badain.

CHAPTER THREE
REFLECTIONS

The Obet sat perched on the highest branch of the signal tree and watched the ships. The Morning Star's approach was very rapid, but she would never get there in time. The girl would be gone before the ship could reach her, taken on the wind by a massive monster of bone and feathers and the madman riding her back.

The Obet watched the two ships, imagining Joshan pacing the deck of the Morning Star, unable to do anything. Even he was constrained by fear. The confrontation was too soon and he lacked the courage to fight. It made them even more kindred spirits.

Beside Joshan stood Trenara, the Provost of Assemblage, the watcher, the safeguard and the lightning rod. She did not know it, but the guider was an Obet herself, of sorts. How would she fare the challenges of loyalty in the end? The Obet did not know; the visions did not reach that far.

On the foredeck stood the giant, Vanderlinden the protector and, if he had known it, the last hope should Joshan fail. The Obet wondered what his response would be if he knew. Again, the visions had been too short.

Then finally, Haiden, the unknown factor, the wild card, mustering his guards and shooting fleeting glances toward the Isle of Dru.

Where does he fit? The Obet asked again. Why is he absent from any of the visions and yet he remains so inexorably within the framework of the story? Haiden, the ultimate mystery.

A head appeared through the crown of the tree.

"Forgive me, Oracle, but the Trillone are mustered and await your command. If we are to arrive in time, we must leave now."

The Obet took one transitory look at the Morning Star and slid from the boughs like a shadowed bird.

"We should have come sooner," Joshan whispered. Tears reddened the already ravished eyes.

Trenara stood beside him, her face drawn and as pale as the moon. "You did not know he would come."

"I knew it would be hopeless." His voice was so bitter Trenara put a tender hand on his arm.

Joshan sighed and turned his back to the sea. "All I can think of is how Ena must feel. Snatched from all she knew of security to wake up in a nightmare that has no ending. Then when rescue seemed an almost hope, to have it pulled away in an instant by what must have been her greatest fear. I can feel her terror, the breaking of her heart. I feel as if—I have betrayed her."

Trenara could not answer. Joshan's words echoed too closely to her own guilt. She took Joshan in her arms, closed her eyes, and they both wept.

Sometime later, Vanderlinden approached them, his face grim, and his voice tight.

"What are your orders, sire? Should we at least go after the ship?"

Joshan looked up wearily. "We will find it empty, admiral. It is useless to search further. Have your crew turn the ship toward Dru. We will dock there tomorrow."

"Aye, sire." Van looked at Trenara who went into his arms. He kissed her gently on the forehead, held her for several seconds, and then turned to his people with quiet orders. Without another word, Joshan folded his arms and went to his cabin.

Although Trenara ached to go with him, to comfort him, to make this better, she could not bring herself to do it. She was afraid her own guilt at the loss of Ena would do nothing more than fuel the flame of uncertainty that she could feel radiating from Joshan. At some point, every guider had to step back and let her student take his own steps. Joshan had to find his own strength, his own path through the darkness. There was nothing more she could do for him now. The thought made her heart catch and she turned to find solace in Vanderlinden's arms.

Joshan sat before the fire and stared at the wavering flames. The golden sword lay on his knees. He caressed it absently, wondering about the future, and wishing it was the past. His mind drifted back to Mathisma and all the words he had said to Assemblage before he left. Empty words? The Crystal had given him the knowledge of Kerillian and Cessas, but he could not use it. Not yet. If he failed, the knowledge would die with him and the empire left with nothing.

He did not want to think about that, so he thought instead of the days that followed.

Trenara woke the morning after the fall of Sanctum and Joshan had told her of Witen's death and the destruction of the Assemblage home. Her grief was so tangible, so difficult that it reached into Joshan deeply, like a wound. In the midst of it, another voice joined theirs. Grandor, the Keeper of the Books, had taken a small boat and rowed to meet the ship. He was perhaps the only other guider who understood the loss. The Mourna had killed Grandor's children that morning and ripped out his heart.

Joshan looked again at the wrinkled piece of parchment clutched in his fist. It had been there for hours now. He was unwilling to keep it or throw it away. When Haiden handed it to him soon after the fall of Sanctum, he knew that it contained something he was not ready to contemplate. Trenara, he whispered to himself, the dread real and unbearable. Written there was the translation from those strange symbols on her forehead that Ena had seen on the ship those many days ago, before the deinos had taken her—an eternity now. That odd forgotten language of Cessas and Kerillian, newly written in Haiden's steady hand. It was a single ancient word.

Sacrifice.

It seeped into Joshan's soul again and as with so many things now, he grappled to understand what it could mean. He feared the worst and forced his mind not to linger on it.

The next days had been anxious in the hopeless task of saving Ena before the deinos reached Badain. Joshan had to try to rescue her for the sake of the crew, even though he knew it was impossible. That was not why he was doing it. If he could save Ena then perhaps not all his actions would be failures. He needed that reassurance. He needed certainty that not everything he touched fell apart.

Despite his efforts, he still failed, as he had on everything. Since the night he had received Vanderlinden's curse, hesitance crept into his mind, eating away at his resolve and confidence, leaving him retched and drained inside. The victories he had with Balinar, the sea demon, and the Crystal seemed nothing more than mockeries of his own deficiencies now.

I do not want to be a messiah! The child screamed inside him desperately.

He wanted nothing more than to be that boy again, to escape his own shortcomings, the awful weight of responsibility that drove him further into despair with each passing day.

Starsight! What a travesty that is. If the gods can see me now, they must be quaking. How Sirdar must have laughed when he whisked the girl away from me. Ena!

He buried his face in his hands.

Joshan heard the cabin door open behind him and the creaking soft footsteps that made their way to his back. He did not turn, but lifted his head and regarded the dying flames in the hearth.

"If you seek companionship, Grandor, I am afraid you will not find it here. I am not in the mood for conversation." His voice was harsher than intended, but he did not amend it.

The old guider slid to the fireside and placed a stringed instrument on his knees that trilled lightly with the motion.

"I could feel your mood through the planks of the ship, sire, and they warranted investigation. Your feelings are… strong. Forgive me if I have disturbed you. I will leave if you wish."

Joshan looked into the jolly round eyes and admired the certainty he saw there. He was grateful for the honesty.

"It is you who should forgive me, Grandor. The loss of Ena has been… well, I should not take it out on you. Please stay." He folded his arms and sat back to stare at the fire.

"Is it only the loss of Ena that weighs on you, my lord?" Grandor gave the instrument an absent caress.

Joshan threw him a stern glance, but the guider merely returned it quietly. Joshan saw himself mirrored in the calm gaze. There was no malice in those eyes, only hope of a listener who could hear without evaluation. Not like Trenara whom he had commanded to judge, nor Vanderlinden or Haiden who could not fully understand. There was serenity in Grandor's eyes and a strong desire to ease the conscience of the speaker, even if only for a moment.

"How did you know?"

The old guider shrugged his heavy shoulders and smiled. "Do you know about historians, my lord?"

"Not really."

"Well then, I should be honored to teach you what I can of them. We are a strange breed, us gatherers of truth, but our craft has given us sensitivity to the nuances of men." Grandor laughed and the sound floated sweetly on the air. "…if not also a disjointed viewpoint of our fellow creatures. Whether guider or king, merchant or lowly peasant, the human plight is the same for each and can be read if you listen well enough or look long enough." His deep gray eyes turned to clouds in the soft light and his jovial brow became serious as he stared back at Joshan.

"I have felt immeasurable sadness in you, my lord, and I have seen so much doubt in your eyes. A devilish thing to play with, if I may be so bold. Doubt of others is one thing; doubt of self is quite another, especially given… who you are." He bowed his head before Joshan. "If I have spoken out of turn, then I sincerely apologize. You may dismiss me, of course."

Joshan shook his head and felt a strange fear this man would leave. "No," he said quickly, "you are right."

"You have no idea how I have wished this was not happening." Joshan's voice was suddenly very young and very fragile to his own ears. He felt a shudder of sadness run through Grandor. "I keep thinking I am going to wake up," Joshan continued, his dark eyes absently watching the flames. "How can I help but doubt myself, when everything I touch falls like sand between my fingers?"

Joshan hugged himself before the fire and tears made stars of the undulating flames. "Sometimes I feel like a small boy, lost and frightened by things I do not fully understand. Yet at other times, I feel like a wrathful god, angry at people's shortcomings. I find it so hard to forgive." When he closed his eyes, the tears escaped and dripped onto his cheeks. "If you want to know the truth, it is not their shortcomings at all, but my own. I am terrified I will make a mistake," he whispered.

"When the people look up at me with pleading in their eyes, eyes that demand that I guide them, my blood turns to water. What if I am wrong? It is not fair. Why me? Why not someone else?" He turned his face to Grandor, but the guider simply looked on sympathetically.

"You do not need to answer." Joshan became thoughtful and ran his fingers delicately over the sword on his lap.

"The Crystal said to seek the Obet. So much will rest on him now. Will he come to our aid? If he does, will we win? If he does not…" His voice trailed off and his eyes became like blackened oil in the flames. "I will not look at that yet."

As the heat of the fire caressed Joshan's face, it seemed as if he drifted away, his brow drawn tightly in the soft golden light. Grandor picked up his lyre and strummed a few minor chords. The music flowed against Joshan's ears like a soft, gentle hand. His eyes closed and somewhere in the back of his mind, it seemed a misty song of enchantment grew out of the quiet room.

He came, they say, from a distant star,
To bring what aid he could.
His thoughts and wisdoms were too far
Above the common good.

He sought to plant a different seed,
Among the chosen few
Who had a gift for seeing truth,
That power cannot subdue.

For many seasons he labored thus
And spread his wisdom wide,
For those who heard the forward thrust
Were those who would not hide.

Then they took the sower's seed,
And brought it forth for all,
But there were met with doubt and greed
Which added to the fall.

When finally the end came near
And all the seeds were spent,
Kerillian put down his fear
And into death, he went.

Some now say, he went not far
But cast aside his flesh
To seek the souls of another star
To spread his seeds afresh.

And though perhaps his words were few
And his visions yet to fill,
With each fresh age we learn anew,
The seeds are with us still.

When Grandor struck the last chord, he put the lyre down and covered Joshan
with a blanket. The emperor would sleep peacefully now, at least tonight, but wished
he could grant him permanent release from his burdens. Sadly, the enchantment of
music was not without limitations. He tucked the blankets under Joshan's chin and
looked down at him, sadly, one more time before stealing away.

When Grandor was gone, Joshan opened his eyes and sat up to stare at the hearth,
keeping his secret safe. Again, he wondered why he could no longer sleep—realizing
now it had been nearly two months since the last time. The mysteries were gathering
momentum as he pondered them unsuccessfully through the long, lonely night.

CHAPTER FOUR
ISLE OF DRU

By morning, they reached the shroud of mist surrounding the strange island. No one among the crew had traveled there before, so knowledge of what lay beyond that cloud was practically non-existent.

The Isle of Dru was not a province and indeed boasted its complete independence from the empire. The inhabitants were an odd sort with primitive customs and strange rituals. There was trade with both Mathisma and the provinces, but merchant vessels were rare to the waters. The natives were not violent—quite the contrary, but neither were they friendly. A ship put to port on Dru once or twice a season.

Van stood on the afterdeck and scowled at the haze. He had heard from one of the merchants that the waters within it were treacherous for a large ship. The coral reefs surrounding the dark blue lagoon were narrow and could tear out the bottom of any ship afloat. Because of the cloud, which lifted only once a season during the primal equinox, shadows covered the bay and made soundings difficult. Ships had to put boats down along the sides to steer though the barbs of coral. Once through the veil, some fifteen spans in thickness, the reefs gave way to a deep harbor.

"Boats are ready, sir," Tam said at Van's side. There was a new crispness about his first mate that Van found a relief. Since the battle with the sea creature, the crew had lost its gangly youth and gained an integrity usually found with a seasoned crew.

He nodded curtly. "Aye. Who do you have to man them?"

Tam pointed to the bustling crew and the boats descending over the sides. "Jak and Thum, abaft port and abaft starboard, Krease and Sores, port bow and starboard bow, Cakins, aft and Toles, fore with the guide rope, sir. The quartermaster will be at the tiller head, and with your permission, sir, I would like to take the helm."

Van could not suppress the proud smirk making its way to his lips. "Thank you, mister, but I'll take the helm this time. You go to the prow and watch the fore line."

"Aye, aye, sir." Tam saluted crisply and turned on his heel shouting orders.

Van mounted the helm and relieved the man at the wheel with a touch. He glanced back to the quartermaster. The man's ancient eyes sparkled gaily from inside the wrinkled face and his grizzled hands caressed the soft wood of the tiller. He was an old timer and Van's original choice for first mate. The man had turned down the merit as he had served this post for nearly forty seasons and did not want to give up the rudder. Van nodded to him and smiled.

"You ready, Hammel?"

He gave the admiral a half-toothless grin and nodded. "Aye, captain. This'll be as easy as laughing, it will. Just like Selas Straights, sir."

Van raised a brow. "This is a tad bit narrower. Don't get cocky on me."

The quartermaster measured the sluggish winds and tested the tiller. "Aye, sir, you can count on that."

Van turned to his crew looking up at him expectantly. "Make ready to sound!" The crew came to life, trimming the sails, readying the poles, and dropping the sound lines.

"Stem," he shouted.

"Ready," echoed the reply in a ripple of voices from fore to aft.

"Port bow."

"Ready."

"Starboard bow."

"Ready."

"Abaft port."

"Ready."

"Abaft starboard."

"Ready."

"Fore."

"Ready."

"Aft."

"Ready."

"Tiller head."

"Ready, sir."

"Foremast"

"Ready."

"Mainmast."

"Ready."

"Mizzen."

"Ready, sir. All trimmed."

"How's the tack?" he shouted to Hammel.

"Slow and even, sir."

Van nodded without looking back and wrapped his hands around the wheel. "All right, mates—hoist anchor. Steady as she goes."

In a fluid movement that made Vanderlinden beam with pride, the crew moved as one and the Morning Star lurched forward.

Joshan, Trenara, Haiden, and Grandor stood atop the forecastle and watched the miracle at work. The ship hummed with life as soundings echoed back and forth, trim orders rose for each of the three sets of sails, and the ship glided toward the misty cloud. When the forward boat disappeared through the dense whiteness there was an anxious stillness for a split second, but the 'all's well' that echoed back animated the crew with renewed fervor.

When the prow went through the cloud, Trenara leaned forward on the railing and strained to see. So many legends and myths surrounded this tiny island, hardly larger than the Keep itself, she felt a kind of schoolgirl excitement as they approached.

For several minutes, nothing broke the silence of the misty world but the muted voices of the sailors as they called out directions and soundings. The haze seemed more like thin smoke than water vapor, as it did not moisten as a cloud would, and it had an odd odor. Not unpleasant, just wholly mystifying.

"What do you make of that smell, sire?" Trenara's words suffocated in the tepid mist.

Joshan shook his head. His smile was wistful, sparking a kind of contentment around his eyes. "I do not know, Trenara. It comforts me, somehow. I feel as if I am coming home."

Trenara glanced at him, but Joshan was lost in his thoughts and said nothing more.

There was a shout from the lead boat. "Through the veil, sir, and the way is clear beyond." His voice was touched with a shaky awe.

The shout rippled back to the admiral and a relieved murmur ran through the crew. They still had yet to bring the full keel through, but the worst was over.

Through the haze, the sound of tide rushing to the shore filled the air. Loud twitters rose from great flocks of sea scalards and sand pips. Joshan suddenly leapt to the prow and stood next to Tam in anticipation.

When the nose of the ship broke through the clouds, the veil lifted. A bright blue sky and lagoon sparkled around the precious green gem that met between them.

Deep, dark green forests covered the island like soft billowing clouds beyond the shining white beaches. Bright colored birds chimed in the trees lending the green a richness of color that moved like a living rainbow. Frothy blue streams ran through the foliage and down to the beach in white crescents. All around the cove, lush flowers bloomed. Beyond the trees that lined the bay, a mountain rose to skim the sky, a magnificent blue giant, its head touched with snow and clouds. At its feet were giant trees that grew side by side towering high above their beachfront neighbors. Their crowns were long and flat while their gray trunks seemed made of smooth seasoned leather.

The wind lifted the imperial banner tied to the mainmast as it broke the cloud and sent the serpent slithering brilliantly in the hot sun.

Joshan wiped sweat from his brow and loosened his leather vest until it opened to the waist. Here on this tiny island lay answers and possibly a kind of relief. He had not felt such exhilaration or desire since before he came to power those many months before.

Trenara joined him on the foredeck, her eyes shining in the bright tropical sun.

"I had no idea it could be this beautiful."

"I did," Joshan replied, scanning the island. "It is as the vision painted it—more so. The colors! I have never seen any more radiant. I am afraid the mainland will seem dull after this."

Trenara said nothing, for the moment content to gaze in wonder at what nature had built from the sea.

When the first mate shouted the Morning Star was well through the coral, the anchor dropped into the middle of the lagoon, the sails furled, and the lines secured, leaving the Morning Star a skeletal image of masts and ropes.

Trenara excused herself to go below to get dressed for the landing as Vanderlinden and Haiden joined Joshan.

"That was brilliant maneuvering, Admiral," Joshan said letting an aide help him into his pack.

"Thank you, sire. But I can't take the credit. The crew did the work, though it was a bit touch and go for a while there."

Haiden looked at the island wide-eyed and shook his head. "Gods! What a sight. If Mati Foresons could see me now, she'd be green with envy. Look at them trees, now. I haven't seen their like—and the flowers. I'd like to get a closer look, if those birds would let me near them." He glanced at Joshan with a half-crooked smile. "If I didn't know better, I'd swear I was sleeping and this was a dream. But still and all, beautiful as it looks, there seems to be a strange kind of enchantment around those trees, like if you asked them a question they'd up and answer you straight away."

Joshan laughed and slapped Haiden on the back soundly. "As for that, my dear friend, you will know soon enough. You can ask them yourself."

Haiden curled the side of his lip and scratched his head. "I thought you and the guider were going to look for the Obet."

Joshan adjusted the strap over his shoulder. "Come now, my fine protector, you do not think I would deny those trees a conversation with the master of words, do you? Besides, we have to find a guide through that forest, and it is said where flowery words and speeches fail, wit will often suffice. If by your character alone, you cannot convince the natives of our sincerity, then we will need to make it through that forest without help. I will need both you and the giant for that."

Haiden blushed to the ears and looked at his hands. "Well, thank you for that. As for character, if they balk at you then they aren't worth their salt, if you take my meaning. I can't see anyone turning you down."

Joshan frowned and looked up at the mountain. "I hope you are right, Haiden."

A longboat slid over the port bow and a shroud fell in place above it to allow the passengers to board. The aides were packing provisions when Trenara appeared from the hold.

Joshan had never seen his mentor in anything but robes since before he could remember, so the sight of the guider in leather leggings, jerkin, and a short-sleeved thin woven shirt was both comical and odd. Her white hair fell in a long braid behind her neck and she looked every bit the thrilling adventurer.

"A vast improvement, I must say," Joshan taunted, echoing his mentor's words when the emperor had first donned an ornate robe. "You are looking the proper adventurer now."

Vanderlinden doubled over with mirth and Haiden was unsuccessful in trying to suppress a smile finding its way around the corners of his mouth.

"Now aren't you the handsome one?" Van chortled, barely able to talk.

Trenara's eyes flashed angrily. "Well, I cannot very well go traipsing through the jungle in my robe. Unless you would like to help me pick my hem out of the foliage."

Joshan put a hand on her shoulder and thought the guider really did look quite beautiful after the initial shock of the change was over. The clothes accentuated a perfect figure, the colors making her blue eyes bright and her face soft and lovely. Trenara cut quite a dashing figure in the tall leather boots and well-fitting woodsman gear. Joshan blushed unaccountably for a moment, her loveliness sparking something deep within him that he could not immediately fathom.

"Of course you are right, guider," he said quietly, clearing the feeling from his throat. "I sincerely apologize. It is just I had never thought what a difference clothes make. You really do look very nice."

Van picked her up off her feet to kiss her. "Very nice indeed!" he said and kissed her again.

"Oh, put me down, you big oaf. You are not forgiven that easily."

Van put her down and bowed his head very low. "I sincerely apologize, my beautiful lady." He held out his arm for her. "Shall we go?"

He escorted her to the boat, then lifted himself over the side and scurried down the lines of the shroud as if his massive bulk were weightless.

When they were all aboard, the oarsmen rowed them to the shore and the four companions got out of the boat slowly, scanning the terrain with wondering eyes. The closer they got to the forest, the more stunning it became.

"Which way now, sire?" Van asked.

Joshan scanned the trees and tropical foliage. "Follow me," he said and led them through the dense brush above the shoreline.

The going was very slow as the brush was thick and impassable in places. The air was alive with stinging insects and soon the paradise became a torture of swatting pests and steaming heat. The only one who seemed unaffected by the bites was Haiden.

"You got some kind of potion you're not telling us about?" Van asked as he slapped at an insect on his neck.

Haiden shrugged and pushed the bushes aside for the emperor. "I guess they just don't ken to my blood."

Trenara snorted. "Well, they 'ken' to mine well enough. Gads, how I wish I had my power. I would give them a taste of guider's blood they would not soon forget." She slapped her arm and trudged along after Joshan.

A short time later, the brush lightened and they found a narrow trail. Joshan took a sip of water from his pouch and wiped sweat from his brow.

"Well, at least we have a clear path. Maybe the insects will let up now. Come on."

Joshan felt a presence the further they moved toward the heart of the island. The brush grew taller and thickened until there was a wall of it on either side of them. A sense of danger started as a pit in his stomach that made its way up his spine. When he slowed his pace, Van almost ran into him. Joshan lifted his arm and stopped them.

"What's wrong?" the giant asked, touching his sword.

"I do not know…"

There was a sudden hiss and then a barely audible whish as something dropped from above their heads and made straight for the giant's neck. Almost at the same time, an abrupt blur knocked Joshan and Vanderlinden back and absorbed the thing before it could hit its mark.

When the shadow stopped some feet from the stunned companions, it stood erect as a man, as tall as Van, with a stern bearded face and a giant serpent held by the neck struggling in his hand. Before the snake could wrap its coils any further up the man's arm, he stepped back and threw it into the forest where it bounced and then slithered away. The man stood at rigid attention.

Appearing out of the darkened forest like a ghost, an ancient woman walked toward them, cackling wildly, her hands and face gnarled. She stopped in front of Joshan and lifted milky brown eyes to stare up at his face. He could not see into her mind, which bothered him. Something hid there under the many wrinkles that lined her face and pinched her lips.

"Are you the one they call the Sight?" The heavily accented voice was quiet and ancient.

Joshan blinked at her. "Some call me that."

She nodded curtly. "You seek the Oracle?"

"We… seek one we call the Obet. A prophet or a wise man."

The old woman chuckled again. "Let me see your hands, child." Joshan took off his gloves and opened his palms for the woman to examine. She touched his palms gingerly and gave him a shaky nod. "Ganafira," she whispered. Blue veined fingers brushed the crystals and a slow smile wrinkled her face. "I will lead you to the Oracle, Ganafira. I and the silent one." She nodded to the man who had not moved.

"Who are you?" Joshan asked.

The woman bowed low and came up with a sparkling eye. "I am called Miere and the silent one there is Porphont. We are servants of the Oracle and are here to greet you. The Oracle awaits you at the Signal Tree. I will take you there."

The companions shifted uneasily behind Joshan. "What is it you called me?"

"Ganafira, my lord."

"Wait a minute," Van said. "Isn't that was Sark called you?"

This caused the old woman's cackle to start anew. "Sark DeMontaire?"

"You know him?"

"Who in Selas does not know the DeMontaires? Yes, I know him."

"Then you are Selasian, not Druan? I do not understand…"

She cocked a naked brow at Joshan and patted his hand. "Enough questions, Ganafira. We must leave now. We cannot travel the jungles at night and it is half a day to the trees." Without another word, she turned on her heel and continued up the path, Porphont a shadow behind her. The companions had to scramble to follow.

Trenara caught Joshan before he could get too close to the strange old woman. "Sire," she whispered urgently, taking his arm, "this is very odd. Did you see how that man moved? As if he had no bones. It is impossible for the human body to do that, at least without…"

"The power?" Joshan shrugged and adjusted his pack. "How do we really know what is possible or impossible without the power? We have known nothing else for almost a thousand seasons. You saw it yourself. I suspect Porphont has no magic beyond his own training. What I could do with an army of people like that."

"But, lad, that strange old woman—she knows who you are. Could she be leading us into a trap? Sirdar knows we are on Dru."

"A trap it might be, but not one of Sirdar's doing. There is another force at work here. This trap has been set for the Obet and me. But it is fate that has set it."

He increased his speed and Trenara followed silently.

CHAPTER FIVE
MIERE

The old woman and the strange silent man walked on as if they did not care if the others followed. Miere came to life once they set out. The deeper the jungle grew, the faster she would walk, as though her urgency was greater than Joshan's.

They stayed to the path, which wound back and forth, roughly following the stream. When they moved deeper into the thick tangle of darkened foliage, any sense of direction was soon lost. Even Vanderlinden, who had hunted every forest and thicket in the provinces, soon became uncertain of their direction until he regarded the plants with a dour suspicion. Stinging insects again accosted them. The swarms of vicious midges were unnaturally clever at finding ways into their clothes and hair no matter how the companions fought them. Again, Haiden suffered little, but Miere and Porphont slowed as the swarms grew. Miere finally stopped and shook an old fist at the air.

"Enough, I say!" Her voice dulled against the dense growth surrounding them, but the black clouds of insects fled in an instant and did not return. She grumbled under her breath in an unintelligible language and increased her speed.

They moved deeper into the island until the forest became a night of dark green trees and stifling gloom. Joshan wondered at Miere's stamina. She walked heedless of the dark on a path that was breaking into rough bushy ground. With an alacrity that contradicted her age, she moved without either sound or stagger, the silent Porphont immediately behind her. Joshan caught up with her and he nearly stumbled himself when he saw her face.

"Miere," he cried, "your eyes are closed."

Swinging around in a delicate dance, Miere's eyes popped open and regarded him wisely from under the naked brows. "Just a game I play, Ganafira. As often as I have trodden this path I find now I see it better with them closed." She laughed at her own private joke and struck the path again.

The trail soon disappeared entirely, leaving them to climb through brush and fallen trees. Miere now had Porphont take the lead and let the companions catch them.

"Come, come. You cannot return to the mainland and say an old woman beat you through the brush." Not a trace of fatigue clouded her brow or her breath, though the companions were gasping for air and soaked to the skin from the humidity and exertion.

"Mother," Van said breathlessly when he reached her. "Either you are a witch or not as old as you seem. I've never met the man who could walk Vanderlinden into the ground. I think today I met my match."

"Ha! Not your match, master giant, but your better. Do not get long-faced on me, man. If you had lived in this forest as long as I, you would then be my match, indeed, my better, for I would long be dust by then, hey?"

Her face then turned very urgent. "Come now, all of you. The darking will pass in another league. Porphont will clear a path through the brush. I would have stayed to the trail, but time is short and the jungles will darken to night soon. We dare not stray for that." She turned to scan the forest.

"I wouldn't think she'd be afraid of a little dark," Haiden muttered under his breath.

The old woman whirled around, fixing Haiden with a keen eye. "It is not the dark I fear, master gray whiskers."

Haiden blushed to the ears and shuffled his feet, but the old woman took off down the primitive path Porphont had cut.

No more than a league away, they came all at once into late afternoon through a breach in the trees. The unexpected sunlight dazzled their eyes. Once adjusted, they stared in awe at what greeted them.

Below their feet stretched a valley of shadowed blue for many leagues in either direction. The cliffs at their feet were shear and stony straight and there seemed no way to scale them. As if a powerful river had once rushed through it to meet the sea, the valley opened before them in an immense chasm. The old river bottom was now an arbor with giant gray barked trees that rose majestically to the sky. Their limbs were as broad as the largest tree trunks in Tola, which boasted the grandest in the empire. The Tolan trees were saplings in comparison. The grove, which stretched as far as the eyes could see, began midway down the valley and then climbed up until it reached the base of the granite mountain beyond. Mt. Diorne towered above their heads and caught the late sunlight in a fantasy of color. At its foot, well above the other trees and so huge it appeared close enough to touch was a magnificent tree. It had to be the largest in the world. It stood apart from the rest, so tall its crown disappeared into misty sunlight.

Joshan's breath caught in his throat. He had no thoughts or feelings, beyond a deep-seated wonder as he gazed at that tree. Nothing in his memory was more wondrous. Without going nearer, he knew a city could rest among those branches that would make the Keep seem a hovel in comparison. Here was real power and it made the star a fleeting candle.

"What do see, Ganafira?" the old woman whispered at his side.

He felt timid and small in its presence. "I see life, mother. I see the dreams and hopes of people nothing more than flashes in time. I see endurance, strength, and power—real power—the power of life."

A satisfied smiled touched the old woman's lips. "As did I, when first I beheld it; power, life… and age."

"No, mother," Joshan said softly. "Not age. Say rather time. Century after century of growth and existence. There lies the father of life."

The words made the old woman scowl. "That is the Signal Tree. It is where you will find the Oracle. Come, we must hurry."

She and Porphont led them to a small ledge that ran to a narrow stair. In single file, they descended with great care, often climbing down hand over hand into the abyss that fell beneath their feet. Soon they were all down and the cliff wall towered above them.

Miere guided them through long grasses that prefaced the trees. Because of the size of the trees, the distance was deceiving. It felt like they were making no progress at all trudging through the stiff tangle of thick grass, their legs aching from the effort. The trees grew larger, blocking the huge mountain beyond as they made their slow way toward them.

When they finally reached the closest tree, they sank to the ground to rest in the coolness of its shadow. The rustle of wind among the branches hissed like tide against the sand. The valley, now dark toward dusk, melted before their eyes.

After a brief rest, Miere urged them on with a sparkle of exigency in her eyes that shone like candlelight in the shadowy twilight. The valley sang with thousands of insect voices, breek-reeking on the evening air until the sound resonated with a dull thud against the forest. The trees filled their vision, a gray wall with gaping breaks of darkness that reminded them of caves. The grasses ended abruptly at the massive trunks and the stark ground was black with rich earth.

Joshan stopped at the wall and gazed up at the tall trees. An eldritch premonition shot up his spine that made him hesitate, but Miere came up behind him and touched his arm lightly.

"Do not fear the trees, Ganafira. They are not your enemy," she whispered. "Take my arm and I will show you my home." She moved through the break in the trees and they plunged at once into almost complete darkness with the rest following behind them.

The only sign of life beyond the trees were thousands of flittering fireflies darting through the trunks, their gloomy iridescence making the forest ghostly bright. The air teamed with energy as though alive with the sap of the towering giants.

As they made their way through the grove, the trees grew dense until there were only narrow aisles between them, making it a maze of thick black walls and distance. Miere pulled them along without hesitation, but with each step, the closeness became more tangible, until Joshan thought he would suffocate in the gloomy dark. His awareness of the life force above his head drowned all other feelings, until his shoulders grew heavy with the weight. Miere's hand on his arm became tight until her nails dug into his flesh, sending sparkling pain up his arm and neck. The sting, sharp on his dulled senses, helped him to concentrate. Without it, he thought he would have simply fallen over.

Without warning, the trees above their heads shifted violently and Joshan's awareness panged at him. He stopped and whirled around to his companions. They blinked back at him.

"What is it?" Trenara asked.

"Did you feel that?"

Trenara and the others shook their heads.

"It is the trees you hear," Miere said reassuringly, "only the trees. Come. We must hurry. Full night is not good here." She pulled him on, but his feet were heavy as they stumbled through the dark.

The ground rose steadily until they were trudging uphill. Their legs ached and their faces strained in the eerie half-light radiating from the dancing moths. Miere would not let them rest until they broke through the trees to stand before a massive wall of a single tree. Here she stopped and allowed them to sink to the ground. With great relief, they took several precious moments to slow their racing hearts and catch their breaths.

Miere signaled to Porphont with a wave of her hand and he disappeared through the trees back the way they had come. Joshan looked up at her from his knees and could not comprehend what he saw in her eyes; they looked full of regret. The sight terrified him.

"What have you done?" he breathed.

"Forgive me," she whispered. "This is… necessary."

Before he could respond, Miere turned sideways and suddenly shot straight up, disappearing so quickly into the limbs, she was no more than a blur. Joshan leapt at the tree where she had been, but his shoulder hit solid bark. He crumbled to the ground as pain immobilized his arm. Van and Haiden jumped to their feet and pulled their swords.

Several faint whooshing sounds echoed around them and the air filled with stinging darts. Three caught Trenara where she sat. She fell to the ground without moving again. Four caught Haiden on the back and he lurched forward at Joshan's feet. He clawed once toward the emperor, his face livid with pain, but then slumped into the ground. Van took several in the back and legs, but his size kept him conscious long enough to pin Joshan to the tree and keep the darts off him. Lights burst in his head again and again, but he fought the drug.

"Run!" he wheezed. "It's a bloody trap!" His body shuddered once. He fell to his knees and then down into the soft earth.

Joshan was unhurt. He gazed at his three friends in shock and quickly dove for the darkness under the trees. The air became silent as he pulled the golden sword from its scabbard. Above his head, he thought he caught a shift in the energy force that hid in the trees, like an inward taking of breath. He tried uselessly to activate the power. Something snaked from his right and wrapped itself around the blade several times. Joshan instinctively tightened his grip. The leather thong jerked once and the sword sailed out of his hand as if he were no more than a child holding a fragile toy. Lights burst in his head when a dart pierced his neck and he plucked it out. The poison became a fiery rush of venom through his bloodstream that burst inside his head. He sank to his knees when the world began to spin. Sounds buzzed in his ears and he thought he heard a woman's voice above him. His eyes burned, his tongue swelled, and his throat ached with thirst. Joshan licked the fire from his lips and tried to see who was kneeling down above him, but it was nothing more than a misty blur.

"What…" he croaked, but could manage nothing more.

"Forgive me, Joshan." That voice—it had haunted his visions from the beginning. "It was the only way."

Blackness took him and the voice faded.

CHAPTER SIX
THE SIGNAL TREE

The Obet ran long fingers over the sword lying on a slab of wood, the gold beauty of the blade looking strangely out of place on the rough lumber. There was a bitter edge to the Oracle's voice as cold steely blue eyes bore into the man who stood to one side of the great chamber in the Signal Tree.

"The people are grumbling that all four should have been tried, Oracle," the man replied stiffly, an echo of their old battle.

"I gave you the leader. What more do you want? If it were up to me, none of them would have been tried."

"I know, Oracle, but our customs dictate…"

"I know the custom, Shadedale. You taught me well. These are not normal people. You will not touch the other three. Do I make myself clear?"

Angry color rose in Shadedale's cheeks, but he tightened his lips and bowed his head in assent. "As you wish, Oracle, but the Ganafira must be tested, so the legend states."

"Yes," the Obet replied wearily, "the Ganafira will be tested. Has the council decided how?"

Shadedale hesitated before speaking. "On the mountain, Oracle."

The Obet bit off a heated reply. The visions had been too clear on this point. The test was necessary; it would force Joshan into his destiny. There would be no turning back. When Joshan was enlightened, the world would be in his hands. The Obet slumped into the chair. "All right, I will take him myself."

Shadedale bowed again with a satisfied crispness. "Thank you."

When he left, the Obet regarded the silent guard, turning words into thoughts the mute could understand.

Porphont, you do not need to return to the mainland. Will you change your mind?

No, Oracle, I will follow where you lead.

The Obet shifted in the chair.

If the visions are correct, you will not come back—unchanged. I could not bear the thought of your death, Porphont. Please reconsider.

I will follow where you lead, was the only reply.

The Obet simply nodded and left to deliver Joshan into the hands of providence.

Trenara rolled onto her side when the drug wore off. She sat up abruptly, trying to piece together what had happened. All she could remember was Miere disappearing, Joshan jumping after her, and a piercing sting that thudded into her back and neck. Where was she? The bars were no more than dense branches attached to a broad platform as if they had grown there. There were no windows or doors; only bright sunlight came through. High over her head another platform sealed the prison. The guider stood up and woozed a bit from the after effects of the drug, but it faded as she tested the bars. They were as solid as the tree from which they grew. She gave the cell a disgruntled look. The only side was leaves that sparkled in the early morning sun climbing into the early morning sky.

When she scanned the cell, her pack, her via and all her weapons were gone. "Hello," she called, but the only immediate reply was the sound of a few birds skittering out of the leaves and her voice bouncing off the distant mountain. All at once, there came a whisper from beyond the wall to her right.

"Trenara?"

She ran her hands along it.

"Haiden?"

"Oh, praise the star and thank the Lady," the Marshal breathed from the other side. "I thought sure I was here alone."

"Are Van and Joshan with you?"

"No, I'm sorry to say. What happened down there?"

"I wish I knew." She leaned against the wall and tried to clear her head. "This is the last thing I expected here. I did not feel any evil intent from Miere or Porphont." She shrugged. "Yet, here we sit. Haiden, do you still have your pack or sword."

There came a disappointed sigh. "Sorry, just the clothes on my back."

"Are there any doors or windows in your cell, anything that might be an entrance?"

"Nothing but these bars. Wait a second—here's a curiosity."

There came a slight click and a grating sound. Extra light flooded through a rectangular patch at the midway point of the wall.

"Trenara," Haiden said excitedly, "is there a twig, about midway down the wall that looks like a small branch?"

Trenara searched the wall and saw it. "Yes."

"Push it down and then pull."

When the guider did so, the door opened and Haiden nearly fell into her cell. He was haggard and blurry-eyed, but otherwise whole and Trenara took him by the shoulders.

"Haiden, I could kiss you!"

"Well, I don't know about that. I think the giant might have a thing or two to say," he said blushing to the ears. "Besides, I haven't solved our problem yet. All I've managed to do, seemingly, is make a bigger prison—wherever we are."

Just then, a loud roar came from beyond the opposite wall. Trenara smiled widely.

"Unless I miss my guess, we have found my wonderful man." They rushed to the wall and found a similar catch on the door. It grated open, but the door to Van's cell would not budge.

"Van? Can you hear me?" Trenara called. "Are you all right?"

There was a groan and then a hoarse bass voice. "You don't have to shout. I can hear you well enough. That must have been some party. I've never been this hung over."

"Are you all right?" she asked again.

"Aye—well enough. Nothing getting out of this cell won't take care of. Is the lad or Haiden with you?"

Trenara and Haiden exchanged glances. "Just Haiden," she replied. "I was hoping Joshan was with you."

"Well, he's not," Van growled. "When I get my hands on that little cackling witch, I'll ring her bloody neck. Are you all right?"

"Fine," she said with a sigh. "Come over to the wall and open your cell door. You will find a latch about in the center."

When Van opened his door, he took Trenara in his arms and examined her carefully, making sure she was unhurt. They searched the cells from wall to wall, but there were no more latches. The three cells were the only ones.

Trenara and Haiden could feel no more effects of the drug, but the giant was still hazy and nauseous. His neck and back were a mass of welts where the darts had hit him. Trenara washed them as best she could with water she found, but the giant would have them for many days.

As far as she could tell, they were toward the crown of the Signal Tree. Far below, she could see the tops of the smaller trees, to the west the distant cliff face that led to the valley, and to the east, the high peaks of Mt. Diorne. Behind them, the branches were thick. Several platforms peeked out from the dense leaves, but only birds were present.

"Why would they do this?" Van asked when they finished examining the cells.

Trenara ran her hand along the bars pensively. "I wish I knew. We know so little about the Druan customs. I wonder how they move through the air as they do. I have never seen control like Porphont displayed, yet without the power—just with training. It is amazing."

"Amazing or not, if they've hurt Joshan, no trick of theirs is going to stop me from making sure they pay for it."

"Guider," said Haiden, "where do they have him do you suppose? Has he been hurt?"

"For what it is worth without the Crystal, my guider's sense tells me he is safe—well, alive at any rate." She could not keep the worry out of her voice and it made her stomach cramp to think of what they could have done with Joshan.

"Well," Van said, "chances are he may have got away. I took most of the darts aimed at him."

"I hope you are right, Van. I do not see how we can escape without him."

Just then, there were several thuds on the roof and long ropes appeared outside the bars. Three men scurried down onto a slight ledge around the cages and flipped several latches. The front slid up and fell onto the top of the cell when they entered.

One was tall and dark, sporting a full beard and crystal blue eyes. The other two were fair-haired and rather slight, with young faces. They were obviously brothers or cousins. All three were clad in green, with finely crafted thigh high boots. None of the three men was armed.

The older of the two blonds bowed low without taking his eyes off them. "If you will accompany me, I will escort you to see the captain now," he said.

"Where is the emperor?" Trenara demanded.

The man smiled amiably. "I am certain the captain will answer all your questions." He motioned toward the entrance. "If you will come with me…"

Van jumped toward the three, but Trenara held up her hand to stop him. "Not now," she whispered. "We need to find out what they have done with Joshan."

"Aye." Van allowed Trenara to take his arm and lead him from the cell with Haiden behind them.

When they came out on the ledge, they threw themselves against the sides of the cage. The distance to the trees below was dizzying and there were no handholds on the platform. The "ropes" were actually thick living vines that had many knots tied an equal distance from one another. The men wrapped their hands around them.

"How are we going to get down from here?" Haiden exclaimed. "You expect us to fly?"

The leader's eyes sparkled with mirth, but his face remained placid.

"Forgive me, but we forget sometimes others are not used to the heights. My brother, Leaflight, will show you how to use the driftlines."

Leaflight sprang to the vine and bore down heavily with his weight. The line dropped several spans and then sprang back sharply, taking Leaflight high over their heads in a swinging semi-circle to the boughs behind the cages. There he landed lightly and threw the line back.

The companions looked on dubiously.

"You got to be out of your mind," breathed Vanderlinden. "How the hell are we supposed to do that?"

"With practice, you could do it very well, I think," replied the young man. "But until you can work the lines, Boughman, Leaflight, and I will guide the lines for you. I must warn you, jump to the limb before the line reaches it. If you miss, it is a long hard fall to the earth." He bowed again and Boughman jumped below the platform. He caught the line and Leaflight came back with another.

"My name is Limbshade and I am to be your host for the time being." With that, he sprang to a third line and slid down about two spans. "Bring your full weight against the line. We will do the rest."

"I'll go first," Van said to Trenara, kissing her lightly and wrapping his hands around the rope. Trenara watched as he scanned the boughs. He seemed startled when he saw it tied to a small limb well above his head. It bobbed and swayed with Boughman's weight teasing it into submission. Trenara could not see how it would possibly bear the weight of both men. Van stepped off the ledge as Limbshade had instructed, and the rope shot down, pulling the limbs after it until the leaves nearly reached the top of the cage.

Just when the vine looked as if it would break, it snapped back up with such a jar to the giant's bones, Trenara could almost hear them snapping under the strain. In a swinging motion that cast the large men like bits of dust in the wind, they angled nearly horizontal through the air and then slowly vertical. Within two hand lengths of the branch, Van and Boughman stepped off the rope and caught themselves on a wide platform. The forest man stood, and Van clung to the broad limb to keep from falling. Boughman smiled and gave Vanderlinden a hand up. Trenara could see the tremble in Van's fingers when he took it.

Haiden was next and he did not do any worse, though he landed on the platform sprawling, misjudging the distance.

Trenara was the lightest of the three and almost made it to the platform on her feet, but stumbled forward to her knee.

When Limbshade scrambled lightly up the length of vine hand over hand, he motioned to the companions to follow him. Boughman and Leaflight brought up the rear.

Despite their good nature, and the cheerfulness that resonated from the trees themselves, Trenara was clearly aware they were prisoners and the forest men were nothing more than guards. None of the men wore weapons and she could see from his face that Van was formulating a plan.

They led them along a broad platform that ran through the Signal Tree like a great boulevard. On either side, Trenara caught glimpses of platforms with decorative matted roofs over them. There were even here and there small thatched dwellings, but no other people appeared. Had Trenara not been so worried, the walk would have been a pleasant one. The sun sparkled through many fingered leaves. There were no flowers, but buds hung like great baskets along each branch.

After a while, the 'road' turned into an even wider boulevard. At a signal from Limbshade, Boughman veered into another lane and disappeared, leaving only Leaflight to cover the companions' flank. The two brothers were shorter than Van and only inches taller than Haiden and Trenara, and their combined weight was probably no more than the giant's. The guider watched as Van examined the young men with trained warrior eyes and managed to exchange a look with Haiden, who nodded.

Once around another bend, well away from the broader path, Van increased his steps to shorten the distance between him and Limbshade, while Haiden slowed his own. Trenara looked from one to the other and inwardly rolled her eyes. She knew the outcome even before it happened. For safety sake, she put as much distance as she could manage from all four.

Without warning, Vanderlinden struck, diving for and catching Limbshade's legs below the knees. The youth hit the limb, caught himself on his hands, and twisted around before the giant could get a good grip. At the same time, Haiden sprang at the young man behind him with a backhand that should have taken Leaflight clear off his feet. The agile Druan ducked under the big hand as if dodging a wayward branch. He turned in a wide circle with such speed even Haiden's well-trained eyes could not see it. The kick landed in Haiden's mid-section, stealing his breath with a power the old sergeant had never felt from men twice the youth's size.

Limbshade escaped the giant's iron grasp in a twinkling, leaving Van to look at empty hands. The boy then did an expert back flip to land on his feet, shaking his head and placing his hands on his hips. He was not even out of breath. Van was on his feet in an instant and dived again at the youth, but Limbshade merely stepped aside. Van crumpled against a tree branch.

As Van was shaking the clout from his head, Limbshade looked on sympathetically.

"I understand your desire to escape the tree, sir, but please understand. We are only doing what is necessary. I do not wish to harm you, but I will take you to my captain as ordered. Please cooperate."

Trenara could see the fury rising in Van's eyes. His pride would not withstand being bested by a youth half his size and a fraction of his age. She looked at Haiden, but he lay immobilized with the Leaflight standing over him protectively. The youth gave Trenara a warning look, but the guider simply curled her lip with no intention of interfering.

Van wiped the trickle of blood running from the corner of his mouth and glared at Limbshade.

Van dived at the youth and missed, but caught himself on his hands and knees against the platform. Limbshade finished his roll through the air over the giant's head to land facing him with a bemused smile on his face. Vanderlinden roared with anger and reached for his sword, but it was gone.

"Please, giant," Limbshade pleaded. "I do not wish to harm you. Despite what you think, we are your friends—and friend of the Oracle who sent us."

Trenara saw the anger flare dangerously in Van's eyes. "My darling, listen to me. As much as this may damage your pride, fighting is complete folly at this point. We will listen to what Limbshade's captain has to say. I do not feel evil here." She glanced into Limbshade's crystal blue eyes. "Besides, I have a disquieting feeling this boy could break you in two, if he wished."

"Listen to your mate, giant. Her words are wise. I could hit you at points in your body that would kill in an instant." He smiled. "Come—get up. Join me as a friend, not as an enemy."

Van lowered his eyes and agreed to the request with a sharp nod of his head and a grunt, but would not allow the boy to help him to his feet. Trenara helped him instead and rewarded him with a kiss, which he returned grudgingly.

Limbshade glowered at Leaflight and scolded the younger man in a strange language. The mortified Leaflight looked at his feet during the tirade; red suffused his cheeks. He leaned down to Haiden and forced air back into his lungs by pulling back on his arms. Haiden came out of the paralysis gasping for air. He coughed violently and then shook his head.

"Forgive my younger brother," Limbshade said, glaring at the youth. "He is young and his training is limited. He should not have harmed you."

With a sad sigh, Leaflight took his station behind Haiden. Limbshade's face smoothed and he spoke again in the crisp language to his brother with a glint of familial mirth in his eyes. Leaflight replied with a shrug and a half smile. Haiden got to his feet with the giant's help.

Trenara realized that unlike Vanderlinden, whose pride often ruled his senses, Haiden knew when to admire a man's strength and training. After all, he had been training boys for many seasons. None of them had the skills of this young man or his brother. He gave Leaflight a smile and shook his head.

"It's not many can wrest Haiden Bails to the ground, lad. How did you do that?"

Leaflight looked at his older brother as if for permission. Limbshade gave him a nod and searched the path before them. "Very well. You may entertain our guests until I return. Mind you," he said smiling to the companions, "my brother can be long winded. I will not be long." With a crisp bow, he dashed down a side path and disappeared.

"Please," Leaflight took his place at the head of the line and bowed. "It isn't far now."

When they settled, Haiden walked next to the youth and scratched his head. "So, you were talking about how you got me to the ground..."

"Yes. I am sorry, sir. I should not have hurt you. As my brother has said, my training is limited. Sadly, I am no more than tyro."

"Tyro? What's that?"

Leaflight looked a little embarrassed. "It is a beginner, sir. Well, less than that, actually. I have only been studying for five seasons."

"Ho, now! Five seasons, you say? Five seasons can make a great warrior."

Leaflight smiled. "Perhaps where you come from, sir, but here, five seasons barely scratches the surface of all there is to learn. Most of the people here have been studying the arts for many times that." His eyes shone in the strange filtered light. "Masters are few, but when they move, it is art in motion."

"But why is it you learn to fight as you do? Does it come in handy for hunting?"

Leaflight laughed. "No, we do not hunt. We are not flesh eaters. Fruits and vegetables, and those things the good Mother provides to us... these things we eat, but no animal flesh. It clogs the mind and congests the heart."

Haiden looked at him uncertainly, liking a stout portion of steak on occasion, and not taking kindly to the fact that it 'clogged the mind,' although he could recall a time or two where his mind did indeed slow a bit after a good meal of broiled bullion and a hearty mug of ale.

"No," the youth continued, "not for hunting. In fact, we learn to fight so we do not hurt any living thing. It is the Philosophy: If you control the body, you control the mind and the mind will control the heart," he quoted solemnly. "It is our way of life. If you wish to control others, you must first control yourself. Violence only breeds violence, hate only hate. If you understand something you can learn from it and grow."

Leaflight glanced over at Haiden who was having some trouble digesting all of this. The youth, who have always been the pupil, looked elated at the prospect of being the teacher for once.

"Perhaps I should tell you something of our history so you can understand us better," Leaflight said to which Haiden nodded.

"We were a warring people... violent, vicious. A tribe of mighty people with nothing to keep them occupied, but their pride and petty desires." He shook his head. "They were consumed by the spark of lust in their hearts and the need for glory.

"But Dru is small, yes? When it was conquered, the tribes built ships, sailed to other lands, and tried to conquer there. The Great Isle, which you call Mathisma, had a civilization once, before the warring Trillone destroyed it. With it went treasure the likes of which no man has ever seen; great works of art and priceless antiquities gone forever, inventions for the ease of man's burdens. We destroyed it all."

"The Trillone then did the one thing that saved them. They captured a man and enslaved him: Conifere the Wise.

"In exchange for his life, he told us he would teach our chiefs an art of fighting that would make them invincible against any weapon and more powerful than any enemy. With it, they could conquer the world if they wished. He set two conditions; no man could use the art until he had completed all the training and at the end of one thousand seasons, they must fulfill a promise. He would not tell them what that promise was, reserving it for when they were ready. The chiefs agreed, knowing they would do as they pleased anyway. Conifere began to teach.

"Many seasons passed and the Trillone learned so much from Conifere. However, their greatest knowledge did not come from the art of war. It came when they realized they had lost their desire for conquest. The fire was gone from their hearts. Many lamented their evil deeds. They swore a Vow before Conifere; all the Trillone would continue with the teaching, until one thousand seasons passed. In those one thousand seasons, the Trillone would spend their days in the aid of mankind, to make up for their evils. The elders handed down the prophecy from generation to generation, keeping the sacred words secret until the Day of Fulfillment. However, just so the Trillone are not headstrong in pride of their strength, Conifere made them swear that only in secret would they aid humans and that no outsider may know…"

"Leaflight!" They all spun around to see Limbshade shaking behind them. Leaflight gasped in horror and then clamped his mouth shut. So caught up in his new role as teacher, he did not realize to whom he was speaking; not a young child in the sanctity of the Signal Tree village huts, but an ancient outsider. Sinking to his knees before Limbshade's blazing eyes, he was too mortified to speak.

"Your flapping tongue has destroyed us both," Limbshade hissed viciously. Leaflight paled under the pronouncement and trembled.

"Ke—kesaimore tisau, Leeafvronnen. An—an ilnokauf vos sae?"

Trenara knew Leaflight had violated some law, the repercussions of which may affect all of them drastically. The dangerous implications grated against her guider's sense like ruin.

"Limbshade…" She searched for words that would not come easily, but pitched her voice to diffuse the situation before it became worse. "Your people have nothing to fear from us. The lad's mistake may not be a breach of your customs because we do not fully comprehend what he has said. We know nothing of your ways. I realize some law may have been violated, but what little Leaflight has said will go no further than us." Van and Haiden nodded in support of the guider's reassurance, not fully understanding what had happened.

Limbshade seemed completely unaffected by Trenara's attempts to soothe him. He shook his head grimly and stared at Leaflight with cold stoicism.

"You do not understand, guider. What my brother has done cannot be undone. This breach has cost him his life and mine as well; honor forces me to join my brother's side for teaching him so poorly. No outsider may hear what you have heard and live. Forgive me," his eyes glazed over with pain, "I have failed the Oracle, my brother, and you. Perhaps I deserve death."

Leaflight let out a cry and tears brimmed in his eyes. "Nay, nay." His voice choked with remorse as he uttered the denial repeatedly.

Limbshade ignored his brother's denials and became lost in thought. The companions did not move.

Limbshade finally regarded his brother and a grim spark came to his eye. He spoke crisply in their language at length. Leaflight said nothing in response. There was a fear in the younger man's face that unsettled Trenara. Leaflight finally nodded and leapt to his feet. He disappeared into a tangle of leaves in a flash of urgency.

"Where has he gone?" Trenara asked.

Limbshade searched the companions' faces thoroughly. "He has gone to seek the Oracle to aid us. The captain will not be lenient with us unless the Oracle intervenes, and even then, I am uncertain. There is conflict between them these days. This matter must be decided by both."

"But what have you got planned?" Van asked.

"There is only one way Leaflight and I may be forgiven this breach. It will depend on you. But it is your choice and I will not gainsay you if you refuse."

"What must we do, lad?" Trenara asked.

"Are you courageous?"

The companions exchanged glances.

"Aye," Van said. "We have proved our courage enough. Why?"

"In the world of outsiders it has often been our experience the proof of a person's courage is limited." Van and Haiden bristled, but Limbshade smiled sadly. "That is not meant as an insult, gentlemen, let me assure you. Compared to our ways, it is often true enough. I am going to ask you to submit to a test of your courage. If the elders accept you into the Trillone, we can salvage this. Be warned; it is a very perilous request. Captain Shadedale will not agree to this test willingly, I think. The Oracle will support it... indeed, she may well sponsor you. If she does, there is a chance."

This made all the companions gape.

"She?" Van exclaimed. "The Obet is a woman?"

Limbshade looked at them incredulously and then laughed.

"You did not know? Yes, a beautiful woman—and perilous. We hold her in high regard. She is exceedingly wise. The Oracle has helped in so many ways—saved so many of us. Even though she has refused training in the gift, we still account her as one of the masters. When you meet her, you will understand why." He smiled softly. "Any man in our company would gladly fall for her or fight for what she professes. It will be a lucky man, indeed, whom she chooses to mate.

"I must ask you now—will you submit to these tests? You may decline, but I do not know what will happen if you do. For an outsider to possess the knowledge you now have is a grave offense. It could mean death for you. That will be up to the captain and the Oracle to decide."

"May we discuss this among ourselves in private?" Trenara asked.

"Certainly, lady, but do it swiftly. Captain Shadedale waits and will wonder why we delay."

Limbshade sprinted off to stand many spans away while the companions gathered.

"I don't like this, Trenara." Van tapped his fingers on his empty scabbard and glared at the young man. "It's all going too fast."

Trenara squeezed her shoulders and furrowed her brow. "I agree, but what can we do? I do not know if these people are friends or enemies. Just from what Limbshade has told us, I think the Oracle is our friend and we need her. Joshan would want us to do whatever was necessary to convince her to join us. There is so much unknown. Where is Joshan? Why imprison us if they are friends? What are the 'tests' he speaks of?"

"If we're here for good," put in Haiden, "it seems we got to play along with their game, guider. For what it's worth, I can't rightly see where they are enemies—and like you said, Joshan is relying on us to sway the Obet. This might be a way of doing that."

"Aye," Van added grimly, "but it also might be a way of losing whatever chance we have. I don't know what this test is—and before we landed on this island, I would've said there wasn't a test made I couldn't pass, but now I don't know. Think of that slip of a boy overpowering me like that and he didn't even touch me. They're way above us, by all accounts. I hate to admit this, but I'm scared."

"So am I, Van." Trenara took his hand and rested her cheek against it. "But for other reasons than that. Something tells me the next few hours may be the most difficult of our journey. I do not see where we have a choice. We are fated to this, I think. It will broach no good to delay what must occur. I say we go with the tests."

"And I say, no," Van said. "I vote for getting out of this accursed tree and back to the ship to get my crew and force them to tell us where Joshan is."

Trenara turned to Haiden. "That is one for and one against. I guess that leaves it up to you."

Haiden ran a finger along his chin and scowled at both of them a long time. "Well," he said at length, "I'm afraid I would have to say go with it—though it will no doubt land us in a pickle, for sure. It won't do no good, I'm thinking, to leave it up to me—chances are I'd lead us to trouble from the onset. But you said it, not me."

"Good," Trenara said. "Van, I cannot force you to go along with this plan, but if you intend to attempt an escape, at least let Haiden and I try this test. If we fail, then you may do what you like."

"No, my love," he said, taking her in his arms and kissing her forehead. "I'd never leave either of you to face that alone. Come what may, I'm with you."

They told Limbshade of their decision, but his face was not hopeful.

"There is indeed honor among others. I hope my brother's folly has not caused the need for your deaths. It would be a heavy blow to lose such valiant folk."

Without another word, he led them to his captain.

CHAPTER SEVEN
CONIFERE

Joshan's hands were frozen. That was his first sensation as he slowly crawled toward consciousness. Deadly warmth was spreading through his back. His legs were numb weights hanging to his hips. Someone had mercifully wrapped a heavy fur around his body, but his legs wore simple leather boots, not thick enough to keep the deadly cold from penetrating his bones. Joshan tried to move his feet, but it was useless. Panic began as a hot flash in his heart. He reached for the golden sword but it was gone, along with his ability to call the power.

He fought the fear by biting his lip until spatters of blood sprinkled his chin and marred the whiteness in front of his eyes. The pain helped. Focusing on the calming exercises, he tried to clear his mind. He took several deep breaths and mentally repeated the chants.

He needed shelter and fire to escape the blizzard that now raged around him, stinging his face and naked hands.

His head pounding, Joshan searched the terrain. The glare of the snow blinded him. It was day. How early or how late, he did not know. He wiped his eyes against the fur. There was something black against the whiteness. A cave? A tree? Lifting himself onto his hands, Joshan dragged his body a few inches closer. Something stood there—a man, dressed in skins and carrying a giant wooden staff. The man clutched the furs more tightly to his shoulders, but made no other move. Joshan reached out to him and the figure motioned him to come nearer. He could only shake his head in anguish. The man disappeared.

Joshan cried out, but the blizzard blew his words to ribbons and scattered them across the featureless peaks high above his head. He sank into destitution quietly, alone in a world of ice. The warmth that had earlier taken his legs, now made a creamy softness in his chest and he could not hold himself up any longer. He wanted nothing more than to drift into sleep. His eyes closed over icicles of tears and he floated into a dream.

The master sat on a throne of gold and crimson fire. In his hand, he held a blackened sword. On his head, a red crown of mist shrouded his face. All around him stood tall black sasarans, heavily muscled, their horns shining in the darkness, their massive legs and hoofed feet as still as statues, armored in bright red livery. To his left the Mourna stood, her beak resting on the master's shoulder, her human eyes on fire. Joshan was naked except for chains that encircled his wrists. They burned where they touched his flesh. His mouth felt parched with fear and anticipation as he waited for the demon to speak.

"Bow to me, Joshan," the creature whispered. "You have chosen a life with the short-lived and will learn to regret this. They thought they could challenge me. I am Sirdar; their efforts mean nothing to me. And you are their champion?" Sirdar laughed until the creatures circling him cringed away from the sound. Joshan stood as still as stone.

"Before this day is through, mortal-friend, you will drink deeply of regret, drink deeply—must drink—you must drink—

"You must drink this."

The new voice impinged on Joshan's foggy awareness. Something warm was flowing down his throat, pungent in his nostrils. He tried to open his eyes, but a rag soaked with something oily sealed them. The scent was sweet like Low Season herbs.

"Keep your eyes closed for now." The strange voice rang like the clang of swords against his eardrums, but it was gentle at the same time. The man's hands were strong, firm, but cold to the touch, as if they contained no blood. Joshan wished he could see the man's face. When Joshan moved to take the cloth from his eyes, the man guided his hands away.

"It is too soon to remove the dressing, young sire. Let your eyes rest. There is much you have yet to see."

"How—how did you find me?" Choked with cold, Joshan's voice came out as a whisper. He heard the soft shuffle of feet and the clink of utensils.

"I think it was you who found me. You were lying nearly on my doorstep, and except for the storm, I would have found you sooner. How came you to be here, on my mountain?"

"Someone must have brought me here," Joshan replied. "We were down below the trees, when we were attacked. I do not remember after that."

"We? You had companions then?"

"Yes, three." But where were they? In a panic, Joshan searched his guider's sense. They were unharmed, although he did not know what had become of them. They seemed millions of leagues away. He relaxed back into the bed, exhausted.

"Here, drink. This will make you strong." The stranger held something under Joshan's nose. The smell was strong with herbs and onions, although where such delicacies could be found on this mountain of ice, Joshan could not guess.

Mountain of ice—

Visions exploded in his head in a lightning flash.

A land of ice, a great chasm, a black sword shot with red—

Then they were gone.

The broth was hot and savory as it slid down Joshan's throat. He had not felt hungry, but once the soup hit his tongue he drank with relish. When he asked for more, the man retreated to the kettle and refilled the bowl.

"How are your legs?" He guided Joshan's hands around the bowl and made him drink.

Joshan swallowed more of the warming liquid. It sent a rush of hot fire through his loins. "Heavy and painful."

"Good," the man said. "If there were greater damage, you would feel nothing. Moments only saved your life, my boy. You are safe."

Another hot flash went through Joshan's body. Safe? Will I ever be truly safe? "I am in your debt... I do not know your name."

The cold hands took away the cup and then helped Joshan to sit. "I think we can remove the dressing. Hold your eyes shut tightly to the count of sixty and then open them very slowly. I am going to move your head to face the wall, away from the light." The big hands began to unwrap the dressing.

A third flash of heat sent Joshan's bowels churning and he thought he might be ill. The old hands slowly unraveled the rags from his eyes.

The light was brilliant at first. Even if he wanted to, Joshan would not have been able to open his eyes before the count of sixty. When they finally did crack open, they watered so much he could not keep them open. Another, stronger flash of fire soared through Joshan's belly. The light faded to acceptable proportions as he turned to look at the man for the first time. He caught his breath in wonder.

The face was ancient; wrinkles, on wrinkles, on wrinkles. There was not a hair on his face or head. A coarsely spun rag hugged the skeletal frame; it was as bent and aged as the wrinkles that surrounded his wonderful smile. It was not the antiquity etched into the old face, nor the seasons of life and experience molded into that smile that startled Joshan. It was the silver-blue eyes staring back at him. They stared from beneath the naked brow and pierced his heart. Even more startling were the crystals that ran in jagged lines along the sides of his neck onto his head. They were not like those on Joshan's hands. These were dull, unlovely, their fire gone.

Joshan both trembled and laughed to see him. How many times had he seen this man in vision— younger, always younger—with those same wise, joyful, and frightening eyes?

"By the gods," Joshan whispered, his heart laboring in his chest.

The old man's smile deepened and the jewels shifted strangely with the movement. His eyes were sad above the smile. "You know who I am."

Joshan could only shake his head. "No. You could not be who I think you are."

"No? Have the visions not been clear to you? I am exactly who you think I am. I have waited for you—for so very long."

Joshan swallowed past the apprehension and pushed down the flashing heat that hurried through his spine.

"But that man is dead," he whispered.

The old man nodded and sang:

"When finally the end came near,
And all the seeds were spent,
Kerillian put down his fear,
And into death he went.

"But some say now, he went not far,
But cast aside his flesh,
To seek the souls of another star,
To spread his seeds afresh.

"Is that the verse still, as it was sung long ago?"

"Kerillian?" Joshan breathed.

"Yes, child, or Conifere as the Trillone call me." He scanned Joshan's face and wrapped bony fingers around his shoulders. "I would have known you, even without the crystals in your hands. How like your great-grand sires you are. Dark, strong." He reached up and touched Joshan's face and his eyes misted. "How like them you are. All the seasons—all the millennium—the planning, the failures, all the progenitor manipulations to come to the finality—the final being…" His voice faded away into private thoughts.

"I… do not understand you, father."

Kerillian's face crinkled into a thousand lines. "No? You do not need to, my boy. What is it they call you?"

"Joshan, sir."

The old man nodded and turned to take a chair. "Well, Joshan, welcome to my mountain."

The burning in Joshan's belly became painful. "How could you be alive?"

"Alive?" Kerillian's chortles filled the cave with joy. "Oh, my boy—I was here when the mountains were young and the trees were not yet seeds on the ground. I have been to the beginnings of the universe—though I shall never see its end for I have other roads to travel."

Joshan held his belly as the hot fire engulfed him. "Forgive me, father, but my insides are…" He groaned and doubled over.

"Yes?"

Then Joshan knew. "You have poisoned me. The soup!" He tried to reach for the seated man, but fell back on the cot, curled into a ball of agony.

"Forgive me, Joshan. The pain will pass. I have not poisoned you, but have attempted, as best I can, to prepare you for what comes next." Joshan looked up at him in torment. "Sit up, child, and breathe deeply as your guider has taught you."

As if Kerillian pulled the strings, Joshan did his bidding. The sting subsided into dull warmth that spread into his arms and legs. Strength radiated from some inner pool. His eyes became sharp and his hearing so acute, the slightest sound shouted at him. Feeling and taste were as keen as the edge of a well-honed knife.

Without calling it, the power awoke around him, white, blue, green, gold, shimmering, and hot as it glanced in showers of embers off the furniture. Joshan realized in a sickening flash, that he did not control it. The power was separate now, wild, driven only by chance. There was no pattern to the lights, no prediction of what level it would be when.

Joshan looked at the veil of random lights and screamed. Charges climbed his body and set his hair alive with sparks.

"Kerillian, help me!"

Kerillian's eyes widened and he shook the old head slowly. "I cannot, Joshan."

Joshan tried to manage the storm of power. Light raced up and down his body. A tomb of glistening power enfolded him in such searing pain he could not get the scream to his lips.

Kerillian, a sudden twinge showing in the silver-blue eyes, leaned on a chair and stared at Joshan's cocoon. Joshan tried to reach him, but the power would not let him. He snatched his hand back to nurse the wound he received. Kerillian fell to his knees. The power grew in strength as the old man weakened.

Joshan watched in horror as the old prophet gasped for air and clutched at his throat.

"Kerillian, run! Get out!"

The prophet lifted his hand. Scales of crystal covered his palm, his wrist, and even his arm. Like his face and neck, skin had grown over the crystals making them dull and blue.

"Listen." Kerillian bowed his head under the weight of the feral lights. "Listen, child. Do not resist the power now, let it control you."

"No!" Joshan screamed. "It will destroy me; burn me to ash as it has the others."

The old man shook his head sadly. "No, Joshan, not you. Not now. Let it touch you and take you where it will."

All the seasons of training, all the warnings against just such a confrontation fought against the request. Every man or woman who let the power control them was dead. Those who faltered even slightly were crippled, insane, or blind. There were no exceptions. Yet, the father of prophets begged him to let the power rule him. Joshan looked at the pulsating lights and trembled.

"Please, child," Kerillian whispered, "I cannot hold on much longer. You must open up to the power and reach the coming to sight, the fifth trial, before I am gone. Take my staff." A limp hand motioned to the tall wooden rod leaning against the stonework around the fire pit. "Take it—it is yours. You will know how to use it when the time comes. And then…" a fit of coughing shook him. "And then, you must go through that door." The hand motioned to a door at the back of the cave. "It will lead you to the Shower Veil and on to the heart of Diorne. It is there you will find the black fire." A spasm shook him and he sank his head.

"Once there," he said with force, "you must cleanse yourself."

Fear wound up Joshan's spine sending pricks of torture down his arms and into his belly. "Father?"

"In the fire, Joshan. It is all I can do. Once cleansed, the rest will be up to the dictates of mankind. It is out of our hands." He sank his head to the floor. "Go!" he rasped without looking up. "Go!" Kerillian shouted with his last strength.

Joshan made his way to the staff, the cocoon moving with him. He doubted he would be able to reach it through the shield, but found it easy to move. Without warning, the barrier opened and the staff flew through the air to land in Joshan's outstretched hand. It glistened there like a star. He looked over his shoulder at Kerillian, but the old man was already on the floor, curled into a tight ball. He tried to move to him, but the power held him fast.

"Kerillian!" he called in anguish.

The old man stirred and looked up at him. "Go, my boy. May the gods be with you."

With that, the power swept Joshan from his feet and carried him through a roughly chiseled stone door that led to darkness.

Kerillian watched him leave and smiled for the last time. His mortal life drained away, fulfilling a prophecy he himself had planted those thousands of seasons before. It was out of their hands—the inbred blueprint of mankind would now shape the future.

With his last breath, Kerillian whispered, "Let not my faith in thee, oh mortal man, be false. Fulfill what I have hoped for thee. All life now depends upon it."

The light faded from his eyes.

CHAPTER EIGHT
CONFRONTATION

Trenara inspected the chamber while they waited for Limbshade's captain to speak. Like the rest of this odd elevated city, the room was a blending of nature and manmade; organic, organized, and altogether strange. It was difficult to get one's wits wrapped around it and Trenara scowled when she tried.

The council chamber was a wide platform domed by a green umbrella of leaves and limbs. About the chamber were tables and chairs of cane, and on the newly swept floor, mats of finely woven rushes graced the hall elegantly.

Six people sat at the largest table... four men and two women. One of the men had gray hair and a silver brow. The women sitting next to him were also graying. One was short and the other tall, each with braided tresses that hung to their waists. All three must have been at least sixty seasons, yet they had firm, muscular bodies erect with a youthful stance.

On the left side of the table sat two other men, younger, their eyes more alive, yet just as grave. One was dark, the other fair. The stern eyes and set of their jaw exuded self-confidence. The sixth man, seated at the center of the table, was neither old nor young, with a crown of fiery hair and green, impaling eyes that flashed at every opportunity. His face was handsome, but weathered by many storms and trials. Trenara, Vanderlinden, Haiden, and Limbshade stood before the six people silently.

"Welcome." The green eyes flashed when the man spoke, but his voice was soft and firm. "I am Captain Shadedale, and with me are Masters Riverill, Hillock, Woodhelm, Glade, and Lark." He motioned to the people from right to left. "We, as the council of the Trillone, have asked that you be brought before us." He nodded toward Limbshade. "Make your report."

Limbshade stepped forward and extended both hands to the council, palms out, and bowed his head.

"Sir, I regret to report..." He stopped to collect his courage. "The Vow has been breached."

The five councilors looked at his sharply, but Shadedale made no outward show of surprise.

"To these people?"

Limbshade licked his lips, but composed his voice. "Yes, sir."

Shadedale locked eyes with the young man and nodded gravely. "I see." He looked at the table. "And the one who breached the secret?"

"My brother, captain, Leaflight the younger. I claim contribution—it was my task to teach well. I have failed in that."

Shadedale's eyes narrowed. "Do you take this burden freely?" he whispered.

"Yes, sir," he replied. "As does my brother."

"You know the law."

Limbshade sighed in resignation. "I know the law, sir. You have taught me well."

The other councilors looked at Shadedale, but the captain's eyes saw only the brave young man. "Where is your brother?"

The young man licked his lips and stared down at his hands. "He has gone to seek the Oracle, sir."

Shadedale brought a fist down to the table. "That was not necessary. You could have come to me first. Again you go to…"

"I know, sir." Limbshade's voice was firm, but his lip trembled. "I think it is necessary."

"You are not yet trained to think! It always seems…"

"Shadedale!" Lark exclaimed.

The captain lowered his head to cool his anger. "Forgive me, councilor. I am forgetting myself."

"If you would like to be excused from this council, no one would blame you." Riverill touched Shadedale's shoulder lightly, but he shrugged it off.

"No," he replied. "I know my duty." He turned cold eyes to Limbshade. "The law is explicit. Your brother's foolishness has killed you both. And as for these strangers…"

"Please, sir, my brother and I are at fault. We do not contest the penalty for our foolishness, but these people are guiltless—they do not know our customs. Punish us for our transgressions, sir, but allow these people the right to fight for their lives. I beg you."

"You beg me?" he spat.

Limbshade lowered his head. "For their sake, yes."

"But they are outsiders!"

"They are people, sir. The Oracle has called them friends."

"This does not concern the Oracle. The law is clear, boy."

"The law is very clear, Shadedale." The voice came from a woman who entered in a flowing white robe. Her hair was dark, braided at her back, and large blue eyes sparkled with anger. Leaflight came to stand by his brother. Trenara gasped as Van and Haiden's eyes went wide.

"Ricilyn?" Trenara exclaimed. The last time the guider had seen the young third-trial starguider was on the Isle of Dru only a few days before. So this is the Obet. A chill of premonition tickled Trenara's spine when the young woman gave her a curt nod and leaned on the table to confront Shadedale.

He stopped himself short of an angry reply, and bowed his head to her. "Oracle, forgive me, but this is a matter for the council to decide. The Vow has been broken."

"So the young one tells me."

"Death is the sum of what they have done today, Oracle. You know the penalty."

Her eyes narrowed. "Could you do that to them?"

His voice was a cold as his eyes. "Yes, I could."

"They are your sons, Shadedale."

A moment of pain passed over his eyes, but he recovered and his voice was stiff. "Within these walls, madam, I have no sons."

"Stubborn…" Ricilyn closed her eyes and turned to the others. "Councilors, Captain Shadedale is correct in stating the law is clear. However, it also states that an outsider may apply for acceptance. If sponsored by one of us, they may attempt the Tri-Test. Is that not correct?"

"You know it is," Shadedale snapped.

She ignored the outburst. "If the council is willing, I will sponsor these people."

All eyes turned to her.

"Ricilyn," Shadedale said slowly. "You will risk expulsion—for these outsiders?"

"You call them outsiders, Shadedale," her voice was soft, "but, as I have tried repeatedly to tell you, the fate of the world rests in their hands."

"More of your prophecy…"

"I would gladly sponsor them," she continued with force, "to ensure their safety. There is more risk than expulsion for me." A flash of anger sparked in her eyes. "As you all know, I have no other choice. I will not impose on our friendship, councilors, by asking you to forego the tests entirely. The code binds you. I simply implore you to give these people a chance to prove their worth."

"Friends, you call them." Shadedale looked over at the companions contemptuously. Trenara watched Van, and Haiden bristled, but they kept silent. "Where I do not doubt the men might pass, the woman has no chance in the Pit. Ricilyn, I will not let you risk your life for these outsiders!"

"Let me?" The words thundered through the room. "You forget yourself."

Shadedale lowered his head and took a deep breath. The awe in his voice was unmistakable. "Forgive me, Oracle. I have let my emotions rule my heart… as always."

She granted him a cool nod in response and turned back to the other councilors. "I have also let my emotions get away from me. I apologize. Will you accept my sponsorship of these three people and with it the pardon from penalty imposed by the law?"

Woodhelm rose. "Your sponsorship is gladly accepted, Oracle. However, we have a problem with Leaflight and Limbshade. They have violated the law and must pay penance for what they have done."

"I can only advise," Ricilyn replied, glancing at the brothers. "Wait until the tests are completed. If these people fail, they will be dead and there will be no threat. If they succeed, again, no threat will exist. I understand you must punish the tyros. Death seems extreme to me." She looked at Shadedale and her eyes became soft. "I think their father should decide."

Shadedale looked to his young sons who stood at stiff attention. His eyes flashed once at Ricilyn before he spoke.

"Should the outsiders fail, then I will call the execution." The brothers exchanged covert glances. "If they succeed, then the tyros will lose their rank and start again from the beginning." The brothers relaxed slightly and Shadedale sat back in his chair.

Lark rose and faced Leaflight and Limbshade. "We agree with your father's decision. Will you accept?"

Limbshade stepped forward and bowed before the council. "We will follow whatever the council dictates, sir."

Shadedale turned to Ricilyn. "Your charges... what do they say?"

Ricilyn turned to Trenara. "Speak."

Trenara stepped to the table slowly and gave them a diplomatic bow. "We are not familiar with your customs, councilors, but we will accept your tests. It would be a great honor to belong to your order. I pray we will be worthy of it."

Shadedale shifted in his seat and folded his arms. "Your words are fair, guider. I only hope our Oracle's trust is not misplaced."

Ricilyn searched each of the companions' faces. "How long will I have to prepare them, captain?"

"You have one hour, Oracle."

She whirled around, but caught the outburst and tightened her lips instead. Bowing low before the council, she strode swiftly from the room, the companions following behind her with a little less confidence.

Ricilyn said nothing as they made their way through narrow complicated twists of road. When they entered a dwelling fifteen minutes later, they followed her up a long rope ladder, passing several darkened platforms on either side, to an isolated room at the top.

The view astonished Trenara when she stepped off the ladder. All around her huge curved windows opened onto a grand vista of the terrain in all directions. The cliffs to the west were a line of blue. Beyond them were forests and then the green sea. Mt. Diorne rose behind the Signal Tree as a snow capped giant, with a wisp of smoke rising from the top like the gnarled wraith of an old guider.

Trenara's eyes stopped when she saw the mountain. Her guider's sense burst open and blackness folded in front of her eyes unexpectedly. She broke out in a sweat and shuddered. The desire to go there was so overwhelming she found herself leaning far out the window.

"Trenara!" Van yanked her from the sill and pulled her into his arms.

Trenara was not with them anymore; she was in a cavern surrounded by molten lava, fumes and smoke, burning and choking.

"Fire!" she screamed.

"Trenara?" Van shook her hard, but it did not break the spell. "What is it?"

Trenara could not hear him. All she could hear was the roar of the flames.

Ricilyn guided Van's hands away and took the guider into her own. She stared at her face gravely and then closed her eyes. Her hands melted into Trenara's terror.

"Trenara," Ricilyn screamed, shaking her violently. She slapped Trenara so swiftly Van had no time to react. Reflexively, he pushed Ricilyn back sending her sprawling across the room.

"Slap her, you idiot! Hard!"

Van took a step toward her angrily. "You are not making any sense…"

"Slap her quickly! You will lose her!"

She did not need to say anything further; Haiden stood before the guider and hit her hard across the face—once. The guider staggered back and her eyelids fluttered as she touched her cheek and slid to her knees.

Van pushed Haiden out of the way and lifted the guider into his arm. "Trenara," he whispered.

A quake ran through the guider. She buried her face into Van's massive chest and wept openly. Van lowered his head to lay it on top of hers.

When Trenara regained her senses, her eyes bore into Ricilyn but her face was as still as stone. "Joshan?" she whispered.

Ricilyn did not respond immediately. "Yes," she said mechanically.

"Why? Why have you done this to him?"

Ricilyn's face was set and icy. "I do not question the tasks the gods lay before me, Trenara. I did not have a choice." Her voice was brittle, fragile.

"He will die in the flames."

Ricilyn searched the floor. "No. He will be reborn."

Trenara's eyes widened. "A new trial—a fifth?"

Ricilyn nodded. "I think so." Her mouth curled into a bitter line. "My visions do not tell me everything. If it is a new trial, a fifth trial, then he is the only one who can reach it. He must, for all our sakes."

"Joshan's there?" Van exclaimed, pointing to the top of the mountain.

Ricilyn glanced up at the giant and crossed to a table to pour mead. "Yes, giant."

Van looked down at the guider. "Why?"

Trenara extracted herself from his arms and went to the window. She folded her arms and frowned up at the mountain. "I do not know why, Van. It is beyond us now. Joshan is being—cleansed, for lack of a better word. It is a new trial, a fifth, born from the flames of Diorne. She took him there."

Van whirled on Ricilyn who was handing Haiden his glass. "Do not accuse me, giant," she said wearily, "I did what the visions required of me. Do you think I chose this? I have never had that choice." She rubbed her face. "Please tell him, guider."

"I am so sorry, Ricilyn. I did not know." Trenara watched Ricilyn pour another drink. "She is a Truthsayer, Van, a person blessed…" Ricilyn glanced at her. "And burdened with a gift. A vision of truth, no matter how ugly it may be. If Truthsayers reveal the vision before it unfolds naturally, the future can be altered—usually for the worse." Ricilyn crossed to the other side of the room. "Most Truthsayers take their own lives—in the end," Trenara whispered.

The glass broke when Ricilyn set it hard on the sideboard, but she ignored it. "Are you at least satisfied he is safe now?"

"Of course. I am sorry."

The young woman smiled a bit and smoothed her face. "It is nothing, guider. As you said, it is out of our hands now. I did not realize your link with the emperor was so strong. I should be the one apologizing." She took a deep breath. "I must prepare the three of you for the tri-test. It is not going to be easy."

"What are these tests?" Haiden asked.

"The first two are not difficult," she replied. "The sighting is easily done, if your eyes are good."

"Now, wait a minute, the giant and me, well, we could see a fly on top of a pile of tar from a league off. The guider can't see more than a few spans in front of her face without her glasses. I'd wager she's not got them."

Ricilyn smiled at the guider. "She is third trial, Haiden. She could pass the test without her eyes."

"Well, I have not tried it yet," Trenara said, "but I am certain that is true."

"And the second?" Van asked.

"A test of courage and faith," Ricilyn responded. "I do not think any of you suffer from lack of either. It is the third one that concerns me. It is a test of strength, and though I have no doubt the giant and marshal could manage it nicely, I have misgivings about our good guider. It takes strength and agility. The Trillone have no respect for weakness, in any form, including age. Nor do they make their tests easier as one grows older. If anything, they require more agility as you approach death.

"Do you feel up to it, Trenara? If you pass the first two, I may be able to talk them out of the last for you." She rubbed her shoulder and stared at the floor. "I am afraid I am not very hopeful. Shadedale can be very nasty when he wants to be. Do not take that personally. Captain Shadedale is a fair man and a good person in most things. But he does not like strangers…" Her voice trailed off as she stared at Mt. Diorne for so long Trenara had to touch her arm to bring her back. "Forgive me." She reached inside a bookshelf and drew out a flask. "Each of you will need to take a dram of this before we go down. It is imaka."

Haiden raised a brow. "Isn't that like cheating?"

Ricilyn shook the bottle. "It is exactly like cheating, father. I am not above a trick or two when the stakes are so high." Off in the distance, a bell chimed. Ricilyn sighed.

"Come on, drink now. That is the signal."

They put the imaka on their tongues and the refreshment chilled them to the core. The air smelled sweeter, cooler, and the life force around them more vibrant when the drug worked into their systems.

"Whew!" Van breathed as the liquid took hold. "Now that is better than any draught I ever had. You put something in it, lass?" He shook out his arms as a chill and a flash of heat ran through his body at the same time.

"Nothing much," she said evasively.

She removed her robe to reveal a green forest outfit and thigh-high boots. Her shoulders were broad for a woman, but her figure was perfect. The green well-worn sash at her waist showed her station as a Starguider, and except for the crystal scepter she kept at her side in a leather strap, it was her only link to the past. She let her hair loose from its bindings and it fell to her waist in dark golden brown waves. The change was stunning. Her eyes shone now with a new fire, a blaze of expectancy. Trenara caught the change, but could not fathom it. Ricilyn slithered down the rope ladder without a word and the companions followed her.

CHAPTER NINE
TEST OF THE TRILLONE

The arena was larger than any Trenara had seen before. At its center was a great pit. A narrow bridge no wider than a man's foot went across it. The sight unnerved her. She turned to scan the multitude of people scattered around the clearing. At one end of the arena was a large dais with a table at its center. The council sat at the table, with Shadedale looking grim at the center. Ricilyn and Miere sat on either side. Mt. Diorne peeked out from behind the massive boughs of The Signal Tree, the early sunlight painting the snow and clouds at its crest a pale pink. The dais was the only structure in the clearing under the trees and the other Trillone present sat on the ground around Trenara, Vanderlinden, and Haiden. Porphont stood in front of the dais with his arms folded, awaiting instructions.

A man named Green stood with the companions. He was an older Trillone with sparkling gray eyes and a stern face. Trenara gathered from Ricilyn during their brief discussion that this man instructed of the unruly tyros. She said he had sharp eyes and keen judgment. Green could spot a mistake in the performance of even the simplest of tasks from a great distance.

He motioned to Van to come and stand beside him, drawing a line in the dirt at his feet. "Stand there," was all he said and the giant moved to the line.

Shadedale signaled to Ricilyn and she nodded. Porphont came to life and produced two objects from a basket on the ground. The distance was well over fifteen spans.

"What does the master hold, Vanderlinden?" Green asked.

Van measured the distance and spoke without hesitation. "A branch in the right hand, a dish in his left."

Green nodded. Porphont removed those items and reached for two more. "Now?"

"A green bottle in his right, a leather hat in his left."

Green signaled Porphont and again the items changed. "Now?"

The items were tiny this time and Porphont held them between two fingers each.

"A pearl in his left, a seed in his right. The pearl is blue, the seed, from a winton fruit, I believe," Van replied smugly.

Green said nothing and motioned Haiden to take Van's place.

Haiden had no trouble with the test. He stated them quickly and took his place back at Trenara's side.

When Trenara approached the line, apprehension seized her, but she quelled her fear and let her guider's sense take over. The first two items she could see with her naked eye—a stool and a book. The second two were a little more difficult, but with a great deal of squinting, she saw them—a cup and a tablet. When it came to the third set of items, no amount of refocusing of her eyes would do. She finally closed them entirely and concentrated on Porphont who held them. The vision came with a wave of nausea.

When she opened her eyes, Green was looking at her darkly.

"A needle in his right, a thread in his left. Hardly a real test, my good man," she said.

The man pursed his lips, snorted an acknowledgement, and turned to cross to three poles lodged in the ground. At a signal from Green, three boys came out of the crowd and bowed low.

"Bind them securely."

The boys led each of the companions to one of the poles and tied their hands behind the rough wood.

"Hey," Van cried, "not so tight."

The boy looked up at his master whose eyes narrowed. "Securely," was all he said. They finished tying their charges and sat back among the crowd.

The companions were not very comfortable, but knew what to expect. At Ricilyn's tutorage, they prepared their nerves.

When Master Green moved off to the side, the morose sound of a gong echoed across the clearing twice and three figures emerged from behind the dais; Limbshade, Leaflight, and Boughman. They were dress only in white loincloths and bands of green around their brows. Each held a long curved blade that dazzled in the late afternoon sun. In exact precision, they stopped, fell to one knee, then lowered their blades before the companions in a ritualistic bow.

Green stepped out and gave Limbshade a dubious look. "You must be mad to do this." His voice was soft but stony.

"It is my father's wish, Master Green," he said tightly.

The master's face softened. "Why?"

Limbshade looked at the companions. "It is our test, Master Green, to prove to him we are worthy of his trust and training. If we succeed without injuring them, we will not have to re-train. If we are sloppy and come too close, then we will. If we injure them…" His voice faltered.

"What of your brother? He is two seasons behind your training."

"Leaflight knows what is at stake."

"Then I will see to it you both come within a hair's breadth before I pass you. Show me you are of your grandfather's breed and that my training has not been wasted on you." Limbshade nodded curtly.

Shadedale stood at the table across the arena and signaled to Green. The older man bowed to him and raised his hand to the crowd. "Let the test begin."

The arena grew very still. The three men got up from their knees and raised their swords to the dais in salute. Shadedale's nod was vague at that distance.

Young tyros carried out three small tables with melons on them and set them before Limbshade, Leaflight, and Boughman. The youngsters scurried to get out of their way. The three men lifted their blades high above their head in perfect unison and swept them through the air four times, their eyes closed and their bodies slick with sweat. In an instant so fast the companions did not see the action, they brought the blades through the fruit, first down and then across the middle. All three melons were still in one piece, until they were touched with the tip of a blade. Each fell into four identical pieces. The tyros appeared again and removed the tables, while the warriors stood still with the blades extended, staring at the bound companions. Other tyros ran to wipe what little juice there was on the blades.

Vanderlinden's mouth went dry. "Guider," he breathed, "I know what the lass said and all—but, ah, them swords ain't exactly butter knives. Are you sure…"

"Shhh, Van. Remember what Ricilyn said. Hold perfectly still, keep your eyes open, and the fear down. They do that only to frighten us. It is their way."

"Some way," Haiden whispered.

Boughman was the first to move. He came forward, jumped, and flipped in the air to land inches from Vanderlinden. The tunics the companions wore were soaked with sweat. Each of them stared straight ahead and did not make a move. They had bound Trenara's breasts flat but that was small comfort.

Limbshade moved next, moving through the air with practiced ease, followed by his brother. They all stood there for a breathless moment, face to face with their respective targets; Limbshade with Trenara, Leaflight with Haiden, and Boughman with Vanderlinden. Their blades ended mere fractions from the companions' noses.

Again, the three warriors glided into a blur of white, tan, and gold; this time bringing their swords across the companions' middles. There was no sound as they finished their sweep, except the whistle of the swords, but the garments parted where the blades had passed. No blood was drawn.

They repeated this process again and again, slashing for a different part of the body, each time coming close enough to rend the material, but not the delicate skin underneath, or in Trenara's case, the bandages around her chest. By the end of the third pass, where the blade did not touch, the fabric clung like a second skin against the companions' bodies.

There was a moment of silence as the three warriors stepped back and collected themselves for one final pass. Tyros came out to wipe their brows as the companions unknotted tense muscles and tried to relax. The gong rang once quietly and all they saw were three circles of killing metal that came at them in a haze. Despite her own warning, Trenara had to close her eyes, but she was not alone—none of them saw what the blades did to the last of the garments they were wearing.

The three warriors used their swords with machine-like exactness and cut the materials from the companions' bodies. When they opened their eyes, the material that had covered their chests was gone. Limbshade, Leaflight, and Boughman knelt before them in a litter of shredded material, their blades buried in the ground before them, their heads down.

Master Green came out and went to Vanderlinden to examine his body and the remnants of cloth on the ground. He held up ten fingers to the dais and Shadedale nodded quietly. Green then turned to Haiden and examined him. On the old guard's shoulder, he found a nick, no larger than a pinhead that had not even gone through the second layer of skin. He turned to Shadedale again and raised seven fingers. Again, he nodded.

When he got to Trenara, the examination was long and painstaking. He covered every inch of her chest and even picked up a scrap or two of the material, checking the edges carefully. He finally shook his head and stood, brushing the dust from his hands.

He looked down at Limbshade and called his name. The boy looked up at him quizzically.

"I know it is unusual, but I wanted you to see this." In a powerful sweeping motion, he lifted up ten fingers to the dais. The crowd, at all other times silent, now let out a cheer that shook the leaves in the trees around them. Shadedale surged to his feet bewildered and ran from the dais with Ricilyn and Miere behind him. When he got to them, his face was pale with wonder.

"Green!" was all he could manage.

The master nodded quietly. "It is true. I have never seen a finer display with the sword by one so young—ever." He put his hand on the boy's head who kept it down obediently. "Limbshade, you have honored your father today. More than that, you have honored me."

"Thank you, sir," Limbshade's voice was tired and slow. "That means more to me than any words you could have said."

Ricilyn had gotten Tyros to let the companions down and they now joined them.

"And you," Green continued, looking over the companions carefully and shaking his head. "For outsiders, your courage is amazing. I myself fainted the first three times I took that test. What about you, Shadedale."

Shadedale's face reddened. "Uh—twice."

"Thanks just the same, master," Haiden said, as a young boy supported him long enough to keep his legs from buckling, "but I think I need to sit down."

Van and Trenara would have said likewise, but they could not manage more than a grunt as Tyros led them to a cool spot to rest. Shadedale and Miere left supporting his two sons. Boughman went with his mate and three small children who beamed at him proudly as they helped him out of the arena.

A pavilion, set with food and drink, had been provided for the companions. It took some time for them to catch their breaths and recover from the ordeal. Ricilyn joined them in the tent as they were pushing plates away and finishing a cup of the heavy tea made from the leaves of the tree.

"Come in, Ricilyn," Trenara beckoned. "You can answer our debate over that pit out there. Vanderlinden seems to think we simply need to cross it. Is that right?"

Ricilyn toyed with a cup on the table and pursed her lips. "Well, in a manner of speaking, I suppose that is essentially correct."

Trenara furrowed her brow. "Go on."

"You do have to cross it—but to make it more difficult a stone collar is placed around your neck and a lot of people throw things at you. As if that were not bad enough, they spin you around several times before placing you on the bridge. Once there, many other people shake it as hard as they can. Just to keep it interesting, there are spikes in the bottom of the pit. From that height, they should kill you instantly."

They all stared at her.

"Sounds charming," Haiden snorted, folding his arms and pulling on his pipe.

"Well, you asked," she said sitting across from them.

"Any advice as to how to do it?" Van said.

"The best way is to not walk the bridge at all, but rather get down and go at it hand over hand, from below. You are less of a target and can keep your balance. The only problem is those stones are heavy—heavier than I think you could manage, at any rate," she said to Trenara. "I really cannot see any way out of it. I could give you more of the imaka, but that will not make this easier."

"Can you talk to the council, lass?" Van asked.

"I have, giant. The law really is quite clear. I cannot push any harder than I am."

Trenara glared at her two companions. "Now, wait a minute. Am I so dotard and decrepit that the three of you think I cannot manage a task such as this? I am not that weak."

"Now, Trenara..." Van began.

"I will not be treated like a feeble old woman! I would like to remind you, Admiral Vanderlinden, I not only ran an empire, but also managed to survive more ordeals than you would care to think about. What I lack in brawn, my dear giant, I am quite capable of making up in intelligence. Or have you forgotten my battles with Palarine, Balinar—and with Sirdar himself," she ended with sudden darkness.

"I am sorry, my beautiful lady," Van kissed her hand. "I almost forgot. But we care about you and where you are great in a battle of wits, you are not as physically strong as this might require. I don't want to see anything happen to you."

Trenara touched his cheek and kissed him.

"I will do the best I can. I admit I am not as strong as I used to be, but I still have a trick or two up my sleeve. If I fail, I fail. There is nothing we can do about that." She stood and looked down at them. "Let's get this over with."

When they arrived at the arena, the council was waiting for them. Ricilyn squeezed each of their hands in turn and joined the council on the high platform. The crowd surrounding the arena now settled around the pit.

Green had three stone yokes sitting up beside him. They were narrow on the sides, but long in the front and back. They looked heavy and awkward to manage. He nodded and then beckoned to Vanderlinden.

As Green strapped the yoke into place, he whispered to the giant, "My advice is to stay beneath the bridge and do not look down. Wait until it stops swaying—we only shake it once. Then orient yourself before starting across. Once started, go as quickly as you can. I have seen to it that people around the arena do not have much to throw. But most of them are expert shots—keep your eyes open."

The yoke around Vanderlinden's neck was heavy, but not as cumbersome as it might be for Trenara or Haiden. He nodded as best he could and took his place before the bridge. He looked down once, but wished he hadn't. The spikes were long, vicious, and so close together, a snake could not get through them. He swallowed past the lump in his throat and waited.

Green saluted the council and Shadedale gave him the signal to start. Two men came from the crowd and helped Green turn Van around several times, until his head spun and his stomach churned. They guided him to the end of the bridge and put him on. Almost at once, the bridge began to sway. He knelt down on the bridge and swung himself beneath it awkwardly, the weighty yoke cutting into his shoulders. He hung there for several seconds, waiting for his head and the bridge to stop swaying. The crowd was very still.

When the bridge stopped, he started across, shuffling his hands one at a time as fast as he could. It seemed like the other side was leagues away.

Then the crowd threw things; fruit, large seed pods, rocks, anything they could find. Green had not been lying when he said they were deadly shots. Most of the items hit Van's hands—hard. The first volley came as such a shock his right hand slipped off the bridge and he almost fell. The crowd took in a hushed breath, but he caught himself in time and steadied himself. More objects catapulted toward him. As big as he was, most of the objects did nothing more than glance off his body. It seemed like an eternity, but he was finally across. The crowd roared with pleasure.

Haiden went through the same process, but being lighter and more agile, he crossed the bridge in half the time. When they removed his collar on the other side, he fell to his knees, exhausted.

When they put on Trenara's collar, her knees nearly buckled beneath the weight. Green held firmly to her elbow to keep her up and looked at her uncertainly. The yoke was immeasurably heavy for the guider, but she stood on her own two feet with a grim look of determination and did not require help again. She nodded stiffly to the master.

Around and around they spun her. With her training, she was able to keep her head level. She felt no more than a little dizzy. When they put her on the bridge, sweat poured from her, the strain of the yoke too much. She almost lost her footing. She managed finally to get to her hands and knees before they swayed the bridge. Back and forth it went, as she tried to maneuver herself beneath it.

She lost her footing and slipped. The crowd was instantly on its feet as the council ran to the pit. It took three of the Trillone to hold Van and two more to hold Haiden to keep them from aiding the guider. In a breathless moment, Trenara reached for the bridge as she fell and grabbed it with her hands and legs, clinging to it like a child to her mother. When the swaying stopped, she lowered her legs and started across.

The weight around her neck was excruciating. It took every ounce of training she possessed to put the pain out of her mind. Her hands were so slick they continually slipped on the thin wooden planks. Her eyes were so clouded with moisture she could not see the other side of the pit. She was never going to make it across.

Her progress was slow and as each hand moved forward, the crowd gave a quiet cheer. Ironically, there was not a single object thrown at the guider. Whether anyone noticed, was later debatable.

She made it to the halfway mark and stopped to rest. Although the sun was nearly gone and the evening approached rapidly, no one left the guider to get lights. Trenara could feel their anticipation like loving hands, and it allowed her to make a few more feeble attempts. It was useless. She could get no farther. The stone was dragging her slowly to her death.

"Help her!" Van cried as more of the Trillone held him back.

Ricilyn squeezed Shadedale's arm tightly and bit her lip as she watched the guider. "Stop this," she hissed at him.

Shadedale looked at the terror in her eyes and turned to seek the other council members. It was too late. Trenara's hand slipped again and she did not have the strength to lift it up a last time. Her world was going black.

Just then, a flutter of wings broke the stillness and a blackened shape plunged out of the air like an arrow. Fiena, Ricilyn's vulcha, flew to rescue the guider, ordered there by a power she would never be able to comprehend. Sleek and black against the coming night, she swooped beneath the guider.

Trenara's fingers lost their hold. When she landed on the bird's back, it jarred her to the bone. She weakly clutched the feathers with her last strength. It happened so quickly, Trenara was on the ground on the other side of the pit before anyone could react. Once her charge was safe, Fiena gave a piercing shriek and flew back to her nest on Mt. Diorne without a second glance at the guider or the crowd.

Ricilyn pushed through the crowd to get to Trenara with Shadedale behind her, beaten there by Haiden and Van. The giant held the guider in his arms as best he could with the yoke around her neck. Trenara was breathing heavily and crying. Green pressed through and removed the yoke.

"Thank you. That was getting rather heavy," she said, smiling through her tears. They were so relieved to hear her voice a great cheer went up from the crowd.

In the midst of the noise, a hush fell. It started as a ripple at the back of the crowd, first a murmur and then a gasp. Van and Haiden looked up to see the crowd parting.

The people fell to their knees one by one, as the silence moved forward. Shadedale stood up abruptly and his mouth hung open.

Ricilyn looked up at their astonished faces, but did not turn to see it. Tears filled her eyes. The guider took her hand not knowing why Ricilyn was so terrified. Shadedale and all those around them fell to their knees.

Trenara looked passed Ricilyn and gasped. "By the gods," she whispered. "Joshan?"

Ricilyn closed her eyes and would not look back.

"Ricilyn," Joshan said from behind her, his voice a haunting echo on the air. "We all have things too harsh to confront sometimes—things which our souls tell us we cannot bear. I have seen my demons. I have seen the path I must travel to destroy them." Ricilyn looked up at Shadedale, but he had eyes only for Joshan, the green sparkling with a devotion she had never seen before. "I cannot do it without you." There was such sorrow in Joshan's voice she thought her heart would break.

She rose and turned slowly to face him, her eyes closed and her voice frozen in her throat. For several heartbeats, she stood there shaking, afraid to look at him... afraid not to.

Joshan reached out to cup her face in one hand and wipe a tear away. Ricilyn opened her eyes slowly and lost her heart.

He was tall, dark, and strong—a mirror image of all her visions. They melted into the man standing before her. His eyes were alive with the black fire he had bested on the mountain. She fell into those eyes helplessly, all fear forgotten. The smile that slowly grew erased all the lingering resistance she had. There could be no more doubt.

When Joshan held his hand to her, she took it without hesitation. Joshan kissed it tenderly, touched her face again, and then took her into his embrace. The torrents of fire rising in her body, the smell of his musky odor, the sound of crinkling fire still smoldering in his eyes, combined to envelop her in warmth, security, and inevitability. She could never go back.

As if it were as natural as breathing, Joshan lifted her chin and pressed his lips to hers, the scintillation soaring through her spine as his touch suffused her with strength, passion, and a boundless contentment. Her eyes filled with the same black fire that lingered in his. The soaring flames that burned around them made everyone shade their eyes against the brilliance.

Joshan held her tenderly in his arms when he broke the kiss and a beautiful benevolence glowed across his face, making him look almost godlike.

"I have one task, beloved," he whispered into her ear and she nodded.

Joshan crossed to the Trillone council looking up at him expectantly from their knees. The fire that surrounded him rolled black and grey on the air, shimmering like electric smoke. When he addressed the people, his voice echoed so loudly through the valley, he had to whisper to be heard.

"All of you rise," he commanded, his eyes flashing. "You are a great people and should bow to no one."

Reluctantly, the people rose to their feet and gathered to hear him.

"I come here as your friend," he said sadly, knowing the demands he would give these people would change them forever. "And to charge you with a mission. On the mountain, I saw many things. Among them, I saw a proud, noble people who have trained for seasons to become guardians of this world." Mutterings ran through the Trillone.

"Please," Joshan said raising a hand, "let me finish." The noise died down and every eye was in rapt attention.

"I know you do not see yourselves in this role—not yet—but it is your first, best destiny and the dream of your prophet, Conifere. He knew a thousand seasons ago when he trained your ancestors that this would eventually be your fate. I have spoken with him," he said, and many gasped. "He has charged me to bring the strength of the Trillone to the world. For generations you have trained for this, even if you were not aware of it. You will now share this knowledge with everyone, as is your duty. Conifere commands you to fulfill your promise to him."

He took the staff from his back and drove it into the ground. A bright amber radiance poured from the top of the staff and spread until it formed the Trillone symbol for their ancient name. The Trillone stepped back when they saw it and shouts went up.

"It is his staff!"

"It is the prophet's sign!"

"The prophecy!"

Joshan regarded them quietly until the noise subsided.

"Here is Conifere's last message to the Trillone."

From out of the top of the staff came a voice all of them knew, although they did not know how. It reached into the souls of the Trillone present.

'For a thousand seasons you have trained, advanced, and grown with the skills I have taught you. I am proud of your accomplishments, your wisdom, and your compassion. You must fulfill your promise. Before you stands the fulfillment of my prophecy. You will follow the Ganafira and take your place as the guardians of the world. Fight for him—protect the world.'

When the voice stopped, the light disappeared and the Trillone looked up at Joshan with wonder in their eyes. He sighed deeply.

"In secret you have built a fleet on the eastern shore of this island—fifty ships," he said and the tribal council looked at each other incredulously. No one knew this secret except the builders and themselves. "You will load the ships with your warriors and supplies within the next two days. At the end of that time, you will sail to the Keep and join the soldiers there to fight our common enemy. Captains," he said reluctantly, "muster your people, arm them and prepare for war."

The council members gasped. These were the signal words. They never thought this would come in their lifetime. Without hesitation, they saluted Joshan, split up, and called out orders to their troops.

The change in the crowd was immediate and staggering. Every Trillone moved like lightning to form columned groups that stood at attention awaiting orders from their generals. The council barked commands in the Trillone language and stood at the head of each column. Scurrying tyros rushed to wrap each commander in gleaming armor. As the companions moved to join Joshan and Ricilyn, deafening horns shrilled loudly through the valley.

Thousands of Trillone appeared from the trees, filling the columns with precision. Rank after rank of fighters appeared as if by magic. The armored men and women, with a staff or lance at their sides, focused on their commanders. Thousands stood in perfect rows answering their generals' orders in unison. The deafening sound resonated to the trees, shaking the leaves with its intensity. After a thousand seasons, the Trillone would march to war.

CHAPTER TEN
THE TAMING OF THE MOURNA

The night was diaphanous and warm, stars spilling across the black sky like jewels and the moons came up, ablaze with light. The meadow was still.

Joshan and Ricilyn knelt together, their hands touching, their lives meshed, and all around them the world turned and the universe spun. The power was only a dark glow now, soft and silent in the night, which flowed like a mist around them. When it finally dwindled, Joshan lowered his head and closed his eyes. Ricilyn gently touched his face.

"You must rest now," she whispered.

Joshan opened his eyes and kissed her hand.

"No. Not yet." He helped her to her feet and walked her through the moonlight.

"You are an enigma, Ricilyn," he said. "In the fire, I saw you, laughing, crying, loving…"

"Joshan…"

He turned to look at her. "…hiding. You are closed to me in so many ways. What do you hide from, Ricilyn?"

She turned away and continued to walk.

"I am a Truthsayer. Did your visions tell you that?"

"Yes," he replied.

"Do you know what that means? What it is like to see truth?"

He took her hand. "I know truth can sometimes be painful, difficult to deal with. But I also know now it is what you do with truth that makes it bearable."

She glanced at him and shrugged. "Perhaps." Ricilyn did not say anything else for a long time as they walked in the moonlight.

"I have seen the future, Joshan."

He kept his pace and looked up at the stars. "I know," he said.

"Do you?" Her voice was very hard.

Joshan grabbed her arms so quickly she winced. He yanked her into his chest and looked deeply into her eyes. She saw such agony there her knees went weak.

"I do not want to know the future. You must never tell me what lies ahead for all of us. Keep it hidden—even if I beg for it—even if I threaten." He shook her with each syllable. "Do you understand?"

"Yes," she whispered.

He took her into his arms and held her head against his chest. "Forgive me, Ricilyn."

She clung to him tightly and grief overwhelmed her. With a clarity that rang in her ears like a warning, Ricilyn understood Joshan, loved him, and pitied him. Within his hands he held the power of the universe, within his mind the knowledge of ages, within his heart all compassion, and yet he was still human, still fragile… still the child. She could feel the injustice of the burden and the price Joshan was paying for humankind. Yet he continued to maintain his sanity. Ricilyn wondered if she would have the same courage were she in his place.

Joshan led her to the Signal Tree and there climbed the limbs as if he were coming home. When they reached her tower, he leaned out the window and stared at Diorne.

"Was it painful for you?" Ricilyn asked tentatively, sitting behind him in the dark.

"Yes, in a way," he replied without turning around. "Have you even been to the mountain?"

"Only once. I saw… well, I guess it must have been Conifere, though I did not know it then. He taught me very much. Is he…"

"He is gone."

Ricilyn felt a tear make its way down her cheek. "I am sorry. I liked him very much. He told me then he would not last the season."

Joshan did not move. "Tell me about Assemblage, Ricilyn. Why did you leave?"

The question startled her, but she joined him at the window and went into his arms. "That is a long story. You need rest, beloved."

Joshan kissed her gently and touched her face. "I can rest later. Tell me about Assemblage."

She folded her arms around his chest and closed her eyes.

"When I was three, the revelations began. Little things at first, about other children—toys or books being lost—things like that. When I was five, I had my first vision; I saw Assemblage falling to disfavor. They would actually be swayed by Sirdar in the end… they would eventually help him." She smiled. "You can imagine they were not thrilled with Saminee's precocious little girl. He nearly lost his post as Provost over it.

"When I turned ten, I reached first trial, which bred a great deal of jealousy among the other children. Not that it was any great loss, mind you. Because of the visions, I knew more than many adults, let alone children. It unnerved people to hear me speak with a high little voice about matters that belonged behind closed doors. They shunned me; not only the other children, but the adults as well. They called me an atrocity," she whispered.

"My only supporter was my father. He trained me himself, when the scholars would not let me into the academy. When I reached first trial, I could not receive my via with the other pre-guiders. My father and I had our own ceremony in the back of the house with just the two of us and several cats. I do not know where he got the scepter. I am certain he stole it." She ran protective fingers over it and touched the orb at the top tenderly. "I never did ask him. I do not think I really ever wanted to know." She laid her head against Joshan's chest, taking comfort in the sound of his heart beating.

"When I reached second trial at thirteen, they had to include me in the ceremonies, Grandor saw to that. He was furious with the guiders for excluding me.

"By the time I reach third trial, a shock to everyone I am certain, the dissension had started. Slow at first, a comment here, a quibble there. Although there was nothing you could put your finger on, no one you could see or blame. The guiders looked to the power and not to their knowledge. Children spent more time with their vias than their books. I tried to get my father and the others to see it, but they ignored me—and worse. There were some very bitter moments.

"Shortly after that, I had another vision." Her voice became brittle as she stared at the stars. "I saw a man with a blaze of fiery hair and green eyes standing on an island. I saw a way of life so like my ideals and hopes for our society I had to go and seek it. I told my father I had to leave.

"Something happened to him then that I could never explain. For some reason he became so angry, I thought he would strike me."

"What did he say to you?" Although Joshan's words were quiet, there was intensity to the question. Ricilyn's mind became exceptionally clear and the scene unfolded before her mind as if it were fresh.

"He did not say anything at first. Then, without warning, he began to cry. I had never seen him like that. I thought it was because I was leaving; I knew he loved me. But this… this was something else and it terrified me. He kept saying over and over again that he was sorry. When I asked him for what, he kept babbling about the Crystal and the vias. He was not making any sense. I almost called Grandor thinking that maybe father was losing his mind. Then he looked up at me with a strange expression on his face and said very clearly, 'He will crawl from beneath his tomb and look for it. Do not let him touch you.'" She shook her head. "It was the oddest thing. Then right after that, he came to his senses. He did not even remember what he had said. When I asked him about it, he acted like I was out of my mind."

Joshan touched her face and kissed her on the forehead. "You are certain that is all he said."

"Yes. Father became adamant about my staying and we quarreled. He had plans for me, he said. With my abilities and control of the power, I could be the greatest Provost Assemblage had ever seen. If I wanted to change things, he argued, I should stay there and do it from the seat of power. His speech sickened me. It stank of the tripe being fed to the students. It split us apart. That wound never did heal," she added with a sad lilt in her voice.

"I was fifteen then," she continued as she closed her eyes and let Joshan's warmth soothe her. "Despite my fear, I became determined to find that island. I stole a boat from the harbor and headed west in search of Dru. It was a foolish thing to do, but I was young and angry.

"That voyage…" Her voice broke off and Joshan held her closer. "I was sick for so long I do not remember most of it. Eventually, the sickness passed and I managed well enough. When the storm hit, I mastered it at first, kept the small boat from capsizing, but then more visions came and I lost control." Her eyes were wide with the terror of that memory. "I do not even remember the boat going under. It was as if another will saved me that night—as if Ethos were there with me. I only wish I remembered more. That strange bird, the vulcha, Fiena's mother, appeared out of nowhere, and snatched me away from death. She brought me to Dru and laid me on the shore. Shadedale and Porphont found me later, half-dead, screaming in terror, they said. What I saw…" She shuddered in his arms. "It drove me to the brink of madness. I remained a prisoner to the insanity for many months."

He did not ask her about the visions; he knew she would not answer.

"They brought me back, Joshan. How, without the power, I could not fathom then. They trained me well and gave me a new life… a new existence here on Dru. They called me the Oracle, because of my sight, my training, and the healing powers. I taught them about medicines, the culling of plants and the use of musical instruments that they had not mastered. I kept their small ones from sickness and their women from dying in childbirth. I gave them everything I could possibly give them—except the power. I would not teach them that. They already had their own. I still owe them so much."

"We will pay them together, my love," Joshan whispered. Ricilyn did not reply, but simply looked at the night. "You are thinking of Porphont. You have seen tragedy for him?"

She looked up at him. "Tragedy? I do not know. Not tragedy, perhaps, but a changing that no one will be able to undo. He is an empath, a rare thing here. A disease at birth left him deaf and mute. The Trillone taught him sign language and the fighting ways at a very early age.

"When he and Shadedale found me and brought me back to life, the two of us developed a strong empathic connection. Since then, he has acted as my protector, my guardian, I guess. Although, believe me, not at my request." She laughed lightly. "Porphont is one of the most accomplished masters in the trees and yet he treats me like… like a goddess. He will not tell me why. I do not really think he knows himself."

A wave of passion fell over Joshan as he looked down at this woman, her hair a dark golden fire in the moonlight, her eyes a wintry blue. He lifted her chin and played his mouth against hers gently, searching, seeking. When she responded to his touch with equal desire, he lifted her into his arms as if she were as light as snow and took her to the bedchamber.

Keenly aware of his inexperience, Joshan allowed Ricilyn to guide him to her body. Every caress of her hand on his flesh seared into his passion like a branding iron. Every touch of her soft hot skin under his fingers bound his soul more tightly to hers. He reveled in the moment, unable to stop the urges rising to consume him. The boy disappeared forever inside the flesh of this woman he loved.

With no more words spoken, their bodies joined and Joshan felt ecstasy for the first time, awed by its command, amazed his heart did not stop at the height of their passion. The power awoke around them intensifying their pleasure. They both knew the challenges that lay ahead, the trials and uncertainty of the future. Knowing there would never be another moment like this, they let the future go and succumbed to the rare joy.

Several hours later, Joshan lay awake and stared up at the darkness. The moons had disappeared and the night was a cold blackness around him. Ricilyn lay in his arms, soft and warm. He sank back into the pleasant memory and then kissed her.

Joshan knew what awaited him in the frozen pre-dawn. He could hear it even now—the low-pitched whines, a compelling desire grating on his guider's sense. He slowed his heart, regained his certainty, and then smiled to think how easy it was. Any other guider would have instantly surrendered to that seductive cry.

Ricilyn stirred and her eyes flickered open. She lay there listening and her breath caught in her throat. Her hands tightened around him. "Mourna," she whispered.

"Shhh, my love," Joshan replied quietly, kissing her face. "It is not here for you."

She looked up at him urgently. "Joshan?"

He touched her lips with his. "Forgive me, my love." He brought his hand over her eyes. The black lashes closed involuntarily and she sank back into the covers. "Sleep now." Her breathing slowed. He kissed her again and arranged her comfortably under the blankets.

The Mourna's cry grew louder as he stood and dressed. He threw a black cloak over his shoulders, grabbed the staff Kerillian had given him and went to seek the golden sword.

When he descended the rope ladder below the tower, he saw it glowing softly in one corner of the room. Next to it stood Trenara.

The guider stared at him, her eyes glazed with sleep, her gray hair mussed and tangled. Joshan returned the look briefly and reached for the sword. Trenara's hand came across his wrist to stop him.

"You hear it. You know what it is," the guider said softly.

Joshan smiled at her and took the sword from its place, strapping it to his waist.

"You are not going out there."

Joshan tied the sash. "It calls to me, Trenara."

The guider's face was incredulous. "Are you insane? That is a Mourna, a servant of Sirdar."

"Do you think I lack the power to handle the demon's messenger?" Joshan's voice held such contempt Trenara took a step back, fearing the barely veiled black fire she saw in his eyes.

She searched his face a long time. "I do not know what power you lack, Joshan. I only know what the Mourna can do. I say again, it is a dangerous animal and serves only its master."

"I know, Trenara," Joshan said softly, "but I have to go."

The guider gave him an aggravated snort. "Very well, I will not try to stop you. If you must do this, look to the creature's heart, if it has any left. It is said they were human once."

Joshan took the guider in his arms and held her. "Thank you, Trenara."

"Yes, well, you may not thank me later. Is Ricilyn…?"

"Asleep. Watch her for me?"

Trenara nodded once and Joshan disappeared into the dark. Trenara buried her face in her hands as Van came out of the shadows and crossed to her. He wrapped his massive arms around her and they both stared out at the night without saying anything.

When Joshan was out on the furthest branch, he whistled for Fiena. The bird came lumbering out of the mountains at his call, the massive black wings shadowing the night, the naked head and neck stretching out toward him.

Fiena was an ugly creature, vulturine, predacious, with marble red eyes, a bumped and knotted head, and a bare and bruised neck. She was the antithesis of Ricilyn. Yet, for all the horror of her looks, the vulcha's good heart glistened from her eyes like a searchlight.

She nestled beside Joshan and allowed him to caress her neck and above her eyes, nudging his hand when he stopped and crooning softly when he found the right spot. When Joshan had ordered her to rescue Trenara from the pit, he did not realize what a bond the mental link would make between them. Fiena, not understanding why, would fight to the death for him.

The Mourna's cry floated like a lament in the unmoving air and each new moan sank deeper into Joshan's awareness as if it were trying to find his soul and capture it. Fiena's head twitched toward the mountains and then back to Joshan uncertainly. He rubbed her head once more, climbed onto her back, and dug his hands into the feathers at her neck.

"Go." With a great sigh of wings, Fiena jumped from the branch and took to the air.

Mt. Diorne loomed before them, black against the sky, the snow at its top a lighter shade of darkness. The trees fell away beneath their feet in a blur of dark green. Nothing stirred in the night except the Mourna's cry and the wind of flight.

Before them in the gloom, a ledge of granite stuck out like a disk from the side of the mountain. It was bare except for a single black figure at its center. Fiena hesitated in her flight and let out a questioning cry, but Joshan allayed her concerns with a hand on her neck and guided her down to the ledge. The Mourna's voice stopped and the night became very still. Joshan slid from the bird's neck, the crunching gravel beneath his boots falling harshly on the silence.

He sent the vulcha back to her eerie with a nod. Fiena looked at the darkened figure ten spans away and gave a soft warning croon in Joshan's ear, but then unfolded the large black wings and leapt into the air. With a final cry, she wheeled around the ledge and flew back to her nest with all the speed she could gather.

Joshan removed Kerillian's staff from its leather housing at his back and opened the sheath that held the golden sword. His robe billowed out behind him when a gust of wind circled the platform. He brought the staff before his eyes with a gloved hand, and singing a somber musical note, thrust it into the rock. It went into the granite as if it were newly tilled soil and hummed like a plucked bowstring. From behind it, Joshan drew out the sword and called the power. It came to him as a fireball from the sky, white and brilliant.

When the light filled him, he waved the sword and called Ethosian moths, bits of light, one by one, and bade them circle the staff. The ledge became an illumination of crystalline beauty when the lights danced in chaotic patterns around the staff. Putting away the sword, he stood back and folded his arms, staring at the giant figure that hid in the shadows beyond the fire.

"Come to the staff, Nissa," he ordered, his voice spiraling along the ledge and down into the valley below.

A deep sibilance snaked from the shadows, the hiss sharp. Two points of lights were all Joshan could see inside the darkness.

"I will not. Send the moths away. I cannot abide the light," it whispered.

"That is because you have been in darkness too long, Nissa. The starmoths stay. Either you can come into the light where I can see you, or I will bring the light to you. Which will it be?"

Again, the Mourna hissed in the shadows, but her wings rustled softly and she lifted herself in the air. She circled three times and then glided down to rest before the staff. Squinting, she brought a wing in front of her eyes.

"Now," Joshan began. "Why have you come here?"

Nissa shied away from his voice. "To help you, sire."

The starmoths became agitated and the staff hummed violently. For a moment, the ledge was a confusion of color and sound. Joshan's eyes turned hard. He calmed both with his hands. Nissa retreated several paces and let out a great cry.

"You lie so easily—like your master," he said coldly. "But the starmoths and the staff do not seem to agree with you. I will ask you once again. Why have you come here?"

The Mourna stared at the starmoths suspiciously and narrowed her eyes. "Send them away. I cannot stand them."

"Answer my question, Mourna."

Nissa preened nervously in the strange half-light. Joshan stared at her, but said nothing.

"The master has sent me to befriend, and in the end, betray you," she whispered.

The starmoths did not change their patterns about the staff and it hummed quietly in the night.

"So I have seen," responded Joshan. Nissa stopped her preening and Joshan smiled. "I know your mission, Mourna, and the plans of the demon that sent you. I also know there is something else in your heart your master could not detect. What is that heart's desire?"

Nissa lowered her eyes and searched the ground at her feet.

"I wish only to die." Her voice had a bitter edge that echoed through the granite. "I wish to die with the monster's body clutched in the talons he forced me to wear. I seek his blood for the degradation he has wreaked on me, and my family. It is the only way I can make retribution for the evil I have done at his command. I do not regret those things he has made me do; I regret only that I have not enough self-will to kill myself... or the devil who rules me." She looked up at Joshan. "You can give me that."

The starmoths and the staff were quiet in the graying dawn as Joshan regarded the giant bird standing before him. Pity swept through him, but it hardened into grim resolve when he thought of the future.

"There is a gift the master has promised that might change the drift of your devotion. Would you not accept this gift in the end and betray me?"

She stared at him a long time.

"Perhaps," she said at length. "As to the end, I can guarantee nothing. For now, I will bear you where you order me and give you what little loyalty I have, if you will help me destroy Sirdar and the magic he wields. What comes in the end comes and I cannot change it. It is all I can give you."

Joshan nodded slowly. "Very well."

The staff hummed violently in protest and the starmoths became a flurry of lights. Joshan waved his hands and the moths disappeared instantly. He wrapped his fingers around the staff and it darkened to a gray stick when he pulled it from the ground.

"But hear me, Nissa," his voice boomed out angrily. "You will follow my orders precisely and obey me in everything I ask of you. Do you understand?"

Nissa lowered her feathered head once.

"You will speak to no one but me, nor raise your voice to lure another guider from this point on. I am unaffected by your voice and can condemn you to an eternity of imprisonment within your feathered shell—just by lifting my hand. I will quell the monster's voice in your mind, but I will not abide your disloyalty. In the end, if you have served me well, I will grant your wish and give you death, if that is your desire. Until then, you will serve only me. Is that clear?"

Nissa closed her eyes in surrender and lowered her head to the ground before him. "Yes, my lord," she whispered.

Without another word, Joshan mounted her and ordered her to the sky. The Mourna leapt into the night and flew where he guided.

CHAPTER ELEVEN
FLIGHT TO BADAIN

"Wake up, guider."

Trenara started out of her slumber to see Ricilyn staring down at her. The guider did not see Van when she lifted her head from the table in the chamber where they had held their vigil the night before. There was a new contentment in Ricilyn's eyes, a beauty that glowed from some inner place and sparked in her eyes.

"Joshan?" Trenara asked.

Ricilyn's smile broadened. "Still in the mountains. We are to meet him at the ship. Are you ready to travel?"

"But the Mourna…"

"He is safe, guider. Get your things gathered and I will have someone bring you tea." With that, Ricilyn scurried down the ladder and disappeared with Porphont close behind her. Trenara rubbed her eyes and left to find her pack and Van.

High atop great Diorne, Joshan was finishing a cairn for Kerillian. The wintry storm was gone and the sky above was blue and clear. The snow at his feet glistened brightly before the cave entrance as he placed the last stone. Nissa stood back from the cairn and preened herself in the icy world until Joshan finished his task. He saluted the grave quietly in Trillone fashion and then studied the cave solemnly. Lifting the staff, he swept it once to the right and the mountain answered with a submerged rumble. The ground shook violently and the Mourna shrieked. A stream of boulders and rubble tumbled down the cliff above the cave entrance and sealed it.

Joshan climbed onto Nissa's back and ordered her to the sky with a touch. The great wings stirred a flurry of snow when she jumped into the air. Joshan ordered her to the ship.

Grandor sat on the prow of the Morning Star reading from a leather bound book of poetry from his own library. If he was anxious about the return of the companions, it did not show.

Tam came up to the guider and stared at the colorful shore. His eyes had dark shadows underneath them. He had not slept since the admiral left the ship.

"Are you certain they will return, Grandor?"

The guider looked up from his book and regarded the young man. "They are safe, that is all I can say."

"We should send a party to find out for certain. The admiral would have sent word. If those people have harmed them..." But his voice trailed off when he saw Grandor laughing and pointing to the forest.

"There is your answer, my good man."

Van and the others were emerging from trees into the sunlight. They all looked robust and healthy. Tam breathed a sigh of relief. He forgot about Grandor and shouted order to his crew to lower the boats to pick them up.

When the companions were all on board and their things settled, Van ordered the crew to their stations, and then ordered the guards to construct a strange enclosure, a cage. The specification included a floor strewn with rushes and a giant perch at its center.

"What is this for, sir?" Tam asked as he came from his station and saw the giant pen.

Van wiped sweat from his forehead with the back of his hand. "You'll see." He called to Ricilyn who was directing the workers from the other side. "Will it do, lady?"

Ricilyn nodded. "It will, admiral. If you will order the workers away, I will call her now."

Van cleared the people from the deck and Ricilyn stood on the prow, staring at the mountains. She was silent for several moments, her eyes closed, swaying in the hot sun. Off in the distance a black speck climbed into the sky, racing toward the ship. The crew exchanged guarded speculations as they watched the black mote grow. Unexpectedly, a second speck appeared next to the first and even Ricilyn was puzzled. As the two figures grew, their wings became visible. The first was small in comparison to the second, but both were black and sleek. Ricilyn stepped back in horror and Haiden exclaimed in alarm. They could all clearly see the soaring form of Fiena with her scarlet neck. Next to her flew the Mourna.

On the bird's back sat a figure, shrouded in darkness, with only gloved hands showing from under a cloak. His face and head were shadowed. Van and his crew were instantly at the ready, brandishing weapons and jumping to the great harpoons. Trenara's eyes went wide in astonishment, but she raised her hands to the crew to keep them from shooting the creature.

"Wait!" she cried and everyone stood breathless.

Moments later the birds flew as one to land on the open deck, the vulcha letting out a great cry at seeing her mistress and the black Mourna silent and nervous. Everyone stepped back from the pair as the figure slid from the nightmare's back. Van drew his blade with a quiet hiss and stepped forward.

"If I were Sirdar, giant, your weapons would be less than effective." The figure lifted the hood from his face and Joshan's eyes shone out darkly as he smiled at his friends. "I did not mean to frighten you. It is cold on the mountain."

Van lowered his sword and snorted an acknowledgment. The rest of the crew went back to their stations.

"You have a strange choice of friends," Trenara said, gesturing to the still Mourna.

Joshan patted the bird's neck and ordered her to fly to the forward mast. Ricilyn examined her vulcha carefully. The bird was in perfect health. She sent the vulcha to the enclosure, but after a cursory glance, the bird went instead to perch beside the Mourna on the mast. Ricilyn ordered her away, but the bird ignored the commands. Fiena stood beside her strange new friend and crooned contentedly. Ricilyn huffed, but let it pass.

"I apologize for my entrance," Joshan was saying when Ricilyn joined them, "but Nissa must travel with us to Badain."

"That bird is a menace." Trenara scowled up at the Mourna and let a shudder run through her. "Are you forgetting what one of her kind did at Sanctum?"

"I have not forgotten, Trenara," Joshan replied. "The Mourna has a role to play in the end. I am not certain what it is, but I know it is vital."

"It will betray you, my love," Ricilyn said going into his arms.

"Perhaps. I have no other choice." He looked down at Ricilyn and ran a rough thumb over her forehead. "Neither us do. For now the Mourna will obey me."

Ricilyn looked up at the black giant and nodded slowly.

"So what happens if she uses her voice against us?" Trenara asked relentlessly.

"There are many here who are not affected by the spell of her voice, even if she could use it. I have stilled it for now and silenced the commands of the master from her mind. As we approach Badain, my hold on her may diminish. I do not know."

Trenara looked at him a long time, but finally resolved herself to the situation with a curt nod.

"And how, might I ask," put in Van, "are we supposed to care for her? What does she eat? How does she sleep? We have hardly enough stores for the crew we got, let alone a giant like that."

"I think I can help," Grandor said, pursing his lips and frowning, "although I do not relish the task. I have learned something of the care of Mournas—at least some things the bird can eat. If the emperor will allow her, she can hunt for herself on the open sea. She and the vulcha can eat scraps from the galley, if necessary. I will see to it that they are fed and cared for."

Van nodded and then looked at Joshan. "Are we ready to sail, sire? The tide is good now."

"Yes, Van. Make for Badain."

Van left with his first mate and ordered the crew to depart. Trenara and Grandor went to check the galley for stores for the creatures and Haiden left to check on his guards.

A dark tremble ran through Ricilyn when she looked at the bird. Something in the Mourna's stance reached a part of her hidden under her consciousness. Joshan took her into his arms.

"Never trust it," Ricilyn said quietly.

Joshan could feel her fear and held her close to allay it.

"I do not intend to, my love. Nissa's fate will affect us all, I think. Your Fiena seems to have taken to the Mourna. Trust the vulcha's instincts. An animal will sometimes sense things even the wise cannot see. Take what little comfort that provides and let the future take care of itself.

He reached down and brushed a wayward hair from her forehead. "There is so much I need to tell you—so much I need to learn. We will take what little time we have left before the battle to find out what we can from one another. There may not be time for it after."

Ricilyn allowed Joshan to lead her to his cabin. The sun sank down on the horizon as the ship lurched toward Cortaim.

CHAPTER TWELVE
THE MERCENARY

No matter how many they killed, the enemy kept advancing. Nothing the imperial forces tried would stop them. At first, thousands came from the south and Sark's army made headway. Then it became tens of thousands, a relentless swarm of southern humans, sasarans, deinos, tarsians, and laminia. The provincial soldiers fell further and further back until Sark and his army stood no more than a hundred leagues from the gates of the Keep. Their forces, which once numbered nearly thirty thousand, had dwindled to less than fifteen. This night would be their last before the desperate race to reach the Keep and sanctuary.

Sark sat on a foaming eecha, shouting orders and rallying his troops. It was an hour before dawn. The enemy had pressed hard, trying to overrun them before the sun rose, before the daligon and his creatures had to retreat from its light, before the southern hoards had to rest.

There was no skill or honor in their attack, no valor, or experience in the way they fought. It was a relentless advance of wave after wave of disposable soldiers thrown at them with little regard for life. Sark lost track of how many he and his captains had killed that night. There were so many, the field was muddy with blood and choked with bodies. Carrion fowl blackened the skies.

Then came a lull in the onslaught and the captains took what rest they could, grimly waiting on their panting eechas. Sark rode through the throng of soldiers and ordered them to regroup and reline. The men and women obeyed without complaint, even though many had serious wounds and all were exhausted. From atop his eecha Sark watched another wave of enemy approaching only a few hundred spans away.

"To the line! To the line!" he cried, galloping past the soldiers and ordering Joshan's banner unfurled. "Steady!"

"Steady!" The reply rang from the troops in perfect unison. They stood at ready stance, their weapons poised.

"Prepare!" Sark cried.

"Prepare!" echoed back across the blood-soaked ground. Every man or woman squared their shoulders, bent their knees in preparation, and cast dour eyes at the enemy.

"Joshan!" The shout sparked a rolling thunder of 'Joshan! Joshan! Joshan!' from the columns. They hit their shields in time and repeated the chant over and over again. The valley shook with the sound. Their weapons sparkled dully in the fire from the torches they carried.

In black livery and darkened helmets, the enemy moved like a wave out of the gloom, outnumbering them ten to one. Without warning, the advancing throng stopped on the field a few hundred paces before the nearly spent imperial army.

Sark stood at the front of his soldiers, staring into the black line of monsters and men before them, wondering what devilry they were up to now.

"Hold!" he cried to his soldiers to ensure they did not break the line. They stood perfectly still.

On the leading edge of the enemy throng, a shadow straddled a great tarsian lizard with massive clipped wings and muzzled mouth. Sark had only heard rumors of this creature and a spark of apprehension filtered through him as he watched the captain of their forces—the daligon, Sirdar's Champion. The blackness held a great spear as large as a small tree and around it were seated four more riders on giant black eechas, all dwarfed by its size. The shadow rose as if standing in the stirrups of the beast and a twisted breeze carried his susurrant voice across the field.

"Hear me, remnants of the Imperium," the sound was a whisper, but all could hear it. "A chance I give you to save your lives. Give me your captain, Sark DeMontaire, and you may return to Thrain unhindered."

Shouts went up from the soldiers cursing the daligon.

"Hold!" Sark cried with such force the voices instantly died. The soldiers stood in rigid readiness. Sark's captains gathered around him protectively.

"Give me this man Sark and you may all go home to your families. Deny me this and you will be tortured and your families enslaved." The sound made their ears ache. The creature moved its mount forward a step.

"Ready!" shouted one of the captains to the troops who replied with a rippling ready through the lines.

"Fools!" the daligon cried as his four captains gathered around him. He held his spear aloft and brought it down, signaling his army to attack. The black wave moved.

"Archers, away!" A brilliant blanket of lighted arrows soared through the night air in an arch of shooting yellow stars. Hundreds of the daligon's troops fell. Hundreds more surged into the empty space without stopping. Four more volleys flew above them and more enemies died. The void filled instantly.

"Forward the mounts!" the captains shouted and every eecha and rider toed the line, their spears or swords drawn, their faces grim.

The shadow and his four captains charged toward Sark.

He raised his hand. "Steady!" he cried and the word rippled back through the rank. The wave was nearly on them.

As the leading edge of the enemy came within spear range, the eechas screamed a challenge. Lancers charged into the line impaling as many as they could, sometimes three or four at a time. Swords flashed in the torchlight as hundreds of mounted men and women waded through the throng of charging foot soldiers before them, killing so many, that the bodies trapped the Badain troops. The battle was a blood bath.

The wave of enemy soldiers skirted Sark and five of his captains, making a great "V" around them with the daligon and his mounted men at its apex. They came at them like a black storm.

Sark's captains forced him behind as they formed a line to shield him from the daligon's attack.

"Stand back!" Sark cried, but they ignored him and brought their spears to bear on the attackers.

Two of the daligon's captains flew from their eecha, a spear protruding from their middles, hanging there lifeless on the deadly barbs. One of the daligon's captains, a large sasaran, breached the line and killed two of Sark's captains with a great axe. He went down with an arrow in the eye slit of his helm. An expert archer lowered his bow from behind the line.

Only the daligon and one soldier stood before the remaining four captains and Sark. The daligon hissed furiously and pulled hard on the reins of his mount.

The tarsian lifted silver clad talons and cut one of the women and her eecha nearly in half. The giant claws then caught another captain, Tige, swiping her from her saddle and hurling her hundreds of spans away. As the woman flew, the last standing captain, Donnelly, heaved his spear straight for the lizard's soft underbelly. The monster shrieked causing everyone within earshot, both friend and foe, to cover their ears in pain. The black shadow that rode its back fell from his mount and sailed back. The lizard died quickly.

The daligon rose like a mist from the ground and stood beside the black armored soldier who survived. Now only Donnelly and Sark stood before the shadow and his captain, while the Badain hordes held back the rest of Sark's captains and the Thrain soldiers who desperately tried to reach their commanders. The shadow lifted its long staff and his captain twirled the two he was carrying until they blurred into wheels of death. Donnelly charged toward the daligon, but was not quick enough. The shadow caught him on the temple before he could get within range to strike. He fell from his eecha and crumbled into a pile on the ground.

Sark stood alone to face his two enemies, one a completely iron clad soldier and the other a menacing shadow. He howled a challenge and charged them, his sword swinging.

The monster's staff caught him on the side and sent him tumbling from the eecha who screamed in terror and fled. Sark lay stunned in the mud, this lance arm broken along with several of his ribs. They moved toward him swiftly, the captain circling around behind him and the shadow standing at his feet.

Sark's arm was useless and all he could do was lift the other to protect his face as the shadow raised his staff. He saw the spinning staffs over his head from the captain behind him. They moved in for the kill.

At the same time the daligon brought down his staff to crush Sark, the captain buried his staffs into the ground on either side of Sark's head and crossed the two pieces of wood above his face. The force of the blow from the daligon nearly splintered the wood, but the staffs held and Sark was still alive.

Before the daligon could respond, the first ray of sunlight broke over the horizon and he shrieked. In a whirling cyclone of blackness, the monster shadow disappeared into a rupture cut into the dawn and was suddenly gone. The rest of the mass of Badain troops fled screaming in the opposite direction, disappearing into the vast plains beyond.

The daligon's captain pulled back on the staffs to let them fall and went to his knees in the mud. Several of the troops ran to Sark. The enemy put his hands behind his helmet and bowed it down low. Many charged to kill him.

"I yield!" the stranger cried. It was a woman's voice. The daligon had no women officers.

"Hold!" Sark cried and everyone stopped. He winced in pain as one of his bloodied captains helped him to his feet. Limping to the kneeling figure, he pulled the helm from her head.

A train of golden hair fell from beneath the iron and folded around her face. She had none of the tattoos associated with Sirdar's forces or the scars that marked someone as servant to the daligon. With his good hand, Sark brushed the hair away from her face. She looked up at him breathing heavily.

"Hello, father," she said.

"Have you completely lost your mind, Sareh?" he screamed. The young woman calmly sat at his feet. "Do you have any idea what the daligon or Sirdar would have done if they had caught you, or what they would have done to you to get to me? Whose idea was this anyway?"

"Mine," she said quietly, letting her father vent his frustration.

He looked at her incredulously. "You are supposed to be on Dru studying! Does your mother know where you are?"

Sareh glanced down at her legs tucked neatly under her.

His arm already wrapped tightly inside a splint, Sark scowled at it and then cursed the healer when he pulled the dressing snugly around Sark's ribs. "Are you trying to kill me?"

"Sorry, sir," the healer replied without taking offense.

Sark whirled back to his daughter. "This is the most foolish, dunder-headed, idiotic, selfish thing you have ever done. And you have done some pretty stupid things, young lady! Do you have any idea what they would have done to you? Any?" He bellowed in pain when his excited breathing caused his broken ribs to ache.

"You feel better now?" There was a twinkle in Sareh's eye and a soft smile softened her lips. She looked so much like her mother Sark had to shake his head.

He took a deep breath and smiled back. "A little," he said motioning her to come to him. Sareh jumped up and gently wrapped her arms around his right side so she would not jar him. Burying her face in his chest, she held him for a long time.

"I have missed you so much," she whispered. "I am so sorry, father. I tried to get word to you, but it was too late. This was the only way I could find you." She stopped and looked at the healer who was finishing up.

"Thank you, Amane," Sark said to the healer, dismissing him. "Please tell the captains we will meet in a quarter hour." Amane bowed, gathered up his materials, and left the tent.

"All right, tell me," Sark said seriously as soon as the man was gone. Sareh went back to her blanket and sat down.

"Shadedale sent me, father—with mother's blessing, I might add—to see if I could help here." His knowing look was dark and Sareh looked down. "All right, it was my idea, but I asked their permission first. I had just reached my masters and I wanted to help. Anyway, when I got to the Keep you had already gone, so I met with Commander Thiels, showed him some of the things I could do and talked him into letting me go south to see what I could find out.

"I traveled through the border woods until I came to their camp three weeks ago. I followed them north until they stopped. An opportunity presented itself, and I took advantage of it," she concluded evasively.

"I see," Sark said, sitting down carefully. "An opportunity?" She simply nodded. "What kind of opportunity?"

She took a deep breath and looked up at him impishly. "The daligon's captain, a southerner, came into the woods to relieve himself and I… well, I… persuaded him to get to know me better."

"You seduced him," Sark said flatly.

Her father was the only man alive who could make her blush, which she did, brightly. "Well, yes, in a way." She looked up at him. "But he did not touch me, father." A bemused smile spread over her face. "As a matter of fact I think he thought I was some kind of forest imp."

Sark nodded. "And he would have been correct."

"Anyway," she said forcibly, "I finally… incapacitated him, took his clothes, and joined the daligon's forces just as they were leaving." She shook her head. "That damned eecha nearly got me killed when I mounted it. That was as close as I got to discovery, but the daligon was entirely preoccupied with his hunt for you and apparently did not notice. I got the animal under control before he caught on." She looked up at her father, her eyes twinkling. "You are the only one I know who can get any man, woman, or beast mad enough to become completely obsessed with destroying you."

Sark smiled. "How is your mother?"

Sareh rolled her eyes. "Never mind," she said, but then knelt in front of her father and took his hands.

"I have seen the extent of their forces. The sortie this morning was nothing. What you saw was merely the beginning of their troops; there are thousands more behind them. You have to get your people to the Keep. You cannot fight this on the field." Her voice was so urgent, her face filled with such pain, his heart went out to her.

"What would you have me do? Run?"

"Yes," she urged. "You have to. Whether you know it or not, you are almost as much a symbol to these fighters as Joshan." He shook his head modestly, but she touched his chin to stop it. "If you die, the heart will go out of these people." Tears welled in her eyes when she caught his eyes. "I know you do not want to hear this, but you cannot win," she whispered. "Turn back now. Go to the Keep and…"

"And hide," he finished for her. She closed her eyes and bowed her head, knowing he would never leave the field. He gently lifted her chin and searched her face.

"Did I ever tell you how proud I am of you? You are my only weakness, girl." She nodded and laid her head on his leg so he could stroke her hair. "I know I was not always there for you, child… or for your mother. I am very glad she found a good man in Boughman on Dru and I am delighted you have completed your training. But, I want you to do something for me."

"What, father?" she whispered from his lap.

"I want you to go back to Dru… and live."

"I cannot do that," she said simply.

"Why?"

"Because now that I am here, I am not leaving again. Whatever comes, father, I will not leave your side."

Sark remained silent and fought back the tears that threatened him.

The captains sat in a rough circle, the argument getting louder as the meeting progressed. Sareh reported everything she had seen. Opinions varied widely on what they should do. Some argued they should stay and fight, while others said they were losing valuable time, should make haste to the Keep and fight from there. Several wanted to take the troops and wipe out the enemy during the day, when they were weakest.

Sark said nothing during the debate, sitting quietly to one side, staring off into the encampment and watching the soldiers as they rested. Sareh was very concerned for her father, but kept her tongue, knowing he would do what he thought best.

At length, he quietly stood before the men and women.

"This is a very difficult decision," he said, wincing a bit from the pain. "But one that only I can make." There were nods of agreement among the captains, but no one said a word. "My daughter has told us our enemy's number and it is beyond our capacity to withstand. The best we could hope for would be to die valiantly and keep them at bay for one more day." He shook his head and looked down. "I, for one, will not leave the field."

"Nor I," called one commander.

"Nor I," called another.

Sark raised his hand to silence them. "That is as it should be," he continued. "But I cannot also spend life like my enemy to gain a day. This is my decision: One thousand will stay on the field to give the others time to reach the Keep. We will hold the enemy back until they ride over us. If we succeed, we should be able to hold long enough to give the others a chance." He stood up straight and gave out orders.

"Donnelly, you and Tige will immediately select one thousand of our finest. Go to the sergeants and have them give you their best riders, archers and swordsmen— only the best. They are to muster here within the hour."

Donnelly and Tige saluted their captain and rushed to the field. "The rest of you, start the others moving. I want every living soul headed for the Keep, and the camp struck within the hour." His other captains bowed and left.

"Healer," he turned to Amane, "get stretchers put together and get the wounded moving now. I want to see them out of here right away." The healer bowed and left for the infirmary tents.

As soon as they were all gone, Sark shakily sat down on a stump and Sareh ran to him.

"Father, are you all right."

"Yes, girl," he said quietly. "I will be fine. Go help the healer, will you?"

She kissed him on the cheek and searched his face, but obeyed his request and went to see what she could do for the wounded.

Sark and Donnelly stood to one side of the field, each silent as they surveyed the men and women breaking camp. Donnelly rarely asked to speak with Sark alone, so the commander knew there was something important on his mind. He also knew he did not have time for Donnelly's usual taciturn replies and pressed him.

"What's on your mind, captain?"

Donnelly scanned the camp and looked behind him before replying. Sark had never seen him so tense. "There's something wrong, Sark." His normally deep voice sounded odd in a whisper and it put Sark on alert.

"Go on."

Donnelly stuck out his bottom lip and gave his commander a long cold stare. "Someone has been issuing orders that are contrary to yours."

Sark scowled at him as his eecha stomped under his legs. "What are you saying?"

"That bastard should never have caught you like that on the field," he said, a look of guilt crossing his face. "There should have been a good six hundred more troops on that front line. He should never have gotten through."

"Don," Sark said smiling, "no one could have predicted that. The troops did their best."

"No," he said adamantly. "When I questioned the sergeants, I am telling you someone changed their orders."

Sark looked at him incredulously. "Who?"

Donnelly shook his head and unconsciously readjusted his reins. "I do not know and no one else knows either."

"Where did the orders come from?"

The captain gave him a bemused smile. "Parchments—signed by you."

Sark blinked at him. "What? I do not give written orders."

"I know."

"So, who..."

"I don't know, but six hundred people were on the flank when they should have been on the front line. I think we have a traitor in our midst."

Sark lowered his head and let the declaration sink in. "Do you suspect someone?" he asked Donnelly and the large man scanned the camp.

"Not specifically. All I know is it must be one of your captains."

"What?"

"Sorry, Sark," Donnelly replied, staring down at his hands. "They knew your codes. They were on the orders—that is why the sergeants followed them. It didn't even cross their minds that the orders were not from you. There are only nine of us that know that code; you and your eight captains."

Sark went through the list mentally. The captains had been with him for many seasons, some as many as twenty. "Three were killed during the battle," he said quietly, more to himself than to Donnelly. "So, who does that leave?"

"Boric, Drisselle, Tige, Shaun and... me."

Sark shrugged and gave him a sparkling eye. "I don't suppose it's you, is it?"

Donnelly laughed quietly. "No, I'm not that smart. Besides, I would look you in the eye to kill you." He spat into the dust and watched the captains as they rallied their soldiers or ordered wagons loaded.

"Maybe it was one of the others; Fluera, Chasel, or Kron," Sark suggested hopefully.

"Maybe. That would make your life easier, since they're all dead. I don't think so. Fluera and Kron only had parts of the code and Chasel couldn't write, remember? So unless he got someone else to do it..."

"Damn!"

Donnelly shifted nervously on his mount. "You got any other ideas? Anyone said or done anything lately that was odd or out of place? Any fights or discipline I don't know about?"

Sark thought a long time. "No. Boric and Tige have been with me longer than you have, my friend… Shaun and Drisselle, almost as long. I can't think of anything that would make them want to betray me. We've been through everything together."

"Well, maybe it's someone else. Maybe somehow the codes got stolen or someone picked them up from one of us…"

"I hope so." Sark turned his eecha toward the line forming behind them. "I will change the codes immediately. Not that it will make much difference. I don't think any of us are coming out of this alive. Just in case, keep your eyes open for me, will you?"

"Count on it, general!" Donnelly spurred his mount to the other side of the line.

Three quarters of an hour later, the exodus to the Keep began. It was just after the noon hour when a thousand soldiers gathered in a line before Sark. Sitting on his eecha, he surveyed the troops with his captains and daughter at his side.

All told, there were two hundred archers, one hundred riders and seven hundred swords and lances. Most of them were seasoned veterans, all of them experts with their weapons and experienced fighters.

The captains had some initial difficulty when word spread that only a thousand were staying. Many protested loudly, ashamed they would have to leave the field. Sark spoke to them, saying if the thousand lost the line, he relied on those left to protect the rest and get them safely to the Keep. It was their duty to the emperor and to him. They did not like it, but they obeyed without further objection.

For the next four hours, Sareh did what she could to prepare the thousand. There was so little time, but she gave them every trick she could think of.

His little girl's abilities amazed Sark. He saw her take on men twice her size and bring them down with no more than a fleeting pass.

She spoke so quickly to the troops, trying to impart as much as she could in the short time allowed that no one absorbed it all. Awed by her knowledge and her fighting prowess, they listened intently to everything she had to say. An hour before dusk, they took what little they could glean from her teaching and slowly formed the lines.

Archers would be at the back where giant oil pots balanced precariously on wagons, waiting for a flame to ignite them. Great bearing eechas bred in Selas, chomped at the bits to pull the heavy wagons forward. Each oil pot was full of arrows with rags wrapped around their barbs and the archers positioned to march next to the wagons in a straight line where one arrow would light the next. Then there were the swords, spread out as far as they could stretch on the open plain. A thin forest rose on one side of them and a cliff on the other, so the line was as solid as they could make it. The gaps between them were unnervingly large. The lancers spread out before the swords, their spears gleaming brightly in the late afternoon sun. Finally, in the front line, were the riders and the sergeants, their eechas screaming for battle and rearing excitedly for the night to begin. In the center rode Sark and his five surviving captains.

Sareh rode up to her father and scanned the plains with him. Behind her were three other scouts on the swiftest eechas they could find.

"We will scout through the forest, father, and come back as soon as we can. You should be able to get at least five or six leagues in. They will not attack until it is very dark which should be in about an hour." She leaned up to kiss him. "We will be back before then."

He kissed her forehead. "Be careful."

She smiled and tightened the grip on her reins. "I always am." Sareh called to her soldiers and disappeared into the forest.

With a deep breath, Sark glanced at his captains and gave the nod. They spread themselves out evenly along the line and started their slow march over the plains to find the enemy.

Such was the precision of their march, that their line stayed almost as straight as it had begun. Drummers pounded the cadence as they moved forward. The only sound on the plains for leagues in every direction was the heavy beat and the dulled pounding of their feet or the eecha's hoof falls on the grasses. When they marched through the battlefield from the previous night, it reeked of feted death and decay. The mud was still slimy with blood, but they did not break their ranks as they marched on, the soles of their boots hob-nailed for traction. The sun sank slowly below the horizon and soon it became dark except for the torches and the pots of fire at their back.

The plain was otherwise silent as they moved forward, but the soldiers readied their weapons. In the cold of the evening, they prepared themselves for defeat. They all knew this would be the last stand.

Twenty minutes into the march, Sark became worried. They had not met a single foe or seen so much as a trace of enemy. He called for a halt and went with his captains further into the night. It was deathly quiet.

Finally, as they walked cautiously to the top of a rise, an incredible sight greeted them. There on the plains were the remnants of a massive campsite that spread out for many leagues in all directions. Campfires were still blazing, tents still standing, pots boiling over small stoves, and tatters of clothes and materials were scattered everywhere. There was not a living creature anywhere among the debris. As they crept forward, they saw bodies—hundreds of them—but these were not victims of war. They were wounded men and women, bandaged or treated. All were now on the ground, their throats cut, or their heads removed. The southern hordes had killed the wounded and then deserted the camp. The sight appalled even the most seasoned warriors among the imperials. None had ever seen such an unspeakable atrocity.

From out of the shadows, Sareh rode her eecha at full speed, the three other scouts following closely behind her.

"They are gone," she cried as she approached. "All of them. We saw the last of them rushing to the north and disappearing into the woods."

"What?" Sark asked, not completely comprehending.

"They are gone. Something has driven them to the north. Their own captains are whipping them, forcing them to run as fast as they can to the mountains. We heard them. Sirdar has ordered all of them to the north. They killed their wounded so they would not hinder their progress—they butchered them like animals. But the rest are gone, tens of thousands of them."

"Why?"

"I do not know, father. But there is something else," her voice broke as she touched his arm. "I heard one of the captains. They march to the white castle of Calisae—they say the emperor is coming and they will meet him there. I do not understand, father. Why would they leave—now?"

Sark shifted in his saddle and surveyed the carnage. "He said this would happen. I did not believe him," he whispered, more to himself than to Sareh.

"Father?"

"Never mind." Sark signaled his captains who rode to his side instantly. He looked down at his daughter and touched her face. "Do not worry, my darling." He looked up at his captains. "Return to the Keep to regroup! We will march to Calisae and bring the war to them."

They bowed to Sark a bit confused, but followed his orders and reorganized their troops to race back to the Keep. Sark looked at the deserted camp a last time and could only shake his head in disgust.

CHAPTER THRITEEN
CORTAIM

The journey from Dru to the mainland was agonizing for Joshan. Every day he spent on the ship was one more day for Sirdar to get his fingers around the provinces... and Ena. The Crystal would not let him use the power to move the ship faster than the improved sails would take it, and there was nothing he could do but wait.

Ricilyn had been his only blessing during those long days. As each hour passed, his love deepened. She was beautiful, brilliant, talented, resourceful, and experienced. Everything, Joshan thought to himself, he was not. Whenever they spoke it was a revelation, whenever they laughed it was a cleansing, whenever they loved it was an awakening. When he was away from her, he felt empty, unworthy, alone. He wondered over and over again why she loved him. When she was with him, he felt fulfilled and did not care why. He could not imagine how he had survived before her.

The third night of the journey, Joshan and Ricilyn stood on the deck looking at the stars. Both were quiet, each lost in thought for a long time. The sparkling universe filled the black of night above their heads. Joshan stood behind her with his arms wrapped tightly around her waist, afraid to let go.

"Vanderlinden asked me a favor today," he said faintly into her ear.

"Yes?"

"He asked if I would perform the marriage ceremony for him and Trenara."

Ricilyn turned around in his arms. "That is wonderful. I am so happy for them."

"So am I," he said leaning down to kiss her and taking her back in his arms.

"When?"

Joshan did not say anything at once and she looked up at him. He stared out at the sea.

"Before we get to Cortaim." His voice was hushed.

Ricilyn laid her head back on his chest. "Oh," she whispered. "Has Trenara seen something?"

"No," he said, "they want to do it—before." He sounded very sad.

"Ricilyn," he said after a long pause.

"Yes."

"I asked Van to return the favor."

Ricilyn's breath caught in her throat and she did not look up at him. His heartbeat echoed in her ear.

"Yes?" The word came out hoarse, without air, and she had to force her lungs to behave.

"He said he would."

She breathed a little more quickly. "Would what, my love?"

He reached down and lifted her chin to capture her eyes. His were almost completely black in the starlight, but they shone like jewels, with a deep submerged light of their own. She would do anything he asked her.

"I love you, Ricilyn," he said quietly, almost painfully, "I want you to be my wife—my consort."

The smile that blossomed from her lips made her blue eyes a bright light to his darkness. He would do anything she asked.

She leaned up and kissed him gently. "Of course I will."

A glorious joy spread over his face that astounded Ricilyn. She had never seen anything more beautiful. He picked her up and kissed her soundly, spinning her around and letting out a very un-emperor-like whoop. For just a moment, a fleeting second, she caught the reflection of the ten-season old boy that still lived far beneath those tragic obsidian eyes. Again, her heart went out to him. Despite their dark fate, it was this moment she would always remember.

The next day there was a subdued ceremony and celebration, first with Van and Trenara and then with Joshan and Ricilyn. Haiden served as best man at both, borrowing formal robes from Joshan, which were too large for him. He looked very handsome nonetheless. Trenara had loaned Ricilyn one of her best robes and had chosen a flowing white gown for herself. Joshan gave each of them lovely hairpieces from the treasures he had brought. He gave Van a priceless wedding wristband for Trenara in brilliant greens and golds and chose one for Ricilyn in whites and blues. The women were stunning.

For the first time in two seasons, Van donned his captain's formal dress uniform, and unlike the admiral's outfit he had worn at the Keep, this one fit him perfectly making him quite a dashing figure. Trenara had never seen anyone more handsome.

Joshan, of course, was required to wear the imperial dress uniform and he looked like what Haiden called 'a proper monarch.' Of course, Ricilyn and Joshan would have to repeat the whole process on the mainland. Traditionally, the emperor and consort were married at the Keep with a four-day celebration where they were married, blessed, and crowned in an exhausting ritual that made the Assemblage dogma seem quick and pleasant. Joshan much preferred the quiet on-board marriage.

After the ceremony, there were many toasts and congratulations, but a shadow shrouded everything. The knowledge that none of them knew how much of a future they had or what they would find when they reached the mainland darkened their hearts.

Despite this small piece of happiness, Joshan's heart grew increasingly heavy as he approached Sirdar.

On the tenth day from Dru, as the Morning Star glided into the Port of Cortaim, every gunner and archer had their weapons ready, every sailor was on high alert awaiting quick orders to change course or retreat at a moment's notice.

When they drew nearer, however, the docks were silent and every mooring slip was empty. Sea scalards darted in and out of the harbor in great flocks, feeding on unknown carrion in the streets. There was not a living soul visible.

Above the docks, the city appeared deserted. There was no smoke rising from the chimneys, no sound save the cries of the scalards and pips. The place was as still as death in the rosy sunrise.

Joshan stood on the foredeck with Ricilyn and Trenara staring at the vacant harbor, all three scowling in surprise. As the brig slid slowly into the moorings, Haiden reluctantly gave the order to stand down to his guards and Van told his sailors to leave the guns. They all stared up at the massive castle that loomed above them, black and menacing in the early dawn.

"They are gone," Joshan whispered.

Ricilyn looked up at him. "What?"

"They are all gone. Except…" He stared up at the castle and a something shadowed his face. "Van," he called, stepping down from the foredeck, leaving the woman to look after him in wonder. "Van, spread your crew out through the town. Search everywhere for survivors." He joined the admiral under the mizzen.

"Survivors?" Van asked tentatively, the deserted dock and adjacent town seeming more ominous than if it had been full of foe.

Joshan gazed up at the high towers. "Someone is alive here—and hurt. Send your crew. Tell them to spread out and search the town from end to end. Now, Admiral."

"Aye, sire." Van shouted orders to weigh anchor and secure the lines to the dock. The crew came alive immediately.

"What is it?" Ricilyn asked as she joined him. The look in his eyes frightened her. She took his arm.

He scanned the high towers looming over them. "Get Fiena down." He squeezed her hand and went to the open deck to summon Nissa.

The Mourna's wings unfurled slowly as she loosened herself from the highest mast. She leapt into the air and glided around the ship to land at Joshan's feet. Bowing very low before him, she raised the human eyes and stared at him quietly.

"Do you know what has happened here?" he asked her. Trenara joined him, careful not to stand too close to the bird. They had come to an icy truce during the voyage, but she still could not abide the creature.

"I do not, master," Nissa replied, lowering her eyes before him.

Joshan scowled at the Mourna, knowing she was hiding something.

"We will try this again." The rising anger was unmistakable in his voice. Nissa lowered her head further. "Do you know what has happened here?" he repeated forcefully.

The bird lifted her eyes to him. "Not entirely, sire," she whispered. "I know the master…"

"I am your master!" Joshan spit the words so vehemently at the creature that Trenara gave him a startled look.

The Mourna cringed and lowered her eyes again. "Forgive me, master. Sirdar told the daligon to send all the troops to crush the mercenary," she whispered urgently.

"When?" he cried.

The Mourna cringed again. "The night we took the girl… fifteen days ago."

"Why did you not tell me this before?" Joshan raised his hand to strike the bird.

Trenara pushed herself in front of him and looked up incredulously. "Joshan!" she cried.

The uncontrolled rage in Joshan's eyes frightened Trenara, but the mad fire melted almost at once into confusion. He took a step back and rubbed his face.

"I am sorry, Trenara… and Nissa," he said softly. "It is this place." He rubbed his hands together and forced his eyes back to the tower.

Trenara touched his arm. "It is all right, lad." She had a difficult time keeping the tremble from her voice. She had never seen Joshan angry and it frightened her.

"Nissa," he said to the bird as Ricilyn and Fiena joined them. "Take me up."

Joshan and Ricilyn circled the city in a low spiraling pattern, checking every home and building they could see for any signs of life. Bodies littered the streets, most of them badly decomposing. The stench was overwhelming and they had to hold their hands over their faces to keep from retching. The only living things were animals that came to feed off the carrion and birds that pecked at the corpses' eyes.

Wagons and carts stood abandoned in the street and debris choked the roadways, evidence of an unscheduled departure. The city seemed completely deserted, but Joshan could feel the pull of a living presence.

"The uppermost tower," he called to Ricilyn pointing to the massive black castle that overshadowed the town. She nodded and coaxed her bird up.

They flew above the great black structure at the top of the castle, but did not land immediately, choosing instead to circle around to make certain there were no hidden dangers.

The place was as silent and empty as the town. They could see Van, Trenara, Haiden, and Porphont winding their way up the massive cobbled street that lead to the tower. After careful examination, Joshan and Ricilyn touched down on the landing at the end of the street in front of a large wooden door. Joshan sent the birds back to the ship.

He stood before the entrance a long time, frowning at the ancient wood and iron framework. This was the entry to the enemy's seat of command, where Sirdar plotted and planned, tortured and abused—the heart of his domain.

Joshan reached for the large brass handles but hesitated to touch them. He pulled his hand back and gathered his courage. Nothing in his experience had ever frightened him more than touching that door; the door that Sirdar had touched and opened countless times, the gate where innocence entered but never left. The life force they were seeking lay behind those doors, calling to him, begging him for help. He had to answer.

Joshan reached again, but Ricilyn cried out and he turned. Behind him, silent as always, but his eyes unusually sad and urgent, stood Porphont staring at the door. The mute moved quickly and pushed the emperor into Ricilyn who was moving to stop him. Joshan would have gone sprawling had not Ricilyn caught him as the others rushed to them.

"Porphont!" Ricilyn cried aloud, but he could not hear her. She took a deep breath and forced her thoughts into his mind. *What are you doing?*

"Ricilyn, what is it?" Joshan asked as Trenara, Haiden and Van joined them.

"I do not know. He will not answer me." *Porphont, what is wrong? What are you doing?*

He glanced back at her over his shoulder and then turned back to the massive doors. Before they could respond, Porphont wrapped his massive hands around the metal loops.

Porphont, no! Ricilyn screamed into his mind, but the large man ignored her and opened the doors with a single tug. A deep rumbling thunder came from the entrance as a massive explosion blew out from the entrance, knocking them to the ground and throwing the mute backwards over the parapet.

Ricilyn screamed and ran to the ledge, expecting to see her friend smashed against the street far below. When she peeked over, what greeted her was the large man smiling up at her knowingly as he hung from a rocky protrusion jutting out of the sheer stone face. His skill alone had saved him. She laughed in relief.

Joshan and the others joined her and helped Porphont back over the wall. Ricilyn examined him thoroughly to make sure he was not hurt. For some reason, she could not reach his mind, which disturbed her. She tried signing, but Porphont only had eyes for the entrance that was now open, its massive doors hanging from broken hinges and much of the stonework from the frame now lying on the ground.

"Is he all right?" Joshan asked when she stood up from her exam.

"I think so. I cannot hear him anymore."

"What?"

"I cannot hear him. He has closed his mind to me."

"What does that mean?"

Ricilyn shook her head and scowled at the man. "I do not know."

Joshan felt a deep rush of pain coming from beyond that entrance and turned to study it. Without a word, he strode toward the door, the group following reluctantly behind him.

Beyond the rubble was a long, centuries-old stone tunnel with a floor smoothed by seasons of footsteps and a wall blackened by millennium of smoking torches. The corridor was dark but at the end was a well-lit chamber. Haiden and Vanderlinden pulled out their blades and the group advanced with caution as they made their way to the light.

The room they entered was immense. The stone tower ended hundreds of spans above their heads. A patch of blue morning sky peeked from a small opening at its apex. There were no windows or openings in the walls of the tower and the only adornments were smoking torches in a line around the perimeter.

In the center of the room was a large dais of circular stone stairs. At its crown rose an intricately carved golden throne. At one time, it must have been magnificent, but now it was dull with age and neglect. At the foot of the throne sat a tiny figure, dwarfed by the immense room and the great throne behind it.

Porphont ran toward the figure, but Joshan caught him with an outstretched arm.

"No." A mysterious light sparked in Joshan's eyes, mirrored in the golden sword at his side. Power surged over his body and he trembled as it took him. "Stay here." The sound of his voice bounced off the somber walls.

Joshan slowly crossed to the figure sitting before the throne. Recognition and grief gripped his heart. She wore filthy, blood stained rags that barely covered her frail gray form. Her matted blond hair was now white and a dirty dressing wrapped around her head covered her eyes. She hugged her knees with bone thin arms and rocked gently as the emperor approached.

"Ena?" he whispered quietly, a few paces from her.

"Ena!" Trenara gasped and ran toward them, but Joshan casually lifted his hand to throw an amber barrier in front of her that effectively cut him off from the others. The guider stopped short and glared at him.

"What the hell…?"

"Stay where you are, guider," he said gently. "I know what I am doing."

Trenara clenched her hands in rage, but was helpless against the barrier. Van came up behind her to take her in his arms. Overwhelmed by Ena's appearance she could only fume in frustration and watch.

"Ena?" Joshan called again taking another tentative step toward her.

The girl lifted her head and turned it from side to side. "I know that voice." Her whisper had no strength.

Joshan crouched down to examine her. Ena's face was sickly ashen in the amber glow. He was appalled at how quickly she had deteriorated. He reached up to touch her face, but stopped short. Something was wrong.

"Ena, it is Joshan. Are you all right?"

"Joshan… Sire? Is this a dream?"

"No, Ena, we are here to help you. I am… I am so sorry we came late."

She gave him a strange smile that shook him to the bone. "Are you really here?"

"Yes, Ena."

"It can't be real." The weak trembling of her body gave her words as odd lilt. "It is you again, yes? You have come to torture me again. Do not hurt me, master, please," she pleaded. "I will give him the message. I promise."

"Ena, it is not Sirdar. We're here to help you." Tears brimmed in his eyes.

Ena's fingers shook as they reached out to find him. When she touched his eyes with a dirty hand, she smiled again, that strange smile. "It is you." She pulled her hand away abruptly.

Something shifted in the light around them as a crimson tinge radiated on the edges of the power. Joshan was instantly alert as the red enveloped Ena. Her face melted into a cavernous horror. Joshan sprang to his feet and stepped back from her. That strange smile turned hard.

"Welcome, Joshan." It was Ena's voice, her vocal cords, her mouth, her lips, but the sound was eerie, making Joshan's sinews tighten. It reached into his heart and squeezed until his chest hurt. "I wait for you in the north. Come to me, Joshan. I will show you your heart's desire and reveal the truth." A terrible laugh shook the room. "If this messenger is not to your liking, there will be others along the way. Come quickly. Each day you wait, more will fall until there are none left to beg."

Joshan sank to his knees, trying to block the terrible voice, but it throbbed in his head.

"If you doubt my validity, perhaps this will convince you."

Ena opened her mouth unnaturally wide and a storm of red smoke poured out.

Catalyst!

Joshan reacted quickly to keep the cloud from reaching his friends. He grabbed the girl off the stairs and pressed his mouth to hers, sucking the smoke deeply into his own lungs. The amber glow around them intensified until they were shadows inside a cocoon of power. Ricilyn screamed and tried to run to him, but Vanderlinden stopped her. She screamed Joshan's name again and again from the giant's impeding arms. The rest of them stared on terrified as Joshan held the young woman in his arms, the devastating kiss filling his lungs with torture. He could feel his trembling mingle with Ena's convulsions.

At length, Ena fainted. Joshan barely caught her. He sank to his knees with her still clutched in his arms and then gently laid her on the stone. Slowly crawling a few paces away from her, he vomited violently next to the dais, the sickness nearly taking his consciousness. The power died as he sank back to his knees and hung his head.

"Let go of me!" Ricilyn shouted. Scowling, Van released her. She ran to Joshan with Trenara and the rest close behind her. She went to her knees before him but he threw up his crystalline hands and crawled away from her. His eyes glowed hideously black and red.

"Do not touch me!" he screamed, drawing further into the shadows. "Let me get it under control."

Ricilyn put her hands to her mouth and tears made her eyes pale blue in the darkened chamber.

Joshan hugged his knees in a darkened corner, trying desperately to fight the catalyst that now rushed through his lungs, his heart, and his blood. There was too much in his system, not a mote or a sliver, but an immeasurable amount coursing through his body and spreading an unbearable fire through his veins. His heart pushed it through his body so quickly there was no time to dispel it. It filled him before he could push it out.

Trenara came next to Ricilyn and clamped her jaw tight, willing herself to remain calm.

"Leea-anu-ema-cha." On her hands and knees, she moved as close as she dared. Joshan looked up at her confused. "Leea—Anu—Ema—Cha." Trenara fought to keep her voice from shaking. "Do it, lad. Deep breath, leea…" The musical notes coming out of her throat trembled madly.

Joshan nodded once and took a deep breath. His face twisted and he screamed in agony, unable to sustain it.

"Again, lad," she said more forcefully. "Leea…"

He took another deep breath and this time the concentration in his face shone above the pain.

"Anu…" she sang and his breath came out raggedly. "Ema…" He took another breath in, this time winning through the pain. "Cha…" she finally sang and Joshan let out a breath of relief as the pain dulled.

"Are you all right?" Trenara stayed away from him and held Ricilyn's arm to keep her still until the crisis passed. The red and black faded slowly from his eyes.

"I think so," he finally said, stumbling as he rose.

Trenara let Ricilyn go. She flew into Joshan's arms and examined him carefully. "What was it?"

He brushed a wayward lock from her forehead and touched her cheek. "It was nothing. Just a little… greeting from Sirdar." It was the first time he had lied to Ricilyn and it took every talent he had to conceal it. Even so, Trenara looked up at him suspiciously.

"What kind of greeting?" she asked.

He smiled at the guider and shook his head. "A little pain to deal with, Trenara. It is gone now." The guider's face was still apprehensive. "You need to trust me."

"Humph," Trenara folded her arms. "You are certain that is all it was?"

"Yes," he lied, "absolutely certain. I am fine."

"Trenara," Haiden called.

Porphont had lifted the unconscious Ena into his arms. Trenara crossed to the mute and examined the girl thoroughly. When Ricilyn and Joshan joined her, she shook her head gravely. Joshan lifted the dressings from her eyes and Trenara let out a cry. Ena's eyes were gone. Only empty sockets covered by sunken lids remained.

Joshan doubted she had eaten in days. It was obvious they had tortured her. Her back was a mess of broken skin where a whip had hit her repeatedly and she had several breaks to her fingers and ribs.

"We need to get her back to the ship, away from this accursed place. I will attend to her there." Joshan took off his cloak and covered her with it. "I can do nothing here."

He went to reach for her, but Porphont shook his head, unwilling to relinquish his bundle. He merely walked through the entrance and down the street.

Once below in the city, Tam and his crew met them.

"There's nothing here, sir," he said to Vanderlinden. "A few bodies, but no one living. It is as if the devil himself chased them out of here. The trail is easy to see; it is wide and heads straight for the north."

Van gave him a curt nod and they all went to the ship.

Once on board, Joshan, Ricilyn, and Trenara tended to Ena as best they could. Joshan was able to call up enough power to ease her pain and heal all the breaks and most of the wounds. However, he could do nothing for her eyes. The monster had taken them. They would never come back. Ricilyn gave her some of the special imaka, which brought the girl out of her sleep. Joshan looked at her ashen face, ashamed at his failure to save her.

"Ena," he said softly, "it is Joshan. Can you hear me?"

"Yes, sire," she said weakly. "I knew you would come for me. He said…" Her voice trailed off into sobs.

"It is all right, Ena. Sirdar is gone. You are safe now. He will never bother you again."

Ena suddenly threw her arms around his neck and it startled him. He held her for as long as she needed. It almost broke his heart. Joshan was grateful she carried no more of the catalyst. Ena's plight was over… as Joshan's began.

Trenara came over to touch her gently, struggling to keep the fear from her voice when she looked at the abuse this poor girl had endured.

"Ena," she said softly, "are you all right, child?"

Ena untangled herself from the emperor and held her hands out for Trenara to take.

"Ma'am? I was so afraid without you. He… he talked about you… a lot. He said awful things. Terrible things about what he would do to you when he caught you. He made me tell him everything about you—over and over again. He said he… loves you," she said with disgust, "but the things he said he would do to you…" She could not go on.

"It is all right, child." She took the girl into her arms. She was amazed how small and fragile Ena was, scarcely more than an armful instead of the robust young woman she should be. "He cannot hurt either of us anymore," she said, rocking the girl gently.

A great sorrow clouded Joshan's face for an instant, which only Ricilyn caught.

"He will never hurt you again, I swear it," Trenara whispered.

At length, she laid the girl down on the clean bed and tucked the blankets around her.

"How about I get you some broth. Could you manage that?"

"Yes, ma'am," Ena said. "I think so." She suddenly tilted her head to one side and smiled for the first time, sitting up in the bed.

"My name's Ena. Who are you?" she said to the air. "I am happy to meet you." She twisted her head again as if listening. "No," she said. Trenara and Joshan exchanged a glance.

"Who are you talking to?" Trenara asked her.

"He says his name is Porphont."

Trenara looked back and the large man was standing at the door, a bemused half-smile curling his lips. Ena laughed weakly and nodded. "We can try," she said lying back down. "All right, I am ready."

Porphont closed his eyes. Joshan and Trenara rose from the bed and watched carefully. Ricilyn went into Joshan's arms.

"It is dark," Ena said. "Oh… all right."

Porphont slowly opened his eyes to regard the companions and Ena gasped.

"Yes, I can see them," she whispered. "Trenara, the emperor, and another woman. Ricilyn is your name, he tells me. Hello."

"I do not understand," said Joshan, but Ricilyn's eyes brightened.

"It is a miracle, my love. They have joined. That is why I could not hear Porphont anymore. He has changed his alliance."

"What does that mean?" Trenara asked.

"It means Ena can now see through Porphont's eyes and Porphont can speak through Ena. It is a kind of merging. The old man told me Porphont had this ability, but since we could not do it, I thought he was wrong. I never dreamed he would link to someone else."

"You sound disappointed," Joshan said.

"Oh, no," she said smiling up at the mute. "I am very happy for him. This means he can speak for himself through Ena and she can see through his eyes. It is wonderful."

The mute went over to the young woman's bed and took her into his arms where he cradled her, tears streaming down his face. She laid her head on his chest and smiled brightly.

"He says he loves you, Ricilyn," Ena said. "But that I need him now. He says you will understand."

Ricilyn touched his shoulder. "Yes, Porphont, I do."

Joshan looked down on them curiously, but a strange light came into his eyes. He helped Ricilyn to her feet and escorted her and Trenara toward the door.

"I think we better leave them alone now. I have a hunch this will do more to heal Ena than anything we have done."

Trenara left them to get the girl some food, reveling in the weak laughter of her student drifting down the companionway. It did her heart good to hear it.

As Ricilyn and Joshan made their way to the deck, she stopped him suddenly and searched his eyes.

"Something happened up there."

He touched her face. "Only a simple trick, which I should never have fallen for, my love," he said. "I am embarrassed, actually. I should have known Sirdar would try something. It was nothing more than a poison. Very painful, very effective. I was able to counteract it. I had to stop it before it reached all of you. I am fine," he finished reassuringly and kissed her. The deceit was getting easier.

She took a deep breath. "All right, if you are sure."

"Absolutely." He took her hand to continue to the bridge.

However, in his heart, Joshan knew there would be no going back. Deeply, irrevocably infected with the catalyst, he had to fight every moment to control it.

He could feel it eating away at his self-restraint, his will, and his desires. When he resisted it, the pain was so intense it was all he could do to keep it off his face. At other times, it spoke to his mind in hideous whisperings compelling him to do terrible things. Joshan realized he was a danger to everyone now. His will was gradually weakening. It would be only a matter of weeks, perhaps days, before the red power turned him. He had to act quickly—he had to act now.

When Joshan and Ricilyn got to the deck, Vanderlinden joined them.

"What now, sire?" he asked quietly. "Do we move to the field and help Sark?"

Joshan leaned against the railing, staring up at the black castle. He knew what he needed to do, but it would take planning and careful timing.

"Sark is no longer on the field, Van."

"What?"

"Sirdar will be moving his forces to Calisae."

"Then we sail to the north," Van said to the quiet emperor.

"I… I do not know. I need to think." Joshan ran a quivering hand through his hair. "We will stay here tonight and I will give you my answer tomorrow."

"Sire, we need to talk tonight. I need to catch the morning tide to get to the Keep and we have to have answers now. I am sorry, lad, but this is not just your battle. It belongs to all of us. We need to fight it together."

Joshan looked up at the giant, moved by his unwavering strength.

"Very well. We will meet in my chambers then." He walked away and Van scowled after him.

CHAPTER FOURTEEN
DEPARTURES

Early that evening, they sat around the emperor's great room and debated their next steps.

"Aye," Van was saying vehemently, "we need to find Sark and take after the bastard! Fight him on the ground."

"I am sorry, Van," Grandor interjected, "but I do not think so. I think this is more about his magic than the war. I think the war is a distraction, something to keep our eyes away from what he is really doing. That is always the way he works. We are so busy watching his right hand, we miss what his left hand is doing."

"I agree," said Trenara. "I think we need to gather as many of the guiders as we can to prepare for whatever he is planning. Pull everyone into the Keep and fight from that strong vantage point."

Van shook his head. "I say once we get to the Keep, we reorganize what people we have left and march to the north to attack him before he is ready. You have no idea what we would be up against if he is allowed to gather his forces. We take what's left of our soldiers, bring in the Trillone, and march to the north."

"And I advise caution," Grandor said. "We were almost defeated last time by running headlong into his trap. I think Trenara's plan is a better idea."

"Hide in the Keep and wait until he comes to us?" Van snapped. "I, for one, will not idle in the castle and let that monster destroy everything else. We must fight and now. Sirdar will have time to gather his forces if we don't and there won't be anything left to fight for."

Trenara shook her head. "It is not a matter of waiting," she said vehemently, "it is a matter of strength. We do not have the Crystal anymore, so we have to gather together to stay strong and we need to stay together, don't you see that?"

The debate went on for a very long time until night fell around them and servants lit the lamps.

Joshan said nothing during the discussions, choosing instead to examine the sea. While others talked back and forth, Ricilyn watched her husband. Something was wrong with him. He had plans of his own that did not include either of the options discussed. Haiden also studied him.

When tempers flared, Joshan brought up his hands.

"Please," he said forcefully, stopping the debate. "Thank you all for your input. I need to think about everything put on the table here. I promise you a decision by early morning."

"Lad, we have to…"

"Peace, Trenara." His voice was quiet and very tired. "In the morning."

She snorted an acknowledgement and allowed Van to lead her away, followed by Grandor. Ricilyn sat next to Joshan and wrapped her arms around him.

"You need rest, my lord," she said, watching Redwyn make his climb in the eastern sky.

"Yes." Joshan lifted her chin and kissed her gently.

They went to their cabin leaving Haiden to find his way to the deck. He leaned back against a mast and took up his vigil. It was going to be a long night.

Around midnight, a black figure flew silently from the uppermost mast to a quiet spot in town. When she landed, a shadowy outline emerged from a doorway and crossed quickly to the bird. She lowered her head to him.

"Did anyone see you leave?" he asked, throwing a pack on her back.

"No, sire," she replied, "they were still asleep. Did you get them all?"

"Yes." Joshan threw back his hood. "They will sleep until morning which should give us a good five or six hours' head start."

"What will they do when they wake?"

Joshan looked up at her. "They will try to reach us, but it will be too late."

"Forgive me, master, but I must ask. Is this wise?"

Joshan tightened the straps holding his pack of provisions. "I do not know, Nissa," he said, "but it is the only option open to me now."

"As you wish, sire," the bird replied bowing her head.

"Come on." He jumped onto her back and the bird rose quickly into the air, disappearing into the darkened night, heading north.

Another figure dislodged itself from the shadows as they left, looking up at them until they disappeared. Haiden shook his head and then ran to the ship.

When he arrived, he saw Ricilyn loading her vulcha for a journey.

"And where are you going?" he said, making her jump.

"I did not see you," she said, but turned around to finish packing her bird.

"You're going after him, aren't you?"

"Yes, Haiden," she said. "He tried to put me to sleep but I was prepared for him. I know what he is trying to do, but he is mistaken. This is exactly what Sirdar wants. He wants him alone and I cannot let that happen. Do not try to stop me, Marshal. I think you will find I am more formidable than I appear."

Haiden reached behind a mast to grab a large pack.

"Stop you?" he said smiling. "No, lass, I'm coming with you."

She whirled around. "What?"

"If Fiena can bear us both. I'm thinking you might need a bit of help."

She studied him, then touched his arm in gratitude.

"Thank you, Haiden. Yes, I think Fiena can bear us both. We have to hurry before he gets too far away. Fiena seems to have developed a link with the Mourna, but her range is limited." She jumped to the bird's back and reached a hand down to help Haiden on. "Stay close to my back and hold on tight." Fiena took a long run and leapt off the deck into the air.

The darkness swallowed them up.

CHAPTER FIFTEEN
DISCOVERY

The next morning shortly before sunrise, Trenara woke up from a terrible nightmare. When she opened her eyes, it was as if the nightmare continued. Something was terribly wrong and her heart pounded in her chest.

"Van," she said, shaking him, "Van, wake up."

"What?"

"Wake up!" She jumped out of bed into the cold early morning darkness and threw her cloak over her shoulders. She rushed down the companionway and opened Ena's door, but the girl was sleeping peacefully with Porphont snoring in a large chair next to her bed.

She closed the door silently and went down to Joshan and Ricilyn's room. She knocked, but there was no reply. Trenara's hand trembled on the knob as she entered their chambers. Both Joshan and Ricilyn were gone and the bed linens tossed. Rumpled on the bed was a note in Joshan's long graceful strokes. With trepidation, Trenara picked it up to read.

My love, you will never understand why I must do this, but please know it is for the best. I cannot watch while all of you are tortured one by one in his effort to reach me. I have lied to you; please forgive me. Sirdar has poisoned me with the catalyst and I am beyond repair now. I cannot stop the forward progression of the disease—I am too deeply infected. Even now, I feel the catalyst destroying my will. It will eventually reach into my mind and I will become as Sirdar is, corrupt and twisted. I could not bear you seeing me when I finally succumb to it. I have to stop this before that happens. Only I can stand against him, as is my fate. Only I can destroy him, as is his fate.

No matter what happens, please know that you have completed me in ways I never thought possible. I will die happy because of it.

Vanderlinden and Trenara will rule in my stead. They know the reason why. Tell Van it is time for him to take his place.

Go back to Dru, beloved, be happy, and tell the son you carry that his father loved him. Love always, Joshan.

Trenara screamed. Van ran into the room and she pushed the note into his hands. She fell on the bed and buried her face in her hands, weeping.

"No!" Van took Trenara into his arms. Tam came running into the room blurry eyed.

"Get this ship to sea, now," Van bellowed. "Get the crew up and get her out of this stinking harbor. Move!"

Without asking why, Tam ran to the alarm bell and rang it loudly, waking everyone and scrambling the crew.

Van led Trenara back to their room where he got dressed. Grandor knocked on their door gently and went to Trenara when Van opened it.

"Stay with her, guider," he said curtly and left.

"Trenara, what is it?" Grandor asked.

"Joshan is gone," she whispered, hardly able to say the words. "He has gone to find Sirdar and Ricilyn has followed him. Sirdar will destroy them," she cried. "He will destroy them both." Grandor folded his arms around her.

A guard came running into the room. "Lady," he said breathless. "The admiral said to give you this." He pressed a parchment into her hands and ran from the room.

She read it quickly and handed it to Grandor. "It is from Haiden," she whispered, rising to look out the port.

Grandor smiled. "But this is good," he said crossing to her and taking her hand. "Haiden and Ricilyn will stop him before he can get to Sirdar. Do not worry, Trenara, if anyone can talk him into coming back, they can."

She stared out the port window watching the graying dawn. Trenara knew in her soul that they would never stop Joshan before he found Sirdar. They would never reach him before the catalyst consumed him. She knew it down to her bones.

"Grandor," she said finally, her voice shaking, "would you please go to the emperor's room and retrieve the gazing for me. You should find it in a drawer next to his bed, if he has not taken it."

Van had been right all along. They would need to gather their forces quickly and fight. She knew in a blinding revelation that the Trillone fleet would meet them at the Keep where the last of the provincial fighters would gather and take their war to the north. She knew they would travel to the cold northern waste to confront the enemy on the field. The fate of the empire would be decided on a field of ice.

Joshan's future was now in his own hands. Trenara trembled for the world.

CHAPTER SIXTEEN
SALDORIAN

As Joshan made his desperate flight to the north, Thiels fumed in his chambers back at the Keep. It was unseasonably cold that night, and he had difficulty sleeping. The commander paced the balcony, but it was a poor substitute for the castle wall.

The Elite had finally ordered him off the parapet after he had been on duty continuously for several days. Jona had quoted some obscure Elite passage that stated any guard caught doing more than twenty consecutive hours of duty would submit to confinement in his chamber to rest for at least twenty. The young man had looked his superior straight in the eye. Jona asserted clearly that if Commander Thiels did not leave the wall to get some sleep they would take him into custody and confine him to his quarters. Jona had gone as far as ordering an escort to accompany the commander. Grumbling and furious, Thiels had done his subordinate's bidding, but he could not sleep.

Thiels ached to be on the field with Sark and his troops, but his duties to the Keep kept him from it. The dispatches that came in daily bore only bad news; the enemy was pushing the army back. The imperials would not last another day. There was no news from the emperor or the admiral, and except for the devastating reports from Mathisma, Thiels could not get anything further. The last thing he heard was they were heading to Cortaim. That was why he could not sleep. It was maddening to sit in the Keep, while the world crumbled around him.

The only consolation had been Saldorian.

Before Balinar's invasion of the Keep, Thiels and Saldorian had actually been very good friends. They had worked together for many seasons in their duties to the Keep and Thiels counted the consort as his closest confidante. Saldorian had seen him through the loss of his wife and child, who both died in childbirth many seasons before. She had known instantly he was covering up the profound loss by overworking himself. When he had taken ill, Sal sent a guider to treat him, even though the healers usually saw the Elite and he did not warrant such extravagant care. The consort's kindness, compassion, and insightful intelligence were evident in everything she did.

Thiels often wondered why she would ever prefer his company when there were so many others to occupy her time. Sal would always seek him out for an energetic debate, an obscure reading, or long discussions on philosophy, religion, science, and art. They would play the scholar's game, Emperor's Gambit, for hours. Equally matched, the game gave both of them mental challenges they had difficulty finding anywhere else.

When he asked her one day why, she had smiled up at the guard and said, 'Thiels, you know as well as I where the real scholar resides in this castle. You cannot fool me. I see you studying, reading, and analyzing everything around you. Everyone knows you are highly intelligent, but I happen to know you are brilliant, my friend. I only wish you could see it yourself. I know you are smarter than the rest; your heart is too pure for anyone else to see it. You hide it very well.'

After the attack, however, all that changed.

What Balinar had done to this remarkable woman was incomprehensible. For the first time in his life, Thiels felt real hatred—unreasoning, primal, all encompassing hatred. It often took everything he had to keep it from consuming him. Even when he found out Balinar was dead, he still harbored a deep loathing for his master.

He stopped by the consort's room when he found time and would talk to her, even though he did not know if she could hear him. As the weeks passed, he found himself spending more and more time with her, reading to her or conducting a one-sided debate on issues he knew she would have taken the opposing side on. He hoped she would respond to challenge him. She never did. Saldorian would lie there in silence, staring at the ceiling, lost in a world where he could not reach her. After many weeks, he realized what he felt for her was becoming much deeper than friendship.

As Thiels paced his balcony and stared at the moonlit sea, there came a thunderous knock on his door. He opened it and Dorthia stumbled in.

"Sir," she breathed. "The consort—she is awake."

"What?"

"Hurry, sir," she panted, throwing frantic looks out the door. "She is on the balcony—I think she means to jump!"

Thiels pushed Dorthia aside and rushed from the room.

When he got there, the Elite had several guards inside the consort's chambers and Jona was standing by the open balcony, blurry eyed, and pleading desperately.

"Please, lady. We're here to help you."

Thiels took the scene in with one fleeting glance and his training shifted his nerves into an acute awareness that was almost painful. Saldorian was shaking, balanced on the top edge of the balcony banister, her eyes languid and dull. She stared at the sea and rocks far below her, swaying in her own world, clearly unaware of her danger. Time slowed in Thiels' mind. Saldorian's sheer nightgown and long black hair flowed like water as he watched. The consort's bare feet were the only things keeping her upright on the old stone.

Thiels turned to the Elite behind him and gave them a crisp silent signal to retreat. They obeyed the fire in his eyes at once and stumbled out the door, taking a nearly hysterical Dorthia with them.

As Jona closed the door, he looked at his commander and nodded. "We will rig a tarpaulin on the balcony below, sir," he whispered.

Thiels did not take his eyes from the consort. "Make it quick."

When everyone was outside, the noise and confusion went with them. Thiels crossed toward the balcony and grabbed a chair from a nearby table.

He did not know what he was going to do. Thiels had never been a religious man, but right then he said a soft prayer to the gods and asked them for guidance. Saldorian was literally on the brink of death.

Approaching cautiously, he stepped out on the balcony and sat down in the chair. All she had to do was turn her head to see him. The commander made his face impassable and folded his arms.

"Evening, Sal," he said calmly.

Saldorian continued to look out at the night, but somewhere deep inside her eyes, there was the slightest glimmer. Had she recognize his voice?

What seemed like an eternity passed without her saying a word, her body swaying gently in the moonlight. Thiels remained frozen where he was, hoping he was close enough to dive and grab her if he had to. He did not dare get any nearer.

He wondered again, what was going on in that sweet, broken mind. Thiels was no guider, no doctor, no healer—he was only a man. But he knew in his heart how strong Saldorian was, how capable, and how brilliant. All he had to do was reach her and she would do the rest; Thiels knew it deep in his heart. Right then, he would have given his soul to take away her pain.

Finally, she very slowly turned her head towards him, but then lost her balance. He jumped up from his chair, but she righted herself and he sat down again, his heart beating wildly. He fought down the panic.

Saldorian's face was strange, pale, and blank, as if her mind were still detached somehow. She did not look straight at him, but rather right above his head. In a very faint voice, she whispered, "Connan?"

"Yes, Sal," he said very gently. "I am here."

She cocked her head to the side and looked very confused.

"Where are you?"

"I am here, Sal, right next to you."

The consort looked down into his eyes for the first time. He watched her struggle for clarity, but then finally, small white teeth showed through her lips and a smile graced her beautiful face.

"Did you want a rematch?" she asked as her eyes cleared.

Inwardly, he took a long breath to calm his beating heart.

"Not yet," he said, measuring how far he could take this. "I thought perhaps—we could have a chat."

She tilted her head and the smile diminished.

"What about?" The question was as innocent as if a child had asked it.

"Oh, nothing in particular," he said casually. "I wanted someone to talk to, that's all." He smiled up to her. "Do you have time?"

Saldorian looked down, obviously trying to place him. All at once, her smile became almost genuine.

"For you? Always, my friend," she said, echoes of their long ago banter.

"Thanks, Sal," he said carefully, slowly leaning forward in his chair. "I... I've got this problem."

"So?"

"Well, you see, I have this friend who really needs me, but... she does not know how to ask."

The consort looked at him seriously. "Sounds like you need to make the first move, my friend."

It was so much like a normal conversation it sounded twisted and eerie here.

Thiels nodded. "That's what I am thinking. But I don't want to hurt her feelings."

"If she is your friend, that will not be a problem, will it?"

Thiels slowly rose, taking his time.

"I think you're right, Sal." He looked up at her sadly and held out his hand. "Would you mind if we moved inside? I'm freezing out here."

Sal looked at him suspiciously and then suddenly turned away. All at once, her foot left the stone railing as if she had decided to take a walk in the night, and she fell. Thiels grabbed her around the waist, barely catching her. Sal almost succeeded in pulling them both over, but she was so thin, he caught her easily and pulled her back over the railing. Holding her in his arms, he tumbled back and hit the balcony wall with a grunt. Thiels waited until he caught his breath, the precious bundle secured in the protection of his arms.

Sal looked up at him and smiled innocently. She reached up to touch his face as if trying to place him again, but then her eyes turned very serious.

"Connan?" she whispered. "What's happened?"

He lifted her into his arms and brought her inside. Setting her on a chair as far away from the window as he could, he knelt and held her hands.

"You have been asleep a long time, Sal," he whispered, turning her hand over and then kissing it gently. "We were afraid you would never wake up."

She looked down at him confused, but then, slowly, her eyes widened and her breath came in sudden, ragged blasts.

"Connan." Her eyes filled with tears and her lip quivered. "He... he..." Great sobs took hold and her body convulsed with panic.

Thiels gathered her in his arms and pulled her down to cradle her on his lap, holding her head against his chest. He held her tightly there on the floor and rocked her gently as she sobbed uncontrollably for a very long time, but never said a word. Thiels had never loved Saldorian more than he did at that moment and his heart broke as he held her. He would not let her go.

The memories all came back to Saldorian is one great, horrible wave, washing over her heart. She remembered it all—the pain—the beating—the rape. All of it flooded back into her mind in a single instant and she screamed, clawing at Thiels, cursing, shrieking her hatred, her disgust—and her own self-loathing. She cried out for Jenhada repeatedly, but he would never answer her again. The despair was crippling, excruciating and Saldorian would have fallen away again—had not Thiels been there with her. He would not let her go.

When the sun rose over the invariable sea, Saldorian finally succumbed to exhaustion and quietly collapsed in Thiels's arms. The worst was over.

Thiels carried her to her bed, tucking the covers around her. He washed her face as best he could, kissed her on the forehead, then settled into a chair next to the bed and watched her sleep. He would not let her go.

"Connan," Saldorian whispered. Thiels woke up instantly and sat next to her on the bed, taking her into his arms again.

"I am here, Sal," he said quietly.

"I…" She stopped, as if her throat closed around itself.

"You don't need to talk."

"But I do," she said. "I need to tell you…" Saldorian stared out at the bedroom with unseeing eyes. "I have to tell you…"

Thiels lifted her face. "You do not have to tell me anything until you are ready."

Saldorian sat back against her pillows, closed her eyes, and balled her fists until they went white. Thiels was afraid she would slip away again. With an obvious effort, Sal hardened her face and opened her eyes. Taking a deep cleansing breath, she looked up at him as if she had made a decision.

"No," she said with passion, but calmed herself. "No." She closed her eyes one more time to control her emotions.

"Where is my son?" she asked, her voice almost spiteful.

Thiels scowled at her, not knowing what he should say. "Joshan?"

Saldorian looked up at him and there was the old spark in her eyes. "Tell me, Thiels. Please," she said touching his arm. "Do not spare me to save me. You will not be doing me any favors."

"All right," he said hesitantly. "He has gone to Mathisma and is now coming back." He stopped and licked his lips. "By way of Cortaim."

He watched her, but she simply nodded, pulled back the covers, and rose to grab her robe. Being in bed for so many months had made her weak and Thiels had to help her to the table, where she sat and he poured her tea. Her face was calm, but her hands were trembling.

"Connan," she began, "I need to tell you something, but I need you to promise me, it will not go any further than you. Trenara knows, but no one else can. Can you promise me that?"

Thiels nodded as he sat across from her. "Of course."

Saldorian took a deep breath and stared out the balcony window. "Poor, Van. I was so… angry with him. I wish I could…"

Thiels smiled at her from across the table. "Sal, Van is alive."

She looked at him with doubt in her eyes. "What? No, he was lost at sea."

"He was wounded by…" But he stopped and looked down at his hands.

"It is all right," she replied quietly. "You can say it. I will be damned if I am going to be frightened by that bastard's name!"

Thiels looked up at her and smiled. "That's my girl," he said proudly. "Van was wounded by Balinar and taken from the city where he escaped. It took him two seasons to get word to anyone. He has lost an eye, but otherwise, he is fine."

"Thank the gods," she said to the table. Then she sat back in her chair and could not look at him again. "I was so angry at him. I thought he was lying to me, but now I do not know. Where is he?"

"He is with the emperor," he said.

A shot of pain crossed Saldorian's face and she bit her lip. "The emperor… you mean Joshan?"

"Yes, Sal, he is emperor now." She did not answer him immediately and continued to stare out at the morning.

At length, she said, "Connan, tell me everything that has happened."

"Sal, are you sure?"

"Please. I need to know."

Saldorian listened quietly as Thiels told her everything that had taken place since her illness. He was tempted to hold back certain aspects, but respected her too much to soften any of it. He did not have to worry; Saldorian listened attentively and seemed to gain strength as he continued. When he finally finished, the consort nodded and sipped her tea.

"My poor Jen," she said at length and quiet tears fell down her cheeks. "I loved him very much."

"I know you did, Sal."

A shadow of a smile covered her lips.

"Twelve seasons ago. He wanted a child so much. It was not even an heir he desired; just a child to love." She looked into Thiels' eyes. "The guiders told us he could not conceive. Did you know that?"

"No… but they were wrong."

Saldorian looked away and took another sip of her tea.

"Yes," she said distantly. "I was so angry at Van…"

Twelve seasons before, it was a cold, rainy Meridian. The hunting party would leave as planned to travel to southern Thrain for the seasonal gathering of the regents, barons, and the provincial hierarchy. Jenhada and his escort assembled outside in the miserable weather and prepared for the trip. Saldorian begged out that season; she hated the hunt and obligatory political intrigue that came with it. Jenhada had not blamed her; had it been possible, he would have skipped it himself, but he was emperor, after all. He could not shirk this one duty. Trenara was away on the island, so he had only taken Vanderlinden for 'moral support,' thinking they could use the time to plan.

Sal kissed Jenhada goodbye and watched as he and Van took off with his troops, his councilors, and his immense entourage, actually pitying the poor fellow. As he was about to go through the gate, he turned on his eecha, gave her a very disgruntled look and threw her a good-natured kiss. Saldorian shook her head and laughed. Gods, how she loved that man.

Three days after the party left, the sun came out, and the weather turned glorious. Sal sat in the sunshine, the gardens surrounding her, and her maiden Trinna sitting cross-legged at her feet. Saldorian tried to read, but it was much too beautiful and she was restless.

"I cannot stand it," she finally said, slamming her book shut. "I need a ride."

Trinna gathered her things and stood up quickly.

"Yes, ma'am. I will have a steward bring around the eechas."

Once out of the stuffy confines of the castle, Saldorian relished the stunning sunlit day, despite her maiden and escort of three Elite guards, two women, Hedda and Wande, and Sergeant Thomal. The old guard fussed terribly over the lady and followed her everywhere. Sal tortured him mercilessly by often disappearing or even hiding from him. She actually adored the old man, but detested his constant watchfulness, which sometimes made her feel like a prisoner.

Saldorian, most times the very epitome of grace, intelligence, and noble bearing, had to let her hair down now and again. She had been a Starguider for a very short time when she met Jenhada and had given it up for him. She always did what was right and expected of her. Saldorian enjoyed her liberties very rarely.

Kicking her heels into the eecha, she thundered through the fields surrounding the Keep. It had been weeks since the consort had been out and Saldorian was in very high spirits. The Elite had a devil of a time keeping up with her; and Trinna, not being a very experienced rider, fell far behind.

"Lady!" Thomal called after her. "Please slow down."

Saldorian laughed and lowered her head into the mane of her eecha. The animal thundered over the open plains and the warm wind was a glorious choir in Saldorian's ears.

When she entered the edge of the woods, she stopped to let the guard catch up with her. No one would wander into the woods alone, even in those days. Thieves were still common in the forests, although the woods were much safer than they used to be; Jen and Vanderlinden had seen to that. When the Elite finally caught up with her, she apologized and then took a well-worn path to the high cliffs, her escort in tow.

Once up on the cliffs, she spent hours staring out at the ocean, meditating, and reading. This was one of her favorite spots. She and Jenhada had spent many pleasurable hours on the high cliffs when they could shake their escort. Saldorian smiled at the memories.

"Madam," Thomal called to her, "it is getting dark. We should head back."

The consort sighed deeply and looked again at the ocean. "I suppose you are right." She got up and turned to go into the woods surrounding the clearing. "I will be right back," she said. When the guard opened his mouth to protest, she simply gave him a warning look.

"Oh," he said, blushing deeply. "Sorry, ma'am, but take one of the women with you, please."

"I am not going more than two spans away, Thomal," she said, lifting her skirt to step over a log and heading into the woods. "I will be right back." The old guard snorted his displeasure, but let her go. He ordered the two guards to watch her carefully from the edge of the woods.

The trees around the clearing were not very dense and Saldorian had to go well away from the camp for privacy.

When she was done, Sal stood up a little too quickly and felt light headed. She shook her head and rubbed her eyes until it passed, but when she opened them again, the woods seemed somehow darker. Thinking it must have been a cloud that passed over, she headed back to the clearing to go home. As she moved forward, a faint mist collected on the ground, making the forest dreamlike.

"Some fog," she called as she stepped out into the clearing.

It was not the clearing at all. If anything, there were more trees and the woods seemed thicker. She thought she must have headed in the wrong direction, so headed the other way.

As Sal plowed through the underbrush, the forest turned very dark and dense around her.

"Thomal!" she called, cupping her hands. Saldorian knew even if she had gone the wrong way, she could not have gone that far. She was sure they would be able to hear her.

"Hedda! Wande! Trinna!" she cried again and then listened carefully. The world became a misty silence around her and there was no reply. Although she called several more times, all she heard was the muted hush of the woods.

"All right," she said to herself, stopping where she was and looking around, "I will stay here and they will find me."

The fog thickened and she found a moss-covered boulder to sit on. Sal shivered as the mist grew colder with evening and she worried that if they did not find her soon, she was not going to last long in the cold with a thin dress on. Her bodice was very low and the sleeves were nothing more than thin lace. The consort rubbed her shoulders and tried unsuccessfully to still the quaking in her limbs. She had never been lost in the woods before and did not care for it much.

The eerie quiet of the forest seeped into Sal as she waited. There should be at least some noise around her. It was as if she had walked into a dark room without any windows or doors. She could not stand it anymore; she got up and paced across the small space to try to warm herself.

Sal stopped when she thought she saw something off to her left just inside the trees.

"Hello!" she called, thinking it must be the Elite and pushed through the brush to follow the movement. "Hello?" she said a little less confidently.

When she stepped over a log, she found herself in another clearing. The darkness enfolded the forest and fear started as tightness in her middle. She had to do a few relaxing exercises to calm herself. Out of the corner of her eye, she caught another movement to her right and whirled around quickly to catch it. She crossed to that side of the clearing and tried to peer through the thick trees, but could see nothing.

Directly behind her a loud snort echoed against the darkness. She jumped a foot and a small scream escaped her as she whirled around. Sitting on a very large black eecha was Jenhada staring down at her.

"By the gods," she exclaimed, catching her breath. "You scared the hell out of me!"

"I am sorry," he said, a handsome smile dusting his lips.

Saldorian caught her breath and looked up at him. "Never mind… I am delighted to see you. I thought I was lost."

Jen dismounted and pulled a lantern from his saddle. "You are not lost, beloved," he said as he struck flint to the lamp, shuttered it, and set it down on a rock. "I knew where you were."

He held out his arms where she went gratefully. Jen rubbed her shoulders and back rapidly until she felt warmth spread through her body.

"Oh, bless you," she said shivering, "I was getting fairly chilly."

"Here," he said, taking off his cloak and enveloping her in it.

Once she was warm again, she looked up at her husband suspiciously.

"What are you doing here? I thought you were still south for the gathering."

He wrapped his arms around her. "Do I have to have a reason to visit my wife?"

"No," she said, "I am delighted." She snuggled deeper against his chest and closed her eyes. "I missed you so much."

Jenhada lifted her chin and pressed his lips fiercely to hers. A wave of passion ran through Saldorian suddenly, startling her, but she let it touch her deeply and responded ardently to his kiss. He wrapped his arms around her tightly and kissed her more deeply. When she broke from it, Sal blinked up at him and smiled.

"My goodness," she breathed. "We should let the others know I am safe."

He smiled at her and ran his hand through her hair, roughly grabbing it from behind and examining her face with a bemused look on his face.

"No," he replied simply, "I have sent them away."

Jenhada kissed her again and brushed the cloak off her shoulder with force. Jen had always been a gentle lover, but from time to time, usually when he had had too much to drink he could be a little rough with her.

As the passion rose, Jen broke the kiss and looked at her quietly. Saldorian thought he would stop now and take her back to the Keep. Without warning, he grabbed the front of her bodice and ripped it open. She gasped and took a step away from him.

"My dress…" she scolded, tugging at the material to pull it back in place.

The fire was unmistakable in Jen's eyes now as he smiled down at her. "I will buy you another," he whispered and swept her up into his arms before she could respond.

She could not stop him. He was all at once like a wild animal; brutal, primal, spontaneous, holding her hard, biting, scratching, draining her of emotion, energy and resistance. Jen touched her in ways he had never touched her before—and it both terrified and thrilled her. She found herself somehow responding to him, as if she had no volition of her own.

Her body was reacting to his stroke like a drug, each caress shooting wave after wave of pleasure through her that she could not resist, making her gasp and moan, which seemed to spark his passion. The world around her became misty and far away as if she were fading into a deep dream. Sal could feel herself falling so slowly it was as if she were floating. The world went away. As she hit the ground, she could feel her will disappear and she gave into him completely—wantonly. When he finally took her, the ecstasy was so overwhelming her scream filled the night.

When Saldorian woke, it was to gray light filtering through the trees around her. Birds chirped on every bough, and rodents rustled in nearby logs. It was very early morning. The woods were still quite dark with a murky dusk.

She sat up and looked around for Jen, but he and his eecha were both gone. When she tried to rise, pain cramped her stomach, arms, and legs and she gasped as a wave of nausea ran through her. She was sore all over and took some time to get up. When she looked down, she was mused, but otherwise whole and she allowed herself a smile. Amazingly, her clothes were intact, although she was certain Jenhada had ruined them the night before. Sal ran her fingers through her hair, dislodging clumps of pine needles and duff. She looked around. From far off, she heard a shout.

"Jen?" she called in response, but it was not her husband's voice that answered.

"Lady?" She turned around to see the three Elite guards struggling to get through the brush to where she stood. Their clothes and hair very disheveled. They looked as if they had not slept all night.

"Lady," Thomal said urgently. "Thank the gods! Are you all right?"

She looked at him strangely. "I am fine. Where is Jen... I mean the emperor?"

Thomal blinked back at her. "Ma'am?"

"You know, my husband—tall fellow, dark hair—leader of the civilized world?"

The sergeant gave her a quizzical look and glanced at the other two guards. "I have not seen him, ma'am," he said shaking his head and looking at her as if she had lost her mind. "Is he not... hunting?"

Sal looked at him incredulously.

"He was here—last night—he said he sent you back to the Keep."

"No, ma'am," the guard said slowly. "We started looking for you as soon as you disappeared. You have been gone almost twelve hours. There are searchers coming up from the village and we sent word to the emperor in the field, but none of us has seen him. Maybe it was a dream, lady," he added cautiously. "Maybe someone else?"

Sal smiled up at him and shook her head. "No... it was my husband; I am sure."

Then she looked around at the clearing, which showed no sign of the eecha's hooves, and at the ground, which looked intact except where she slept. Sal sighed and shook her head.

"Maybe you are right. Maybe it was a dream. It seems very strange now. Some dream," she said wistfully.

"Ma'am?"

"Never you mind, sergeant. Come on. Let's go home."

As Sal traveled back to the Keep, the incident became more and more real to her. By the time she arrived, she was certain Jenhada had been with her that night, even though no one else had seen him. He never came to the Keep or to any of the gates from what she could gather, so he must have gone directly to her without anyone seeing him.

The next day she received a message that he was returning immediately to make sure the consort was all right. That afternoon, Vanderlinden approached her in the garden.

"Sal?"

"Hello, my friend." She smiled up at him. "You are back early."

"Came up yesterday to get the ship ready for the sweep," he replied, sitting down next to her and turning down tea offered by Trinna. "I, uh... heard about your adventure in the woods yesterday."

"Oh?" she said.

"Are you all right?"

"I am fine, Van," she said and then laughed. "But you might want to ask that husband of mine how he is."

"What?"

"Well, he must have had to fly back to camp."

Van shook his head. "What are you babbling about?" he teased.

"Oh, go on... I am certain you were probably in on it."

"In on what? Sal, what are you talking about?"

She scowled at him and a tremor of fear touched her heart. "I saw him, Van, night before last—in the woods."

"Saw who?"

"Jen, of course. I think I know my own husband."

The giant sat back. "Sal," he began slowly, "it must have been a dream. Jen's been down at the camp this whole time."

"Oh, don't be ridiculous," she said lightly, thinking he was teasing her. "I knew you were in on it! You two…"

"Sal," he said seriously, "I think you better tell me what happened."

"Well, maybe you did not know—maybe he left without telling anyone."

"It's a day's journey from the Keep to the hunt, both ways. Jen wasn't out of my sight more than maybe six hours, tops. Sal, he couldn't have come up here. It's not possible."

"Why are you saying that?" She stood and glared down at him. "If this is some kind of joke, it is not very funny!"

"Sal, calm down," Van said rising and lifting his hands. "Tell me what happened in the woods."

She tightened her lip and scooped up her book from the table. "I do not think so! Good day, captain." With that she scurried away to go to her chambers.

Thiels stared at her now, small, thin with swollen eyes and pale face. Although something in the story deeply disturbed him, he said nothing and let her finish.

"I did not speak to Van for weeks after that, thinking that he was making fun of me. Poor Van. Jenhada returned the next day and said nothing about his visit to me in the woods. I never brought it up." Sal lowered her head and looked at her hands. "I do not know why," she whispered like a confession. "It was as if I still wanted to believe it was real, I guess. After several weeks I convinced myself it was a dream, that I must have fainted or hit my head or something and had dreamt the whole thing. The only other person I told was Trenara when she came back from Mathisma and she agreed with me. It could not be anything more than a dream."

Saldorian's eyes misted as her voice shook. "When I finally did talk to Van, I apologized to him for getting so angry and we decided never to talk about it again, although once in a while he would ask me about that night. For some reason I never told him. Too embarrassed I guess. Anyway, soon after, I found out I was pregnant with Joshan."

Sal reached for the teapot again and Thiels gently took it from her trembling fingers. She smiled sadly, gently touched his cheek, and leaned over to kiss him softly.

"You are too good to me," she said with tears in her eyes.

Thiels shook his head and poured her tea. "Probably not as good as you deserve, my lady."

"I wonder," she whispered, looking deeply into his eyes. "I wonder if you will think so, once you know the truth." She turned away and stared at the unlit fire.

"What truth, Sal?" he asked, kneeling down in front of her and taking her hands again. They were getting nearer to her secret and it somehow frightened him.

"After—Balinar," it was very hard for her to get the words out and she became nauseous, "hurt me… he told me…" Sobs took her again. Thiels wrapped his arms around her.

"Sal," he whispered in her ear, "it is too soon. You do not need to do this now. Wait until you are stronger."

"No!" she said, pushing him away. Her eyes were still full of tears, but she looked at him with a stony, determined face. "I have to tell you."

She took a shaky breath and squeezed her eyes shut. "Balinar knew about that night in the woods," she began. "He knew all about it; every nuance, every word, every movement, as if he had been there, as if he'd been watching," she said in disgust. "I screamed at him that Jenhada or Trenara must have told him about it." Her face became suddenly very painful. "But, he said…" She almost lost control again, but willed her face to behave. "That it was not Jenhada in the woods… it was not a dream. Van had been right. Jen never left the hunting camp that night. It was someone else…" Saldorian buried her face in her hands and all Thiels could do was look on in horror.

"Who?" he whispered.

She looked up at him like a child on the verge of tears. "He said I was so easily tricked, that someone disguised as Jenhada had come to me. He said that I had acted like a… harlot for another man and had allowed him to…" Saldorian looked up at him, her face contorted with deep regret. "He was right, Connan." Her words were so full of terrified softness, he barely heard her. "I did… I thought it was Jenhada, but he said it was…" She broke down into tears then and looked away from him. "Sirdar," she whispered through her sobs.

"No," Thiels said, taking her by the chin and making her look at him. "No, I do not believe it. He lied to you, Sal. It was a dream. It had to be."

The consort returned the look sadly and touched his face. "No, Connan. As soon as he said it, I remembered everything. It was Sirdar in the woods and I knew it then. I could not do anything to stop him. I knew his face, his touch, his whispers in my ear telling me to forget… forget until the time was right. He wanted me to remember, don't you understand? He wanted me to remember so he could claim that Joshan was…"

Thiels stood up suddenly and stared down at her in horror.

"No!" The information made him weak. He wanted nothing more than to run from the room. "It is a lie, Sal! It was a dream! Joshan could not possibly be…"

As he watched in horror, Saldorian shrank into herself and rocked softly in her chair, humming quietly. She was quickly slipping away again and Thiels yanked her from the chair.

"I am not going to let you do this, Sal!" he screamed, shaking her with each syllable. "I am not letting you go. Do you understand? I love you! I am not letting you go away again! Do you hear me?"

All at once, she looked up at him and whispered, "You do not have to shout, you know."

Thiels took her in his arms and held her tightly. "Don't scare me like that," he murmured.

"I am sorry," she replied and buried her head in his chest, feeling the strength of his arms and allowing herself to be comforted.

"I am here, Sal. We will get through this together. It is one of Sirdar's tricks, I am certain of it. Let it go for now. Just let me hold you until it passes."

Saldorian moved deeper into his arms and let the grief wash over her unabated. She cried there quietly for a very long time, until the fear and pain melted into the strong arms of her companion, until her mind dulled the ache of her guilt and allowed her a moment of peace.

Finally, she spoke quietly against his chest, her voice sad and tired. "Did you… mean that?"

"What?"

"What you said about… loving me?"

Thiels looked up at the ceiling, closed his eyes over the guilt, and took a deep breath. "May the gods forgive me," he whispered, "but yes… with all my heart. I have always loved you, Sal."

The consort smiled and tightened her grip. "That is good. I was afraid I was the only one."

Thiels' heart skipped a beat and he swallowed. "What do you mean?"

Sal pulled herself out of his arms and looked up at him. Touching his face, she leaned up and kissed him softly, the light in her eyes unmistakable.

"You know," she mused, "for an intelligent man, you are not very bright." She then laughed for the first time in many months. "I have loved you for longer than you could possibly imagine, my sweet friend. We are kindred, you and I. It is only now we can share that."

He looked down at her seriously. "But you are in mourning. We cannot…"

"I know," she said, breaking away from him and settling back in her chair. "We have waited this long, we can wait a little longer, for the future." She looked off into the sky outside her balcony and tears began in her eyes again. "If we have a future. If it was Sirdar in the woods and he…"

Thiels stared out at the morning with her. "Maybe you are wrong, Sal. It would not be the first time that bastard lied to us, made things appear different than they actually are. He rules by deceit, by manipulating people into doing things, saying things, and even remembering things falsely. His strength lies in our gullibility. You need to keep that in mind." He turned to take her hands. "You may be wrong."

"I hope to the goddess I am wrong," she said softly. "For all our sakes."

Just then, there was a knock and Thiels went to the door to find Jona standing there with a group of blurry-eyed Elite.

"Commander," he said urgently, "the consort, is she..."

"She is fine, Jona," he replied, stepping out into the hallway.

"Good," he breathed, but then looked up at Thiels urgently. "Sir, the troops are returning from the field."

"What?"

"Yes, sir. They are passing through last gate and the scouts say General Sark and his escort are close behind them." He took Thiels' arm. "They are saying the enemy has retreated to the north."

"The north? You are certain?"

Jona swallowed. "Yes, sir."

Thiels looked through the door at the consort. "They are going to Calisae," he whispered.

"Sir?"

"Never mind. Get my gear, wake the chancellors, and have them meet me in the East Hall at the noon hour. When Sark enters the gates have him come immediately to the Hall."

"Yes, sir." Jona saluted and turned with his guards to run from the hallway.

Thiels spotted Dorthia peering around a marble column.

"Dottie," he said taking her arm, "you stay with the consort." He scooted her through the door and bowed to Sal. "I am sorry, my lady," he said formally. "I have to go."

Saldorian lowered her head by a fraction. "Thank you, commander." Her facade was cool, regal. "You have been very helpful. I am grateful."

Thiels gave her a crisp bow. "It was my honor, Your Highness," he replied and quickly headed for his chambers.

CHAPTER SEVENTEEN
MARCH TO WAR

Sark, his captains and Sareh drove their animals at break neck speed to get to the Keep. They arrived there so quickly, the last few soldiers Sark had ordered back the previous evening were just going through the gate. When they passed through Last Gate, Sark reined in, but a guard saluted him and held onto his eecha's bridle.

"Sorry, sir, but Commander Thiels orders you to the East Hall as quick as you can get there. We will take care of the rest of your escort."

Sark nodded once and turned to his daughter. "Sareh, you stay here."

"I could help."

"No," he said gently, "Thiels and I know what we're doing and you'd only get in the way. I want you to rest for a bit, and then I need you to organize the captains and gather every man or woman who can carry a sword or bow. Anyone with experience, I do not care how old or young. Do you understand me?"

Sareh looked up and shook her head. "No, father. What are you up to?"

He leaned down and kissed her lightly on the forehead causing his ribs to ache. "Don't worry," he said. "I need you to gather every person who can carry a sword, spear, or bow. You are to rally them in front of First Gate and begin immediate training. I need you to do it without question." He grimaced in pain slightly as he adjusted his broken arm.

"Father, you are scaring me."

"Good! You need to be scared. You also need to do your job. Follow my orders, soldier."

She heard not her father, but General Sark, her commander. Sareh gave him a rigid salute. "Yes, sir."

Without another word, Sark turned his exhausted eecha toward the castle and raced down the cobbled roadway.

When he arrived, he dismounted carefully, knowing he had to save what little strength he had left. The ride had not done anything to improve his broken arm and ribs. It was everything he could do to manage the marble stairs that led to the castle doors. At the top, leaning casually against a pillar, stood Thiels smiling down at him.

"You look terrible," he said.

Sark gave him a derisive snort. "Thanks," he said, climbing the rest of the torturous stairs. "You could have had the meeting down below."

"Yes, I could have," Thiels said, "and you could have come back earlier." Sark winced when Thiels hit him on the shoulder good-naturedly. The mirth faded from Thiels's face. "You're hurt."

Sark shook his head, and took the proffered hand. "It's nothing," he said, his tired eyes glancing up at the looming castle above his head. "I just need some rest—and so do my people." He jerked his head back toward the village. "We're exhausted, commander," he said, following Thiels through the door. "We have more wounded than whole right now."

"I know. I heard." Thiels was having problems keeping the regret out of his voice. He stopped Sark outside the East Hall. "Can you hold out for a little longer? It will not start for a few minutes. Take what rest you can here and then I think we can manage a few hours."

They sank down on the benches outside the chamber and Sark put his head back against the wall. "The emperor was right," he said softly. "He was right about everything."

"I am sorry, Sark." Thiels rubbed his arm and then tented his fingers. "I am sorry I could not be there with you—could not be on the field."

Sark turned his head toward Thiels and lifted his brow. "Commander, it wouldn't have made any difference. The same people would have died, the enemy would have moved just as swiftly, and disappeared just as quickly. We all serve the emperor, as we must. You know that." He smacked Thiels on the back and gave him a roguish smile. "Besides, it was more glory for me, yes?"

Thiels laughed. "Yes, indeed, my friend."

He settled into the seat, but his thoughts kept going back to Joshan. The emperor told both of them about this moment.

"How did he know?" Thiels whispered, staring off into the corridor.

"The emperor is a great man and a great Starguider. I do not pretend to understand his powers—or his wisdom—but this…" Sark stared down at his hands. "That day in the forest I never thought I would feel that way about anyone."

Their minds wandered back several weeks, two days before Joshan had left for the isle.

Thiels and Sark sat on impatient eechas for a very long time, each having ridden to a secluded spot in the woods. The note from the emperor had to the point. They were to ride to the woods just before dawn and wait for him. They were not to speak to anyone about where they were going. He would explain when they met.

Sark arrived first and searched the surrounding forest for any trespasser. This was more out of habit than necessity. When Thiels arrived some minutes later, they exchanged greetings, but said nothing about why they were there. The woods were lightening when they saw the emperor on his eecha, with Marshal Bails following behind him.

Sark was amazed at the difference in the young man he had seen only a few weeks earlier. He hardly recognized Joshan. The fatigue and sadness he saw in those eyes disturbed him. At the same time, he found himself drawn to the strength and maturity that had not been there before. Sark had sworn allegiance to Joshan and now remembered why. Joshan was a great man; a man who had sacrificed his childhood, who had a vast, terrible power, and who was leading the civilized world against an enemy that could destroy them all. Yet, there was vulnerability about the emperor that went to the heart. Sark would follow him anywhere.

"Good morning, gentlemen," Joshan said, dismounting and motioning to the clearing. "I apologize for the earliness of this meeting and the secrecy. It is not my wish to be deceptive. Believe me, it is warranted in this case. Please," he said, taking out a bundle from his saddle, "I have brought some strong, hot tea. Would you join me?" There was such grace in Joshan, a natural humility that the older men trusted implicitly. They dismounted and joined Joshan and Haiden on the ground to sip tea.

"I am not going to mince words with you. I need your help and your guidance," he began slowly, staring down at his drink. "I have come to rely so much on your strengths and I honestly do not have the right to ask you what I am about to. Please consider well before answering. If it is too much, then you have no obligation to me. I come to the two of you now as a friend not as your emperor."

They glanced at each other, but did not answer at once. Thiels looked up from his tea and smiled.

"You have but to ask. I think I speak for both of us. We would do anything for you." Sark echoed the sentiment.

Joshan sipped his tea, but there was no humor in his face. "Thank you," he answered slowly. "What I am going to ask may be too much. You must promise to let me know if it is." They nodded gravely.

"I need to tell you that there are some… difficult times in store for all of us. I will be leaving within the next few days to travel to the isle. I may not be returning." Haiden scowled at him and Joshan touched his arm. "You need to let me go," he said to him and then turned to the others, "all of you. My journey may lie on another road. I need you to plan for that. You have prepared my armies as I requested and I am amazed at what you have accomplished. Unfortunately, I have to tell you that more than half of that army will not return from the field." Sark looked up. "There is no way to win this battle. If you were to fight it to its logical conclusion, the Keep would fall. However," he said with intensity, staring hard at Sark, "you have to fight it regardless. It is imperative you stand your ground, no matter what happens, even knowing you will fail." His eyes took on an amber glow as he looked at the mercenary. "Can you do that?"

Sark knitted his brow. "I honestly don't know," he finally said. "How could I know until I am on the field?"

Joshan's face became intense in the morning light. "But I do know, Sark. I have seen it."

His dark eyes became shadowed and the three men looked on in wonder at the glow that radiated from them. His voice became an echoing chime on the air instilling strength and courage as they listened.

"You will be a mighty champion to your soldiers, General Sark, and strike terror in the hearts of the enemy as you take the field. People would follow you into death—thousands of them, without a second thought. Your soldiers will take up your cry until the battlefield rings with it. You will lead them to honor and glory, and withstand forces that would ride over any other army. The field will be yours again and again and the enemy will not be able to move you. Tens of thousands of Sirdar's troops will fall against your strength like waves against the stone. Nonetheless," he said as if he were far away, "they will eventually move you back. A multitude of enemies will come. They will drive you to the north. Nothing you can do will stop it. Well over half of your people will die on the field. Finally, the troops will have to retreat to the Keep. You yourself will fall, but a mysterious champion will save your life. When the imperials finally make a last stand, the enemy will be—gone."

"Sire?" Sark whispered, clinging to his every word.

Joshan came out of his trance and gave the mercenary a wary smile. "I cannot say more than this," he said slowly. "You need to be prepared."

"For what, sire?"

Joshan shifted his eyes from man to man. "To go on," he said quietly. "The war will not be over. Indeed, this will be just the beginning. When the field is clear of foe, the two of you must gather every hand—young, old, man, or woman—and arm it. Any who can walk and carry a sword, a lance, a bow or means to carry an army, must be mobilized and very quickly. You will find skills and means to train them, but they must march within two days."

"March to where, sire?" Thiels asked anxiously.

"To Calisae."

The two men sat back confounded.

"Calisae?" breathed Sark. "It is a field of ghosts. There is no one there."

Joshan nodded. "Unfortunately, there will be, Sark. The southern hordes will take it. There they will prepare a throne for Sirdar where he will rule—and destroy this world. If you let them get a foothold in Calisae, there will be no defeating him. Sirdar will roll over this land like a plague and nothing will stop him this time. You must stop the armies of Sirdar before they get that foothold. I rely on you to do this for me. Lead my army to Calisae. Hold back the hordes of Sirdar, and retake the castle. If you do not, our civilization will die. Do you understand?"

The men could not speak at once as the finality in Joshan's voice chilled them to the bottom of their hearts. Finally, Sark looked up at him.

"I do understand," he said and then bowed his head to Joshan. "I swore my allegiance to you, sire, and I will do anything you ask. Tell me what I must do."

Thiels also bowed his head before Joshan. "Sire, I pledge my life, my soul, and my heart. Let them serve you."

"There is such valor in the soul of noble people. I will take your allegiance," Joshan said quietly. "And I will require your absolute obedience. If you falter from what is required of you, you will doom the world and everything we love. The task will prove daunting, I assure you, and I say again, do I ask too much?"

"No, sire," they both said at the same time.

"Very well. This is what you will do…"

Thiels and Sark sat in silence remembering that strange morning long ago. They were amazed at how accurate Joshan's predictions had been and how much he knew about the strengths they had shown. The noon bell rang and they stood to enter the council chambers.

They went to inform the councils that the twenty-three of them were now in charge of the Keep. The Chancellor of Justice, Harlane Granaire would now be the Emperor's Regent. The appointment was supported by documents Thiels held tightly in his fist, which had been signed by Joshan weeks before; documents he thought he would never have to serve. They went to tell the councils that the only people to be left in the Keep would be the very old and the very young, that it was now time to stand and bear arms against their enemies. They went to tell the councils that they had to hold the Keep until the army returned.

They entered the chamber to a confused, noisy chaos. As usual, the councilors bickered and fought with one another. But when they left the chamber nearly an hour later, they left a group of people standing straight and tall, their faces grim but determined, their spirits united to fight for the emperor and their world.

Sark went back to his mount to return to his troops. When Thiels grabbed his pack from behind the pillar where he had met Sark earlier, he descended the steps to inspect the six hundred Elite dressed in full field uniforms, standing at rigid attention in the training grounds below the castle. Pulling on his helmet and gloves, Jona and his other three captains joined him, and they briskly walked through the ranks to take their positions at the head of the columns.

"Present!" yelled Jona and every guard raised his or her weapon in perfect unison, the present echoing from every voice.

The columns were as tight and straight as a finely tuned machine. Every pair of eyes stared ahead—resolute, confident, and obedient. The countless seasons of training showed in their stance and exact rigor, in the noble carriage of their heads and weapons. These were the Elite, the best of their times, hand selected, highly intelligent, extremely skilled, and the greatest of all warriors in the provinces. For one thousand seasons, generation after generation, they had prepared for this day.

"Salute!" yelled the next captain and each weapon whirled in precise movement from left to right, from front to rear and back again, the wave unflawed as it undulated perfectly through the ranks. The replied salute was deafening.

Thiels glanced up at the castle and saw the slight figure of Saldorian, dressed now in royal regalia, standing proudly in the consort's parade review seat with the new Emperor's Regent standing at attention next to her. The other council members spread behind them, but each stood tall in the sunlight. Thiels caught Sal's eye and, with great formality, saluted the consort. Saldorian nodded to him once and he whirled around.

"Elite!" His voice echoed like a trumpet call across the troops and they replied in kind. "Forward!"

With that, the columns moved as one, the imperial banners flying proudly side by side at the front. For the first time in a thousand seasons, the Elite marched to war.

CHAPTER EIGHTEEN
MT. CÁISON

Nissa soared above ragged mountains buffeted by relentless winds. Joshan clung to her neck peering through the clouds to look for the higher peaks of Mt. Cáison. There was nothing but vast sheets of white and craggy heaps of black rock.

His strength waned as they moved forward and Nissa quivered beneath him. They had been flying for four days and nights now. Joshan knew they needed to land soon or Nissa would simply fall out of the sky.

Nissa's stamina, strength, and perseverance amazed Joshan. The Mourna had not complained once during the journey and he knew she was starving and thirsty. Finally, he spotted a lake beneath them and turned her to dive for it. He thought she could find fresh fish in the water and he could gather his strength for the last leg of the journey.

When they finally landed, Nissa stumbled on the icy ground, jarring her wing badly. Joshan rolled off and fell. When he tried to stand after he hit the freezing earth, it was too much for his weakened legs, and he struggled to his hands and knees at the water's edge. Crawling the rest of the way, he finally made it to the bank and reached down for a sip of water. The lake was frozen solid.

Joshan made a fist and shrieked out at the night, his tears turning almost instantly to ice. He closed his eyes against the cold and shivered in the darkness.

It was not the lack of water, food, or exhaustion that haunted him; he needed those things less and less, as the days passed. It was the rage of catalyst as it grew like a cancer in his body, the blinding pain that made the world dull and unreal. When he retched from the overwhelming sickness, the heave was empty and destitute. Joshan could only cough violently and close his eyes until the dizziness went away.

There was no one there to be strong for, no life that rested in the palms of his crystalline hands. He was alone with a companion that could kill him with a swipe. With no one there to be responsible for, Joshan completely let go.

He sank his head and great overwhelming sobs shook him. Despair enfolded him like a shroud and he bowed to the ground as if worshiping.

Joshan howled in the darkness, cursed the stars, the crescent moons, and the invisible gods, shaking his fists at the fates until they bled, screaming as loud as he could until he could scream no more.

"I hate you!" The sound echoed up to the cloudy sky. "It is not fair! It is not right! Why should I suffer? Why should I have to save them? I cannot do it! I cannot stand it! Make it stop—make it go away—it is not fair, damn you—I hate you. Make it—stop—please…" he finally whispered. "Please… make it stop."

A deep weariness came over him, engulfing his mind like a potent drug. He had not slept in weeks. This was something else. It pulled him out of the world effortlessly. Joshan collapsed in the snow and the only sound was the reverberating echo of his voice cascading back from the lake.

When he opened his eyes, he was no longer on the mountain. The night was black around him and he could not see anything at first. A distant light sparkled in the darkness, growing as it approached. When it was near enough, it transformed into a figure. Joshan's legs gave out when the shadow came near him and he fell to his knees. Looking up, he saw a woman. She was breathtaking, with locks of finest gold, injected with silver. She had huge violet eyes that glowed down at him benevolently.

"Ethos," he whispered and then bowed his head.

"Rise, child," she said, her voice the most amazing sound Joshan had ever heard. He struggled to his feet and stared at her.

"Why are you here?"

"I heard your cries in the wilderness, your desperation. I cannot bare it any longer, Joshan, to watch you suffer... and so needlessly. What we asked of you is too much. I have come to help you, child, to take the pain away."

She lifted her hand toward him and he saw crystals glistening brightly on her palms. They were a hundred times more brilliant than his. The tiny lights traveled in delicate tendrils up her arms, sparkled gloriously at her temples, and framed her face in soft illumination. Her delicate fingers drifted toward his face and a ghost of a smile touched her lips.

"Please, Joshan. Let me help you."

Joshan's eyes filled with tears and he reached out to her. "Please," he whispered.

Something in his guider's sense shattered like a falling icicle, ringing in his ears. Fear prickled in his arms. He quickly withdrew his hand.

"Wait," he said, taking a step back. He searched her face carefully, trying to clear his mind. It was clouded and confused. "This is wrong."

"Everything will be all right. You have but to touch my hand and you will be free of pain and suffering." Her violet eyes were calm with compassion. "It is not fair, is it? What we have done is cruel and vicious—stealing your life, your love, requiring you to suffer—every day. I want to give you rest, Joshan, as you deserve. You have done enough. Let me ease your pain. You can rest for as long as you wish."

Joshan took another step away from her and shook his head to clear it. He remembered what it was, what was wrong. "You are... you are early," he said to her.

"I have come when you needed me. Will you not let me help you?" She raised her hand again and glided toward him.

"No," Joshan said, pulling the sword out of its shaft. "Stay away from me. You are not Ethos."

The goddess stopped where she was, but her face did not change. "You must listen to me now." Joshan could feel his eyelids drifting down and shook his head again to get the lull of her voice out of his mind. "Come with me, child, and I promise you will be happy. I want to take away your agony, your sorrow, and grant you your deepest desire. I know what it is you wish, what is in your heart."

She motioned to the night and out of the darkness, images grew, surrounding them with clarity. It was as if he had stepped into another place, another time, and he gazed around himself in disbelief.

He was back with Ricilyn. She cradled their son in her arms, nursing him as she sat in sunlight from a broad window, more beautiful than he could remember. It was not the Keep; it was a small farm somewhere in the plains of Palimar. The cottage was neat, comfortable, and peaceful. The warmth of love and sunshine enveloped him in a sweet embrace and he rushed to hold his wife and baby in his arms. When he reached her, it all disappeared, leaving only aching loneliness.

"This is the gift I can give you, Joshan," the goddess whispered in his ear. "Lay down the sword and I can offer you peace, love, and eternal tranquility. All you have to do is let go."

When Joshan turned to the woman, his eyes were a black blaze. The figure stepped back and shrank from the light. Joshan became suddenly cold, his jaw set, his eyes a furious fire.

"Get away from me," he hissed. "I know who you are. Get back to your hole, Sirdar. Take your tricks with you—leave me!" He lifted the sword and drove it straight into the woman's heart. The blade hit air. The woman dissolved into a million motes of light, blinding him for a moment.

"Fool!" The voice was deep, male, and malevolent. "What I offer is genuine, Joshan, and you spurn it. I have the power to give these things to you. Do not fight me, boy, or you will regret it. Come to me now and I will teach you."

The voice had no affect on Joshan and he laughed at the sound. "Your arrogance will destroy you, Sirdar. I am coming," he said grimly, putting the sword back at his side. "When I get there, the lesson will be mine."

There was a sudden lightening of the darkness and a picture appeared before Joshan. Seated on a giant bird he could see Ricilyn and Haiden flying high above the mountains, cloaked against the cold and speeding through the night.

"She is coming to me, Joshan; or did you think she would not follow? Love has made her blind and her fate now lies in my hands, not yours. Come to me and save her… if you can."

The image faded. Joshan screamed and everything went black.

Joshan came out of the dream slowly. Someone had wrapped a blanket around him and a small fire crackled at his feet. The Mourna sat close to the flames, preening one of her wings, the other lying unnaturally askew at her side. He sat up groggily and looked around. A pot of boiling stew rested on a spit and the scent of savory herbs drifted through the air.

Joshan rose stiffly and warmed his hands above the fire. He looked up at the Mourna suspiciously. "How did you manage this?"

Nissa bowed her head and nodded covertly to her right. Coming out of the woods, a man approached them, his arms full of firewood. Joshan instinctively pulled the golden sword from its shaft and lifted it against the stranger. The man stopped in his tracks, dropped the wood, and raised his hands.

The hood covering his head made it difficult to see his face. He was thin toward emaciation, filthy, and his clothes were nothing more than rags that hung off his bone thin arms.

"Please, your majesty," he replied meekly. "Do not hurt me."

Joshan lowered his sword at once. "I know your voice. Who are you?"

The man reached up and removed his hood. Smiling at him broadly from under a wild mane of black hair, he reached down to pick up the wood. "Don't you remember me, sir? I am a friend of Vanderlinden's."

"By the gods," Joshan stared at him wide-eyed. "Wert? What the devil are you doing here? We thought you were dead."

"No, sire." He crossed to the fire and dropped the wood. "Just gone, I guess." He picked up a worn bowl and ladled out a portion of the stew. "Here," he said, relaxing a bit. "I made this for you. It's not much, but should warm you."

Joshan frowned at him and grabbed his staff from the ground. "Come here, Wert."

The little man set the bowl down and nervously crossed to stand before Joshan.

"This is nothing personal," Joshan said, burying the staff in the ground and flexing his hands, "just necessary. Hold absolutely still?"

"Yes, sir." Wert wrung his hands, squeezed his eyes shut, and grimaced in the cold. "Will this hurt, sire?"

Joshan smiled down at the little man. "It should be painless," he said, lifting his palms and placing them on either side of Wert's head.

When Joshan called the power, the white tendrils mingled delicately with the frozen air around him and illuminated his hands. The staff hummed loudly, silencing the noise in the surrounding forest. Joshan pushed quiet musical notes from his throat. When the white flashed into brilliant amber around them, Wert let out a yelp.

"Do not move."

Concentrating, Joshan let his mind drift into Wert's thoughts. The feeling was strange, tactile, like reaching through someone. Joshan pushed back his own hesitancy and probed further. All he found there was deep regret, quiet humility, and a profound experience. He could not see the latter clearly, but whatever it was, it had changed this man's life. It was not the loss of his daughter or the betrayal of himself and Van those many months ago. This was something that happened to him very recently. Regardless, it was clear Wert no longer served the enemy.

Joshan stopped the fire and pulled the staff from the earth. Wert went to his knees and blinked up at the emperor.

"What did you do to me, sire?"

Joshan smiled. "Nothing, Wert. I looked into your mind to make sure you were… safe."

Color rose in Wert's cheeks and he rubbed the back of his neck with a thin hand. "I could have told you," he said softly. "After what he did to my daughter."

Joshan sat by the fire to warm himself. "How did you get here?"

Wert picked up the wooden bowl, dumped the content back into the pot, and stirred it briefly.

"Usual way, I guess," he said, ladling another serving into the bowl. He handed it to Joshan and picked up another to fill.

"Something happened to you, didn't it?"

He looked up from his bowl his mouth fell open. "How did you… I mean no one was there, except…"

Joshan pitched his voice carefully. "Tell me what happened, Wert."

"Aye, sir." Wert stirred the stew pensively and spooned some into his mouth.

"After I left the Village," he said around the food, "I was so ashamed. I hated myself for what I'd let Balinar do to you, Van… and to my daughter. I wanted to die." The whispered voice sounded as faint as the white breath drifting from his mouth. Tears welled in his eyes as he swallowed. "I stumbled over the plains and into the northern woods. I didn't eat nor drink for days, but I don't remember how many. I didn't care.

"When I reached the snowline, I fell and decided that was it. I closed my eyes in the snow and went to sleep."

He took another bite of stew and absently played with the rest.

"I didn't die," he said softly, tilting his head to the side. "These people… they found me, took me in, and nursed me back to health." He smiled to himself. "They didn't have two pennies to rub together, and hardly any food, but they shared what they had and helped me." Glancing up at Joshan, the sides of Wert's mouth curled into a sad smile. "I've never seen such kindness in people, or such greatness of spirit. But these men and women, they weren't from the provinces, sire… they were northerners, every one of them." He stuck the spoon in his mouth until it was clean. "You know, I've been raised to hate their kind, from the time I could walk. My father fought with your grandfather, sire, at Calisae. He was a sailor and came on one of the ships.

"These people took me in, shared what little they had, and showed kindness I hadn't earned. When I was better, they led me to this lake, showed me a cave where I could live, gave me weapons to hunt with, and told me the lake was full of fish. I asked why they led me here. They told me it was because… I needed to wait."

"For what?" A chill snaked up Joshan's spine.

A kind of contentment softened Wert's face. "For a visitor, they said."

"What kind of visitor?"

The thin man's eyes dulled in the firelight as he stared at the lake.

"He came to me night before last..." his voice trailed off at the memory.

The sudden urgency that coursed through Joshan's blood startled him. He went to his knees before Wert and tried to see into his mind again, but he could see nothing. "Who came to you, Wert?"

"He came to me, sire," he finally said. "He came in the fire in the cave and talked to me a long time."

"Who was this man, Wert? Was it Sirdar?"

Wert tilted his chin to the left and smiled.

"Oh no, sire, not him." He licked his lips and swallowed hard. "It was... well, at least I think it was Eraze, sir, himself."

Joshan blinked at him in disbelief. "The king of the gods?"

"Yes, sir. And he talked to me a long time."

"What did he say?"

Wert shook his head and contorted his face in concentration. "He said a lot of things, sire. A lot of things I didn't understand entirely. He talked about a war fought in another place. It lasted for many seasons, he said. It was bitter and bloody. People died, sire, lots of people, he said. He was very sad. I couldn't understand everything he told me. Sometimes he'd talk in a language I didn't know and then tell me things that... well, that didn't make sense, if you take my meaning."

"What kind of things, Wert?"

His voice lowered into a quiet awe. "He said the war was fought three thousand seasons ago. Then something about a leader, and a keeper—then some kind of cover. I'm sorry, sire, it didn't make a whole lot of sense. That's about all I can remember."

Wert grew pale in the firelight. "He did tell me one more thing."

"Go on."

Wert licked his lips nervously. "He said I was to go down to the lake and wait for you. I would find you asleep next to the lake with a Mourna standing guard over you. At the time, that didn't make any sense either, but here we are. He said the bird would be lame and not able to fly. That I was to take care of you and make sure you were safe. You see, he said you had something to do. Said I needed to lead you somewhere."

Joshan sat back on his haunches and took a deep breath. "Where?"

Wert shifted uncomfortably and set the bowl down. "I'm to lead you to the temple, on the mountain."

Joshan scowled at him. "What temple?"

"The Temple of Cáison. Ethos' temple. He said it was there you would find..."

"Sirdar," Joshan finished for him quietly. "Did he say I would win?"

"I'm sorry. He didn't say anything else after that."

Joshan nodded and brushed his hands as he rose. "Then you will lead me, Wert, as the gods have commanded. In this way, you will repay your debt to me and to Vanderlinden."

"Yes, sire." Wert lowered his head away from the emperor's grim stare. "But I'm afraid for you. I'm afraid he might…"

"Do not be, Wert," Joshan said, crossing to Nissa to check her wing. "How long a journey is it?"

"Four or five days, if we don't hit snow too low on the mountain; six or eight, if we do."

Joshan looked at him sharply. "How do you know this? Have you been to the temple?"

"No, sir," Wert said, taking the pot from the fire. "The northerners taught me before they went back to their homes. Said it was what they'd been told to do."

"By whom?"

Wert dropped the hot pot onto the dirt and sucked a scorched finger into his mouth. He glanced up at Joshan and then scratched his head. "They were told by the goddess. These people are priests and priestesses, Ethos' people. The temple was hers, too. They lived there, until… well, until he drove them out."

Joshan rubbed between the Mourna's eyes. "Are you all right?"

The bird looked over his shoulder at Wert and then back to Joshan.

"It is all right, Nissa, you may speak."

"My wing is damaged from the fall," she said, wincing a bit at his touch.

Wert's eyes widened. "It speaks?"

Joshan smiled back at him. "Yes, she speaks. Are you in a lot of pain?"

The Mourna lowered her head and sharpened her beak against a rock. "Not so much. I can walk, but I think it will be several days before I fly again. I am sorry."

Joshan reached up to pat her neck. "Do not be. You have been a true and valiant companion. I do not know enough about your anatomy to heal the wing, but I think I can at least relieve some of the pain, if you will let me."

Nissa looked at him a bit confused and then suspiciously. "You will not punish me?"

Joshan was horrified. "Punish you? For what?"

"For failing."

"What kind of monster must he be to punish a brave and valiant creature like you? I am not Sirdar and will not punish you for carrying me. Hold still." Joshan's hands glowed in the firelight and he very gently ran his fingers over her wings.

"That should help," he said when the power dwindled.

Nissa looked down at him and her expression was hard to read; something foreign softened those soulless eyes. Joshan smiled at her and then crossed to pick up his staff. Standing on the edge of the lake, before the amber fire was completely gone, he lifted the staff and sang toward the water softly. He pulled his cloak in front of him and made a basket out of it.

There was a sudden crackle and then a deafening swoosh. A hole appeared at the water's edge and several fish jumped out and landed in the outstretched cloak. Once it was full, Joshan crossed to the injured Mourna and poured the squirming mass on the snow before her.

"There," he said, straightening this cloak. "Eat now. We have a long journey ahead of us tomorrow."

Nissa lowered her head almost to the ground before him.

"As my master wishes," she said and then turned to devour the fish.

Two days later, Wert, Joshan, and Nissa were nearly half way up the mountain approaching twin spires that rose to a great height above them. The towering rock statues had been there for hundreds of seasons, carved in the likeness of gods, worn and white with snow. Glistening in the sun as it rose over the horizon, they were now no more than pillars against the sky.

"Where are we, Wert?" Joshan adjusted his gloves and pulled his scarf tighter around his throat.

"These are The Twins, sire, the entrance to the gorge of the temple."

"Good. Are there any other forks in this road?"

"No, sire. There is only one path on Cáison and it leads to the temple."

"How do we find it?

"Beyond The Twins is a very deep ravine that runs up the mountain. The path runs along the cliffs and follows the ravine almost to the top. At the end there's a cave called Eraze's Den. You have to travel through the cave to get to the temple. The entrance is just on the other side. The temple stands on a tongue of rock that juts over a great chasm called Temple Deep. There is only one road leading to the temple with cliffs on all sides."

"Then I will not need you any longer."

"Sire?" Wert exclaimed.

"I have to do this alone."

"No, sire. I swore I would keep you safe."

"And you have. You have helped me more than you know. Go now. Go back to your lake and live happily. Perhaps one day, when this is all over, you will come and visit me in Thrain. Yes?"

"Sire, please," Wert wrung his hands as tears filled his eyes.

"You cannot go with me, Wert. He would use you to get to me."

Wert looked at his hands and sighed deeply. "It does not seem right," he said quietly. "The god, he said to keep you safe…"

"Please, Wert, go now," Joshan said, using his voice to manipulate the man. It came so easily to him now. Wert nodded once and turned to head down the path.

When he was about twenty spans away, he twisted back to Joshan. "Be careful, sire," he called. "Don't let him get the drop on you."

"Count on it."

When Wert disappeared around a corner, Joshan fell to his knees and vomited into the snow, shaking uncontrollably for a long time. When the nausea passed, he sat back on his haunches and took several deep breaths to still the quaking in his limbs. He was running out of stamina and the pain was increasingly demanding. Nissa looked down at him until he could get himself under control.

"Master," she said quietly. "I could carry you."

Joshan struggled to his feet and adjusted his clothes. "I will be all right, Nissa," he said. "But if you could carry the pack, that would be most helpful."

Nissa bowed her head low. Joshan slid the heavy pack off his back and tied it between her wings. He scratched between her eyes and even managed a smile. "Thank you, Nissa. I honestly do not know what I would have done without you." The Mourna returned the look sadly.

They made good time at first. The pass was relatively level and the snow on the ground was well packed. At the end of three hours, they saw signs of the gorge Wert had spoken of and the trail became narrower as they proceeded. All at once, when they turned a corner, the canyon opened up in front of them and they stopped to take in its magnificence.

The gorge was deeper than even the High Cliffs in Thrain and Joshan inspected its grandeur quietly. It must have been two leagues deep and as wide as the Keep where they stood, broadening even further along the trail. The rock face was sheer and conical icicles hung in huge spirals down the cliff wall. At the bottom, barely visible at that distance, was a ribbon of river that must have been very wide. The narrow trail continued along the cliff wall, winding to end around a corner several hundred spans away.

Joshan took the weathered staff from his back, gazing at this creation of ice and stone. Had he been feeling better, it would have made more of an impact. With the sickness clouding everything he saw, it was only another barrier to overcome. Snowflakes fell around him and he pulled his hood forward to cover his face.

Joshan could feel Ricilyn as an ache in his heart. She was in front of him, high in the mountains, possibly even with Sirdar already. He had to force down the crippling concern. He wrapped his gloved hand around the staff and trudged forward. Joshan became a black speck in the whiteness, the Mourna a silent shadow behind him as they began the arduous climb to the Temple of Cáison.

Starsight Volume II
BOOK IV – THE Gods

BOOK IV – THE GODS

CHAPTER NINETEEN
THE DEN OF ERAZE

When Fiena landed, Haiden slid off the bird onto the icy ground and stumbled to one knee. Ricilyn fared better and landed on her feet, but she slid onto a nearby rock.

"Haiden, are you all right?" she asked breathlessly.

"Fine," he said, struggling to his feet and taking in a lungful of icy air. He beat the cold from his arms, then reached up and took the packs from Fiena's back. The bird shivered in the darkness and shook out her feathers, almost falling off her feet.

Ricilyn rose and stroked Fiena affectionately. "It is too cold here for her. She is used to the heat of the island. She cannot stay here."

"Send her down, lass," Haiden said, shouldering his pack and then helping Ricilyn with hers. "There's nothing more she can do up here, anyway. It's too cold to fly."

Ricilyn threw her arms around the bird's neck and closed her eyes, listening to the quick beat of the vulcha's heart.

"Go down now," she whispered. "Go down to the lake and stay there. I will call you when we're ready."

The bird ruffled her wings and leapt into the night. She glanced back at the two once more, but did her mistress's bidding. They watched as she disappeared and floated down the mountain.

"Where to now?" Haiden asked, giving the mountain a dubious look.

"Up," Ricilyn said with a sigh and then climbed the path.

Ricilyn's heart became heavier the further into the mountain they traveled. It was not from the biting cold that found its way through thick leggings and layers of protection or the aching weariness that was becoming a serious burden for them both; it came from the certainty that inevitability hunted her. The closer she came to her future the more like an illusion it became.

Where once Ricilyn saw the vision with clarity, now each step brought her closer to something resembling a dream. There was nothing she could do to stop it, had she the courage to try. Her awareness was becoming more and more clouded the higher they went into the mountain. For the first time in her life, she was alone and it felt like a black emptiness inside her. She could not feel anything and it left her drained and desperate. Hours passed without a word.

"Lass," Haiden finally called from behind her, "how about a break?"

"I am fine, Haiden," she said.

"Aye, but I'm not. Would you mind? I really need to take a breather."

Ricilyn nodded and searched the snow in front of them. "There is a cave ahead," she said. "We will rest there."

The snow came down in swirling eddies around them, making their progress very slow. Howling wind made speech impossible and the oppressive cold made their feet leaden. The path was extremely narrow here and difficult to see in the snowstorm. As they moved along, Ricilyn missed a step and almost tumbled over the cliff. With a remarkable swiftness, Haiden caught her and pulled her back hard against the cliff wall. Ricilyn had never seen anyone move that quickly. She clung to him until her heart stopped racing. Even in the cold mountain, Haiden wiped sweat from his forehead and took in a shaky breath.

"By the gods," he said breathlessly. "Are you all right?"

"Yes." Ricilyn swallowed and glanced behind her at the fathomless distance to the bottom of the ravine. She was exhausted and had to fight to stay alert before she killed them both.

Staying close to the cliff, they edged their way to the distant cave. When they finally reached it, the darkness opened like a giant mouth to swallow them.

They fell to their knees a few feet inside the entrance. The storm quickly faded, leaving a frozen white landscape and piled drifts to line the opening. They watched for several long minutes as the wind died down and everything became very quiet. When they finally recovered their strength, Haiden stepped out of the cave to explore the path.

"This is the end of the trail, lady." He rubbed his hands together and pulled the pack from his back. "Let's get a little light going so we can see where we're at."

He dug through his pack and finally pulled out a lantern and flint. Shouldering the pack again, he struck flint to the lantern and turned to explore the back of the cave.

"Careful!" Ricilyn called when he disappeared behind an outcrop of rock.

"It's all right. Come here—you've got to see this!"

Ricilyn followed Haiden, careful on the thick sheet of ice that served as a floor.

When she rounded the corner, she stopped in amazement.

All around them, as brilliant as a million candles, the frozen cave walls reflected the light like a great mirror, illuminating a huge wintry chamber. The floor and walls were exceptionally smooth blue and white ice, so pure, it was difficult to determine where one ended, and the other began. In sharp contrast, the ceiling, hundreds of spans above their heads, fell in jagged, dripping white cones, the water drifting from them as a fine snow that swirled through the air. The cave tunneled so far away from them, they could not make out the other side. Both of them looked around in wonder.

"By the gods," Ricilyn whispered, awed by the spectacular beauty of this earthly shrine.

"Aye," was all Haiden could manage when he lifted the lantern. The light moved the shadows strangely and sharp ghostly images danced on the walls. Their silhouettes cast from the light sent a chill of fear through Ricilyn.

Stooping, Haiden set the lamp down. He began rubbing and blowing warm air on his frozen fingers.

"Lady, we got a choice in front of us. My guess is, the path continues through the cave. We either go forward or back. What do you want to do?"

Ricilyn again tried to find her husband with her dwindling sight. Her guider's sense was as dead as it had been for the last four days. She could feel nothing.

Something was blocking her abilities, making her as helpless as a child in this strange cold world. Ricilyn had never felt this out of touch and wondered again how people could stand it—this loneliness, this isolation.

She was afraid to go forward and could not bring herself to go back. Joshan was here somewhere; Ricilyn had seen it the first day they had flown toward him, when her sense was sharp—indeed sharper than it had ever been. The gods had touched her that night and Joshan was on Mt. Cáison. Now all she knew was doubt.

"I think we need to go on, Haiden," she said, adjusting her pack. "He is here somewhere. We will go through the cave and see where it leads."

"Aye," Haiden said, eyeing the cavern with doubt.

At first, the cave proved extremely difficult to navigate. They slid over the slippery floor on their backsides to get through the large chamber. On the other side of the chamber, the ice disappeared and the cave funneled into a long, winding tunnel, with a rocky frozen pathway. People had cut it into the rock as evidenced by several torches lining the walls. Haiden took one down to save his lamp oil.

They trudged along the tunnel for a good two hours, amazed at how long it was. When they finally emerged into a small chamber, Ricilyn was relieved to see a running stream to one side. She tested the water and then took a long drink.

"Fresh water," she said taking off her pack. "Let's fill our water bags."

When Haiden approached, he kicked something on the ground.

"Bless the gods!" he exclaimed, stooping down in the darkness. "Firewood and a pit. I think this might be a good place to stay the night, lady. We need rest."

Haiden searched the cave and found several more pieces of wood. He soon had a small fire going and they were both grateful for its warmth and light. They prepared a small meal of bread, water, and smoked meat Haiden had tucked away in his pack. Both of them felt much better for it.

"You best get some rest, lady," Haiden said repacking the food. "No telling how long it will be before we get another chance."

Ricilyn smiled at him. "I think you need the rest more than I do, my sweet friend. I do not think you have had more than a couple of hours in the last few days. I can stay awake for a bit and keep watch."

Haiden gave her a parental scowl. "Not likely. I will take the first watch. I am not as feeble as all that."

Ricilyn opened her mouth to protest, but smiled instead. "All right. Two hours on and two hours off—good enough?"

"Aye."

Ricilyn curled up into her bedroll, leaving Haiden to stare absently into the fire.

About an hour into the watch, Haiden felt very sleepy so got up to explore the cave. Over in one corner was another store of firewood, so he gathered a few pieces and went back to build the fire back up. As soon as the pieces ignited, Haiden saw a pale blue flame rise from the wood. He scowled at the odd color, but his eyes drooped. Without warning, he fell onto his side sound asleep.

Sirdar stepped from the shadows. He stood over the sleeping Ricilyn for a very long time, several large, black sasarans appearing behind him. They arranged themselves around the edges of the cave, their massive black horns reflecting the fire like blood.

The hooded figure knelt next to the beauty and ran his hands slowly above her. "Sleep, my lovely." The fire threw twisted shadows against the cave wall.

Sirdar hissed his passion when he touched her face, brushing the hair from her eyes tenderly, and then running his hands down her body. He stopped at her belly and smiled. The mist disappeared from around his head when he pulled his hood back and again laid his hands on her middle.

"A child," he whispered. "Joshan's child—a boy. How wonderful. It will be two lives instead of one." When Sirdar pressed her belly, there came the unmistakable hiss of a sword pulled from its scabbard behind him.

"Get your hands off of her, you bastard!" Haiden said.

The massive sasarans were instantly alert and ran toward them.

"Stop!" Sirdar cried and all froze where they were, their human faces wrinkled in surprise and their hooves sparking to a halt on the stone floor.

Taking his time, Sirdar rose putting his hands out to his sides. "You have resilience," he said without turning around. "Few escape the sleeping vapors. I have always known you were special."

Reaching faster than the eye could see, he pulled out a long blade and raised it above his head before Haiden could plunge his own into the monster's back. The sparks flying from blades cascaded around them and Haiden fell back from the force of the blow. When Sirdar finally looked into the old guard's eyes, his face for the first time unveiled, Haiden took two steps back.

"Not what you expected, old man?"

Haiden lifted his sword. "A lie," he whispered incredulously.

Sirdar smiled back at him. "The truth."

The sasarans moved again, but Sirdar held up a restraining hand. "No. This one is mine. You can have him when I am finished."

Sirdar circled Haiden, his blade spinning. "It is said you are the best, old man. Do you think that is true?"

Cinching up on the hilt of the sword, Haiden smoothed the lines of his face, spread his legs in ready stance, and narrowed his eyes in concentration. "I guess we'll find out."

Sirdar stopped his circling and advanced on Haiden. The old guard parried the thrust before it could hit its mark.

Sirdar's blade was very long and light, with sharp spikes that ran along the back of a razor sharp blade. He held it so nimbly in his hand it seemed an extension of his arm. The sword gave the taller figure the advantage of speed and control. Haiden's blade was shorter, but stouter, giving the old soldier more power in the lunge. The clang of metal meeting metal was deafening in the echoing chamber.

Even though Sirdar was incredibly fast, Haiden was a master, seeming to predict exactly where the monster's blade would land before he himself knew it. The duel was an intricate dance of parry, thrust, counter thrust, and blurring ripostes. Sirdar pressed hard, but Haiden was surprisingly quick on his feet and moved with an alacrity that belied his age and size. Every time Sirdar thought he had the advantage, the little man would not be where he expected. The marshal even got close enough with one lunge to rend the material of Sirdar's cloak.

Despite the success Haiden was having, Sirdar was too powerful. This was merely a dalliance for the monster, a deadly game he was playing to prolong the old guard's death. Haiden was not going to give him the satisfaction of going down without a fight. He used every skill and trick he possessed, even managing to drive a point into the monster from time to time.

In a sudden unexpected move, Haiden feigned expertly to the right and Sirdar attacked from the left. The old guard had him and wasted no time in running the blade across the monster's throat, mortally cutting it through the windpipe and both jugulars. Haiden fell back to watch blood gush unabated from beneath Sirdar's chin. When Sirdar fell to his knees, the old guard thought he had killed him.

Sirdar raised his hand to his throat. Red power curled like smoke around his head, the smell hanging hot and putrid in the air. When he pulled his hand away, it was as if the blade had never touched him. The wound and the blood were completely gone, only crimson stains on his shirt remaining.

"Do you begin to understand, old man?" Sirdar hissed at him, rising to prepare another attack. "I cannot be killed—not by you."

He circled Haiden and smiled. "Your skill is unsurpassed," he said persuasively, the tones of his voice making the old guard glare. "I have never seen better. Bow to me and I will spare you. Join me and your uncanny ability will earn you a very high place."

"Not bloody likely," Haiden hissed back, adjusting his blade.

"Do not turn me down so quickly, Marshal," Sirdar said, the tones becoming very compelling. "Think of what I offer. Think of what I could do for the empire. I do not intend to harm Joshan. You see, I need him, just as he needs me. I do not expect you to understand. Trust me, Haiden. Join me now and if what I say is not true, you can help him when he arrives. I will not even disarm you. I give you my word; I will not hinder you in any way."

"Your word?" For the first time Haiden laughed. "Not today, demon. Kill me if you can."

Sirdar pushed him hard.

Haiden fell back. Sirdar ran the red tinted blade into his shoulder, driving Haiden to his knees with a searing pain that made him scream. The old guard glared at Sirdar and fought bravely, but Sirdar pressed his advantage before Haiden could recover. He flicked the blade out of Haiden's hand and it sailed across the floor to the other side of the cave.

Haiden panted from his knees, Sirdar towering over him. Sirdar raised his blade to sink it into Haiden's heart.

At that moment, there was a cry from across the cave. "Haiden!" Joshan shouted, running toward them and sweeping the sasarans closest to him into oblivion with a wave of his hand. The others fell back in terror. Black fire blazed around him as he tried to reach his friend.

It was too late. Sirdar drove his blade to the hilt into Haiden's chest and he fell to the ground.

"No!" Joshan screamed. His eyes blazed as he raised his hands against Sirdar.

The monster pulled his hood back into place before turning around to confront Joshan, and at the same moment lifted his hand to throw up a red shield. He threw down his sword and scooped Ricilyn into his arms in one flowing movement. Joshan stopped instantly and glared at Sirdar. Behind Joshan, Nissa stood at the entrance, motionless.

"Put her down!" Joshan screamed, channeling the power to take down the shield.

As the power flowed almost opaquely, Ricilyn screamed in the monster's arms. The red eyes glared out of the hood. "You are killing her, boy. The more you use the power, the quicker she dies."

The fear of losing her made Joshan reckless and he sent another blast that tore a hole in the shield, his own eyes suddenly blazing with red fire. A sickly glint came over Sirdar's face when he saw it. Ricilyn let out an ear-piercing scream and writhed in Sirdar's arms.

"I am telling you. If you continue, she will succumb very quickly. I have tied her to your power and she will die if you use it again. Understand me, boy," he shouted at him. "If she and the child die, it will be because you killed her. Stop it now and I swear they will both live."

Joshan stopped and glared at him. "Let her go," he demanded, breathing heavily. "Let her go and I will... surrender to you."

Sirdar nodded. "A wise choice, boy. Throw me the sword and the staff—slowly."

Joshan could not move. His duty to the empire and his love for Ricilyn tore at each other inside him, ignited by the catalyst, and fueled by his hatred. A quick red spark ignited in his eyes as he glared at Sirdar and then glanced at Ricilyn lying unconscious in his arms. For one fraction of a second, he considered destroying them both, sweeping them into oblivion with a single wave of his hand. The desire became so strong it took all his will to quell it. He almost dropped the sword when he realized what the catalyst was doing to him, to his abilities. Finally, he reluctantly slid the golden sword along the frozen floor to Sirdar. Without taking his eyes off Ricilyn, Joshan took the staff from his back and threw that as well.

Sirdar motioned to one of the sasarans. "Take those to the temple and leave them next to my throne." The servant bowed, scooped up the weapons, and ran through the tunnel exit.

Sirdar handed the unconscious Ricilyn to a large sasaran whose tattoos marked him as one of Sirdar's commanders, then motioned to the giant bird. "Come here, Nissa," he said seductively.

The bird took a few slow steps into the chamber and stopped. She stared at her former master, hatred burning in her eyes.

Sirdar raised his hand toward her and she cringed, letting out a loud shriek. "Come here," he hissed, moving his hand slightly.

The Mourna flapped her wings and shivered, not able to resist his will. She moved toward Sirdar. The red fire flared again in Joshan's eyes.

"Does that make you angry?" Sirdar asked quietly. "When I hurt her? That is very interesting. It is getting stronger... I can see it in your eyes. You should have succumbed long before now. Your resistance to the catalyst is—remarkable."

Joshan said nothing and forced his fury down.

Nissa crossed to Sirdar and bowed her head. He grabbed a handful of feathers from the back of her neck. Lifting her head, he stared into her eyes.

"Remember your loyalties, my pet." A red light encircled him and Nissa writhed in pain. "You have brought him to me. For this, I will do as I promised. When you have fulfilled one more mission, I will reunite you with your precious body. Do you understand?"

"Yes, my lord," she whispered shakily. He rubbed her neck and then mounted her with a practiced grace.

Sirdar signaled to the remaining guards. They approached Joshan slowly, obviously reluctant to touch the powerful young man. Heavy chains hung in their hands.

"Bind his hands, his mouth, and hood him. I want no one to see his face," Sirdar said at the guards, "then bring him to the temple." He turned Nissa to the cave exit.

Haiden let out a moan and Joshan tried to go to him. Surrounded now by eight sasarans and Ricilyn as a hostage, Joshan screamed in frustration.

"What do we do with him, sire?" one of the guards asked, nodding to the dying Haiden.

Sirdar glanced back and shrugged. "Leave him. He is of no more use to me."

"For pity sakes," Joshan cried when they gripped his arms, "he has been like a father to me. At least let me say goodbye!"

Sirdar nodded once and then left with his captain and Ricilyn.

When the sasarans let him go, Joshan rushed to Haiden, kneeling in a puddle of his blood.

"Haiden?" Joshan lifted the wounded man into his arms and held him to his chest. "Haiden…" The light faded from the old eyes.

"It's going to be all right, lad," Haiden said hoarsely as color drained from his face. "You can do it—don't let him tell you—otherwise. Fight it, no matter what—don't let it get to you." He reached up to touch Joshan's face and gave him a half-crooked smile.

"No, please," Joshan sobbed.

"There's nothing for it—but to do it," the old guard whispered. His breath gave out and he slumped in Joshan's arms.

"No!" Joshan threw back his head and screamed in grief, clinging to Haiden.

Without compassion, the sasarans tore him away and brutally bound and gagged him. The last thing he saw before they hooded him was Haiden's glassy eyes staring lifelessly into the dying fire.

CHAPTER TWENTY
THE GAZING

Trenara would not eat or sleep. She paced back and forth on the open deck, watching futilely for Joshan, Ricilyn or Haiden's return. She never felt more helpless—useless—and it ate away at her moment by moment. She blamed herself for Joshan's departure, as if she had driven him off. Though many tried, there was nothing anyone could do to soften her mood.

Vanderlinden became increasingly anxious about her depression, her angry outbursts, and the long silence. Grandor brought her food, books, and even played music for her, but nothing reached her. She would simply grunt an irritable acknowledgement and ask that they leave her alone. The guider barely accepted a blanket against the cold night as she sat out on the deck of the ship and stared night after night into the sky. Her eyes had become swollen red rings of stern self-abuse and she had not said more than ten words in the days following Joshan's disappearance.

To make matters worse, the ship made very slow progress up the coast as if something was holding them back. The winds were sluggish with barely enough strength to fill the sails. The delay terrified the guider. She watched the endless coast. After four long days, Van told her it would only be a matter of hours before they reached the Keep.

Trenara had tried many times to look into the gazing. It had revealed nothing. Both she and Grandor had taken turns with the relic, but it remained gold and opal, ivory and glass, and nothing more.

When she looked out at the sea now, trepidation was becoming an all-consuming obsession.

"Ma'am?" The voice broke sharply into her reverie. She whirled around to stare into the beautiful, eyeless face of Ena carried in Porphont's strong arms. Ena still lacked enough strength to walk on her own, but that did not stop her and Porphont from exploring every inch of the ship, and each other. Their bond was so strong now it was difficult to remember they had even been apart. Even though Ena's body was still weak, her spirit had soared over the last four days, and her face radiated a pureness that Trenara had never seen in another. Even without her eyes, when she was with Porphont, you forgot she no longer had them.

"Quit sneaking up on me like that," Trenara hissed and turned back to the sea.

Ena and Porphont both smiled. "Grandor has made you lunch, guider, and asked that we fetch you."

"I am not hungry," she whispered.

"Nonetheless," Ena replied, touching Porphont's face tenderly, "he says you need to eat something. Starving yourself is not going to do anyone any good."

Trenara gave them a stubborn huff and folded her arms. "You can tell Grandor…"

Without warning, Porphont swept her up in his free arm and threw her over his shoulder. At a silent command from Ena—at which he smiled broadly—he turned around and headed for the cabins.

"Put me down, you big oaf!" Trenara cried, kicking and screaming. "Put me down at once! I will have your head for this!"

Of course, Porphont could not hear her and strode across the deck. As they passed Vanderlinden, the giant kissed his wife quickly on the forehead, ducking out of reach of a flailing arm.

"Now, why didn't I think of that?" He slapped Tam soundly on the back and went back to work.

When they reached her cabin, Porphont unceremoniously dumped Trenara at the dinner table and then gently set Ena down across from her. Just at that moment Grandor swept into the room carrying a large tray laden with food.

The old guider had a well-earned reputation for being one of the finest cooks in the provinces, having given up a successful career in the culinary arts to take up the guider's wand full time. It was the major cause of his girth and he was quite proud of it. It was rare he cooked for others, so everyone considered his meals quite the treat.

"Wonderful, guider!" he cried, tucking a napkin under his chin and taking a seat next to her. "I am so glad you could join us."

Trenara snatched up a large serving knife and fork from the tray. All three of them lost their smiles and leaned as far away from her as they could.

"Do not worry," she groused, "I never spill blood at the table."

She dove into the tender fish in front of her and took a large portion. She was suddenly famished and certain Grandor had put something in the food to make it more alluring. It went a long way to improve her mood.

After they had eaten, Grandor cleared the table and the other three went into the parlor. When he returned, he had the worn out velvet bag containing the gazing.

Trenara glowered up at him. "It does not work," she said testily, "not without the power."

"I disagree," he said, taking his seat next to her and carefully sliding the mirror from the bag. "The Crystal was not even here when Kerillian used this. Please," he said, touching her hand, "will you try it again?"

Before Trenara could touch it, Ena reached out across the table and took it into her own hands. Without saying a word, she ran delicate fingers purposefully over the mirror.

"What is this?" she asked, running the smooth surface across her cheek. The kaleidoscope colors glistened beautifully against her skin and naked ivory gods and goddesses danced shamelessly around the frame. They seemed alive in her hands.

"It is the gazing, child," answered Grandor, watching Ena carefully. "It is used to see many things."

"Yes, of course," she said to Porphont and passed the relic to him. When his hand brushed hers, there was a sudden spark of static, and both of them jumped. Looking startled, Porphont quickly lifted Ena to his lap and wrapped his massive hands around hers as she held the mirror in front of her face. They both stared into the mirror, caught by something glistening there. Ena gasped and a tear fell down Porphont's cheek.

Getting to her knees in front of them, Trenara forced her voice to take on the guiding tones.

"What do you see?" she asked, knowing the girl and the mute both saw the same thing.

"It is dark," Ena said in a very low voice, a voice foreign to Trenara, with an accent she could not place. It must be Porphont speaking. "It is dark, but white at the same time." A multi-colored light radiated from the mirror, illuminating their faces in reds, blues, yellows, and greens, swirling and undulating, making their eyes dark and vacant.

"It is cold," said the voice and then another took its place. "It is very cold." It was Ena's voice. "We are in a dark place—a cold place—the walls are stone, the ground frozen. We see a man—no, a woman..." Then the other voice continued. "It is the Oracle. She is asleep in a cave. There is a fire and—wait, another—there is another in the cave—Haiden. He is also asleep. The fire dies—it is so cold—so cold." Then Ena's mouth widened and Porphont's eyes became confused. "There is another," she said, her voice breaking. "There is another with them..."

Her breathing stuttered in frightened gasps. "It is him!" The gods and goddesses continued their ivory dance around the mirror. "He has found her." Tears glistened on Porphont's cheeks. "He is reaching down to touch her. He is reaching down to take her..." A scream pierced the quiet air. "He has killed him! He has killed the marshal! Run! Run! Lady, run!" They both stayed frozen, only their faces moving. "Run, lady!" This was Porphont's voice. "Do not let him touch you! Run! Run! Run!" They both shuddered in horror.

"He sees us," they whispered, a strange twisted sound as if two voices were talking in harmony. "He knows we are here." The shriek from the eerie double voice made both guiders cover their ears. Trenara snatched the mirror from their hands and looked into it briefly before Grandor threw the cover over it. In that instant, sitting in the darkened cabin, what Trenara saw was unmistakable.

Grandor helped the guider to her feet. Trenara stared blankly into the room. Porphont had wrapped his arms around Ena and was rocking her quietly, his face surprisingly pale. Ena buried her own in her hands. They both wept. Grandor turned his attention to Trenara and took her hands. They were ice-cold.

"Trenara, are you all right?"

"He, he…"

"What is it? What did you see?"

"He…" Tears soaked her gray lashes. "He killed him. He's killed Haiden."

"What?" Grandor whispered, looking back at Porphont who nodded agreement. "Sirdar killed him?"

When Trenara's eyes widened, the dammed up tears fell apart. She slowly shook her head. "No, not Sirdar." She looked like she would be sick. "Joshan," she hissed.

Grandor blinked several times, slowly.

"No," he said, squeezing her hand. "You are mistaken. It is a trick—a trick of Sirdar's."

"It is no trick. It was Joshan's face behind the blade. I saw it… Haiden is dead."

When Trenara sank her head and collapsed, Grandor barely caught her. The vibration of the keel hitting the currents of Keep Harbor shivered in Grandor's bones and he pulled her tight into his arms.

CHAPER TWENTY-ONE
THE TEMPLE

The manacles sliced into Joshan's wrists as a rope pulled him stumbling along a rocky path he could not see. The gag tasted foul in his mouth and he saw little light from the black hood they had thrown over his head.

They yanked him mercilessly through the ice and snow that led to the Temple of Cáison. On both sides of the road, he could hear jeering men cursing him. Small rocks propelled by the mob stung his head and hands. Several times, he fell to his knees and they dragged him several spans before he could regain his footing. His body became bloody and bruised from the assaults. Compared to the catalyst that now ruled his awareness, the pain was nothing.

The guards forced him up a torturously long stairway. He stumbled many times, cutting deep gashes into his shins; his wrists became bloody where there were no crystals. By the time they reached the top, they had to half drag, half carry Joshan through the immense marble doors and down a long corridor.

When they reached the end, they ripped the bag from his head and forced him to his knees. In front of him, sitting at the top of a very high dais, sat Sirdar looking down at him. Ricilyn was awake, but unaware of her surroundings. She sat at the monster's feet with unseeing eyes. On Sirdar's right stood Nissa, resting her chin on his shoulder and glaring at Joshan. He thought he saw pity in those eyes.

Behind Sirdar, rising almost a hundred spans above his head was a great white stone statue of Ethos. Her hands rested before her in the classic gesture of peace, her hair carved as a flowing mass over her shoulders, and her eyes staring sightlessly straight ahead. The sculpture was a stunning masterpiece with gold and silver glistening from her gown and face. All over the statue, however, there were large chunks of marble that had been hacked away by heavy blows, all at arm's reach. The statue had been defiled repeatedly. Despite the damage, the piece was an incredible achievement.

Joshan could do no more than glance up at it for a fleeting second and then bow his head before Sirdar.

The hooded figure lifted his hands to his guards and they quickly removed the bindings from Joshan's wrists and mouth. With another silent signal, the guards bowed very low and retreated to the back of the temple, where they turned their backs on the dais.

"Look at me," Sirdar whispered. Joshan lifted his chin slowly, his eyes blazing. He wanted nothing more than to destroy this creature, but knew Ricilyn would die if he used the power.

"Do not be discouraged, my boy," Sirdar said. "You see, despite what you may be feeling right now, I am not your enemy. In fact, I am probably the only friend you have. I know it does not seem so now, but it will—later."

"You are wasting my time, Sirdar," Joshan said through his teeth. "Get on with it. What do you want?"

Sitting back against the throne, Sirdar folded his hands and a soft chuckle escaped the hood. "Tell me, how do you like my little gift? You should feel honored," he added slyly. "I share it very rarely. All you need to do now is let it touch you, Joshan. Let the catalyst touch you. You will feel pain—terrible, terrible pain—but I promise it will pass very quickly." He laughed. "That is what she said there on the cliffs—at first trial—I promise it will pass very quickly. Trenara lied to you. It was only the beginning of pain."

Joshan gaped at him. "How do you know?"

"I know, my boy. I know everything. It will pass very quickly—so it is with the catalyst."

His voice became low and dangerous, echoing persuasively through the air around them. Red sparks of static hummed from his hands as he leaned toward Joshan.

"Let me guide you, Joshan. The catalyst is more powerful than you could possibly imagine. I know you can feel it, coursing through your blood, your brain, your heart, releasing useless inhibitions—setting your mind free to do what it wishes. Is that not worth little pain—a little torture? It calls to you. I can see it in your eyes, telling you to do whatever you wish; telling you of the dark pleasures that you have yet to experience—pleasures unknown to mortals. If you let it take you, if you let it touch you. There will be no more pain, only pleasure. The pain is in the resistance. It must be very difficult for you; the ache must be excruciating. Let me ease your pain."

"Save your breath, Sirdar," Joshan said. "What do you want from me?"

Sirdar chuckled quietly from the mist around his head. "I have a mission for you, my boy; one that will make our happy little family here complete. In exchange, you and Ricilyn may go on your way. I will not hinder you." He reached down to stroke Ricilyn's hair gently.

"Get your hands off her!" The unmistakable red hue rose in Joshan's eyes.

Sirdar lifted his hand to caress the arm of the chair.

"Forgive me," he said with mock penitence, "I did not mean to offend you. But it is very important you understand your position."

"What mission?"

"You will take Nissa and go to Thrain where you will retrieve something I lost."

Joshan scowled at him. "What?"

"My queen, of course."

Joshan tightened his lips. "You are not serious. She would never come to you willingly."

Sirdar leaned forward on his throne and sparks of crimson lights popped all around him. "Trenara must come and you had better be very persuasive," he spat back at him. "You will take her by force, if need be. Otherwise, Ricilyn will be mine to do with as I please."

Joshan could feel his heart sink in his chest. "I will not. You cannot ask me to choose."

"I can and I do," Sirdar hissed back at him. "You bring me Trenara and I will give you Ricilyn."

"And if I refuse?"

Sirdar lifted his hand and Ricilyn rose. Without hesitation, she crawled onto his lap and rested her head against his chest. He caressed her seductively, running his hands along her neck and shoulder.

Joshan tried to run up the stairs, but the shield hit him hard and he fell against the stone.

"If you refuse, Ricilyn will take her place. You will die and your son will become mine. Do I make myself clear?"

Joshan screamed in frustration, but could only ball his hands into fists.

"I take that as a yes," Sirdar said, releasing Ricilyn. She crawled back down at his feet.

"Go to him, my pet," Sirdar said to Nissa and she descended the stairs to stand by Joshan's side. Joshan mounted the bird.

"Oh, and one more thing," Sirdar said chuckling. "I do not want my bride—distracted. Kill the giant," he said slowly, his red eyes blazing from beneath the cowl, "and bring me his heart."

Joshan's mouth hung open as he looked up at the hooded figure. "What? No!"

"Yes," Sirdar replied simply. "And to make certain… Nissa, look at me." She lifted the almost human eyes.

A fine red mist flowed from his hands to settle around the Mourna's head. She shrieked and shook violently, almost throwing Joshan from her back. When the pain passed, she lowered her head.

"What Nissa sees now, I will see. What she hears, I will hear. If you leave her sight at any time or for any reason, I will kill your wife and child instantly. Is that clear?"

"Yes," Joshan hissed, touching Nissa's neck tenderly, wishing he could relieve her pain.

"Kill the giant, then bring me his heart—and his wife."

"He will not go down without a fight, Sirdar," Joshan snapped back at him. "I am no match for the giant in a fair fight. How do you expect me to accomplish this without my power?"

"I will grant you that," he said, throwing the golden sword to him. "You may use your power for this and this alone. I will not let it hurt the girl. But hear me… if you use it for anything else, she will suffer, I promise you."

"And what of Trenara? I doubt she will come to me willingly after I have killed her husband. Should I use my power on her as well?" He slammed the sword into its scabbard.

"No," Sirdar said slowly, relishing the moment. "Nissa knows Trenara's song. I taught it to her long ago. She will make the guider obedient to your commands, as she will become obedient to mine. I have planned this for a very long time."

The weight of Sirdar's words made Joshan sick to his stomach as he looked down at the bird and she nodded shamefully.

"Now go! Bring me back my treasure."

Without hesitation, Nissa leapt into the air to fly down the long corridor, a silent grieving Joshan clinging to her back. She glanced once at the massive throne with the two figures near it and then ducked out the entrance into the cold frigid night.

CHAPTER TWENTY-TWO
VANDERLINDEN'S CHOICE

As Grandor quietly closed the cabin door, Van came up behind him expectantly. "Is she all right?"

Grandor nodded grimly and crossed to pour himself a drink. "I gave her a strong sedative and she will sleep now for several hours—at least until tomorrow morning. It is the strongest one I have. I should have done this long before now," he concluded as he sat on the divan.

"What was it she saw?" the giant asked, taking the offered drink, and sitting across from the guider. "Ena would not say anything."

Grandor took a long drink before answering. "She says she saw Joshan in the gazing. She said…" The old guider looked down and rubbed his eyes.

"What?"

The guider took a deep breath. "Trenara saw Joshan in the gazing. She said she saw Joshan—kill Haiden. Ena and Porphont said the same thing."

"What?" Van said, shaking his head. "Haiden's dead?"

"I am sorry, Van. I know he was a good friend. That is what they all saw. They all saw Joshan kill him."

"It's a trick, it's got to be. Joshan would never hurt Haiden. It's a trick of Sirdar's, I'm sure of it."

The old historian stared into his drink. "It is possible, but Trenara was certain and so were the others." He looked down at his hands. "Admiral, we have to be prepared for the possibility that we have lost him; that whatever Sirdar did to him in Cortaim has done exactly what Joshan said it would. For all we know, the emperor may be as twisted as—Sirdar."

Van stood up and threw his glass into the fire. "I don't believe it! I won't believe it! Joshan is no more evil than you or I. In fact, that boy's better than any of us," he said, sweeping his hand across his chest. "I can't believe the gods would give him to us, just to take him away like this. I'm not a religious man, Grandor, but I absolutely know that that boy was sent here to save us! No one can tell me otherwise!"

"What did they see then?"

Before Van could answer, there was a soft knock at the door. Van opened it.

Ena was nestled comfortably in Porphont's arms. She looked paler than she had earlier and Porphont's usual robust face was drawn with lines of fatigue.

"Forgive us, admiral," Ena began as Porphont bowed his head politely. "But, Porphont insisted we come to see you. Is her ladyship—?"

"Asleep in the other room, lass. Come in." Van allowed the pair to enter and they sat across from Grandor.

"I must speak with you privately, admiral," Ena said in Porphont's voice. "Can the Starguider hear us in the other room?"

"I shouldn't think so," Grandor replied when Van shook his head and sat down. "I gave her enough sedative to put her out for quite a while. Why?"

"It is important she not hear us, sir," that voice continued urgently. "He will know what she knows—later."

Grandor shook his head. "Who will know what, Porphont?"

"The Ganafira has sent a message for the admiral."

"You are speaking in riddles. Speak more plainly."

"I am sorry, sir," it was Ena's voice this time, "he will not let me see what he saw in the gazing after Haiden died."

"I do not understand. You saw more?"

"He did, yes—Porphont saw much more. But he will not let me see it. He asks me to withdraw. I have agreed. I will not speak again until he calls me."

Ena seemed to fall asleep in Porphont's arms. Only her mouth moved, but the expressions on his face were his own.

"After the marshal died, there was blackness—a gap I cannot see. But after, there is another image. The master… forgive me that is Ena's word. Sirdar sits on a throne in a great temple in the ice and snow. The Oracle…that is Ricilyn sits at his feet, but she is asleep. No, not asleep, awake, but not awake. I do not know the word. "

"In a trance?" Grandor ventured.

"Yes," Porphont replied, nodding. "The lady is in a trace and the bird, the great black bird that was under the sire's sway now sits with the monster, the master— Sirdar. In front of him, on his knees is the Ganafira. He is beaten, bloody… angry. Something eats away at him. His eyes are red. He cannot use the magic—the power. It will kill the lady."

"Kill her?" Van asked, startled. "How?"

Porphont shook his head. "Joined—no, linked—Ricilyn is linked with the power. Sirdar did this. If the emperor uses the power it will take away, drain away her life. Is that correct?"

Grandor nodded and leaned in closer. "You mean, if Joshan uses the power, Ricilyn will die."

Porphont nodded and pulled Ena closer to him. "Sirdar gives the Ganafira a mission. He says he will release the Oracle if the sire finds something the master has lost." He took a moment to sip some water.

"What has he lost?" Van asked.

Porphont took a deep breath. "I do not know the word. A royalty, a queen. A woman he has lost."

"That bastard," Van hissed, sitting up abruptly. "I should have known. He wants Trenara! He bloody well won't get her."

"There is more, admiral," Porphont continued, that strange voice echoing from Ena's lips. "He will take the Oracle if two tasks are not completed. The sire must bring a heart to the temple. He must bring a heart and the guider."

"A heart? Whose heart?"

"Yours, sir," Porphont said.

Both the men stared at the mute.

"Are you certain, Porphont?"asked Grandor.

"Yes," he said through Ena. "The sire is to bring the giant's heart to the temple with Trenara. If he fails, Ricilyn will take her place and the sire will die. The child she carries will belong to Sirdar. The bird, the black bird has been enchanted. Sirdar's eyes will see what her eyes see. His ears hear what her ears hear. If the sire leaves her sight the lady and the child will die."

"By the gods," Van hissed, rising to shake his fists at the air. "That stinking bastard!"

He sat down slowly and shook his head. "What a choice; to kill me and betray Trenara in exchange for the life of his wife and child." He ran a hand through his hair.

"Please, admiral," Porphont continued urgently. "There is more, much more."

"After the emperor left, he felt us—me—in the glass. He knew I was listening. He told me to say exactly this to you, made me memorize it."

Porphont's eyes flickered and then closed. There was a long silence when both Porphont and Ena appeared asleep. When he finally spoke through Ena, it was an odd sound coming first from Joshan into Porphont, both of them using Ena's voice.

"Van, I have ordered Thiels and Sark to move my army to the north, to Calisae. The enemy has taken the fortress and must be expelled. Nothing else is more important. It is why I am here... to keep him from Calisae. If this does not happen and quickly, the world will fall. I am coming for Trenara and you cannot stop that. You must believe I would never harm her. If you are there when I arrive, I will kill you. Please do not make me do that, I beg you. Leave—leave before I arrive. You will find the Trillone fleet close behind you when you get to the Keep. Dock, leave Trenara, and then turn the ship to lead the fleet to the Bay of Calisae. You must trust me once again, old friend. Without you, Sark will never take the fortress. You must obey me in this."

Porphont and Ena both woke up with a start. Van and Grandor looked at the two in disbelief. Van turned away from the group and stared out at the lights of the Keep.

"My god, man," Grandor said to him quietly. "What will you do?"

Van shook his head and scowled at the approaching port. "I don't know."

Grandor crossed to him and put a hand on his arm. "Will you do what the emperor asks?"

"And let that monster have her?" The giant stomped out the hatch to order the ship to dock.

The old guider looked at the fire a long time. Many possibilities went through his head, but each of them was extremely dangerous and could get anyone participating killed. Finally, he looked long and hard at Porphont. A slow smile spread over Grandor's face.

"Will you help?" he asked the giant mute.

Porphont blinked a few times before answering through Ena.

"He says if he can he will do whatever it takes." She reached up and touched the guider's arm. "So will I."

He patted her hand and rose to get his cloak. "My friends, we have work to do." He turned back and looked at them seriously. "Are you certain? This will be extremely dangerous."

Ena smiled up at him and though her smile was weak, her face was bright with fierce determination. "Absolutely," she said. "What have you in mind?"

It was near midnight when they docked, but a group had gathered at the pier to meet them, headed by Saldorian surrounded by both councils.

When Van saw her, he did not wait for the gangplank to fall, choosing instead to ride the ropes along with several of his mooring crew. He crossed to Saldorian and without ceremony, picked her up in his arms, swung her around quickly, and squeezed her tightly.

"Thank the gods!" he cried and kissed her forehead. "Are you all right, Sal? We thought…"

"I know, Van. I am fine." Although Saldorian was very pale and thin, she was awake and seemed herself again. "I am so glad to see you. You look like you have been through a lot."

"Aye," he said gently, "but we'll have to exchange stories later. Have Thiels and Sark…"

"They have marched north to Calisae."

Vanderlinden nodded. "How long ago?"

"Yesterday. They took everyone except the children, the old people, and us. Had I been stronger…"

He smiled and kissed her hand. "I know, Sal."

The crew was pushing the gangplank in place and Grandor appeared at the top of it with Trenara in his arms. Before he descended, he looked at the giant. Van nodded and motioned him down.

"Oh, my god, is she all right?"

"Fine, Sal. She's sleeping. When Joshan disappeared…" She looked up at him sharply. "He left without telling us. Trenara took it hard. Grandor had to give her something so she'd sleep. She'll be awake in the morning." He looked down at his hands and then nodded toward the guider. "Sal," he began very quietly, "Trenara and I..."

She put her fingers on his lips mouth and smiled. "I know, I saw the band," Sal said. "I am very happy for you. It is about time—for both of you. Come," she said, taking his arm and leading him from the dock. "We will put up food for everyone."

Sal ordered a litter for Trenara, which appeared quickly, and led the group up the long winding pathway to the Keep.

When they finally reached Trenara's chambers, Van placed her in bed and closed the door behind him. As soon as he could, he dismissed everyone and sat down next to the fire to think, the flames making his eyes sparkle darkly.

Van did not know what to do, who to believe, or what to think. It was happening so fast and the world was leaving him far behind. He was only a simple man, who loved one woman very much. Van stared at the embers.

How could he leave Trenara? Could he trust Joshan? Was it possible the emperor was as corrupt as Grandor suggested? Or was Joshan right? If Van stayed, what would happen to the Imperium? If he went, what would happen to Trenara? Could he hand her over to a lunatic? Van buried his face in his hands and thought long and hard about his choices, his duty, his life—the woman he had waited for almost thirty seasons—the man he had sworn his life and loyalty to.

Van reviewed Joshan's message repeatedly in his mind and finally slammed his fist in his hand, not believing what Joshan was asking. He stared at Trenara's bedroom door. When he sank his head before the hearth, he heard a quiet knock.

"Come in," he called to the door, standing up to pour himself a drink.

"Admiral?"

When he turned, there was a very old guard standing in the doorway. "Yes, Thomal, what is it?"

"Her majesty says they have spotted a fleet of ships coming from the southeast," he said urgently. "She wonders if this might be an attack by..."

Van laughed and shook his head. "It is no attack. Tell the consort not to worry, these are friends and very welcome. I will go down to the dock presently to greet them."

He looked again at Trenara's door. Sighing deeply, he licked his lips and downed his drink. "Tell the consort, the Morning Star and the rest of the ships will be sailing to the north immediately."

"Yes, sir." Thomal saluted and left.

Van opened the door to Trenara's room and knelt next to her bed. Taking her small hand in his, he kissed it gently and then held it to his cheek, closing his eyes. He wished she were awake, but it would be several more hours.

"My love," he whispered gently, "I hope to hell I'm doing the right thing. It feels right, but what do I know? My gods, I'm so lost without you. Despite everything that's happened, despite everything… oh, gods," he moaned, taking her limp body in his massive arms and holding her tenderly.

"Please let this be the right choice," he prayed to the air. He looked down and kissed her closed eyelids. "I love you so much. I would give my soul for you. Ethos, please… let this be the right choice."

He kissed her lips and gently laid her back on the bed, then left the room to greet the Trillone.

CHAPTER TWENTY-THREE
THE MISSION

When Trenara woke several hours later, it was dark. She found herself in her own bed and for a fleeting moment, she thought she was dreaming. When her mind cleared, it all came rushing back. She sat up and grabbed the robe lying at the end of her bed, tucking Andelian inside the pocket. She did not know why—after all, the via was useless—but the habit was difficult to break and having it close comforted her. Slipping on the robe, she rushed out to the living room.

"Van?" she called, but the room was dark and quiet.

Something was terribly wrong. Trenara could not feel anything and she had to stop a moment to wrap her wits around it. It was as if a veil fell in front of her eyes, only vague images coming through like ghostly shadows. She stood in the middle of the room shaking, unable to clear the stifled awareness. Glancing up, the moonlight streamed in from the balcony and she scowled at it. There were answers on the balcony. She was not certain what that meant, but the urgency to look propelled her forward.

Before she could reach it, a sound surrounded her, making her giddy and then numb, stopping her.

It was a song for her alone. The last time she heard it was in a crimson cave many, many seasons before. The Mourna's cry soaked into her awareness, saturating her with euphoria until the craving to follow it eclipsed every other thought. There was nothing except that sound. Without thinking, she turned to the door and quietly left her chambers.

As she walked through the hallways of the Keep, Trenara heard people talk to her, but it all seemed vague and distant. She acknowledged them politely, not even knowing what she said. They left her alone to walk in the glorious sound that possessed her and made her aware of nothing else.

In a dream state, the guider ascended the cold marble stairs that led to the parapet, her naked feet blackened by the ancient stone, the air like faded smoke around her.

When Trenara passed through the stone archway into the frozen night, the Mourna stood like a shining beacon at the uppermost wall, the sound swirling around her. The guider smiled up at the creature and lifted her eyes to the man who sat on its back.

"Trenara, come here."

Her hair and gown flowed like soft fire behind her as a cold wind whistled through the stonework. She crossed to that wonderful voice, surrendering completely to its soft embrace.

When she was half way to him, a giant hooded figure rushed from the shadows and stood between them. Drawing a long blade and holding his arms in front of her, the figure spread his feet and would not let her pass.

The spell broke when the Mourna's voice stopped. Trenara was very confused and fought to make sense of what was happening.

"Van?" she cried, staring up at the dark figure in front of her. Grandor jumped out of the shadows to clasp her in his arms and pull her away.

"What are you doing?" She struggled against him.

"Get her back!" Joshan shouted as he slid from Nissa.

He slowly approached the giant. "I warned you!" he screamed. "You fool! Do you realize what I have to do?" Red fire burned in his eyes for a fleeting moment.

There was no reply. The giant stood up straight and held his sword before his face, the hood hiding his expression in the darkness.

Joshan drew the golden sword from the scabbard at his side slowly, reluctantly. The two men circled, their boots scrapping dully on the stone, their robes whipping in the wind. Grandor moved Trenara out of the way.

In the starlight, it was very difficult to see the two men as they crossed blades. Joshan brought his sword down, sending golden sparks around them, but the giant moved quickly, spinning even further away from the onlookers. Grandor moved back, pushing the Mourna against the wall, his large form blocking her.

The men circled back and forth, each an expert with his weapon. For every move, there was a stunning countermove and the deadly weapons left no mark on either of them. Back and forth they fought, each determined. The more they danced around one other, the further away they moved. Then suddenly the giant pushed into Joshan and grabbed his hands, trying to wrist the sword away from him.

For a long time they were locked face to face, their hands tangled together, the hilt of the blades clashing noisily, their cloaks swirling around them until it was difficult to see which man was which and where one began or ended.

In a flash, power erupted from Joshan's sword and the giant fell back, landing in a heap on the stony parapet many spans away.

When the hood fell away revealing Vanderlinden's terrorized face, Trenara screamed and fought to get away from Grandor. Grandor held her firm and Joshan crossed to the fallen giant. In a swift motion, he plunged his sword through the giant's chest, the power erupting in a maelstrom of black energy that circled into Van's body, making him contort savagely. Van's scream echoed through the stonework.

Trenara shrieked at the top of her lungs viciously fighting to get to her husband. She scratched and beat Grandor frantically. The old guider wept but would not let her go.

When Van's body stopped writhing, Joshan went to one knee, his back to them, his cloak making a pool around his legs. His hand glowed with black power as it reached into the giant's chest, the flesh melting like butter at his touch. With one pull,

Joshan ripped out a blackened mass, his form silhouetted by the deadly light. He rose from the body, holding the thing out to his side, squeezing the quivering knot until its contents spilled noisily on the stone at his feet, clouds of heat rising from it in the cold. He then fell to his knees next to the body and screamed until the sound echoed to the sea.

Guards poured onto the rooftop, but Joshan lifted his hand, throwing up a barrier that kept them all from interfering. When he looked up, it was to gaze into his mother's face. She watched from the other side of the barrier, her eyes brimming with tears. He said nothing as he rose and pushed the bloody mass into a fold in his robes. Joshan turned away from the mutilated body and the accusing eyes of the crowd. He crossed deliberately to the Mourna, his boots scraping the frozen stone beneath them.

Trenara finally broke away from Grandor and tried to run to the giant. Joshan grabbed her arm as she passed, leaving a bloody handprint on the sleeve of her evening robe. He whirled her in the other direction, toward the bird. She stumbled and fell to the stones, scraping her hands and knees.

Grandor helped her to her feet, but she brushed off his hands and tried again. This time Joshan glanced at the Mourna with red, blazing eyes, and Nissa opened her mouth.

Trenara froze in mid-stride and became very still. When Grandor tried to go to her, he could not move, the Mourna's cry freezing his blood so he could only look on helplessly.

Joshan mounted Nissa and moved the bird to where Trenara was standing, staring glassy eyed at her dead husband. Joshan reached down and tucked his arm around her waist, lifting her to sit in front of him. Running his hand over her face, Trenara slumped forward. He folded her into the crook of his arm and grabbed the reins. Glancing once more at his mother, he kicked the bird. They lifted off the tower and disappeared into the night.

CHAPTER TWENTY-FOUR
EVE OF BATTLE

The journey through the passes of the North Range had been a bitter one for the imperial troops, but few complained and they made good time to the north.

Sark thanked the gods for Molly and her crew. They had come along to keep food, drink, and supplies running through the moving host. She was a genius at organization. The machine that kept the army on its feet was finely tuned. Suddenly conscripted and pulled from a warm bed, more than half of these people found themselves freezing in the harsh northern climate. Because of Molly's guidance, morale was still very high.

In the two days allowed to get stores and materials ready for the march, Molly had organized her impromptu crew to clean out every warehouse, restaurant, and pub in the Keep. Even the castle's Lead Steward, who found herself partnered with Molly, was amazed at the Mistress's aggressive command and abilities. The steward was an older woman who had been running the underpinnings of the castle for twenty-five seasons, but Molly put her to shame. When she asked Molly where she learned this, the robust young woman smiled as she counted the crates coming in from a distant warehouse. "It is no different than running the House, darling—it is just bigger, that's all." The wagons were ready for the trip before the troops were.

Sareh had been up for several days, and had done everything she could to get the masses ready for battle. She spent the journey up the mountains sleeping in her saddle.

All told, they had gathered ten thousand people for the march, many of them with limited or ancient experience carrying a rag-tag of weaponry from long sickles to rusted antique swords.

Even though the Elite and Sark's people divided the troops among their own seasoned veterans to bolster the ranks, training merchants, innkeepers, teachers, healers, prostitutes, and barkeeps had been daunting. Many of these men and women had not lifted a weapon in thirty seasons. Children rounded out the troops, ranging in age from twelve to eighteen. They had only the mandatory Keep training as youngsters. Sark had little choice and demanded as much from them as he did from his seasoned troops.

On the second day from the Keep, Sark, Thiels and their captains stood at a hidden vantage point overlooking the field before Calisae. Their resting army waited behind them.

The enemy spread like a black blanket up to the white castle's western barbican gate. It was dusk, so hundreds of torches sparkled from the castle.

Sareh galloped up behind them and pulled in her reins next to her father.

"General," she said pointing across the valley, "you can see from here what the odds are. They spread back into the western forests as well. We are estimating twenty-eight to thirty thousand, give or take. About a third are sasarans, laminia, and deinos. The rest are humans, some from the south and some from the north, we are guessing. They seem to have reinforced their numbers since the march. They must have conscripted as they passed as they did in the south. Most of the people are on foot and carry only swords, but others are very well armed. In addition, they have weapons we have never seen before.

"We must be very careful, father. This army is much more prepared than what we saw on the field in Thrain. The only advantage we have is the forest that surrounds the valley floor. It is deep, tangled. We should be able to get troops spread in a wide line without anyone seeing us. The sentries do not seem well trained and should be easy to take out. I would suggest using in and out tactics—demoralization—hit tactical targets in the forest. We will never gain in a frontal attack."

Sark merely nodded and surveyed the throng pensively. His ribs and arm were aching, but he would not let the healers give him anything for pain. He wanted to keep his wits. Sareh worried about the grim wrinkles that lined her father's face and dark circles that devastated his eyes, but said nothing.

He glanced at Thiels who gave him an agreeable nod.

"We camp tonight," he said to his captains. "We will set up maneuvers tomorrow. Get your people fed and bedded with sentries posted within eye distance. Two hours on, two hours off to keep them sharp. I want you all personally patrolling after council." They saluted their general and went to organize their troops.

Making her way past the galloping captains, Molly carried steaming clay mug. She sat astride an old eecha. When she reached them, she pushed the mugs into their hands.

Sark looked at the drink suspiciously. "What's this?"

Molly smiled as she dug into a bag tied to her wrist. "Just drink." She pulled bread out of the bag and tore it into three equal parts.

"Molly, I appreciate this, but..."

"I'm sorry, general, but my job is to keep this army on its feet and that means you. Drink up or I'll have a couple of lads hold you down to make sure."

Sark looked at her incredulously as Sareh smiled and Thiels suppressed a smirk. "I can have you court-martialed," he blustered.

"I'm a volunteer—sir—now drink up." She threw them each a piece of the bread, turned her eecha around, and headed back the way she had come. "Thank you, general." Her laughter echoed after her.

Once the camp settled, Sark and Thiels met with their captains and outlined the strategies for the next morning. Close to midnight, Sark sent his captains to rest and finally went to his own tent. When he arrived, Molly was there setting his table.

"Molly? You should be resting," he said quietly, taking off his sword and grimacing when he loosened his belt.

"As should you, but here we are." She ladled stew into his bowl.

Sark sat down to his late dinner and closed his eyes for the first time in two days. "That smells marvelous," he said. "I am famished." Without another word, he dove into the stew and made short work of it.

Molly sat across from him and watched him eat, resting her chin on her hands. She looked exhausted, but her beautiful face stood out against the drab tent. After several bites, Sark looked up.

"Aren't you eating?" he asked around a mouth of food.

"Already did."

He reached for the decanter of wine but Molly beat him to it and stood up to pour him a mug. Setting down the decanter, she got behind him and massaged his shoulders, mindful of his broken arm and ribs.

Sark sat back in the chair allowing her to dig deeply into the tense muscles. "That feels wonderful," he whispered and closed his eyes.

Molly then kissed the top of his head and held out her hand. "Come on, darling," she said seductively, "let's lie you down so I can do this properly." She gave him a saucy wink.

"All right," he said, allowing himself to be led to his bedroll.

Around two in the morning, the darkness was absolute when someone entered Sareh's tent. Her training woke her instantly and she had a deadly grip on the intruder's throat before she was even fully awake. The woman lay sprawled at her feet.

"Tige?" she said, letting her go instantly. "I am sorry. Are you all right?"

The larger woman rubbed her neck and got to her feet. "I guess I should know better than to get within arm's length when I wake you. It's your father," she said, opening the flap to the tent. "He's called for you."

Sareh was up quickly and threw on her boots. "It's dawn already?" she asked, throwing a heavy cloak over her shoulders.

"No," Tige said mechanically. "It's several hours before dawn."

Sareh frowned at the woman. "Why would he call me at this hour? He should be asleep."

"I don't know, ma'am," the captain said quietly. "He told me to fetch you and bring you to a clearing in the woods where he has gathered the other captains."

Sareh merely shrugged and followed Tige.

They threaded their way quietly though the sleeping camp, until Tige led Sareh well to the back of the troops. Sareh stopped and looked around. "Where are the sentries?" she asked, but Tige reached back and patted her hand.

"They are in the woods protecting the captains, Sareh. The line is still intact, I promise. Come on. We'll be late and your father'll have my head if we are." Sareh nodded, letting Tige lead her into the woods.

Several hundred spans into the forest, Sareh finally stopped and called to the captain. "Tige, where are we going?"

"There's a clearing just there," she said, pointing through the darkened woods. "It's a few more spans."

Sareh looked suspiciously at the woman, not moving from the spot. "Why would my father have a council out here in the woods?" She searched the dense trees surrounding them. "Something's not right here."

Sareh stepped back from the woman, but too late. Tige pulled her fist out of her pocket and blew fine dust into Sareh's face before she could respond. Sareh managed to land a crippling blow to Tige's face, but was unconscious before she hit the ground.

"Damn it!" cried Tige from where she had landed. The kick had opened her lip and bruised her cheek. She stood up and kicked the unconscious Sareh hard.

"Bitch!" she screamed and prepared to kick her again, when someone grabbed her from behind and restrained her.

"The master said undamaged," the man whispered in her ear. "Don't make me kill you," he said, running a hand down her throat. "It would be such a pity."

Tige pushed away from the man and pulled her sword from its scabbard.

"Touch me again," she hissed, "and I'll see to it you never touch another."

The man smirked back at her, making the tattoos on his face curl upward, and his shaven head wrinkle. He was a large brute with massive hands. He picked up the unconscious Sareh as if she weighed nothing. Throwing her over his shoulder, he gave Tige a mock bow and pulled himself onto a large eecha standing next to him.

"It's been a pleasure doing business with you," he snorted. "You've been very helpful. When her father comes for her, you'll get your reward."

"I don't need a reward," Tige snarled at him, "just make sure she doesn't come back."

The man kicked the animal and disappeared into the forest. Tige sheathed her blade and made her way back to camp.

When she left the woods, a figure was sitting on a stump looking up at her. Tige stopped abruptly.

"Molly? What're you doing here?"

"Just taking a breather. How 'bout you?"

Tige adjusted her belt self-consciously and looked at the woods. "Checking the perimeter. You should be asleep."

"I was." Molly twisted her neck and flexed her shoulders. "But something woke me. Two women passing the tent. Could've sworn I heard Sareh's voice." Molly adjusted herself on the stump. "I followed, but lost them in the woods. Pretty sure it was you and Sareh. Where is she?"

Tige ran her fingers closer to her blade. "I took her to a meeting with her father in the woods."

Molly nodded. "I see. Funny thing that…" A smile curled the sides of her mouth, "…since I've been with her dad all night." She nodded at the tent behind her. "That's his tent, case you didn't know… and by the way, he's in it." Molly rose slowly from the stump. "I think you and I are going to have a little chat with Sark."

Tige's eyes narrowed and she pulled her knife instantly. "I don't think so, Molly," she said, shifting the knife to her right hand. "This goes no further. You've got no knife. Even if you did, you wouldn't know how to use it." She crouched down for the attack.

"As to that," Molly smiled back at her, "you're probably right."

In a quick flash, Molly brought a long handled black skillet from behind her back that landed with a smack on the side of Tige's head. The warrior went down without a struggle.

"But I'm damned handy with a pan."

When Tige came to sometime later, it was to stare up at the dark face of Sark looming over her. She shook the daze from her head and reached for her knife, but it was gone along with the rest of her weapons. Tige struggled to her knees. Sark's other captains formed a circle around them, holding torches. Molly stood in the shadow of the trees, watching intently. There was no one else around and the group was well away from the camp, more than likely so they would not disturb her troops. Tige knew this was going to be a private affair and prepared herself for it.

Sark crouched down to her and grabbed the front of her uniform with his good hand, his breath punctuating the cold night air with whiteness. "Where is she?" he growled through his teeth.

Tige looked up at him and a small smile dusted her lips. "Who?"

He brought the back of his hand hard across her face opening the lip again, a ring on his finger cutting her cheek. She hit the ground hard. The other captains took a step forward to intervene, but Sark flashed them a warning and grabbed her to set her up on her knees.

"Tell me," he whispered, his eyes smoking with rage.

"Sark," whispered Donnelly at his back, "why don't you let me… there are laws to address…"

"Not for traitors, there aren't!" he snapped back at him. "Where is she?"

Tige searched for a sympathetic face, but all the eyes looking back were cold and angry. She would never leave the woods alive. "Probably half way to the daligon, by now," she whispered, the words lisping slightly from her damaged lip.

Sark's shoulders slumped and anguish twisted his face. "Why would you do this? We have been friends for twenty seasons!"

Tige hung her head and did not say anything at once.

Something snapped inside her. Tige swallowed hard against the euphoria crawling up her throat. She stared at the dirt at her knees and let out a guttural moan, the sound strange and frightening. Sark's cold, unloving eyes, the pain, the betrayal—the shame finally wrapped around Tige's mind, distorting her awareness until everything turned into a dream.

When her face changed, Sark stood up and his nostrils flared. He drew his sword.

Tige stared at a blank space in front of her. Sitting back on her haunches, she tilted her head to the side. The words coming out of her mouth were unintelligible, babbling oddly against the vacant night. A laugh started in her throat and crept out of her mouth in staccato patches of white until it turned hysterical. Sark and the other captains took a step back.

"Sark?" she whispered. "You know why."

Sark shook his head holding his sword up a few inches from her as if it would hold back the insanity contorting her beautiful face.

"Because I love you," she said distantly. "You should have been mine a long time ago. You were mine." Tears fell from her eyes without passion, leaving lines in the dirt and blood. "She took you from me. I never got another chance; not with your daughter in the way, not with the other captains, not with my—cowardice." A deep pale turned her face ashen, accentuated by the red rising in her cheeks. "Now you are mine. No one will keep us apart. I love you so much, Sark." She slowly rose to her feet. "I have always loved you. Now we can be together."

Tige impaled herself on his outstretched sword so quickly Sark had no time to react. Grasping his hands to hold the sword in place, she squeezed them until her nails dug into his flesh. Her strength was startling. He could not pull his hands away. With precise determination, Tige pulled herself along the sword, the blade finally popping from her back, black with her blood. Tige crushed against him, the hilt of the sword the only thing between them. Her blood coated his hand and soaked the front of his cloak; he could feel the warmth trickling down his chest and legs. Sark could not move. The color drained from her eyes as he watched.

"The master said I could have you," she whispered, "if I would help him."

The madness left her voice and she gaped in terror up at him.

"No," she whispered, her mouth twisting oddly, "Sark—I'm sorry."

Tige slumped against him, laying her head against his chest, almost tenderly. As her last breath hissed from her throat, a red vapor dripped upward from her mouth and dissipated in a wisp on the cold air. Sark jumped back from her before he inhaled any of it.

He quaked uncontrollably, not believing what had just happened. Tige fell into a heap on the ground, embracing the sword like a lover.

Sark fell to his knees. Grief clouded his eyes. Throwing back his head, he screamed at the trees, sending birds skittering from the branches. The other captains lowered their heads and mourned their fallen comrade.

"Where are you going?" Thiels asked quietly when he entered Sark's tent. Sark strapped a second sword to his waist and attached a knife to his upper thigh. He was dressed in his old forest clothes, obviously preparing to slip into the woods for a quiet mission. Sark looked again like the mercenary he used to be.

He glared at the commander, his face a red challenge. "Do not try to stop me, Thiels," he hissed, searching for a third knife that had fallen from the table.

Thiels stood at the entrance and watched him. "What do you think you can do?"

"Bring her back," he said quietly, throwing an old cloak around his shoulders.

"Sark, you can't leave here—not like this."

"What would you have me do?" He plunked down on the bench to pull on his boots. "Sit here and do nothing?"

"No!" Thiels shouted back, matching his intensity. "I would have you lead your army to take the castle… as you have been commanded, general!" He handed Sark the fallen knife. "She is gone. There's nothing you can do about that now, except lead your troops."

"You don't know…," he whispered back.

"I do," Thiels spat. "There isn't a man or woman on this field who hasn't lost someone they loved. That is war! That's what it does! It kills people—people who are loved." The energy went out of him with a soft shrug. "He's not going to kill her, Sark, you know that. They took her to lure you, to weaken you, to make you less of a symbol to these people. He's taken her to stab at the heart of this army. This attack must make this army stronger, not weaker."

Sark scowled. "You will not make my daughter a martyr!"

"She already is, Sark!" Thiels nodded to the entrance. "Listen to them. They're furious! Not just for Sareh, but for what she represents; the cowardly rape of our valor—our honor. That's what this act is. With it the enemy has made us stronger than he could possibly imagine."

Thiels suddenly stood at rigid attention before a befuddled Sark. "Get on your feet, general!"

Sark's eyes were red with grief. "I can't!"

Thiels addressed him sternly. "You can, and by the gods, you will!"

He crossed to where Sark sat, pulled the chair out from behind him, and reached to the table to grab his helmet and armor. Pushing the uniform into his hands, he saluted sharply.

"Your troops wait for your orders, general."

Sark nodded once and took off his cloak to don his armor. Outside, the trumpets called the morning rally.

CHAPTER TWENTY-FIVE
THE DALION

When Sareh regained consciousness, she was lying on the cold marble floor of the great room in the White Castle of Calisae surrounded by hundreds of spectators and fifty guards in black armor. In front of her on a low platform sat the daligon's shadowy form, undulating in the twilight room. Few torches flickered around them and those only for the benefit of the minority of humans that stood among Sirdar's monsters. Black curtains shrouded the high windows to keep the deadly sunlight out of the hall. The once beautiful white pillars rose black above her, tarnished by seasons of neglect and smoky torches. Behind the shadow, there was a huge hole roughly cut into the floor, filled with a glowing red substance that smoldered behind him. Its perverse contents made the room stuffy and close. The smell was pungent, stinging her eyes with its putrid scent.

Sareh lifted her head and sat up to confront the menace before her. Her weapons were gone. They had stripped her to just thin under layers, now black and dirty. She shifted slowly to her knees, never taking her eyes off the daligon. The creature was by far the most dangerous in the room. Sareh concentrated, letting her skills work through her body, stiffening to the challenge.

A small smile graced her lips in the darkened room when she lifted herself to her knees.

"You should have tied me up."

Sareh moved so quickly five guards went down before they even knew she had stirred. She rushed toward the daligon, now armed with a heavy spear. The rest of the guards charged quickly to stop her. She killed ten more before they were able to halt her progress, scant inches from where the daligon's face would have been, if he had one. It took six of the most skilled to wrench the weapon from her hands.

With just her head, she killed three more during the struggle, driving two of their noses through their skulls, and breaking the windpipe of another. There were then eight of them on her. She continued to fight, removing a mouthful of skin from one large sasaran, and managing to poke out the eye of another with her toe. His screams echoed through the chamber as he ran blindly into his comrades.

They had her pinned to the cold marble floor, covered in sasaran blood. Her thin clothes clung to her skin and her long yellow hair was drenched with gore.

The daligon lifted from his seat and drifted to Sareh. It reached a dark tendril from the shadow to cover her face, cutting off her air until she blacked out. The remaining creatures fell away from her exhausted.

When Sareh woke again sometime later, they had bound her securely in heavy irons. The guards stood further away from her now, all of them holding spears or arrows aimed at her.

Sareh was already on her knees and could not move an inch in her bindings. She tried to move her head, but even it had a band around it attached to the chains holding her hands at her back. She had to lower her eyes to see the black shadow in front of her. The menacing red pit behind him roiled crimson fire, giving the chamber a perverse, sickly color. It was the only thing she feared in the room.

"I needed to see just how skilled you were," the shadow whispered and the creatures gave each other fleeting looks. All told, twenty soldiers died or sustained serious injuries. It had taken Sareh only a matter of seconds. These were the daligon's personal guard, his best. The rest stared at her now, their lips tightened in anger.

"You deceived me on the field, little girl. Had I been less preoccupied you would not have found it so simple."

Sareh shrugged as best she could in the confines of her chains and smiled at him. "Had I been less preoccupied, you would be dead."

The shadow floated to her. A black strand snaked out of the darkness and slid into her chest. The pressure on her heart was instantaneous; she fought not to scream. The pain was worse than any she had felt in her life. Clamping her mouth shut and glaring at the creature, she did not cry out. It pulled the tendril out of her chest and she let out an unguarded huff of air, knowing she had come very close to death.

"It is good to know you are not impervious to pain, child," it whispered into her ear, the cold wisp brushing her cheek like a caress. "If I had time, I would teach you pain. I am the master of anguish and relish its dark degrees. I would love to watch as you learn them all. Perhaps later."

It ran another strand around her throat, cutting off her air long enough to send shooting sparks through her head. It pulled back before she passed out.

"Unfortunately, my time is short. Your father is coming for you and I have plans."

It sailed back to the basin and hovered over the edge, reaching into the hole with another dark wisp. When it came out, a red fire coated it, sparkling through the translucent blackness. The menacing shade drifted back to her.

"This, my dear, is catalyst. It will make you…" It paused, hypnotically passing the red tendril back and forth in front of her eyes. Her heart pounded in her chest. "It will make you pliable, willing, submissive to my commands. You have skill, girl, and we will use it for the glory of my master—your master now."

He called two of the guards who were at his side instantly.

"Open her mouth."

Holding her nose and staying well away from the business end of her teeth, they forced her mouth open and the tendril went down her throat. She gagged on the violation and tried to scream, but the poison forced into her stomach muffled her voice.

When the shadow withdrew, she retched violently, dryly. Sareh spat in one of the sasaran's eyes, but it was her last act of defiance. Her face softened into a docile mask within seconds. The creature slapped her across the face, bruising her cheek, making her nose bleed, and cutting her lip. Sareh stared silently at an empty space in front of her.

The daligon shadow encircled her several times, making certain she was completely under the influence of the catalyst, and then rose above her and slithered out a strand of darkness to touch her face.

"You were my captain for a very short time," he whispered at her blank face. "It is time you were so again. Shave her head, mark her with my personal symbols, give her the standard conditioning, and then..." It hovered above her and ran a tendril down her still body. "Then put her on the front of the line. She is not to be helmed or armored. I want the bastard to see my marks on her."

They dragged her from the chamber, the spark now gone from her eyes.

CHAPTER TWENTY-SIX
THE FLIGHT TO SIRDAR

Trenara woke to the sound of a living heart beating its rhythm into her ear. She was laying in someone's arms, a heavy cloak enfolding her in softness as the wind hammered against her.

At first, the guider could not remember where she was, forgetting her anguish for several exquisite seconds. Then it all came back in one stomach-turning rush.

Van was dead.

The memory flashed so quickly, her chest heaved and grief clogged her throat. Joshan had killed him—taken—

—his heart.

Her mind went numb, unwilling to allow reality to intrude.

"Nissa, the guider is awake. Take us down."

Trenara could feel the muscles of the bird shift beneath her as it descended from the frozen altitude, the wind finding its way through the cloak to chill her. Reluctantly, she held onto Joshan and shivered uncontrollably.

When they landed, Joshan gathered her in his arms and dismounted. They had landed in a clearing in a forest where snow piled around the rough trunks of evergreen trees. It was dawn, making the trees black against the graying sky.

Joshan set her on the cold ground, his face grim and angry. A stab of icy pain shot through Trenara's naked feet. She folded her arms and shivered in the darkness, not knowing what else to do.

She gazed at Joshan, the child she had raised, the boy she had loved above all else in her universe. The agony was immeasurable. This stranger had wholly betrayed her.

Without saying anything, Joshan went to the bird and pulled a bundle from the pack. He tossed it to Trenara who caught it awkwardly.

"Put that on." She looked at the bundle in her hands as if it were something foreign. "Put it on before you freeze."

Trenara stood, shaking in the cold, her face hard and grim, her jaw set. "Go to hell."

Joshan grabbed her upper arms and lifted her off her feet. Glaring down into her face, his eyes mere inches from hers, she saw the red fire and almost screamed. His face was shinning with rage.

"Put the clothes on or I will do it for you."

He squeezed her so tightly she let out a cry. Hot flashes of agony went through her head, his hands like scalding vises on her arms, his fingers bruising her fragile flesh. He threw her down and the rocky ground scraped her already tender hands. Joshan picked up the bundle where it had landed and smashed it into her arms.

Trenara struggled to her feet and turned to walk into the woods, holding her head up and refusing to cry.

"No," he called to her, "here."

The guider narrowed her eyes and clamped her teeth against her rage. Taking a livid breath, she unceremoniously peeled away the flimsy nightgown.

Joshan ran his eyes over Trenara's naked body, smiling strangely. That odd seductive glance frightened her more than anything else he could have done. She quickly donned the oversized robe, leggings, and boots to stop the unwanted stare.

When she finished, she forced herself to look at the robe in her hand—the robe with the bloody handprint on the sleeve—Vanderlinden's blood. Trenara's lip quivered, despite her efforts to stop it, and large tears rolled down her cheeks.

"Come now, Trenara," Joshan said quietly, ripping the nightclothes from her hands and tossing them into the trees.

Trenara looked up at him. "You killed him. You bastard!"

"Van was a fool. It was so easily done," he said quietly, sneering down at her.

She screamed and lunged at him, but he caught her wrists and twisted her around as if she were as light as the snow at their feet. He crushed her to his chest with such force Trenara could barely breathe. Joshan lowered his mouth to her ear, his quiet laugh vibrating as he pressed his lips against her flesh and whispered.

"His heart belongs to me now."

The insidious words cascaded over her senses like rubble. Her outrage knew no bounds and for a split second, she could not breathe for the ache in her heart. The betrayal was unbearable.

"You monster," she hissed through her teeth.

Joshan released her, sending her flying across the clearing. When Trenara turned, the face looking back at her was a quiet ruin, but his own again.

"Trenara," Joshan whispered, his voice trembling. "I am... so sorry. I do not know what I am saying. I did not mean... it is the poison."

She looked at him utterly mystified, a drop of pity touching her for an instant. What he had done, however, hammered against her mind and the pity turned to loathing.

"He trusted you," she said, her small fists turning white. "He loved you. Why would you do this?"

Like a curtain falling, his expression melted back into black brutality. She stepped away from that face.

"Because it was necessary," he said mechanically. "Because if I did not kill Van, Ricilyn and my child would be dead. What the hell was I supposed to do? Sacrifice them for him? Or you?"

Trenara blinked back at him. "Sirdar has Ricilyn?"

"Brilliant," he snarled at her. "So you see, my dear Trenara, I did what I had to." He raised his eyes from under his brow. "Just as I have to now. Come here." His voice was softly ruthless.

Trenara turned to run into the woods and hit the tangled foliage at full speed. The darkness was complete as she fought to get through it. It tore at her skin, but would not yield.

Nissa's voice enfolded her like a warm breeze and she stopped, snared by desire. Trenara fought to shake the embrace, but it was impossible. Joshan appeared behind her and grabbed her by the hair to drag her back to the clearing. Nissa's voice stopped.

"Is this what you want? I can hurt you! Don't you understand?" She could see the poison in his eyes running like a bloody river through his consciousness.

Trenara cringed away from him, grasping handfuls of duff between her fingers. "No. I do not understand. I have never seen you like this," she whispered, terrified. "This is not you, Joshan. This is the catalyst. It is destroying who you are. Can't you see that? You have to resist it, for all our sakes. Fight it, damn you!"

His lips became a hard line and then slowly curled into a strange smile. "Still guiding, guider?"

His eyes now glowing, Joshan reached down and grabbed her wrist. With a force she had never felt before, he pushed Trenara's fingers back until shots of pain traveled up her arm into her head. She shrieked in panic, fighting to get her hand away.

Without warning, something of absolute malevolence flashed across his face, and for a moment, Joshan completely disappeared. That monstrous face gritted its teeth and grinned down at her. With little effort, he pushed her fingers all the way back to breaking, sending black dots flashing before her vision. A muted scream escaped her, and a wave of nausea coursed through her bowels. Trenara almost lost consciousness when he threw her down.

"Do you understand?" he hissed through his teeth, the redness in his eyes flashing.

The pain of the wound was nothing compared to the realization breaking her heart. "Yes," she whispered, sobs shaking her body. "I have lost you."

Again, the dark light lifted from Joshan's face and he stepped away from her. "By the gods, what have I done?"

His hands shaking, he removed his gloves and pushed back the sleeves of his robe. The sheeted crystals completely covered both palms now and flowed in long graceful tendrils up his wrists and well into his forearms.

Trenara cradled her broken hand and struggled to crawl away from him as he approached. With little effort, he caught her in his arms and ran his hand gently over her face. She calmed at once and he lifted the blackened fingers. Amber light flowed from his hand, and in a twinkling, the pain was gone, the fingers healed.

"I am so sorry, Trenara," he whispered softly, kissing the hand tenderly and taking her in his arms. "You are right. It is not me. It is the catalyst. It is destroying me."

When he set her on the ground, the fog lifted from her head and Joshan rose to cross to the Mourna. "We need to go."

Trenara did not move. "Why are you doing this? Where are you taking me?"

That other creature turned back to her. Trenara's heart sank when Joshan's head tilted oddly and he glanced at the Mourna again. The bird's voice echoed from that beautiful purple throat.

"No," Trenara whispered.

Joshan lifted his hand toward her. "Come to me." The timbre of his music changed.

"Oh, my god. No, Joshan. Please."

"Come here!"

Trenara felt that euphoric longing, compelling her irresistibly to rise and walk to him. Trembling uncontrollably, but unable to move away, she could do no more than look up at that odd, twisted face—that stranger's face. The catalyst shone in his eyes so brightly now, they were a bonfire to his soul.

Joshan pushed one hand into her hair and forced her face back to stare longingly into her eyes. She could not move to push him away. Tenderly, Joshan pushed the robe off her shoulder and traced her skin with his fingertips. The guider had never been so terrified.

"I know what Sirdar desires in you." Joshan's voice was a hot caress against her ears. He ran his hand up to her neck, tracing the muscles under her ear. The touch sent unwanted waves of pleasure through her. "Why he craves you as he does. Why he would risk his empire to have you—to own you, to rule you. You are an addiction, Trenara—an aching need that must be fulfilled. Do you know that?" His face blazed with that twisted light. He sucked air through his teeth and pulled her head back to run his lips and tongue along her neck, biting the flesh seductively and then whispering in her ear. "Sirdar will have to wait."

The Mourna's voice stopped and Trenara struggled to get away, but he held her firmly.

"Stop this!"

He took her face in both hands and pulled her toward him.

"Please, Joshan. Do not do this…"

He forced her lips to his, stealing her breath, wrapping one hand around her throat, and crushing her against his body with the other.

The kiss sent a wave of revulsion through her. Beside it pulsed that same deep, irresistible passion she had felt in Sirdar's arms thirty seasons before—the enticing touch of the catalyst. It took every skill she had to resist it.

Desperate, Trenara did the only thing she could think of; she bit his lip as hard as she could. Joshan's blood gushed into her mouth. She could taste the bitter poison burning her tongue and lips. Her stomach churned and she almost wretched.

Joshan pushed her away and slapped her hard across the face, sending her sprawling into the clearing, her hair a storm of gray, the crystals leaving bloody lines across her cheek.

"Bitch!" he screamed and lit his hands with black and red fury. Trenara threw her arms in front of her face and shrank away.

The fire did not come. Instead, she felt a massive presence in front of her and looked up to see a mountain of black feathers. Nissa had moved between them.

"No," the Mourna whispered. Joshan melted under those soulless eyes and the fire died within him. "What I see, he sees," Nissa said sadly. "What I hear, he hears. Please, sire. Bring him what he has asked for. He will destroy you... have no doubts. Please."

Joshan lowered his head when Nissa moved away.

"Trenara," he said hoarsely, "I am..."

"I know—sorry." She gritted her teeth and pulled the robe back over her shoulder. Touching her cheek carefully, she looked at the blood smeared on her shaking fingers. She spit out the poison and it steamed on the snow.

Joshan stepped toward her but she held up her hands again.

"Please let me help you," he pleaded.

She shook her head. "I have had enough of your help for one day."

The guider rubbed her chin and looked at the bird. "What does she mean, 'bring him what he has asked for'?" Even though her voice was trembling, she would be damned if she would let him make her cry again. "Where are you taking me?"

Without looking at her, he mounted the Mourna. "I am taking you to Sirdar, in exchange for..."

"Ricilyn," Trenara finished. "I see. You take me to him and then what? He lets you go, just like that? Is that what you think?"

She could not read his expression, a strange mixture of confusion, anger, and determination.

"I want my wife back, Trenara, and a little peace. That is all. It is you he wants and my power. He can have them both."

Trenara shook her head, the shame overwhelming. "And this is worth your loyalty, you friends, and your world, is it?" The guider's face was red with anger. "Coward," she hissed.

When Joshan raised his hand to strike her, she faced him without flinching. Instead, he grabbed her by the front of the robe and tossed her behind him on the Mourna. He smashed his heels into Nissa's sides making her shriek, but she obeyed his command and leapt into the cold air to fly to Sirdar.

CHAPER TWENTY SEVEN
THE TRAP

"Steady as she goes," Captain Elts screamed at his crew, his voice bellowing over the wind. He shook the massive black horns on his head and watched the retreating ships, his black eyes almost invisible in the darkness.

"We've got them on the run! Get her turned. We'll box them in."

The sasaran sauntered across the deck, his hooves scraping the wooden timbers and his great hands cradling the glass as he held it up to his eye.

He ordered signals sent to his other fourteen ships to close the circle around the fleeing imperial armada. His large face wrinkled into a broad smile.

"Bring her in, lads," he yelled up at his crew. "We've got 'em now!"

The storm howled around them. He squinted up at the pelting rain to see huge black clouds rolling from the south. They would have lightning soon.

They had chased the five ships for hours, getting almost close enough to board, but then losing the advantage. The imperial ships kept slipping through their fingers.

After the long chase, the northern fleet finally closed in, positioning itself to sweep around the pathetic imperials. They would kill the bastards before they even saw the shore.

The captain of the larger brig, the one flying the royal crest, was smart, the sasaran thought. The master's meddling had nearly destroyed the imperial fleet. Stupid humans had only gotten five of the ships back on their legs. Five! He snorted to himself. And they dared to challenge my northern fleet? An insult! Elts had twenty of the best ships on the north coast; larger, faster, and much better armed than the puny imperials.

He leaned against the railing to examine the torches of the five vessels plowing through the water less than a league away. Waves crashed against his deck.

He watched the small clipper, a beautiful boat that moved through the water with little effort between her larger sisters. Then there were the three brigantines, swift and sure in the currents, all with the emperor's serpent snapping in the storm, their bows bouncing in the waves, like a swift and flowing dance in the water. He would love to get his hands on any one of those ships, just to find out how they were built. Imperial ships were the best in the world. Balinar's men had stolen several when he infiltrated the southern scum. None of those ships was anywhere near as valuable as what he could see in his glass.

The one he really wanted—the one that sliced through the water like silk, her sails filling seductively before him—the one he craved almost as much as a woman, was the giant brig, the imperial Morning Star. That was the trophy he was after, the gift he would present to his master along with the head of the captain that commanded her. There was a genius at that helm who had managed to evade the sasaran's every maneuver, moving the ship through the water as if by magic, always seeming to be one step ahead of him.

They had chased them all night. But now seven of his swiftest ships were driving the imperials toward the other eight, waiting to the east in deeper waters. The sasaran's fleet would surround and capture those beautiful ships, enslave the human scum that manned them, and take the head of the man who ruled them.

He smiled to himself when he finally saw the torches from his other vessels bearing down on the imperial fleet from the east. Elts threw back his head and laughed, then ordered his crew to trim the sails to slow his ships. The imperials had taken the bait. There was no chance of escape. The sasaran licked his black lips hungrily.

The Morning Star turned suddenly to starboard, feebly trying to outrun the maneuvering ships. Elts knew it was much too late. His other eight ships filled the gaps around her and her sisters, trapping them efficiently. The maidens were ready for his advance.

Elts ordered his ship to come along side the large brig, the storm raging around them with increasing fury. His ship was much taller than the Morning Star and he had them pull within hailing distance. He sneered arrogantly at the giant man who stood unmoving on the brig's prow.

"Surrender!" Elts shouted above the wind that blew with fury around them.

The man smiled up at him, the rain slicking down his black hair and beard. A smaller man came behind the imperial captain and handed him a glass, then went to help the other members hoist huge white flags to the top of the main mast. The man ignored the demand and swept the glass up to inspect the ships that surrounded him. He lowered the glass and then raised his brow at the sasaran. He cupped his hands.

"Fifteen? You haven't enough ships!" he yelled, distant thunder accentuating his word. "If you turn around now, you may escape."

"Arrogant human," the sasaran shouted back, laughing as he pulled a sword from his side. He pointed it at the white flags hoisted on all five of the ships and gave the captain a derisive snort. "You fly the flag of surrender. I accept!"

The man glanced at the large white piece of fabric whipping wildly in the wind. "No," he shouted back. "You misunderstand. In our country, this is the signal for peace. They are used so friendly fire will not destroy our ships."

"Friendly fire," Elts shouted back, hitting a massive muscular leg with a hand the size of a roast. "You call us friendly fire? What is your name, human?"

The captain gave a sailor a quiet order and looked up at his own masts, now skeletons in the storm. "Vanderlinden," he called up casually, giving yet another man a quick hand signal.

The sasaran's raised brows made wrinkles around his great curved horns.

"You are Captain Vanderlinden of the imperial fleet? Well, your legends account you with more intelligence than you appear to have. This is indeed a pleasure, sir. Your head will delight my master."

"Well, as to that," Van replied, his eyes for the first time blazing. "I guess he will just have to wait. Steady!" he called to his crew over a nearby thunderclap.

Elts put his hands on his hips and blasted a scornful snort from his nostrils. "You are a fool, Vanderlinden. You are grossly outnumbered. Do you yield?"

"Yield?" Van called back. "That wouldn't be my first choice, no."

Captain Elts threw back his head and roared with laughter. "Fool! Ready to board!" he called to his crew who waited with swords, grappling hooks and chains.

"Captain," Van called.

"What is it, silly human?"

Van smiled. "Watch your head!"

At that moment, a huge fireball plummeted out of the sky charging at the sasaran's ship. It crashed through the deck, splintering the timbers. Silhouettes of humans and creatures diving out of the way froze for an instant against the brilliant firestorm. A blinding flash of lightning illuminated the sky and a great peel of thunder shattered the night.

When the sasaran whirled around, he saw fifty Trillone ships sparkling in the sudden luminosity. The tall gray ships surrounded them on every side, heavily armed, and bearing down on them. Out of nowhere, a dozen burning globes lit the stormy sky, hurtling toward his fleet.

He screamed orders to unfurl the sails, but too late. A barrage of flaming destruction rained down on his ship, turning it into a floating conflagration.

The Trillone fleet moved in for the kill as Van moved the Morning Star away from the burning ships. The last thing he saw before the fire engulfed his enemy was Captain Elts's silent roar of frustration, drowned out by a rolling clap of thunder that emphasized his failure. Van shook his head and ordered his crew to move the ships out of the way.

CHAPTER TWENTY-EIGHT
THE BATTLE OF CALISAE

From his hiding in the trees, Sark pulled back the bowstring until the arrow was taut in his hands. He carefully aimed it at one of the several sentries patrolling the west section of the forest around the enemy encampment. It left his bow with a stinging ping and sailed alongside a dozen more at precisely the same moment. Every enemy went down with a shaft protruding from his eye or throat. The mercenaries jumped from the trees, finished the job quietly, and then disappeared like smoke into the woods.

This was the twelfth such excursion in the last two days for Sark and his handpicked team, and it was making an impact on the enemy troops.

They had heard many arguments from the enemy soldiers as they covertly observed them from the trees.

None of Sirdar's troops wanted sentry duty. Soldiers did not return from such an assignment. Morale was disintegrating and many humans tried to desert the ranks. Sirdar's creature hunted those that did and slaughtered them for their efforts. The enemy killed more of their own than Sark and his troops had.

Sark mounted his eecha, and sprinted off to return to their hidden meeting place in the mountains.

The plan was working well—at least from his perspective. It had been nearly five days since he had talked to anyone but his mercenaries. Sark wished he had news from the other factions. He had been awake now for two days straight and would be for another two, if he had anything to say about it. Sark was afraid to lie down—afraid to think about what they were doing to Sareh.

Shaking the thought from his mind, Sark concentrated on the plan. The woods were too dense for a direct onslaught and they knew a frontal attack against such odds was impossible. The plan was to strike and go. Hit the enemy in several places at once, demoralize their troops, and create chaos. Thiels and some of his elite went to the southern edge of the fortress, coming up on the enemy's flank. Sark and his mercenaries took the west, using the skills that came to them naturally.

Sark's mission had been daunting at first; the woods were full of enemies, many more than they had expected. With some very clever assassinations, they were able to finally get the humans encamped in the woods to move out to the field and desert their advantage in the forest. Too many of them were dying in their tents and rumors were going around that the imperials had magical ghosts that were smothering their comrades in their sleep or enchanting them to wander into the woods at night. Many soldiers had suddenly disappeared as well. The reality was that most of those were simply deserters who got away.

In fury, the daligon sent in large bands of seasoned soldiers to rid the woods of these assailants, but every time he did, they never returned. By the fifth day, the woods were at last deserted. No threat could motivate anyone to enter that forest.

Thiels was having problems of his own. The daligon had sent two ships up the coast with a handpicked group of trained warriors to try to approach the imperial army from the east. This group contained none of the cowardly laminia, deinos, or conscripted humans; instead, it consisted of three hundred sasaran warriors riding clipped tarsian lizards. They carried strange weapons that expelled clouds of red vapor that instantly killed anything it touched.

Thiels lost fifty people to the weapon in the first assault and had to leave several more to the mercy of the brutal giants. The imperial elite guards were butchered like bullions, and worse. Thiels swore he would never make the same mistake twice and reverted to covert maneuvers after that.

Although he had his people set traps in the woods in front of Sirdar's troops, they had only killed twenty and the enemy was advancing swiftly. Thiels had to do something he swore he would never do against another living creature. As their position became almost impossible, he had no choice. He ordered fire trails cut and the forests torched around the advancing sasarans. The ensuing firestorm killed every living thing within ten square leagues and only two sasarans escaped to return to their ships. Thiels lay awake at night regretting the life he had destroyed in the forest that day.

The act, however, sparked a more insidious consequence when news of it reached the castle at Calisae.

The daligon was outraged. Sark's men had driven his troops out of the woods, had killed thousands with nothing to show for it. Moreover, three hundred of the daligon's best soldiers had died in a cowardly act at the hands of the elite. The humans were making inroads he thought impossible. The shadow gathered his captains and outlined his retribution. He had to fight down the urge to skin Sareh alive and hang her where Sark could see her. Instead, he ordered her training increased.

Donnelly, in charge of the standing army up on the mountain, was not idle. He spent day and night working with the troops left to him. Despite the fact that these were mostly conscripts, the capture of Sareh had galvanized them. He was amazed at how able they became in the very short time allowed. Men, women, and children worked day and night to perfect their skills. He had to order many of them to sleep or eat. By the fourth day, he had a real army.

The troops had no illusions about the odds; the enemy host outnumbered them a hundred to one and wielded a dangerous weapon. To Donnelly's amazement, however, it united them as nothing else could.

To prepare for the battle, Donnelly had traps set throughout the woods and a series of ditches dug at the entrance to the mountain pass. He recruited engineers who had never built anything but ships, buildings, and bridges. Donnelly ordered them to build weapons, design trenches, and devise deadfalls.

Chief among the engineers was Prentice Ilina, head of Vanderlinden's imperial ship builders. At first, Prentice was adamant about not using her skills to create weapons, but Donnelly convinced her of the dire necessity. At his urging, she created some of the most ingenious traps and weapons her age had ever seen, including portable bridges for the trenches, new catapults with ranges unheard of to that day, and a new arrow launcher that shot multiple barbs without having to reload for a dozen volleys. It could kill fifty without missing a beat. This is what kept her up at night.

On the sixth day the sun set like a red fireball to the west, sending bloody clouds to ripple across the sky. Sark and his people were sitting on their eechas on a high clearing in the woods, watching as the enemy troops rallied. Rank after rank formed on the frozen field. When it became dark, the daligon's creatures emerged from the castle to lead them. They gathered directly below where the imperial army was encamped. Sark knew their time had run out.

He ordered his troops to gather as he watched the enemy enter the woods. He guessed fifteen thousand plowed slowly through the forest, trampling anything in their way. Ten thousand remained on the field in a wide semi-circle around the castle. The daligon was not among the advancing army.

Thiels and the elite that remained to him, had made their way through the woods to the west, sneaking through the trees and skirting the advancing army as it passed. The night made their passage easier and they lay beneath the underbrush watching the thousands of troops crushing the foliage under their marching feet.

Many of the creatures carried the strange weapons Thiels had seen with the sasarans, the weapons that spread poisonous catalyst as a vapor. These were much larger. A lump of apprehension stung his throat. He scowled at them when they passed, knowing the devastation those weapons could cause on an isolated enemy. If the size of the weapon were any indication, they could take out thousands at a time. For the first time, he doubted their position.

Thiels and his guard crossed the wide trail left by the advancing army, deciding to follow out of sight along the woods. When they entered a large clearing, Thiels heard something and stopped them with a hand signal. All at once, people dropped out of the trees to surround them.

Thiels' people drew their blades in the darkness, prepared for a final battle. As the advancing figures came out of the shadowed trees, their leader pulled back his hood and smiled at the commander.

"You are lucky I know your voice." Sark said, sheathing his sword.

"Damn." Thiels barked an order to stand down. "I am very happy to see you." He dismounted and ordered his people to do the same. "You've seen them?"

"We saw them leave the field about an hour ago. I would say fifteen thousand, give or take," Sark replied, signaling to his people to gather. "I think we can take out quite a few from the back. I sure as hell hope Donnelly has those people prepared. They will have a heavy battle before the end of this night."

"Sark," Thiels replied reluctantly. "They have something new with them. We saw it in the eastern woods, a weapon that dispenses a cloud of poison. Catalyst."

Sark's eyes sparked in the moonlight. "Catalyst? Are you certain?"

Thiels nodded. "A smaller version of the weapon took out fifty of my best in less than a second." He tightened his lips. "These weapons, the ones this army is carrying, are huge. They could annihilate our entire army in a matter of minutes."

Sark blew out a slow breath as the soldiers around them muttered among themselves. He gripped the handle of his sword and scanned them.

"It looks like we have our work cut out for us. We'll take out these weapons before they get to the encampment. Agreed?"

Thiels nodded and mentally counted their number. "What do you have in mind?"

"Same as we have been doing. Follow them, watch for an opportunity, and strike as many times as we can," he searched the faces of his soldiers, "before they kill us." Without reply, the men and women cinched up their swords, stretched their muscles, and mounted their eechas to follow their captain.

The strikes were small at first. Sark sent in three or four of the soldiers with bows to hit the tail end of the march and take out specific targets. The first five attacks were swift and successful. They managed to kill over a hundred soldiers and destroyed three of the larger weapons. But the enemy reinforced the rear with tarsians and more of the massive sasarans who were tougher than their human counterparts. Arrows often bounced off their thick hides and had very little effect on their beasts. The sasaran commanders sent in a search crew that caught several of the mercenaries before they were able to scatter and hide in the woods.

Thiels and Sark watched in horror as the women were raped, tortured, and beheaded and the men disemboweled, then burned alive right on the trail. Thiels had to hold onto Sark for a long time to make sure he did not rush to save them when the sasarans called and jeered. They danced around the bodies of the valiant soldiers and desecrated their remains. It was an unholy bloodbath and Sark vowed revenge for his fallen comrades. There was little left to bury.

After that, the mercenaries and the elite watched more carefully when they followed the horde deeper into the woods. As they moved toward the mountains, the ground became increasingly steep and the army slowed. The climb was arduous. Finally, around midnight, a few leagues from the imperial's hiding place, the marching army abruptly stopped. The elite and the mercenaries had to scatter to hide themselves. Sark and Thiels watched the daligon's troops from the safety of the trees.

At their head, a giant sasaran spoke to the captains surrounding him. Sark and Thiels could not hear what he said, but the captain gathered many soldiers from the ranks and handed them torches. The break in the trees they had come to was not large, but it was clear of underbrush. In the middle of the clearing, the sasaran had ordered a bonfire started. The flames reached up to the sky sending creeping shadows dancing against the trees on either side of the road.

As the imperials watched in horror, the sasaran ordered hundreds of torches lit and thrown into the forest on the other side of the clearing. They ignited the woods and raced up the hill through the tangled foliage. Heading up the mountain, it moved so quickly, it was difficult to track its progress. Soon the woods were a blazing firestorm, the flames jumping from tree to tree. The enemy laughed, clapped, and screamed obscenities at the flames. The firestorm raced up the mountain to trap the imperial army.

Sark and Thiels gathered their remaining soldiers and made their way to the back of the march to confer. They both knew that Sirdar's army would wait where they were until the fire burned out their enemies and then march in to finish the job. Then they could take their time to find Sark, Thiels, and the rest of the fighters.

"This is bad," Thiels said breathlessly when they found a quiet spot away from the enemy.

"Organize your people to form a line directly behind the enemy and I will do the same. We will give them back a little of their own," Sark said angrily, the image of his dying comrades still vivid in his memory.

"What are you saying?" Thiels asked.

Sark's face was cold in the dark forest as he shouted orders to his troops and finally turned to glare at Thiels.

"They want to play with fire, we will accommodate them." He mounted his eecha and led his soldiers well behind the enemy line.

Standing in a line that spread for nearly a quarter league in both directions, the silent soldiers each lit a burning torch and threw it in the tangled brush before them. The fire took off so quickly, the soldiers had to retreat several hundred spans back.

The firestorm that ate away at the mountain before them roared to life, growing to hundreds of spans in moments, trapping Sirdar's army with a ring of destruction that even the hardy sasarans and tarsians could not avoid. The wind created by the fire blew with such fury it obscured the sky with billowing black smoke and red destruction. The mercenaries and elite tried to follow, but it was impossible. Sark ordered his people to stand back until the fire had finished its gruesome dance.

When the sun came up several hours later, the forest was a graveyard. They picked their way through the carnage. Charred masses of blackened humans, laminia, eechas, deinos, tarsians, and sasarans were scattered everywhere, the smell of cooked flesh and burned wood sickeningly sweet.

As the men and women of Sark's command made their way through the forests, many of them wept or became ill. Sark himself would not look at the corpses. Deep remorse threatened to weaken him. Thiels looked down at the spent lives. He let tears fall down his cheeks for a brief moment, but then took a breath to ease his guilt.

They killed many who had not died in the conflagration, humans and creatures who begged screaming as they passed. Sark's people put them out of their misery as quickly as they could. There were many wounded wailing far into the woods where they had fallen, but there were too many, and the group could not stop to help them all. They let them scream.

When Sark finally looked up toward the gap where his troops hid, black trees smoked and red ash fell like grotesque rain out of the sky. He did not expect to find anyone alive.

Sark wondered if the only living creatures were now the ten thousand who remained at Calisae's gates and the thousand he had with him now. He hoped that some of Thrain's people had escaped to the other side of the mountain where they could live, until Sirdar finally swept over them in the end.

Sark would find as many as he could and make a last stand at Sirdar's door.

CHAPTER TWENTY-NINE
SIRDAR'S TREASURE

When Trenara managed to look at the great temple, the sight should have filled her with awe. From their height in the sky, it glistened on the mountain like a brilliant jewel. Twelve golden turrets spiraled around the roof, ending in fine points at the top. The design of the temple was almost organic. Intricate carvings of deities and reliefs danced everywhere around its façade, the gods frolicking in the snow.

The building itself was an engineering marvel. It stood tall and fragile on a long narrow jut of protruding rock with cliffs falling on three sides into vast, endless distance below and a narrow road that led to its entrance. The white columns surrounding the structure were elaborate with fine lines and patterns, fluted at the top and bottom and so close to one another, two men side by side would not be able to pass through.

At the back of the temple, was a long thin walkway with a golden domed structure at its end. A filigree bridge curved back to the temple roof. The domed structure appeared even more precarious as it expanded out far beyond the cliff. It floated there, delicate, intricate, suspended over the abyss beneath it, defying gravity and reason. The temple was older than legend.

Trenara appreciated none of this. Fear tainted everything, making the beautiful structure look shadowed and horrifying. She fancied she saw the face of Sirdar glaring out at her from every opening. She shut her eyes. She was helpless, bound by a paralyzing apprehension that made the normally aggressive woman weak and tearful. Trenara hated herself for not being stronger, for letting grief and betrayal consume her, for not pushing back the terrible thoughts her imagination was now sparking.

The ever-mounting pain and loss was too much; the deaths of Van and Haiden, Joshan's betrayal, his cruelty—her mind could not manage it all.

The catalyst was meticulously driving Joshan insane. The thought sent a wave of nausea through her, the failure tasting bitter in her throat. She could see it growing in his face, in the red eyes getting brighter every moment, in the angry outbursts, in the abuse and perversion. It all came out of him so easily now, as if it had always been so.

What will Sirdar do to me? The question echoed behind her eyes so many times it was almost a mantra now. Will he kill me? Will he torture me?

He had told Ena he was in love with Trenara, cared for her—did he? She doubted it very much. How could he? She had spurned him… opted for death over his touch. The irony mocked her like the beauty of the temple.

What will he do to me?

Without saying a word, Joshan guided the giant Mourna to land on the roof of the structure.

Trenara tried to see his face, tried to fathom what was happening to him, why he frightened her so. He was so different from the child she had loved, the man she had respected. It was as if he were a completely different being… tempestuous and dark, angry and violent.

Joshan had hurt her in so many ways. The betrayal stung so freshly she had to wipe angry tears from her face repeatedly. She could never forgive him. Yet, for all that, she felt a twang of compassion when she looked at him. Trenara allowed her outrage to kill her moment of weakness.

There were hundreds of heavily armed guards on the roof of the temple. Joshan slid off the bird, pulling Trenara after him, and tightly gripping her in his arms. Because the sun was still very high, the guards were human. Sirdar's creatures could not stand the light.

Their leader was a large man with the typical shaved head and tattoos. Sneering up at Joshan, he then greedily ran his eyes over Trenara. Joshan pushed her behind his back.

"Give me the woman," the man commanded.

Joshan pulled the golden sword from its shaft; his eyes sparked with black and red fire. "Stand away!" That voice echoed over the rooftop, and Trenara was amazed at the compelling tones. The guards stepped back. "No one will touch this woman save Sirdar or me. Is that clear?"

The men went so easily to their knees, it was as if it were more natural than breathing. Joshan completely ignored them when he grabbed Trenara by the wrist and pulled her toward an open hatch.

As they descended, he glanced back at Nissa. "Leave. Do not return until I call you."

Nissa lifted off the roof in one swift jump, her massive black wings disappearing into distance quickly.

Joshan climbed down the ladder with Trenara in front of him, very careful not to let her wander more than a few inches away. He stayed so close she could feel his breath on her neck, could feel the heat of his body close to hers, hear the rustle of his robes and the vibration of his boots as they ticked on the ladder and then the marble floor. Trenara knew it was an attempt to ensure she did not try to end her life before he had paid his debt to Sirdar. Joshan could read her. He always could. He would know how desperately she wanted to flee, how she would do anything to escape. The guider felt like a caged animal as her captor bruised her arms trying to keep her in line.

When they reached the large central chamber there were hundreds of sasarans lining the walls, each armed with a long silver spear and armored in gold and red. Their massive bodies, deeply muscled, stood straight and tall around the perimeters of the chamber. Their black human faces and great curving horns lay motionless in the darkness. A few weak torches cast little light in the enormous room.

At the end of the column of creatures was a high throne surrounded by twelve more sasarans, these in red and black armor. Each carried a naked silver sword across his chest. Behind them, sitting on a golden throne, sat Sirdar.

He was as tall as Joshan, clad in a crimson hooded robe. A red mist hung as a shroud around head, flowed down his shoulders, and swirled like a raging storm. Behind him, stood the immense statue of Ethos. Although the sight of the goddess inspired brief hope in Trenara, it washed away in despair when she looked again at Sirdar.

A soft laugh escaped the shroud. An old memory reached into Trenara's soul. She shuddered and fought to pull away from Joshan. He tightened his grip. She could not control the fear; her training had deserted her.

Sirdar slowly rose from the throne and descended, his guards parting for him at once. He stepped through and lifted a red-gloved hand.

"Bring her to me." Sirdar's voice was a quiet seduction, sending a tremor through Trenara's heart. She stepped back into Joshan. He shoved her forward until she stood so close to the monster, she could hear the air rushing into his lungs, feel the gruesome chill of the mist as it licked her face.

Sirdar looked down at Trenara and reached out to touch her. When she tried to pull away, the back of her head hit Joshan's chest. He squeezed her shoulders, trapping her.

Sirdar held her chin casually and forced her head back, turning it from side to side to examine her. Trenara could only see bright red eyes shining lustily from inside the hood and mist, the rest of his face in shadows. He took in a deep breath as if drinking in her scent.

"Ah, beloved." The touch made her writhe in agony… and then pleasure. "How I have missed you. How I have needed you," he said, looking at Joshan. "I am apparently not alone in my desire. That was quite a scene in the woods. It is fortunate I am not a jealous man." He so suddenly slapped her that Joshan pulled her away and took a step back.

"Enough, Sirdar! We had a bargain. Where is Ricilyn?" Joshan's voice echoed strangely and Trenara suddenly did not know whom to fear more.

"She is here. Come out, my dear."

Ricilyn emerged from behind a pillar and crossed to them in a daze.

"Did he hurt you?" Joshan demanded.

"No," she whispered and then lifted her hand. The fingers were mangled and blackened, swollen and bruised. Her voice trembled with accusation. "You did."

"What have you done to her?"

"I have done nothing. This is a result of your healing the guider after you broke her hand. Very enlightening. I did not realize how far things had gotten. I warned you if you used your power for any other purpose there would be consequences. You did this to her, Joshan, not I. Let it serve as a reminder."

"Let me help her!"

There was a long pause as Sirdar stared at Trenara. "No," he said finally and grabbed Ricilyn's wrist.

She tried to pull away from him. Joshan pushed Trenara out of the way and lunged at him, but Sirdar threw up a shield and laughed. "Turn about is fair play, boy," he whispered and red vapors poured from around him to encircle Ricilyn's hand.

Ricilyn screamed when pulsating ruby filaments wrapped themselves around her fingers. She felt the touch of the catalyst and her stomach clenched at the wrongness of it. It coursed through her body, sending hot flashes of pain through her limbs. It was like the power—flowing, strong, potent, but unlike the power it was strange and perverse, conveying feelings of degradation and shame through her mind. Ricilyn cried when it touched her intimately and forced her to yield.

The catalyst spun into the mist surrounding Sirdar's head. When Ricilyn fell to her knees sobbing, the shield was gone and Joshan rushed to take her in his arms. Ricilyn looked at him in fear and then at her hand. The injury was gone.

"You see," Sirdar said folding his arms above them. "I can heal as well as you, when I am motivated."

He signaled to a guard. Trenara was running as fast as she could down the long corridor of pillars, the large clothes, and boots making her progress awkward.

"Leaving so soon, my dear?" Sirdar laughed when a guard tackled her and wrestled her to the ground. The sasaran caught at her legs, but she fought and kicked him hard in the face, sending the large creature sprawling. Trenara scrambled to gain her footing, but the sasaran was too fast and had her in his arms. She kicked, scratched, and bit him. He grabbed her by the hair and slapped her across the face, stunning her. She crumbled to the ground.

Sirdar's face twisted into rage when he saw Trenara go down. With a crack of ear-numbing thunder, a crimson bolt exploded from his hand hitting the sasaran between the horns. The creature flew into the air and then skittered across the marble landing next to Trenara.

When she sat up and shook the daze from her head, the sasaran guard lay next to her in a black pool of blood, the top of his head gone and his brains splattered over the cold stone. Trenara screamed and scuttled away from him, looking back at Sirdar in horror.

Sirdar's steps were dead slow, calculated, intimidating. He was obviously relishing her terror, drinking in her fear with a sigh of satisfaction. Without saying a word, he stood over her to prolong her agony, his eyes hungry, his breathing hard.

"No one else will ever harm you, Trenara," he whispered, the words a quiet insanity that seeped into her resolve, "unless I order it. Any man who touches you dies. You are mine and only I control you."

Whether it was the numbness taking over and making her careless or a compelling wish to die to end the torture, Trenara rose slowly. "You will never control me." She said it simply, quietly.

Sirdar chuckled. "You think not?" He touched her face tenderly. "Kill them. Kill them both," he called to his guards.

Eight of the guards broke ranks and surrounded Joshan and Ricilyn so quickly, they had no time to respond. Joshan pushed Ricilyn behind him and drew his blade, knowing their position was impossible. The creatures rushed in to cut them down and Joshan raised his sword.

"No!" Trenara cried.

"Stop!"

The guards took a step back from the couple, waiting for Sirdar's command.

He circled around Trenara as she stared at the couple, tears staining her cheeks. "No, what?" he asked.

She closed her eyes. "Do not hurt them." The words were very quiet.

"I cannot hear you," he replied, circling her again, his arms folded.

"Do not hurt them. Please, Sirdar, let them go," she said more distinctly.

Sirdar stopped behind her and pulled the hair from her neck. A shudder coursed through her body. He ran a gloved finger along her skin and leaned down to whisper in her ear. "And what will do you for me?"

Trenara swallowed hard against the sickness building in her stomach. She could not breathe, the revulsion making her throat hurt.

"Tell me," he said, wrapping his hand around her throat and forcing her head back against his chest.

"Trenara, stop!" Joshan screamed, but the spears around him made it impossible to reach her.

Her eyes were still. "Anything," she whispered.

Sirdar brushed the hair from her face. "I have waited so long to hear those words flow from this lovely throat. You are lying, of course." He leaned closer and spoke quietly in her ear, the red mist clouding her vision.

"You have a weakness, my dear, and it has made you vulnerable. What happens when that weakness is gone, I wonder? What happens when I let them go? Will you be strong again, prideful, resistant to my requests? Shall I take others to replace them? There are so many others; Ena, Porphont, Grandor. There are so many more I could bring here to make you dance for my pleasure. It does not even have to be someone you love. Just an innocent. An infant? Perhaps Ricilyn's child..." He spread his hand over Trenara's belly and pressed hard, making her gasp, "...or your own."

Her mouth fell open as the information sank into her numb awareness. It was not possible...

"You did not know." Sirdar's laugh was cruel in her ear. "It is my pleasure to give you such joyous news. Vanderlinden's child. An heir to the throne? The next empress, perhaps? You did not think I knew about Vanderlinden's lineage, did you? About the tragic story of his mother and father? Who do you think whispered into Norsk's ear?" Trenara was unable to believe what she was hearing. Sirdar tenderly ran his hands through her hair, down her face and over her lips.

"It would be so easy," he whispered in her other ear, "to control you with this weakness, this compassion, this misguided kindness. That is not what I want, my love." He pushed the robe off her shoulder. "I want you to bow to me of your own free will, without a threat over your head, without using my power. I will make you my consort, take your pride, your anger, your indignation, and turn it against your will. Your compassion will be mine." He blew air behind her ear and lightly brushed her naked shoulder with his gloved hand, making her tremble in disgust.

"In the interim, I am no fool. Shall I kill them and make you watch?" He tightened his grip around her throat. "Or shall I have them watch while I make you dance for me?"

He shifted against her body and pulled her to her feet. She could feel the crimson clouds move with him. It made her skin crawl.

"Perhaps I should make you dance for him. For both of us?" he said suddenly, viciously. "Joshan loves you, you know, in so many ways it is often difficult for him to be around you. He does not understand his passion, his desires for you. He pushes them away. He does not know as I do that delights are sweeter when taken forcefully." Sirdar squeezed her throat until she could barely breathe. "Joshan was right; you are an addiction, a disease that gets under the skin, a maddening desire that will not go away, no matter how hard you try. I know," he hissed seductively. He put his hand on top of her womb again and painful cramps made her sick from his touch. She struggled to take his hand away, but it was too strong.

"There is less and less of Joshan every second the catalyst burns in his body, in his loins, in his mind. He only brought you here because he thought it would delay me, giving him the advantage. Fortunately, he has underestimated my abilities and my control of the catalyst. All I have to do now is wait for him to succumb. Then he will be mine—as you are mine—as your child is mine."

Sirdar turned her around to face him. She saw in the blackened hood only those blazing red eyes. He squeezed her shoulders until tears came into her eyes. "Shall I kill them?"

Trenara shook her head.

"What should I do with them?"

She swallowed hard. "Let them go. Please, Sirdar."

"Not Sirdar, beloved. You know what you must call me."

"No," she said, shaking her head.

"Ah, that pride again. It is going to get them slaughtered—or worse. Say it!"

"Please, no."

"Say it!" He shook her violently, sending her head spinning.

Trenara sank her head, hating herself. "Master," she hissed.

"Louder."

"Master," she said through her teeth.

Sirdar pulled air through his nose as he circled her waist with his arm. Lifting her off her feet, he took her easily into his arms and carried her to the dais where he set her before him and sat at his throne. "Get on your knees." His voice once again boomed against the marble, echoing off the walls.

With a deep shaking breath, Trenara went to her knees. Ricilyn tried to go to her, but Joshan held her back and shook his head, watching the guards around them.

Sirdar leaned forward and pulled Trenara's face close to the hood, tenderly wiping away her tears with his thumb, and then brushing her lips gently.

"I could make you see whatever I wanted you to see," he said. "I could easily convince you that I am Vanderlinden, taking you to my bed without you suspecting a thing. I could make you believe whatever I wanted you to believe, for as long as I wanted you to believe it. You are an intelligent, powerful woman. In truth, you are a queen among mortals, stronger, my dear, than almost any other. I could make you stupid, weak, and perversely licentious with a glance. I could make you beg me to beat you, to torture you, or even to kill you. I could make you worship me, even... love me. You know that."

Trenara nodded stiffly and tightened her lips.

"Then, what stops me?" he asked, letting her go and sitting back in the throne.

She could not stop the tears flowing down her cheeks. "Because you do not want another slave..."

"Very good. Go on."

"Because you have too many slaves."

He looked down at her. "Keep going."

Despite her fear, something crept from some deep recess of her will. She narrowed her eyes. "Because you are scared and pathetic," she continued, warming to the subject. "Spite has taken over your heart—if you have one—and you sit by yourself season after season without anyone to talk to, to cherish, or to love. Because you are jealous of those who do and know, deeply, that you will never find anyone to more than fear you. Because you know deep in your soul, it would be better spending the rest of existence with someone who loathes you—than spending it alone."

Sirdar folded his hands and lowered his head. A quiet hum rose from behind him. A fine mist of catalyst swirled and surrounded Trenara. She looked up at him with wide eyes and screamed. It was as if molten fire consumed her, constricting her into a ball of sobs on the marble floor before him.

When Sirdar raised his head again, the catalyst fell away. Trenara rose to her hands and knees panting. She went back to her knees angrily, wiping tears from her face with her sleeve.

"There is that pride again, beloved. It will be the death you, I am sure. That was a little taste of things to come, my dear," he said quietly, taking a deep breath. "You are wrong, of course."

He rose from the throne and grabbed her chin, forcing her to look at him.

"I will not make you a slave with my power or threats because I want you to feel everything I am going do to you. I want you to experience every degradation with full perceptions, every anguish, every pain, every perverse pleasure until you surrender to me willingly. I will not let you become a martyr, Trenara, so you can justify the pain. No. I will break you and you will beg me to fulfill you. This I swear." A laugh sounded in the back of his throat. "Call it my wedding vow. You will be the only one in the universe to receive my special attention."

"Why?" Trenara asked.

"Because, my dear, I love you."

The twisted confession hit hard against her ravished senses.

He leaned into her slowly, the mist touching her face.

"I will show you how much—very soon."

"That will never happen, Sirdar," Trenara whispered. "I will die first."

She thought she saw the flash of teeth through the haze. "Or I will kill you. We will have to see."

He reached down, grabbed her wrists, and pulled her to her feet.

"But before that, I need to make a few alternations, just so we have many more seasons to explore our—love."

He put both hands in her hair and tilted her face back, bringing the hood down until her face almost disappeared inside it. She fought violently to get away from him, but he blew into her face and a heavy mist of red catalyst engulfed them.

Joshan tried to run to her, but the guards held them back.

The catalyst coalesced until the cloud was an opaque curtain around them, like a brilliant cocoon, pulsating with flashing sparks of fire. They could hear Trenara's muffled cries from the vortex, could see her silhouette struggle in Sirdar's arms, see the monster throw back his head at the climax and scream his passion. With a loud blast that shook the room, the catalyst shot up like a fountain and then disappeared in another explosion that knocked dust off the pillars and added cracks to the marble walls.

When the fire was gone, Trenara lay limply in Sirdar's arms. Joshan gasped when he saw a flowing mane of auburn hair and the guider's pale face smooth and beautiful with youth again. She looked no more than twenty.

Sirdar reached down to touch her face until her eyelids fluttered open. Trenara pushed herself away and then saw her hands.

"What have you done to me?"

"Done to you? Why, my dear, I have given you a great gift," he said smugly, brushing red powder from his gloves. "It is a benefit of the catalyst that I have found most useful. I can make you younger—or older," he added, glancing at Joshan, "at my wish."

"Change me back!"

"Do you not care for my gift?" The contemptuous edge to his voice was sharp in her ears.

Trenara backed away, her aplomb shaken by that tone and the anger she felt radiating from him like waves of heat. She hit up against a sasaran guard who stood perfectly still. Sirdar grabbed her wrists.

"You will come to appreciate what few favors I grant you," he whispered maliciously, pinning her to the creature. "You will learn to thank me when I bestow them."

Sirdar pulled her into his arms and then pushed her face inside the hood to force her lips to his. The kiss was violent, passionate, and terrifying. The catalyst swirled around them. Trenara fought desperately to get away from his touch. She had never felt anything like this. It was ice cold and then blazing hot, pulsating from pleasure to pain so quickly, it was difficult to tell which was which. The feeling became more and more intense until she screamed against his mouth.

"Sirdar, stop this!" Joshan called to him. "We had a bargain, remember? I have kept my part. Now it is time for you to keep yours."

Sirdar released the kiss and Trenara slumped in his arms. "Such concern, Joshan. I thought, after that little confrontation in the woods, you did not care what happened to her. Was I wrong?"

"Let us go, Sirdar," Joshan demanded tightly.

Sirdar lifted Trenara easily into his arms and crossed to the throne. "Go? Not just yet. I had hoped you would stay. Please, I must insist. We will retire to my chambers. The guider does seem to need some rest. Will you join us?"

"We had an agreement. Let us go."

Sirdar's eyes sparkled from beneath the cowl. The air seemed thick, pressing down on the couple as Ricilyn folded herself into Joshan's arms, frightened by the intensity.

"Are you not curious?" Sirdar asked slowly.

"What?"

"Curious..." Sirdar's voice became lyrical and commanding.

Joshan licked his lips, trying to shake off the compelling words. "About what?"

"About it all, my boy. About who I am—who you are..."

"I am not interested in your lies, Sirdar."

"Lies? Ah, yes, I almost forgot. That is what they call me—the deceiver? The father of lies? It was not always so!" Sirdar paused, swaying near the throne, his prize clutched in his arms.

"I swear to you there will only be truth between us. It is important you know the truth, Joshan. To ensure that, Ricilyn will need her abilities restored."

He nodded casually and Ricilyn gasped. She touched Joshan's arm.

"I can feel you again," she breathed. "My perceptions are clear. Sirdar has done something to them. They are—stronger. What have you done?"

"Nothing, my dear. Just a gift."

Joshan took a step toward Sirdar. "I am not falling for your tricks, Sirdar. We are leaving." He took Ricilyn's hand and turned for the exit.

"Have you even wondered why you are so powerful, Joshan?" Sirdar called after him.

Joshan stopped and his eyes flared.

"Would you like to know why we are here? How all of this could come about? I can tell you that. No one else can. It is time you heard the truth, boy. Of course, it is your choice. It has always been your choice." Sirdar turned to a curtain behind the great statue of Ethos and disappeared behind it.

Joshan tilted Ricilyn head back to search her face. "He is lying," he said uncertainly.

Ricilyn bit her lip and brought her brows together. "No," she whispered. "It does not matter, Joshan. We need to leave, now, before it is too late. Please. Call Nissa. We will get help. We will come back for Trenara. We will bring an army. Oh, god, please!"

He pulled her into his arms and squeezed her gently. "I have to go with him. You know that."

Ricilyn listened to his heart. "I saw you in the woods with Trenara," she began. "He made me watch you."

Joshan kissed the top of her head. "It was a trick, Ricilyn, a ruse to convince Sirdar that I am changing, to keep him off balance."

Ricilyn pulled back and touched his lips. "I saw it in your face, your eyes, heard it in your voice. When you broke Trenara's hand, when you tried to—when you kissed her—that was not a trick, was it?"

He tucked his hand under her chin and made her look into his eyes. "Yes, it was."

She ran a finger across his brow. "Sirdar has given me back my perceptions. I can hear the lie in your voice. You have deceived me too easily, Joshan. Not any longer." A tear rolled down her cheek. "The catalyst is consuming you."

Joshan released himself to his fate. "Yes."

"And you are… allowing it."

"Yes." He pulled her into his arms and held her tightly, knowing the truth would terrify her. "It is the only way I can defeat him without destroying the two of you. I must let the catalyst combine within me; merge with the power, so I can become stronger. It will happen very soon now. I need to delay him until then."

Ricilyn's lips stretched taught in pain. "You will die," she sobbed.

"Yes," he replied quietly, "and you help me. You have seen this from the beginning."

"There has to be another way."

"No, my love," he whispered back, "but you already know that, as well."

Ricilyn nodded. Joshan lifted her face and pressed his lips to hers, the salt of her tears tasting bitter on his tongue. When he pulled away, a black mist fell from his eyes to drift into hers. "You need to be brave for me. This will help you."

She gave her hand to him and together they went into Sirdar's chambers.

CHAPTER THIRTY
REUNION

Sark and Thiels could not believe their eyes. Tired, some burned and all black from the smoke, the rest of their army came marching toward them. The imperial soldiers walked in perfect unison behind a white eecha with a fully clad Captain Donnelly leading them. The army that had been a rag tag of civilians, frightened, angry, and for the most part, unwilling mere days before were now sharp and organized. All had that dedicated gleam in their eye that came with hard campaigns and experience. They were still angry, but the anger was for an enemy without honor that had stabbed at the heart of their valor and stolen their innocence.

When Sark, Thiels, and what was left of their company came into view, a deafening roar ascended from the crowd that a strange southern wind made echo down to the fields before Calisae. That sound made the daligon uncertain of the future. It did more to demoralize the enemy than anything else could have; it convinced Sirdar's conscripted hordes that they had perhaps aligned themselves with the wrong side. Many deserted—many died. That roar made the daligon careless and opened the door to possibilities.

"Present!" ordered Donnelly, standing up in the stirrups and swinging a large sword above his head. The deafening present that went up from the six thousand rippled like water down the ranks and deep drums pounded in reply.

Sark made his way slowly up the hill to the waiting commander and took his hand gratefully, shaking his head.

"You wily bastard," Sark said to Donnelly as he stared proudly at his army. "We thought for sure you were burned or gone. How the hell did you manage this?"

Donnelly smirked at his people. "They did it, not me, general. The engineers, Prentice and her group, had us build trenches and traps all through the woods in front of us. They saved our lives, kept that fire back until it burned itself out. That was not why we built them, but I am sure as hell glad we did. The fire would have razed us to the ground. We would have been trapped in that valley and cooked."

Sark searched the number of his army. "How many?"

"Six thousand plus what you have."

Sark scowled at him. "What happened to the rest?"

Donnelly shook his head. "I can report to you at council, sir," he said quietly. "I would rather not here."

"Very well," Sark said simply.

Donnelly ordered his new lieutenants to get the army to rest until they were ready to continue the march, and then followed Sark into the woods, well away from the troops. Thiels and the other captains followed close behind him, sending the rest of their people to merge with the standing army, ordering most to get cleaned up, rest and then armored before the final battle.

"Report," Sark said to Donnelly.

"The fire did not kill them all, general. About a hundred of the sasarans and perhaps another hundred humans, deinos, and laminia came through the fire wielding weapons we have never seen before." He shook his head and ran a shaky hand through his hair. "About three thousand went down in an instant," he whispered, swallowing hard. "So many, they could not get to the rest of us quickly. Bodies clogged the ground, some devilry burning them slowly. I can't even begin to describe it. The next line was too far away and, thanks to the gods, the weapons didn't have the range. We showered them with arrows from Prentices' new launchers and slaughtered them before they could get any closer. Her new weapon is amazing; it can take down a hundred in two volleys. But it is nothing compared to what the enemy has.

"The sight of our people dying in the woods from this abomination stirred these soldiers as nothing I have even seen. They lost their innocence last night, Sark. We got damn lucky, if you want to know the truth. We could have lost a great many more." He looked down at his hands and shook his head.

"Sark, if the enemy has more of these weapons on the open plains, if they expend their troops as they did in Thrain, without regard to life, we haven't a chance in hell of winning this." Donnelly searched Sark's face. "I don't care how many people we have or how good our weapons are, we will all die within sight of Calisae. All he has to do is stay behind its walls and fire those weapons until we're all dead, then come out on the field to finish us off. I don't know how we're going to take that castle, unless the daligon is fool enough to give up his advantage and meet us on the field. He has no reason to do that."

Sark bowed his head, Donnelly grew still, and the other captains became lost in their own thoughts. Finally, Sark looked at the roughly seven thousand troops he had: men, women, and children. Something sparked in him when he thought of his daughter in the hands of the enemy and her words many days ago. It seemed like an eternity now.

You are the only one I know who can get any man, woman, or beast mad enough to become completely obsessed with destroying you.

Sark missed Sareh so much he could not breathe for a moment. He set his jaw, knowing full well the only thing the daligon would come out to retrieve himself; Sark's head. He would make certain it was right where the monster could reach it.

"I will give him a reason to leave his gate," he whispered quietly. His captains scowled at him.

"Captains," he rose and adjusted a glove, "muster your people, mount them, and prepare for battle. Arm them to the teeth, as much as they carry. Everyone is to polish their armor until it gleams, not a speck of dirt on any of it. Same for their helms and their weapons. I want this army shining when we hit that field.

"Donnelly, gather the engineers and send them to me immediately. The rest of you, gather your people, fan out through the legion and each of you take a contingent. Thiels, I want your elite spread through the front line." He set his jaw and stared out at the woods. "We will give these bastards something to come out for. Now, move!"

Ten minutes later, the engineers stood before Sark as an aide helped him with his armor in the open woods.

"You called for us?" Prentice Ilina was short, yet willowy, with thin graying hair tied tightly behind her head. She looked out of place in military leggings and tunic, which were a bit too large for her. She held several scrolls in her arms and two of the engineers pulled a wheeled weapon behind her. Prentice was focused and straight in her manner, at times very sharp in her replies, extremely intelligent and forthright. Now, she seemed a bit put out. Being summoned perfunctorily, she had to scramble to gather her information and her other engineers.

"Yes, Prentice," Sark replied as the aide pulled his armor into place around his chest. "Tell me about this weapon."

"I am certain others have told you of its ability," she snapped. "What would you like to know?"

"How many have you?"

"There are six, general."

He scowled back at her and winced when the armor bit into his sore ribs.

"Six? I need at least a dozen more."

Prentice lifted her chin haughtily and stared back at him with cold eyes. "You are joking, of course."

Sark smiled down at her. "No, Prentice, I am quite serious."

The woman calculated quietly. "It took us three days and five catapults to build these six, general," she said slowly, as if talking to a child. "Perhaps if I had more time…"

"You have no more time, Prentice," he said. "Take what people you need from the line, use what materials you have at the camp, and build the other twelve. They are to be on the field by nightfall." He glanced up at the graying sky. "I would say you have about nine hours. You had better get started."

Prentice Ilina pulled herself up to her complete height, quite short of a full span. "I cannot guarantee accuracy, general," she said crisply. "Not with that kind of timeline. The machines will be faulty. I would estimate perhaps… eighty percent accuracy, if that."

"Eighty percent?" Sark looked at her incredulously. "How accurate are the six you have?"

"Why, a hundred percent, of course," she shot back, her look comically shocked that he would expect anything less.

Sark shook his head and tried to suppress a baffled smile. "Eighty percent is acceptable, Prentice. Please see to it they are completed as requested."

"Very well," she said with finality. She gathered her engineers and quickly departed, shouting orders as she went.

"I would take ten of her for the elite in half a heartbeat," Thiels said staring after the engineer when he came up behind Sark. Sark dismissed his aide and turned to the commander.

"So would I," he said, sheathing his sword.

They walked to where their eechas were tethered and mounted.

"How are we doing?" Sark asked Thiels quietly as they moved their animals to the front of the line. Soldiers were finishing the formation of the columns and the captains were already in position. The shields, armor, and weapons gleamed brightly even in the shadowed, charred forest.

The commander scanned his elite down the line, giving a couple of them a quiet hand signal. "As well as can be expected, I suppose. You know we have less than two thousand with any real experience. The three thousand Donnelly lost to the catalyst, they were all veterans."

Sark nodded to a group of nervous soldiers. "I have seen worse odds," he replied quietly.

"So have I. Do you honestly think the daligon will come out on the field to kill you?"

Sark smiled back at him, his eye twinkling. "Wouldn't you?"

Thiels laughed and pulled his reins to the left. "Ask me later!"

He yelled to his eecha and galloped off to take his place on the left flank of the army.

Sark turned to his troops. The columns formed quickly before him and the captains galloped to stand on both sides of him as he reviewed his army.

There were so many young among them, no more than teenagers, their innocent eyes staring straight ahead, as they had been commanded. They reminded him so much of Sareh that a pang of grief touched his heart for a fleeting moment. He pushed it down. His eyes turned grim. This fight would be for her.

"Legions!" His voice sounded full and sharp in the late morning. A fitful gray light clarified the blackened forest around them. The red and blue of their uniforms looked oddly out of place against this distorted graveyard. "I will not lie to you," he said dourly. "The chances of us winning on the field are small. They have superior numbers, greater weapons, and more experienced troops. They wield a weapon of incredible power. You have seen it. Yet," he said with certainty, "we have something they do not." He looked carefully over the columns before him. "It makes us stronger, more able, and better equipped to fight this battle than any other army. We have honor!"

A shout of honor went up through the troops in one voice.

"We have valor!"

Valor! echoed through the woods and out to the plains, making the enemy grumble in response.

"We have courage!"

Courage!

"And we fight for our freedom!"

Freedom!

"Captains!" he cried, turning his eecha and placing a bright helm on his head. "To war!" Sark led his army to take the field of Calisae.

CHAPTER THIRTY-ONE
THE TRUTH

When Joshan and Ricilyn moved through the entrance, Sirdar and Trenara were gone. They found themselves passing through a long, dark hallway where hundreds of strange old paintings and sketches hung on the walls. Most tilted in haphazard fashion as if a child had placed them.

Tortured faces stared out of those paintings, haunted, perverted, and cadaverous. It was obvious a single artist had painted them. If these were indeed a window into the artist's soul, that soul had surrendered to depravity long ago. The portraits of these inconceivable atrocities sent shivers of disgust through Joshan. Ricilyn moved closer and kept her eyes closed.

Sirdar suddenly appeared out of the darkness in front of them. "Do you like my little gallery?"

Trenara was no longer with him. He reached to touch Ricilyn's face and she pulled it away.

"My art is one of my few pleasures," he said quietly. "Perhaps you would be interested in posing for me, my dear. You would make an excellent subject."

Joshan stepped between them. Sirdar smiled at him and straightened. "No? Pity." He turned abruptly on his heel and moved quickly down the hall. Motioning to a large curved opening at the end of the gallery, he respectfully tilted his head. "Welcome to my humble home."

Joshan stopped when he passed through the arch, appalled at what he saw.

The room was huge and at one time, it must have been splendid. A circular chamber towered up around them ending many stories above their heads. A great crystal dome capped the room. The walls, the floor, and even the doors were rare marble fitted so precisely a piece of parchment would not pass through the cracks. It was so similar to the Sanctum Library on Mathisma Joshan was certain it must have been designed by the same architect.

In the precise middle was an immense spiraling staircase, broad, intricate, and magnificent. Its finely carved railings twisted up the staircase, covered in beautiful sculptures. Thousands of intertwined people, eechas, wagons, and war machines filled the balustrades on both sides. It was a mural of the history of the north, carved in precious woods and polished to perfection. It ended in a large glass platform at the top, covered by the crystal dome.

Although this piece was immaculate and well cared for, everything else in the room was gray with seasons of dust and dirt. Cobwebs hung like great tapestries from the ceiling. Against the walls were hundreds of shelves, obviously designed to hold books. But there were no books. What they housed was something all together different.

At first, it was difficult to make out. The chamber was so dark. As their eyes adjusted to the gloom, the glass vats and multitude of jars became very distinct. There were literally hundreds of strange clear containers, each filled with a viscous yellowing fluid containing unimaginable horrors.

Creatures floated in a filthy liquid Joshan had never heard of. There were parts and pieces of humans, animals, and abominations scattered everywhere in the room, on the shelves, on the floor and stacked up in areas one on another. The smell was putrid, sharp, and strangely antiseptic like a badly maintained healer's lodge.

Centuries of experiments, dissections, and terrible tortures, rested in the macabre museum. It represented thousands of living souls, now dead and cut apart in this gruesome exhibition.

Where the gallery of twisted paintings had shown into the mind of madness, these opened the heart of that same insanity. Hands, eyes, brains, every part or piece imaginable glared out of the yellowing liquid.

"This is my inner sanctum," Sirdar said with a wide sweep of his arm. "This is where I work. These are my failed experiments. I keep them here as reminders. It motivates me to excel to greater heights." His laughter sent a tinkling echo through the glass containers.

In one far corner, looking oddly out of place, there stood a tall table and on it a beautiful crystal casket, as immaculate as the stairs had been. Inside, reclining as if asleep, lay a naked young woman. Golden hair cascaded down her body, ending in delicate curls at her hips. Her deep blue-green eyes were open, lost in an enchantment as they stared without life at the ceiling.

Joshan gasped when he saw it. "Nissa," he whispered.

Sirdar stopped and looked back, his head tilted. "Yes. How did you know?"

Joshan set his face into stone. "It does not matter."

Sirdar crossed and ran his fingers seductively over the glass. "It does matter, Joshan. I want you to see there are successes. This is my crowning achievement, one of my greatest contribution. Even though she breathes, grows, and has life, it will be empty until I place a soul within her." He grew quiet as the red smoke curled around him.

"Where is Nissa?" Sirdar asked.

"I sent her away, where you cannot reach her."

There was a soft chuckle on the air. "You are wrong. I have already called her. She is flying back to me, where she belongs. Nissa is mine, not yours and this…" he spread his arms wide above the enclosure, "is why. You do not know her as I do. I am her father, her guider, and her family. It is my heart that beats in her chest, my voice she hears in her ears, my commands she follows. You need to remember that.

Do you honestly think a few days of kindness can undo the seasons of… love I have given her?"

Sirdar stopped and looked up at the jars above his head, suddenly leaving the reclining form, and crossing to an empty one on a shelf. He turned to Joshan and held out his hand.

"Give me his heart," he whispered.

Joshan reached under his robes to retrieve a bloodstained pouch. Ricilyn looked at him in horror when he handed it to Sirdar.

"Whose heart?" she whispered, stepping away from him.

Joshan's eyes blazed red and he turned away angrily to cross back to the staircase, trying to get his fury in check.

"It is the giant's heart, Ricilyn," Sirdar said suddenly in her ear, making her jump and step away.

"What?"

"Vanderlinden's—and lighter than I would have expected," Sirdar said, weighing the horror in his hand. "Did he not tell you, my dear? He killed the giant, cut out his heart, took Trenara, and then brought them to me, all to save you."

Ricilyn's lip trembled when Sirdar poured the grisly contents into his hand and casually dropped it into the jar where it floated in the contaminated liquid.

"No…" The uncertainty was tangible in her voice. "He would not do that."

"Wouldn't he?" Sirdar came up behind her, breathing in her anger, her loss. He slowly wrapped his arms around her waist and rocked her tenderly. "He betrayed them all. Do you now begin to understand what is happening to him… what he is becoming?"

"Get away from her, you bastard!" Joshan appeared behind him, his sword drawn.

Sirdar stepped back and lifted his hands. "Just a friendly conversation. No need to get angry."

Joshan grabbed Ricilyn's wrist and pulled her away from Sirdar, setting her behind him. "Let's get on with this, Sirdar," he hissed. "No more of your games."

Ricilyn broke away from Joshan's grasp.

"You killed him. You killed Van," she whispered. "I heard the truth in his voice. Please tell me he is lying."

Joshan sheathed his sword and took her shoulders in his hands, squeezing her so tightly she winced in pain. "You will do as I say," he said, shaking her with each word. "Whatever I say. Do you understand me?"

Ricilyn nodded numbly, the pain shooting into her head. Anger radiated from him like a storm.

"What I do, I do for you and our child—for our future. You will obey me!"

He released her shoulders and took her hand, turning back to Sirdar. "Let's get on with this!"

Sirdar nodded quietly and turned to cross the chamber.

He led them past the staircase and into a smaller door on the other side of the room. When they entered, this at least, seemed almost normal. Luxuriant couches and chairs dotted the small study, set around a great fireplace.

When they rounded the corner, Trenara was sitting on a chair, glaring up at Sirdar angrily, her eyes now a vivid blue. She wore a beautiful flowing gown that emphasized her graceful figure. It was the same color as her auburn hair, and cut to expose her shoulders and naked back. Around her wrist, where her wedding band had been, was another bracelet of precious red and black jewels. Attached to the band was a short chain that ended in an old loop set securely in the floor behind her. Standing straight and rigid behind the chair stood an immense sasaran in full armor with his arms crossed.

Sirdar crossed and lifted Trenara's chin. "That is much better, my dear. You look exquisite." He glanced back at her guard. "He did not hurt you, did he? Sasaran appetites for young, lovely creatures can be quite extraordinary. I will be happy to show you one day. Did he touch you?" His eyes blazed lustily.

"No," Trenara said flatly. "He was a perfect gentleman."

Sirdar threw back his head and laughed. "I doubt that, my dear," he said, motioning for the others to sit.

Joshan and Ricilyn sat guardedly on the couch. Sirdar motioned to the sasaran, who crossed to the table to pour wine, his massive hands amazingly graceful with the fine, delicate wine glasses and crystal server.

"I must apologize for the wine," Sirdar said. "We left Cortaim rather quickly. I am afraid I had to leave some of my more favorable amenities behind. But this is good northern stock, hearty and robust, like its people." He looked down and caressed Trenara's face, making her shiver. "Are you cold, my dear? How thoughtless of me. It is rather chilly in here." He crossed to the fire.

"All right, Sirdar," Joshan said, trying desperately to keep control of the anger. "We are here. Say what you have to say!"

"You are so impatient, my boy." Sirdar stoked the fire. "Are you certain you want to hear it? The truth can be very enlightening, don't you think?"

"No more games, Sirdar," Joshan said through his teeth.

"No more games," Sirdar whispered with his back to them.

He rose, slowly reached up, and pulled the hood off his head. The smoke around him swirled into nothing, exposing a long expanse of white hair that fell almost to his waist. He shrugged out of his robe, letting it fall around his boots into a pile on the floor. Tilting his head back, he ran his red-gloved hands through his hair. Then, he turned very slowly to Trenara.

"By the gods," she whispered throwing her hand over her mouth. "It was you I saw in the gazing. You killed Haiden."

Sirdar turned to look at Joshan and he gasped. Except for the large blazing red eyes, the long white hair, and the scars that ran down both sides of his jaw, the face was so like Joshan's it was as if he were looking in a mirror.

"No," Joshan breathed, standing. "A lie."

A slow smile spread over Sirdar's full lips—Joshan's lips—and the madness shone from his eyes like a search light.

"Tell him, Truthseer. Tell him what he sees is real."

"No," Joshan shouted, looking at Ricilyn pleadingly. She could not speak.

"Tell him!" Sirdar commanded.

Ricilyn folded her hands around her shoulders and trembled. "He is as you see him," Ricilyn whispered, glancing back at Sirdar. "This is his true form."

"I do not understand."

"You wanted the truth, boy," Sirdar said softly, stepping over his robe and pouring a glass of wine. "You wanted to know who I was, who you were, did you not?" He sipped the wine slowly, never taking his eyes off Joshan.

"Why do you look like me?" Joshan demanded.

"Actually," Sirdar replied, taking a sip of his wine, "it is you who looks like me. Well, almost. It is only a family resemblance, after all." He set down his glass and crossed behind Trenara to place his hand on her naked shoulders.

"Trenara knows," he said slyly, bending down to kiss her neck. "Don't you, my love?"

Joshan eyes blazed. "What does he mean?"

Trenara searched those same eyes that hurt her so deeply before. She could not find her voice. Sirdar reached down to take her wrist and pulled her from the chair, the chains releasing at once. He wrapped his arms around her protectively.

"Come, my dear," he whispered in her ear as he forced her toward Joshan. "He is entitled to the truth, isn't he?"

She struggled to get away from him but he pulled her arms behind her back and pushed her forward until Joshan loomed over her.

"What is he saying?" Joshan forced her chin up.

"You are hurting me." Trenara tried to sound courageous, but fear rippled through every muscle.

Ricilyn reached up to Joshan, but he pulled his arm away violently. "Tell me what he means."

Trenara set her jaw to confront him. "Your mother," she began, controlling her voice with effort. "Your mother told me about something that happened twelve seasons ago. She was lost in the woods, and your father came to her... took her there in the forest by force. We both thought it was a dream." Trenara bit her lip to try to keep it from trembling.

"But it was not, was it?" Sirdar licked the outside of her ear. Trenara turned her head away in disgust.

"Tell me," Joshan's voice was so compelling, Trenara calmed immediately and would have told him anything he asked.

"After Balinar abused her, he told her it was not Jenhada in the woods—it was Sirdar who raped her."

Crimson fire rose in Joshan's eyes when he wrapped his hand around her neck. "My mother told you this?"

"No," she whispered, terrified by the growing fire. "I saw it in her mind, when I was trying to help her. I did not know what I was seeing. The sight just opened up. I am not even sure it was real, Joshan. Please believe me."

"And you did not tell me?" His hand squeezed slowly around her windpipe.

"I thought it was a trick, Joshan," she pleaded. "I thought Balinar had planted the memory there, for me to find. I never thought it was true. I never thought it was Sirdar who raped her!"

Sirdar suddenly pulled her away from Joshan and wrapped an arm over her chest.

"Hardly rape, my dear," he said. "You will forgive me my infidelity, won't you Trenara? It was necessary to ensure my legacy."

He propelled her into the arms of the sasaran who forced her back into the chair and reattached the chain to her wrist. Trenara buried her face in her hands and wept.

Joshan's eyes blazed, but his face remained stony, as Sirdar crossed back to the fire and stirred it again.

"So you are telling me you are my father?" Joshan finally asked quietly.

Sirdar turned around and eyed him darkly. "Is it not obvious, Joshan? You must see the family resemblance?"

"The truth, Sirdar! That is what you promised."

For some reason, the red moved from Sirdar's eyes for a brief second leaving them a very pale blue and almost sad. The smirk filtered back into his face when he turned back to the fire.

"The truth. All right. Ask me your questions and we will let Ricilyn decide if the answers are true. Fair enough?"

Joshan nodded and crossed to the back of the couch. "What are you?" he asked simply.

Sirdar smirked and moved to pick up his wine glass. "Very good. Straight to the point." He took a long drink, set the glass down, and raised his eyebrows at him. "I am a god, Joshan."

Joshan scowled. "What?" He looked to Ricilyn for an answer. "Is what he is saying true?"

Ricilyn nodded slowly. "Yes."

"What does that mean?" Joshan asked Sirdar.

"A god, a supreme being." The humor on his face turned malicious. "Just as you are, my boy. You see, my blood runs through your veins. You are also a god."

"No," he whispered.

Sirdar changed the pitch of his voice. "You must have wondered about it. Why it takes so little to nourish you." He crossed behind Joshan and spoke deliberately, quietly. "Why you hardly drink. Why, without even trying, you can hear the voices of others, even though they are not speaking. Why you feel an uncontrollable longing inside your loins to release the power that sleeps within you. But you will not—you cannot—it would destroy everyone around you, wouldn't it?"

Sirdar circled in front of him. "Why you do not—sleep." Joshan's mouth opened and Sirdar seemed satisfied. "How long has it been? Weeks? Months? How long has it been since you slept? That night—that last night when you reached first trial—it was the last time, wasn't it?"

"Is this true?" Ricilyn whispered, not remembering when she had actually seen him sleep.

Joshan folded him arms.

"You are a god. Ask her if I am lying to you."

Joshan looked down at Ricilyn and she quietly nodded.

Joshan's world crumbled beneath him, reality suddenly shifting. The monster circled behind him and gripped his shoulders.

"Accept it," Sirdar whispered in his ear. "It is who you are. It is why you have such power, even without the Crystal, even without the catalyst. Your human blood will soon succumb to the holy blood that flows through your veins, and you will be complete. You will become the god. With the Crystal and the catalyst, you will become more powerful than any of us."

Joshan stared into the fire. "Who are you?"

"They used to call me Lughati. No one has called me that in a very long time."

"The Fallen One," whispered Trenara.

Sirdar crossed to yank her out of the chair. "No one calls me that!" The catalyst spun around her in a torrent until she screamed in agony.

"Sirdar, stop it!" Joshan shouted, involuntarily sending a tendril of red out of his own hands that took the fire away from Trenara. Joshan's breath came out in ragged, agonized gasps. He fell to his knees and looked up at Sirdar in horror.

Sirdar took Joshan's face in his hands and searched his eyes. "You are so close now... so very close." He let him go and crossed to the fire

Joshan struggled to stand. "Why are you here?"

Sirdar leaned against the mantel and a light came slowly to his large pale eyes. "I was imprisoned here three thousand seasons ago..." His voice trailed off as the fire leapt suddenly in the hearth.

"Imprisoned? Why?"

"I was once like you," he whispered at the fire. "We were powerful beings; advanced, talented, immortal..." He looked at his gloved hands and chuckled, "... flawed. We ruled planets, star systems, galaxies; hundreds of thousands of them." He lifted his eyes to Joshan. "We were more advanced, you see? With great power over the millenniums we ruled. Our subjects were mortal—sentient beings, all of them, without power or knowledge." Sirdar paused to stare at the fire.

"And what did we do with these billions and billions of beautiful creatures? What else?" A strange twisted laugh escaped his throat. "We enslaved them, of course. We made them serve us, degraded them, adjusted their minds, tampered with their bodies and their sentience. In other words, we destroyed them—billions of them for many long centuries." Sirdar lowered himself to the hearth and hung his head.

"It was wrong," he said softly. "I tried to help them."

When Sirdar looked up at Joshan, there were tears in the monster's eyes. "I gathered as many as would follow me." His voice was strange and far away. "My own people and many of the slaves. I incited them to riot. That was one of the charges; insurrection. What I actually did was start a holy war." He looked again at Joshan. "A civil war that we fought for a thousand seasons. Billions of beings died; countless civilizations disappeared. They killed them all without mercy—without warning— they destroyed them all," he whispered.

He looked again at his hands. "In the end I was betrayed." Sirdar stood up and crossed to Trenara, standing behind her. "By a human, a fiery haired, blue eyed mortal," he said, putting his hands in the guider's hair and pulling her head back. "So much like my beautiful Trenara here I sometimes wonder if she is not that child reborn." Sirdar leaned over to kiss her on the forehead.

"What happened after they caught you?" Joshan asked quietly.

"They sent me here," he said simply, crossing back to the fire. "They stripped me of my power, tortured me, and abandoned me." He looked up again, his eyes a red blaze as he slowly removed his gloves. "They took the one thing I most valued."

Sirdar held his naked hands palms up so all three could see them clearly. The hands were long-fingered and large like Joshan's, but unlike Joshan's, they were a mangled mass of scared flesh and destruction. The crystals that once must have covered his palms, his wrists and much of his arms, had been scraped from his flesh, leaving it tattered and disfigured. He brought one of his hands up to his face and pulled away the hair from his ears. The scars that ran along both sides of his face ran well into the hairline and through to the back of his neck.

"This is what they did to me," he said bitterly. "They destroyed my power and three thousand seasons ago left me at the top of your world, in the frozen north. I had only a keeper for company who was charged with torturing me for as long as he could make it last; a demigod—the daligon. They sealed this planet with a layer of crystal to make certain and then—they forgot me." He crossed to pour himself another glass as the three looked on in horror.

"The daligon did his job very well," Sirdar continued, looking down at his drink. "The first hundred seasons in the cold north were agony." The memory sent a scowl over the spoiled face.

"Then salvation came," he said, his eyes sparkling. "I discovered the catalyst deep in the frozen north, a power that I could harness, control, and use to escape this hell, this planet of yours.

"At first, all I wanted to do was destroy that creature, keep him from torturing me. Soon I found I could actually control him, so I turned it against him and he became my slave. With the catalyst, my world became bearable again and I relished its wonder, its beauty, and its terrible gift." His eyes became distant and almost painful again.

"And it is a terrible gift. Is it not?" Joshan felt a sudden compassion for this being. It made him sick to his stomach. "With the catalyst, I discovered I was not alone." He looked up at the ceiling. "I could find companions, someone to talk to, someone to make my imprisonment tolerable. We traveled south. In time, I became a king among the northerners. I experimented with the catalyst to bring creatures back from extinction—the sasarans, the tarsians, others—creating faithful companions for me, soldiers for my developing armies. I ruled the north, Joshan, for two thousand seasons." His eyes sparked. "And we began our plans to invade the south.

"Then something happened that would change the future of this planet forever. While experimenting with the catalyst there was an accident. It caused such a conflagration that the fountain of catalyst that ripped through the sky tore through the crystal dome, sending a piece of that precious commodity down where I could reach it."

Sirdar looked down at the scarred flesh and made fists. "It was not to be," he said through his teeth. "Someone else found it first and gave it to the humans."

"Kerillian," Joshan whispered astounded.

Sirdar licked his lips. "Yes," he hissed, "Kerillian. I did not even know he was here until then. He found the Crystal of Healing and gave it to undeserving mortals whom he trained. Kerillian was my brother and one of my lieutenants in the war," he said bitterly. "He turned on me. He gave the greatest gift we could have—our one chance to escape our prison—and squandered it. Without even thinking, he gave it to mortals."

"That was a thousand seasons ago. That was when I finally surrendered to the catalyst and let it make me strong. It took me four hundred seasons, but I finally controlled it and discovered its secrets. I realized then that the catalyst could make me every bit as powerful as they are," he said bitterly.

"You started the war with the provinces," Joshan said.

"Yes."

"Attacked the fledgling Assemblage."

"Yes."

"Organized the north. Killed Vanderlinden's mother."

"Yes, that was me, as well—a quiet whisper in Norsk's ear."

"Then why did you fail?"

Sirdar rested a hand on the mantel. "I underestimated Thoringale's passion and overestimated the ability of my humans." He stared back at the fire.

"After the defeat at Calisae, I left the north, realizing the northern people were simply not strong enough to defeat those who held the Crystal. I knew without the Crystal I could not win, so went to the south to regroup and start again." He looked up at Joshan. "I think you know that story, so I will not bore you with it."

"But you failed again," Joshan said coldly, quietly. "What happened thirty seasons ago in Badain?"

Sirdar stared at Trenara. "Again, I was brought down by a young thing with auburn hair and dazzling eyes.

"I thought the only way to activate the catalyst to its full potential was with a true piece of the Crystal. I knew where one was. I had seen it at work on the plains of Palimar. It had bested my champion." He smiled at Trenara. "Andelian."

"No." Trenara hugged her arms as she looked up at him.

"Yes," Sirdar replied quietly. "I know my own, my darling." He held up his devastated hands and crossed to her slowly.

"How you ended up with it, I am not entirely certain, but there were two vias missing from the original Crystal and Andelian was one of them." He glanced at Joshan. "Perhaps your boy here knows. In any event, I had Andelian in my grasp. I should have destroyed Vanderlinden and forced you to give it to me. I was weak. I threw it all away for a woman with beautiful eyes." He stopped in front of her chair and then reached down to lift her to her feet. "And now I have it back."

Sirdar grabbed her wrists and spun her around, pinning her hands to her chest with one scarred hand. Reaching into the front of her gown, he pulled Andelian from its hiding in her waistband, and then threw her back into the chair.

Trenara rubbed her wrists as Sirdar turned to pace before the fireplace.

"When the guiders came to destroy me, had I possession of this little trinket and the other missing via, it would never have happened. You see, there was one survivor. It was not, however, one of the guiders who came to destroy me. It was a guider who worked for me."

Trenara looked at him confused. "Balinar?"

Sirdar snorted a huff of derision. "You are joking, of course. No, as soon as Assemblage stepped onto the province, Balinar deserted me and went to hide with his brother in the north. No, not Balinar." He suddenly gazed at Ricilyn. "It was Saminee."

Ricilyn's mouth fell open and angry tears filled her eyes. "You are lying!" she screamed. "My father would never betray Assemblage!"

Sirdar crossed to her slowly, seeming to relish her anger, drinking in her fear. "What does your awareness tell you, Ricilyn," he said softly, kneeling down in front of her and touching her face. "You know what I am saying is true, my dear. Your father served me for many seasons. It was Saminee who stole the Crystal and brought it to me." He looked deeply into her ravished eyes. "And when the other guiders came, my dear, he helped destroy them. As a matter of fact, he killed two of them with his own hands."

Ricilyn screamed and buried her face in her hands. Joshan pushed himself between them. Sirdar stood laughing.

"Get away from her!" Joshan took a step toward Sirdar, the red light in his eyes now unmistakable.

Sirdar frowned at him and took a step back, doubt seeping into his cruelty.

"Now," Joshan said, "tell her the rest, Sirdar."

"You are perceptive, my boy. Remind me not to underestimate you.

"He is correct, my dear. It was Saminee who betrayed me," he said. "He used the Crystal to bring my mountain down and then returned it to Sanctum. He reconsidered, you see? He was a fool!"

"You could not corrupt him," Ricilyn whispered.

"He was corrupt or he would never have given me the stone. That never changed. He continued to do my bidding."

"You are lying," she said softly. "I can hear it in your voice."

"Saminee repented," Joshan whispered to her, touching her chin. "He never told anyone what he had done and he spent the rest of his life making up for that transgression. He never forgave himself and put every talent he had into you, to make you strong, to make you ready for what must be done. That is why he wanted you to be powerful, because you had to be."

"Touching," sneered Sirdar savagely. He twirled Andelian in his hands.

"Why are you telling me all this?" Joshan asked. "If it is true, you do not need us." Joshan knew there was something missing, some larger truth Sirdar was not sharing. "Or do you?"

Sirdar smiled back at him and tilted his head. "I believe my darling Nissa has come back."

They all turned to see the giant bird standing shyly at the door. Joshan's eyes blazed when he saw her and he crossed to her quickly. "I ordered you to stay away!"

"Do not blame her," Sirdar said. "You see, she has a weakness, as you all do. And now, I would like to show you yours."

At a signal from Sirdar, the sasaran undid Trenara's chain and then pulled her roughly from the chair. Sirdar pulled Ricilyn from hers and grabbed Trenara's hand.

"My dear?" he called to the Mourna.

Nissa stared down at Joshan as she opened her mouth. Her sweet seductive sound filled the chambers, making the women docile in Sirdar's hands. They obeyed him without protest.

"Just a precaution, my boy," he said. "I do not want them hurt and this will make things easier. Please, come with me and I will show you what you really want to see. I will show you the why of all of this."

His face was suddenly calm again, as if the catalyst did not stir in his blood. "I think it is time you knew the truth, Joshan, and it is appropriate that I show it to you. Please," he nodded toward the staircase and casually walked out of the room with the women on his arms.

Joshan did not follow at once, knowing they had come to the end of all the futures, knowing that what he did now would save or destroy them.

The little boy inside him cried out to run away; the man inside him ordered him to stay and fight; but the god inside him raged like a demon. The catalyst at last merged with the crystals on his palms turning them into a crimson fire and colored his eyes a bloody red. A sharp pain ran down his jaw, and when he touched beneath his ears, the pain went away. He could feel the delicate row on row of crystals as they grew along his jaw, down his neck and into his hairline. They glowed with red fire as well.

All around him, a black and red smoke gathered slowly, like building storm clouds, and he could feel the madness crawling up his spine and into his mind. A quiet awful laugh echoed in Sirdar's chambers and Joshan realized all it once it was his own voice. He followed Sirdar to face his future.

CHAPTER THIRTY-TWO
THE FINAL STAND

Sark and his scant troops stood on the field before the castle of Calisae, bloody and exhausted. They screamed up at the white wall from the frozen midnight plains. Black clouds moved in to cover the night and everything was as dark as pitch around them. The only light flickered fitfully from the few torches they dared to light.

At first, they had swept relentlessly over the enemy. Many had died on both sides. Although the weaponized catalyst took out hundreds during that first push, Sark's people were prepared and quickly pulled the improved catapults to the field. Volley after volley smashed into the unsuspecting rival soldiers, destroying most of the machines and hundreds of the daligon's troops. The arrow launchers killed hundreds more when they charged the field. The few of Sirdar's troops left after that assault quickly retreated into the protection of the great white fortress.

Now the imperial troops stood before the gate, their numbers depleted tragically. They gathered far enough away that the enemy troops soon abandoned feeble attempts to use the catalyst.

With a hand signal, Sark quieted his soldiers. He stood at the front, proud and straight, his eyes glaring hotly up at the gate screaming his challenge. It was two hours before dawn.

"Hear me, daligon!" Sark called, knowing the monster was listening. "Do you hide from me? Do you lack the courage to fight me eye to eye? Will you hide behind your wall, terrified a mere human will defeat you? Why use your cowardly poison to kill me when you could take my life with your bare hands? Show me you are not a coward that trembles in fear, daligon! Meet me here if you have the courage. I will show these people how easily you can be defeated and what a weakling you really are!"

There was a vicious response from the castle wall when thousands of Sirdar's troops bellowed in response. Their torches glimmered like daylight from the parapet. They could not see the shadow of the daligon, but Sark knew he was there. He could feel it as a deeply buried aching in his heart; the monster stood on the wall. Arrows and other projectiles came streaming down, but they all fell short. Sark brooded about how to break this impasse.

Exhausted, he had been at this for hours and was afraid they would have to storm the castle, losing many more soldiers and precious time if they had to siege. He had made a promise to Joshan and he would keep it. Thiels rode up and regarded the castle with him.

"It is not working," Sark said to him quietly, signaling to his aide. "The bait has to be better."

"What do you mean?"

Sark's small smile appeared strange in the torchlight as he removed his helm. "I intend to make the target more enticing."

As the other captains joined them, Sark whispered quietly to Thiels who nodded grimly. "I can do that, but how will I know when?" he asked.

"You will know when the time comes. In the interim, get the troops ready, commander." Sark loosened the catches on his armor, signaling the aide to help him. "If this does not work, you are in charge."

Sark removed his armor, sighing deeply. It had been slow torture having it cinched tightly around his ribs. He gave it to the aide, called for a torch, and then quickly removed his sword and belt.

"I've always liked that sword," he said as he handed it to Thiels. "Make sure it is put on the wall at Pap's, will you?"

"What the hell are you doing?"

Sark grabbed the blazing torch from the soldier.

"I am giving him a better target."

With a cry, Sark dug his heels into his eecha and charged toward the castle before Thiels could stop him.

"This is suicide. You know that, don't you?" Thiels screamed after him, shaking his head. "You will never survive this!"

"Just think what a great looking corpse I'll make," Sark called back, and then he disappeared quickly into the gloom.

"Crazy bastard," Thiels swore under his breath and signaled the captains to gather. A deafening roar went up from the fortress when the enemy realized what Sark was doing. Thiels gave out the general's last orders.

Sark drove his beast forward as quickly as he could, digging his heels deep into the sides of the eecha, miraculously dodging falling arrows, rocks, and spears thrown from the parapet. It took every skill he possessed to maneuver the animal through the rutted field and avoid the deadly projectiles that he could not see until they were almost on him. It seemed his luck was holding or the gods were with him, for nothing hit him on the way to the gate.

He pulled hard on his reins forcing the eecha to climb its hind legs and snort a complaint. Sark stopped so close to the gate, he could see the intricate iron details of the hinges, lighted only by the enemy torches above. Putting his arms out to the side, he howled with laughter.

"Is this better for you, daligon?" he shouted up at the wall. "I stand almost naked before you and still you fear me. Now will you come down?" Sark thanked his stars that no more arrows rained down, but the daligon had something else in mind.

"It is your master who is the coward, daligon! He leaves his mongrel to fight, staying far away to cower in fear. Perhaps he has abandoned you. I do not blame him. Your soldiers have burned, your people have died on the field like insects, and they fight worse than children. There is not an ounce of nerve among them. Your soldiers are no more than curs—stupid, weak, and spineless. Come out and fight me if you have the audacity."

In response, the enemy let up a deafening roar that reverberated over the plains and well passed the harbors behind the castle. So intent were the enemy hordes on the lone figure standing before them, they did not notice when the plains went dark.

Out of the noise from the wall echoed the unmistakable sound of one of the daligon's new weapons booming well over Sark's head. When he looked up, all he could see in the darkness was a great writhing mass of faint red mist as it charged like a fireball from the sky. All he had time to do was look up in surprise and realize his life was over.

All at once, the cloud of mist stopped. It floated in the air above Sark's head, doing an intricate, slow dance as it undulated in the night. He scowled at it in confusion. It swirled suspended and then spiraled up, like an upside down whirl of water. There it paused and was joined by huge masses of red catalyst as it funneled out of the castle from every opening. The combined mass, strangely lighted by the enemy torches, jetted suddenly to the west and disappeared in an instant.

For one breathless moment, a stunned silence emanated from the castle wall and every creature stared at the sky where the catalyst had been. Then murmurs and cries went up. Sark could hear shouts of panic and angry orders from the hordes.

In relief, he threw back his head and laughed. "Yes!"

When he looked up, the walls were deserted and the castle gates grated open. The enemy was coming out to meet Sark on the field.

The gate was only a few spans from where Sark's eecha stomped in the darkness. When the thick wooden beams thundered against the ground, a throng emerged. At its head was a huge sasaran riding a giant tarsian. There were hundreds of creatures behind the leader. They crossed the drawbridge intent on destroying the unarmed man. As they drew nearer, the light from their outstretched torches illuminated the night behind him. They realized all at once, he was not alone.

Behind Sark, having come forward in the darkness while he held their attention, were his remaining five thousand troops, with Thiels and the other captains shouting quick orders to strike.

As the provincial troops moved quickly passed them, Thiels flew to Sark's side with his sword and helm.

"You are one lucky bastard!" he said handing Sark his sword.

"I'm just glad you were back there." Sark threw the sword around his waist and donned his helmet, then kicked his eecha.

The imperials hit the line of surprised enemy troops so quickly many had no time to draw their swords.

Sark's soldiers made good progress at first, but the enemy numbers kept growing until Sark realized he had underestimated their reserves. From behind the castle and out of the woods on either side, poured thousands of troops. They were outnumbered at least ten to one and still more soldiers appeared.

Despite this, Sark and his army were making headway toward the castle as they fought through the hour. The catalyst was now gone and the enemy troops had to rely on conventional weapons, leaving the imperials with an advantage since they had the arrow launchers and improved catapults.

As Sark scanned the fighting, he suddenly saw off to his right an enemy soldier with no helm, although her head was shaven and she bore the slave tattoos of the daligon. His own troops were staying well away from her, knowing first that she was deadly and second, that she was the daughter of their general.

Tears of joy sparkled in Sark's eyes as he watched Sareh screaming in frustration when no one would fight her. He pulled up on his reins and swore under his breath. He would never be able to reach her. She stood next to the giant sasaran who led the troops from the castle. There were several hundred spans of distance and a multitude of fighting between her and Sark.

"You need to focus!" Thiels screamed at him as he cut down two laminia who had nearly reached Sark. "Let us win the battle and then we can help her!"

Sark nodded grimly, shouted to his troops, and dove into the fight. The enemy fell back.

Although they made their slow way forward, another menace loomed large from the castle wall. When Sark looked up from his eecha, he could see a great shadow rise and hover way above the melee. Seated on the back of a fully functioning flying tarsian lizard, the daligon rode to the attack.

The creature wasted no time in driving the lizard to devastate the imperial army. It killed as many of Sirdar's troops as it did the imperials, but the daligon seemed unmoved. Flames erupted repeatedly from the tarsian's mouth. It would burn as many as it could reach and then swoop with its immense claws to cut down any survivors.

Sark watched as hundreds died in agony from the tarsian's flames. He was about to give the call for retreat, when he looked back and realized they were surrounded on all sides. The enemy had outflanked them. There would be no retreat; they would have to fight this to the end.

Sark gripped his sword tightly and shouted to his troops. "Fight until there are none left standing! For freedom!"

A great roar rose from those who remained of the imperial troops. They redoubled their efforts and charged into the roiling mass of enemy. It was an hour before dawn.

CHAPTER THIRTY-THREE
TRANSFORMATION

When Joshan entered the chamber, Nissa had stopped abruptly at the glass casket and stared down at it. She looked almost frightened. Her voice faded and the women came out of the enchantment. They fought to get out of Sirdar's grasp. He called two sasaran guards and quickly handed the women to them.

"Take them up and secure them." He glanced back at Joshan and then whispered something into one of the guard's ear. The sasaran nodded his obedience and they forced the women to climb the spiraling staircase.

Sirdar crossed to the Mourna and caressed her head as she examined the lifeless figure, her eyes difficult to read.

"I told you, my dear," he whispered in her ear. "It is as I promised. Now it is time for you to change, to have the beauty and the life you have so desired, to take your place at my side." He ran his hands down her neck. Nissa shuddered when he whispered something into her ear Joshan could not hear. Tears of hate filled her eyes. She looked down at the woman before her and Sirdar smiled with satisfaction.

"I told you Nissa had a weakness." The bird flinched. "Her love for you is trivial and fleeting. The creature has no heart—nothing to make her in the least bit human anymore. This will complete her. Her soul belongs to me. I can give her something that you cannot; life and beauty." He smiled up at her angry face.

"Do not look at me so. I know you better than you know yourself. She is creature of horror, Joshan," he said quietly. "You have no idea what she has done, the atrocities she has committed with but a whisper from me, the innocence she has destroyed. Shall I tell him? Do you honestly think he could possibly love a monster like you?" He laughed cruelly and Nissa wept. "Shall I tell him about the children, the infants?"

"No!" She looked at Joshan pleadingly, but then bowed her head before Sirdar. "Please do not, master."

Sirdar lit his hands with red fire and ran them along the glass. Nissa watched as the clear substance melted under the flames, leaving the reclining figure real and warm in front of her. The eyes closed when Sirdar touched them and he lifted her porcelain-white hand to touch the bird's chest. Nissa gasped.

"It will be painful at first, but it will pass. When you awake you will be human again. You will then come to me, won't you?" She nodded reluctantly, wincing in pain. "For all you have done for me, Nissa, for all the seasons you have served me well. For all the eternal seasons you will continue to serve me," he finished with an ardent glare.

A cloud of crimson encircled both figures and Sirdar stepped away to stand next to Joshan. He watched for only a moment. Nissa screamed in pain, but did not move.

"Come," he said quietly, taking Joshan's arm. "This will take quite some time and there is something I need to show you above." He motioned to the staircase and Joshan reluctantly followed him.

As they climbed the stairs, Sirdar waved his hand and dome rotated. As it spun, it opened from the middle and disappeared into the wall around it on all sides, leaving the black sky and billions of stars that shone brilliantly above their heads. It was a moonless night.

When they reached the landing, Joshan saw that the floor was crystal, so pure that is was completely translucent. When they stepped out onto the platform, the hole where the stairs had been disappeared.

A delicate railing circled the platform, so intricate and clear it looked like a sculpture of ice. On the eastern side, a beautiful translucent bridge fell gracefully back to the temple roof. It looked as if a note could shatter it. At each compass point, north, east, south, and west was a tall, golden spire, thin and fine, that reached high above their heads to the sky. Tied to the north and south spires were Ricilyn and Trenara, struggling vainly to free themselves and shivering in the freezing wind. There was a tear in Ricilyn's shirt, exposing her side where a bloody scratch swelled. The sasaran standing before her held a slender rod in his hands while the other held Kerillian's staff.

Joshan scowled and tried to cross to her, but something emerged before him and he stopped.

In a ring that almost filled the circumference of the platform, a profound, bloody fire appeared. It became deep, wide, and spellbinding in front of Joshan's eyes, growing larger as wisps of catalyst circled in from the night, gathering to make the fire hotter, higher, and more alluring.

Before the circle completed itself, the two sasarans approached and bowed to their master. Sirdar took the offered wand and staff from them and then opened the entrance to the stairs to send the sasarans away. He then closed the hatch and turned to Joshan. The wind of the catalyst howled in the dark night. Red tendrils appeared from everywhere, filling the circle and coalescing into a liquid flame.

Sirdar held both crystal vias, Andelian and Crystara, up to Joshan and leered at him. "You knew she had the other original piece of the Crystal, didn't you?"

Joshan tightened his jaw. "How did you know?"

"I told you, I know my own. Balinar brought it to me from Sanctum and Saminee stole it along with the Crystal. I assumed he would have given it to his daughter."

"No!" Ricilyn cried.

"Yes, my dear," Sirdar called back to her, not letting Joshan out of his sight. "And your husband has known it since the beginning, along with many other things. He knew where the true via was—it was what brought him to Dru. You were simply an afterthought."

"Is that true?" Ricilyn asked Joshan.

He lifted those blazing red eyes to her.

"Yes, in part. I did know you had the true crystal. I saw it on Mathisma the first time I saw you. But that is not why I traveled to Dru."

"Semantics." Sirdar laughed. "Now, the final question—why?"

Joshan tried to take a step back, but something in Sirdar's eyes stopped him; a truth Joshan could see, and the answer he had wanted from that first day. It terrified him.

"Why?" The whispered words drifted through the wind. Sirdar gently touched Joshan's face and smiled.

Instead of answering, Sirdar opened his mouth. A single deep note erupted from his throat, beautiful, perfect, making Joshan's head explode with pain, and the women scream in agony.

The pull of that sound was stronger than anything Joshan had ever felt in his life. It held him forcefully in its embrace, as tightly as the Mourna's voice could hold a guider, allowing the catalyst to cascade into his eyes and seep into his mind. He fought to break away from the sound, desperately trying to lift his hands to dispel it. They hung traitorously at his sides, useless.

Joshan panicked at its touch. He opened his mouth to sing, to shout, to make any kind of noise to stop the forward progress of the entrapment, but his voice was mute and his throat closed on itself. He was helpless to stop it. Before he could respond, as the sound and the red fury consumed his will, he suddenly lost the fire in his eyes and stared out at the night with no more volition than a puppet. Slowly, he fell to his knees before Sirdar.

The music stopped when Sirdar chuckled down at him. As the catalyst swirled thickly around him, he casually reached down to the quiet figure and pulled the golden sword from its place, caressing the metal. He set the vias down and raised the sword to the staff, slicing it in two as if it were soft bread.

From out of the center of the staff fell a crystal sliver, no larger than a stylus, which he picked up along with the other two vias. In a quick movement, Sirdar closed his eyes and another note escaped his lips. He laid all three elements on top of the blade. There was a small explosion that shook the sword in Sirdar's hands. When the smoke cleared, the vias were gone and the sword contained three new jewels.

Sirdar looked down at the kneeling Joshan. "Raise your hands."

Joshan lifted the crystalline palms up. Sirdar laid the sword almost tenderly into the outstretched palms. Almost as a father would, Sirdar touched Joshan's face gently.

"It is time for you to complete your journey, my boy."

"What have you done to him?" Trenara screamed. "Let him go!"

Sirdar turned to the guider. "Are you only now beginning to understand?" he said, slowly crossing to her.

Trenara cast a frantic gaze at Joshan and then to Ricilyn. The young woman's head was now resting on her chest, unconscious.

"Do what you like to me, Sirdar, just do not hurt him, please," she pleaded.

Sirdar casually stepped through the fire without injury. Trenara could feel the heat of it, even from her far distance. She struggled to free her hands at her back, but it was useless. She could not escape.

Sirdar pressed his body close to hers and grabbed the back of her head. She could not move when he forced his lips to hers and ran his scarred hands over her neck and exposed shoulders.

"I am not going to hurt him, my dear," he said gently. "You need to understand finally, why he is here."

She pulled her face away.

"You sick bastard!" she screamed at him. "Why are you doing this?"

"Ah," he said, touching her face with the back of his hand. "There's the question." He looked a long time into her eyes, sending a wisp of catalyst to touch her lightly as he probed her mind.

Without warning, seasons of degradation and torture flashed through Trenara's head. Sirdar's mind probed her deeply, violently, reaching into the dark depth of his own insanity to show her his black inner soul. Dark perversions invaded her mind like poison. He made her confront his madness, presenting her with revelations of experience that any sane person would quickly reject. The visions, like the abominations in the viscous liquid, floated in his awareness, gruesome, twisted, and warped beyond her wildest imagination.

Trenara closed her eyes against the abuse and sobbed. "Get out of my head!"

He touched her face and the visions faded.

"Look at me!" he demanded and she had to open her eyes. "You are an intelligent woman. You begin to see the truth, don't you, Trenara?" He leaned in to whisper very quietly in her ear. "Joshan is one of my creatures."

"No!" she screamed, trying to escape his embrace, but he pushed his body harder into hers.

"Yes, Trenara, I created him. I needed a child with the strength of a man and the blood of a god. A child would be easier to control, you see. So, I stole his childhood taking him from you that night in the woods when he reached first trial." His eyes shone with such madness, Trenara trembled, more afraid of him now than she had ever been. There was no telling what he was capable of now that the fire consumed him.

"You were so lovely lying there asleep, in the rain. You remember it was raining, don't you? It was a pity to put you to sleep. I did not want you spoiling my plans. I should have slit your throat that night," he said casually running his hand over her throat. "But, as I said, you have always been my weakness.

"I brought him to the top of the cliffs and turned him into the man you see before you. I put the visions into his brain and I lured him here to complete the process.

"Very soon, his body and the crystals that they took from me will be mine again. You see, I know how to use them." He laughed quietly in her ear. "He and I will possess it all; the Crystal, the catalyst—everything. We will rule the universe, my dear. You and Ricilyn and Nissa will join us." He licked his lips. "Joshan and I will share you all."

Again, he pushed perverse thoughts through her mind without mercy and she screamed, suddenly realizing what he meant to do.

"With the power and the catalyst, we will become the most powerful being in the universes. We can get off this accursed planet and I can take my rightful place among the gods. I will give you immortality, my love, and we will spend it together."

Tears made muddy trails though the dirt on Trenara's face as she stared passed him at Joshan, trying to deny what he was saying. Joshan knelt there unmoving, staring into the sword, completely devoid of self-will.

Sirdar ran his hands lightly over her body and then stood away from her.

He crossed back through the fire and rolled up his shirtsleeves, revealing the grossly mangled scars on his arms. He then reached over and rolled up Joshan's sleeves as well, uncovering the beautiful gems as they glistened brightly on his arms and wrists. Kneeling before him, he touched the crystals very lightly and pulled in a shaky breath.

Sirdar pulled the sword from Joshan's hands and set the tip against the crystal beneath it. Sparks spewed like a fountain when they met. The blade hung suspended between the two men. Sirdar took Joshan's hands and wrapped them around the naked blade, squeezing them until blood flowed from his palms. Amber and black light radiated from the blade in giant currents, like ripples in water. Sirdar finally wrapped his own hands around the blade beneath Joshan's and more blood spilled. The golden sword turned crimson in the sudden light from the power.

"Listen to my voice, Joshan. Do exactly as I tell you," Sirdar said with such force, the light vibrated and the spires hummed. "Let the power take you, let it touch you, let it complete you and we will be joined in your body." His eyes grew in color and size as he looked at Joshan.

"Sing for me! Let me hear that glorious voice. Make the power dance for you. Bend it to your will, Joshan. This is your purpose. This is why I created you. Open your soul and let me enter so we can rule the universe together. In this way, we will both be strong. Sing for me!"

Trenara screamed at Joshan, trying to get him to stop, but he could not hear her. He lifted his chin to the stars and opened his mouth to let a note fall into the darkness like a sun. It was a brilliant tone. Trenara's heart stopped for a moment, lost in the sound.

As the note climbed to the heavens, another voice joined his and doubled that sound as if it were one voice. The catalyst fell from the circle into the sword that now lay gleaming between the two men, filling it up, turning it black. The red vapors poured out of Joshan's mouth, his hands, and every pore of his body. Catalyst bled from Sirdar. His eyes got wider with pain and it all poured into the sword unabated, unchecked, until the blade gleamed so brightly it was as if a red sun stood on the platform.

Just as the crescendo radiated to the sky, for a brief moment Sirdar was himself again and deep tears flew from his eyes propelled by the furious wind of the power. He watched in amazement as the sword filled. He concentrated and began his invasion, the thing he had planned for, his salvation, and he finally realized it as he dominated Joshan's mind.

But it was, after all, a mortal woman who betrayed Sirdar in the end, as had been his fate from the very beginning—as had always been his fate.

She loomed up behind him as he forced Joshan to surrender his soul. Sirdar was, for the first time in his existence, mortal. He had poured his immortality, his history, his powers into Joshan and would have easily stepped into his shell.

Nissa stepped up behind Sirdar and slowly, almost tenderly embraced him with two taloned claws. They sank deeply into his mortal flesh, bloodying the ground and spraying the clear crystal with a spin of red. It surged out of his outstretched body.

Nissa gazed with gentle eyes at Joshan as she squeezed the lifeblood out of his enemy. She sacrificed her dream of humanity for the dream of freedom. The monster would never rule her again.

Joshan became instantly aware of his surroundings. Sirdar's eyes were masks of pain. Without hesitation, as if the motion were an instinctual first breath, Joshan seized the sword and ran it to the hilt through Sirdar's heart. Nissa screamed in pain. The sword sank through Sirdar's flesh and then buried itself in the Mourna's heart. The god's eyes closed and the catalyst fell out of him in a torrent that engulfed Joshan, forcing its way uncontrollably back into his body.

Sirdar's consciousness was gone—the monster was dead.

The power burned Nissa quickly, her wings a blazing mantle of fire. They stretched behind her, the feathers curling and popping loudly in the night as she flew away from Joshan. She made it no further than the edge of the platform.

When Joshan's eyes fully cleared, when the catalyst finished its deadly possession, when the black sword sat on his knees and the power fell away, the last thing he saw of his beautiful friend, were those almost human eyes filled with grateful tears. She stepped back in a graceful dance. The dead body of Sirdar clenched tightly in her grasp, Nissa broke through the delicate crystal railing to fall into oblivion down the endless chasm that surrounded the temple.

As she succumbed to death, she smiled sweetly, her wish at last fulfilled.

CHAPTER THIRTY-FOUR
THE SHIPS

The tarsian was almost on them as Sark and Thiels fought against the multitudes pressing in. All around were the remnants of the imperial army, back to back, the cold air steaming from their mouths and sweat freezing on their faces. The daligon shadow clinging to the flying lizard diving from the heavens seemed frantic to reach the two men who straddled bloodied eechas.

There was little time left. The imperials squeezed tightly into the center of the advancing army. Dawn was only moments away, but Sark knew none of them would see it. He cut down yet another of the sasarans, his hands numbing from the weight of his sword and his eyes blinded by blood dripping from a wound on his forehead. The tarsian with the shadow on its back was nearly on them.

In an instant, the enemy troops that had surrounded the two standing captains pushed the imperial troops back. Sark and Thiels stood in a circle of blood, the ghastly torchlight illuminating their panting mounts. The general and the commander looked around madly searching for an escape. They lifted their eyes to the darkness and saw a blazing fireball of flying death falling toward them. As one, they lifted their fragile shields to stay the heat of the beast's deadly breath. The poor eechas they rode put up a valiant fight, before being roasted out from underneath them.

Both men slid off their rearing animals and fell with a thud onto the muddy ground. Instinctively, they huddled together at the center of the clearing, their blackened shields a delicate membrane of fragile metal briefly saving them from death as their soldiers fought urgently to reach them.

As the shadow of the daligon rose up on the diving beast, now so close to them they could hear the rustle of the leathery wings, from out of nowhere, a single flash sparkled to the lizard's right. Caught by the sudden movement, it turned its head slightly scorching the daligon's own troops holding the imperials back. The indiscriminate flames burned both friend and foe.

Lit now like a blazing torch, the flash became a single gigantic arrow that flew through the darkness so quickly it was a blur of wood and feathers. It moved with such force it pieced the tarsian's eye, went through its brain as if it were molten, and came out the other side of its skull sending bloody shards of bone into the daligon on its back.

The creature had no time to scream. It crashed into the earth on the other side of Thiels and Sark, covering them with dirt as it plowed through the earth. It left a trench many spans wide and killed several of the daligon's troops, impaling them on the splayed iron clad claws.

When it finally stopped against a mound of earth the daligon flew through the air and landed several hundred spans away from the two standing captains.

When the shadow rose, furious at the death of his mount, a sound suddenly stopped him. The bray of triumphant singing voices and the cry of hundreds of soldiers in unison screamed Trillone! Trillone! Trillone! For the first time in his millions of seasons of existence, the daligon trembled.

It turned to confront the source of the sound. Fifty ships slammed against the docks one after the other and countless troops poured from their bows.

The Trillone had landed at Calisae. Like insects, they became a massive swarm that poured into the daligon's army, killing so quickly and so many it was as if a great wave of death ebbed from the ships.

There standing at the top of the mast of the lead ship was a giant of a man with an immense bow still singing in his hands.

Vanderlinden looked out at the daligon and laughed as he slid down the mainmast in one fluid motion and bounded across his beautiful Morning Star in three steps. He rode the lines to land on the deck and pulled his sword. With a battle cry that grated against the monster's ears the giant led his troops to charge.

It was not a fight at all—it was a slaughter. The catalyst now gone, the human enemy had fled the field and only Sirdar's creatures remained.

The Trillone were masters of demise. For the first time in their existence they displayed the exact precision of their deadly craft, the product of a thousand seasons of endless training all culminated in this one devastating annihilation.

Men, women and even children, some no older than ten seasons, killed with no more than a touch, with merely their bare hands. There was little blood. They flooded over the enemy overwhelming them so easily even Sirdar's best had no chance. The exhausted imperial troops could only watch and stay out of the way, astonished beyond measure at the skills and fatal exactness of these fighters.

In one final act of desperation, the daligon turned from the advancing Trillone and charged toward the figures of Sark and Thiels. Bringing himself up to his full measure, he flew suspended above the air. The two men had no time.

Just as the shadow loomed above them, a piecing battle cry echoed across the field. A great fishing net sailed over the two men's heads. The net fell squarely over the massive shadow in an instant. Weighted all along the edge, the net twisted around the swirling shadow until it completely disappeared into the cloud.

A screaming figure appeared with a spear in her hands. Sareh charged into the shadow and disappeared into its darkness.

"Sareh!" Sark tried to follow her, but an immense hand on his shoulder held him back.

"Wait!" Van had appeared as if by magic out of the pre-dawn.

Pushing Sark back, Van grappled the shield out of the mercenary's hands and ran toward the now swirling shadow. He lifted the shield well above his head and then drove it with one swift movement to bury it several inches into the ground. When

Sark looked, he saw the bundled edge of the net trapped under the shield. A great force tried to pull it free. The net did not budge.

Another cry went up and a terrible rending crunch echoed around them, followed by an ear-splitting shriek. Everyone close by covered their ears.

A strong wind blew around them, a great maelstrom of air tugging at their clothes and weapons. The last of the enemy lay dead at their feet. The wind settled around the shadow surrounding the daligon and pulled it into a whirl that quickly disappeared into the lightening sky above their heads.

What remained when the smoke cleared was Sareh with a dripping spear in her hand, her head bent as she stood over a feeble black creature squeezed tightly in the net anchored by the shield into the ground.

The thing was tiny, no taller than Sareh's waist, mortally wounded. It lifted what must have been its head, a mass of blackness, and opened a hole that served as its mouth to let out a frail moan. Sareh gave the creature a glance of pity, and then casually put her spear through it one more time. The thing died with a shudder. Sareh fell to her knees and wept.

Sark rushed to his daughter and swept her up into his arms. The sun broke over the horizon sending its first wave of rays onto the battlefield. Any enemy that remained alive screamed briefly in agony and then in an ear-splitting rumble, dissolved almost instantly. The dusty remains spun into a blackened fog that hid the imperial troops and the Trillone warriors. When a sweet morning breeze flowed from the east, the fog vanished into the reddened sky, leaving the humans on the bloody field of victory—alone. The enemy was gone.

CHAPTER THIRTY-FIVE
THE GOD

Joshan's eyes blazed. There were no pupils or irises, only the pulsating glow of crimson. He rose and surveyed the carnage where Sirdar had been. There was blood everywhere. It looked as if Joshan had bathed in it.

He threw back his head, laughing hysterically as if he could not contain the sound.

It frightened Trenara. It was loud, echoing, startling in its insanity, almost musical as it rolled out of his throat and reverberated across the valley—stronger than anything Sirdar had done. The guider trembled uncontrollably when Joshan lifted his arms to the heavens and let the laughter take him.

Just as quickly as it had come, it stopped and Joshan crossed to Ricilyn. "Do not be frightened, Trenara." The whisper of his voice reached so deeply inside her, it was almost a violation. Pricks of fear raced up her spine. "Wake up, Ricilyn."

Ricilyn's eyelids fluttered. He ran his hands over her body and the bindings disappeared. She floated into his arms and he kissed her deeply. "Are you all right?"

"Yes, my love." She touched his face as tears streaked her face. "I thought he had killed you."

He set her down and crossed to Trenara. Once the bindings were loose, he caught her as she fell from the spire and held her tightly. "Say nothing," he hissed into her ear when he set her down.

Joshan caught Ricilyn in his arms and twirled her around, his face exuberant in joy. Then Trenara heard it, the sound of drums bouncing off the roof of the temple and over the bridge. Just at that moment, they all heard the flutter of wings and Fiena appeared out of the heavens to land on the roof.

Ricilyn looked at her friend and smiled. "Fiena!" When she tried to cross, Joshan took her face in his hands and looked deeply into her eyes.

"You are to take Fiena and fly to Calisae as quickly as you can. Do not stop for anything. We will meet you there later."

Ricilyn's brow furrowed. "We? I do not understand..."

"Look at me." He forced her eyes back to his. "You are to fly with Fiena to Calisae and wait for me. Obey me." His voice deepened as the drums grew louder. Ricilyn's face became docile.

He swept her up to set her on top of Fiena. Ricilyn nodded back at him. He smacked the bird on the back and she screamed as she jumped into the air. "Fly, Fiena—as quickly as you can." The bird let out another shriek and took to the air.

They disappeared into the heavens as hundreds of arrows came showering down from over the bridge.

"Joshan!" Trenara screamed.

He lifted his hand and the arrows fell to the ground. "Do not worry, Trenara," he said, touching her face. "I will not let anything happen to you."

"Yes... well." She took a step away from him and brushed the auburn hair out of her eyes then rubbed her hands together as she crossed to the center of the platform.

"You are frightened of me."

"Yes."

Trenara moved around the platform, looking for a way off. Down below the crystal floor she could see several darkened shadows trying without success to break through the closed entrance. Across the extended bridge, hundreds of sasarans were making their way over the long span, crouching low as they advanced.

Without taking his eyes off her, Joshan lifted his hand and in a thundering blast, the bridge exploded into a million shards sending screaming sasarans and humans to their deaths down the endless cliffs.

"You should not be afraid of me, Trenara," Joshan said, his eyes flashing.

When she glanced up at Joshan, his face had not changed. "Right," she said doubtfully.

"You have to know I would never hurt you," he said softly, crossing to her. She took a step back.

"You already have hurt me."

"That was not me, Trenara. That was the..."

"The catalyst?" She searched his face. "You should see your eyes. There is nothing there but the catalyst now. I can hear it in the timbre of your voice; feel it in the waves of heat coming off your body. It exudes from you like a disease when you speak of trust. This is what I see now. Not the child or the man I used to love, but this other creature, this extension of Sirdar, this—god. And yes, you frighten me."

There was a sudden loud pounding against the crystal floor. Joshan's eyes flared dangerously and his hands became fists. A surge of power unlike anything Trenara had seen before fell away from Joshan in a great translucent wave. It knocked her from her feet and rippled through the air to encompass everything for many leagues in all directions.

In one instant every sentient creature touched by that wave burst into flames whether friend, foe, human, or creation. The screams of the living souls echoed against the air and Trenara sobbed in the night, holding her ears to rid the sound from her head—a sound that would haunt her the rest of her life.

When it died down, she struggled to her feet and stared out at the roof of the temple. Every living creature was a charred lump of flesh as far as her eyes could see. She trembled.

"How many?" she whispered, more to herself than to Joshan.

"All of them, I think," he said quietly at her back, making her jump and whirl on him.

"What?"

"I am sorry, Trenara. You need to understand… they do not matter."

"They do not matter? Are you insane?"

"They are enemies. I did what I had to."

"How many?" she demanded, not even sure she wanted to know.

He looked down at her and brushed a wayward auburn hair from her forehead. "You should not bother yourself with trivialities, guider."

"How many?" she grated through her teeth.

He flashed an angry look at her and she stepped away. "All that fought us."

"Just—just here?"

"No," he said without looking away. "Everywhere."

Trenara swallowed hard for the first time realizing the extent of his power. "Humans, too?"

"Yes," he replied without apology.

She could not speak for a moment. Her eyes brimmed with tears and she stepped back into the railing. "You have killed thousands of sentient beings—you have killed them all?!" She raised her hands to strike him. Joshan pressed her into the railing and took her wrists easily into his hands.

As he stared down into her eyes, she realized for the first time her danger and the danger for her world. He was immeasurably more powerful than Sirdar could ever have been.

"You must trust me, Trenara," he said. "Those people would have ruined us later. I had to destroy them. It is naïve to think otherwise. I know with certainty that those people would have banded together in twenty seasons and attacked the provinces again. I have seen it."

"You are insane," she whispered, trying without success to escape his vise-like grasp.

"No, Trenara," he said calmly. "The crystals in my hands will not let the catalyst rule me as it did Sirdar. Had they allowed him to keep his crystals, he would have been a blessing to this world, not a curse. The catalyst and the torture by the daligon drove him mad and he had no chance. That will not happen to me. You see, I have you to guide me, to keep me from making the same mistakes."

"I doubt my ability extends to gods."

Joshan threw back his head and laughed, the peels sounding almost normal for the first time in so many days Trenara had almost forgotten the sound. He took her in his arms again and squeezed her tightly.

The guider managed to break from him. "Why did you send Ricilyn away?"

"I need to tell you what I have become and what the future holds for all of us."

"I know what you have become, Joshan," she said pensively. "You have become a god like Sirdar—like his kind."

"No," he replied simply. "I am so different from them. It is as if they are no more powerful than—humans." He said it with such contempt a chill went up Trenara's back. "There is so much I can accomplish with these new abilities," he continued, looking at the crystals in his hands. "You have no idea…"

A strange light glowed in his eyes, so dark, the red was almost indiscernible. "It is time for you to relax, Trenara."

"What does that mean?"

The red flowed beautifully in his eyes and she could not look away. "It is time for you to stop fighting me, to stop fighting the inevitable. It is time for you to spend the rest of your life making your husband happy and bringing up the next Empress."

With a jolt, she focused in on what he was saying. "Van?"

A spark of hope kindled in her heart. "He is dead. The fight in the Keep…"

"An illusion. It was Porphont you saw me fight."

"Is he…?"

"He is fine. The heart I gave Sirdar must have come from one of the healers. It was in Porphont's hand. I imagine Grandor planned the whole thing. All I did was add a bit of flare."

The relief was overwhelming, but it did nothing to stop the fear still gripping Trenara's heart as he pulled her closer.

He turned her around and showed her the endless mountains that drifted to the horizon. "This is your world, Trenara. I leave it to you, Van, and your child to watch for me."

She could feel his lips vibrate on her ear as he hissed the words.

"You have fought so hard for so long, it is time to forget doubt. Let yourself be free, at peace."

"I do not understand you…"

"You do," he said, touching her face. The touch sent a wave of tranquility through her and she gasped. "You need to let go and trust me. You need to take that lingering doubt and abandon it. I know you think I am a monster, a mirror of my father…"

"No, Joshan, I…"

"Yes. Even now, you are conjuring your next lie to put me off, to convince me you trust me, when you do not. You need to hear me and understand this; it is time for you to let that go forever."

"You commanded me to doubt and to question, remember?

Joshan laughed quietly in her ear. "And now I am commanding you to stop."

"You could… make me, like you did Ricilyn…"

"Yes, I could."

"Then, why…"

Joshan wrapped his arms around her. "Then, why?"

Trenara gasped and tears came into her eyes. "Because then I would not be free…"

"Yes, I want you free—completely free…" Joshan turned her around. "I am not Sirdar. I will never trick you. I will never lie. I will never hurt you again. I truly, desperately want you free and at peace." He took her shoulders and pulled her into his arms.

"In one thing Sirdar was right; you are a singularly incredible human being, more powerful than any in this or other worlds. There is a spirit in you that speaks to us all, a reality that reaches deep into our souls and makes us both question and revel in our existence. Yet you yourself have never seen it. You have fought from the very beginning for all of us and died a little every day. I want more than anything to finally give you happiness."

He held her at arm's length and his eyes were no longer red, but black and opalescent. It was Joshan she was seeing, if only briefly.

"No matter what happens in the next few hours, remember that," he said urgently, as if there were no time. "Remember also that I love you. No matter what it may cost, you must be my salvation. Will you remember that?"

For the first time in months, she could finally believe him, at least about this. "Yes," she said simply.

"Good." He smiled at her, but as she watched, his eyes turned a bloody red and the smile became a passionate fire. "When it is over, we will rule together."

Those words turned her blood to ice. She suddenly realized how very precarious her position had become. Just as the guider had saved this child from insanity when he came to power that eternity ago, now she would have to save the world from an even more devastating lunacy. Joshan was already so far gone. He would never return except for fleeting glimpses like the one she just saw. These would dwindle. Trenara knew she had to destroy this creature.

"If you are ready, I think we can get you back to where you were before all of this started."

Without waiting for a reply, he lifted his hand and ran it down her body. In a swirl of red power her youth disappeared replaced by the more familiar façade she was used to. It was small consolation, but it felt good to get back to her old self. In a twinkling, the flimsy dress she had on turned into her comfortable robe and she was again back to normal, even if the situation was not.

"Thank you," she said.

"It is time to go." Joshan pushed the black sword into its scabbard and took her hand.

CHAPTER THIRTY-SIX
THE SACRIFICE

The ground disappeared beneath Trenara's feet. The sensation was as if someone had tied a rope around her waist and pulled it hard. What happened next was so unreal, she was never certain it actually happened.

At first, all she could feel were Joshan's strong arms around her waist holding her warmly. Her head rested on his chest and she listened to the beating of his heart.

There was nothing around them except absolute blackness—she could not even see her hands in front of her eyes. Then out of the darkness, a blurring of lights, incredible pinpoints of brilliance, millions of them. They clarified into suns.

Unlike the stars of the night sky, these were strange and close, the blackness between them so absolute it was as if they were surfacing through ink.

Colors appeared all around them in great sweeping clouds; reds, blues, and brightest whites with frantic stars peering out at them from inside. Out of the vast darkness, a great blue sphere grew until it filled the sky.

Trenara had to close her eyes as they fell and the wind whipped around them blowing her hair into a storm. Just as quickly, they stopped and there was a hush around them.

When Trenara opened her eyes, the first thing she saw was Vanderlinden. Her heart almost stopped. Joy poured into her, sending pricks of scintillation through every inch of her skin.

She and Joshan stood on the highest tier of the platform at the heart of Calisae. Standing all around them in the great white hall were soldiers of the imperial army. Most froze where they stood. They had been tearing down the darkened tattered curtains to let the sun through the high windows, but now stared up at the two in wonder. Joshan and Trenara appeared out of nowhere and the red and black glow that now shone from Joshan like a torch made all of them step back.

Trenara broke from Joshan and ran down the stairs to Vanderlinden's arms. Not believing her eyes, she inspected him thoroughly to make sure he was not an illusion.

Van gazed at Joshan suspiciously, but there was awe in his face as well. Just at that moment, Fiena flew into the room and deposited Ricilyn on the dais, then flew away without missing a beat.

Sark and Thiels made their way to the front of the crowd and joined Van and Trenara. They turned to Joshan when he stepped to the large blackened hole where the catalyst had been and shook his head. When he finally looked up at the crowd, the glow around him was now a flame and they could barely see him.

"Forgive me." Joshan's voice echoed through every corner of the immense chamber, making the pillars shake and the windows rattle.

He threw back his head and breathed deeply. The power faded and they could make out his form inside the red light. The crystals on his arms and face sparkled like the trillion stars Trenara had seen in the heavens, but now they ran down his neck and disappeared under the crimson robe. The stones saturated his hands; you could no longer make out the flesh beneath them.

Like drifting water, his hair and robes flowed around him even though there was no wind. A red mist appeared like a thundercloud above his head and he glanced up at it with a magnificent smile on his face. His eyes became brilliant and expanded to twice the size they had been. All gasped at the beauty of the creature standing before them.

"Forgive me," he said again, his voice now quiet and exquisite.

The music in it was unmistakable. There were no more spoken elements in that magnificence as it made everyone it touched peaceful and happy.

"I did not mean to frighten you. I am so proud of what you have accomplished here. You have destroyed an evil that will not come back," he said, looking straight into Sarah's eyes as she joined her father. "You have withstood adversity, pain, and loss to make my reign possible. No one, not even the other gods, will be able to move us. We will conquer the universe together!" There was such a thunderous cheer from the crowd that it would have been heard for several hundred leagues in all directions—had anyone been alive to hear it.

"Vanderlinden and Trenara will rule here in my stead as we take our war to the stars. We will destroy all who oppose us. You will become my warriors, my soldiers, as we take our holy march to the other worlds where they will join us. Yours will be a glorious life and you will receive riches beyond your wildest imaginations. You have but to fight for me and bow before my command."

Such was the power of his words, so magnificent and persuasive were the emanations that flowed unabated from his hands, that the ripple of power flowed like honey from the platform and touched every soul in the room. They filled with boundless joy.

Every man, woman, and child went immediately to their knees before Joshan, bowing low to the ground, crying in worship. The room became a sea of backs and bowed heads. The smile of beneficence on Joshan's face shone like a mad flame that radiated through the room, painting everything it touched red.

In that sea of prostrate worshippers, standing tall and erect at the foot of the dais stood Trenara.

Her face was as cold as ice and her jaw set with such strength of will, those bowing beneath her trembled in fear. A deafening silence burned the room of sound as the two regarded one another. With a small flick of his finger, Joshan pulled back the red power and everyone was completely still. Van, Sark, Thiels, and Sareh could not move to help her had they the will to try.

"How dare you? You will bow to me." His voice snaked out like a whip and Trenara flinched.

"I will not! I am done with gods and demons. We are free men and women here. We have no need of gods anymore."

"You will destroy everything I have planned—the world I wanted for you—for all of you…"

"We do not want that world. You do not want that world. I know it as I know you. Despite your power, your knowledge, you are still a child… desperate, angry, and so terribly frightened. You are so afraid you will make a mistake, do the wrong thing, as we all are. Don't you understand? You do not need to be a god, Joshan. You only need to be a little stronger—a little less afraid…"

The anger in his eyes was all consuming as he lifted his sword.

"I am not afraid of you!" he screamed, his voice now so much like Sirdar's it made her take a step back. In a flash, she saw that horrible black and red sword lifting high above Joshan's head and twirling toward her. All Trenara could do was close her eyes.

But the point of the blade did not come. When Trenara opened her eyes, the vision before her forced an ear-piercing scream from her lungs.

Ricilyn was on the stair before Joshan with the black blade protruding from her back. She had thrown herself between them and taken the full brunt of his thrust through her womb. The two of them were standing in front of Trenara, frozen, face to face with the sword now buried in her belly.

Joshan's mouth and eyes opened wide in terror as he watched his wife and child die on his sword. As if in slow motion, Ricilyn glanced down at the sword hilt as it rested on her belly and then up into her husband's eyes. A slight smile dusted her lips. She touched Joshan's cheek tenderly.

"I always thought it would hurt," she whispered, "but it doesn't really. The visions were so clear. I never thought I could do it, that there was anything worth my life. I was wrong." She winced slightly and sighed. "I only regret having to leave you, my love."

Joshan immediately pulled the sword out of her belly and threw it toward the pit where it landed with a clatter against the stone. He swept her into his arms and held her so tightly the blood flowed like a fountain from her back.

"No, no, no, no!" he screamed over and over again.

"I love you," she whispered in his ear as she died.

Joshan staggered back from the edge of the dais with Ricilyn in his arms and for the first time, the red left his eyes. His face was awash with grief and guilt. There was a terrible moment when he stared at Trenara.

She knew what he meant to do.

"No!" she screamed and rushed toward him. It was too late.

Joshan swept up the sword from the floor. As gently as rain, he fell backwards into the bottomless pit, the lifeless body of his wife and unborn son clutched in his arms, and the blackened affliction that was the Crystal of Healing dangling from his crystalline hand.

Vanderlinden barely caught Trenara before she could follow him and pulled her with all his might away from the edge of destruction.

A sudden roar rose from the very bowels of the earth. It thundered and rocked the floor beneath their feet, knocking everyone to the ground. Following the deafening roar was a rumbling fireball that exploded out of the pit. It destroyed the platform in an instant and opened a gigantic hole in the ceiling of the castle.

Shards of marble fell on the spectators below, wounding many. Van pulled Trenara well away from the platform and miraculously the explosion hurt neither of them.

The astonished crowd watched as the fire bolt shot from the castle and continued to the bright blue sky until it disappeared into the heavens.

Many seconds passed as people picked themselves up from the floor and aided the wounded.

Sark helped a shaking Vanderlinden to his feet as he held Trenara weeping in his arms.

Just as the soldiers got their bearings, another earsplitting thunder shook the castle sending more marble down on their heads. When they looked up through the hole in the ceiling, they were amazed at what they saw.

The sky was on fire.

Millions of fragments of crystal burned above the world. For one beautiful, brilliant moment, the sky lit up in a spectacular show of colorful lights. The flames moved across the world, from far distant Mathisma where they were rising to sweep the debris from their homes, to Dru, where loved ones left behind were starting a quick breakfast, through the provinces, the northlands, and into the west.

The lights blazed in the heavens for a full six minutes as humanity watched the shield fall from their world, freeing it for the first time in three thousand seasons.

When the brilliance passed, the next spectacle was even more breathtaking. The sky turned from the pale blue they had always known to the deepest royal blue.

In a heartbeat, the sun flared from pale yellow to a brilliant gold, bringing out colors they had never even imagined. Crops quadrupled that season and rains came early filling the parched lands of the south to heal it. The Imperium would remain changed forever.

CHAPTER THIRTY-SEVEN
THE GODDESS

Van, Sark, and Thiels rushed the people out of the castle as the building crumbled under its own weight. They dispensed help quickly to the wounded.

The three looked over Trenara with the most concern. Van carried her out of the building and tried to talk to her, but nothing seemed to get through to her. She stared unseeing and unmoving into the morning.

A caravan approached the field from the west and Thiels jumped to his feet to run to his eecha. Without another word, he disappeared in a spray of mud to meet it.

Sark stared after him and shook his head, laughing when he saw the flag flying above the procession. He ordered his crew to finish the makeshift pavilion and other tents for the soldiers and wounded.

"Trenara." Van set her on a bench under the canopy and took her into his arms. "It was not your fault. Don't leave me, my love—not like this. Come back to me." He held her tightly, tears streaming down his face.

"I… I am all right, Van," she whispered softly. He held her out by her shoulders and searched her face. "I am all right."

"Thank the gods!" He took her in his arms again where she cried deeply. For the first time in many months, Trenara let the grief wash over her and she wept without stopping as Van held her.

When the caravan reached the camp, Saldorian and Thiels tentatively approached the couple with Porphont, Ena, and Grandor coming quietly behind them. Van motioned them to come in and leaned Trenara back to kiss her gently on the forehead.

When she glanced up at the others, she could see her own grief etched in their faces. They were quiet for a long time, each weeping, as they needed.

Trenara finally left her husband's embrace. A soft calm pressed against her swollen eyes. In wonder, she realized something was coming. She could feel it in her shoulder blades and as an electric shock that spilled down her arms. The well-known kiss of Ethos flooded her awareness, stronger than it had ever been before. Her mind reeled with the implications.

She thought the gods were dead—killed from her belief at the hands of Joshan's betrayal and their abandonment after the battle on the field at Mathisma. Trenara had not felt them since then and thought they had died with the Crystal.

Without saying a word, she wandered out of the pavilion.

"Trenara?" Van called after her.

She stepped into the mocking sunlight and regarded the new bright sky, Van and the others following her.

As Trenara stepped onto the bloody field, she saw crews burning what little remained of the countless bodies of their enemies and burying the bodies of their friends. Hundreds of tents sheltered the countless wounded. She ignored it entirely and made her way to the castle with the broken roof that loomed over the field.

The drawbridge hung loosely on ancient rusted chains, so huge that the maw of blackness dwarfed her small form. She stopped expectantly before the entrance and lifted her eyes to take in the crumbling structure. Van joined her and saw the look of ecstasy on her face.

"What is it?" he asked as the others joined them.

"Wait," was all she said.

Taking a step toward the castle, Trenara slowly closed her eyes and lowered her chin until it almost touched her chest. When she raised her arms from her sides, palms out, people gathered. Van, as always, stood like a giant monolith directly behind her, protecting her as he had always done—loving her unconditionally. He would never leave her again. Then Saldorian and Thiels, standing close to one another, touching, yet not touching, their love shining from their tired faces as they shared a surreptitious glance. Porphont had Ena in his arms, smiling up at the great white building seeing for them both. The girl became their voice and softly sighed in wonder. Grandor looked kind and confused at their side. Sark and Sareh limped up slowly, each a whisper of their former self, thin, tired, and grateful it was over. The tattoos on Sareh's face would always be with her, a badge of her courage and strength. They would always be with Sark as well, a scar on his soul. Behind them, all those who could, gathered to watch.

Trenara lifted her chin with the grace of a cloud and a single clear, perfect note flowed from her throat. It started as a whisper, and then grew stronger as the seconds went by until it resounded like a clap of thunder. Every ear rang with that beautiful sound.

A flickering mirage appeared on the drawbridge as they watched. Within that shimmer, two tall, graceful figures emerged. As the note faded, Trenara's breath unable to sustain it any longer, the shadows solidified until they stood clear and real in the morning sunlight.

The woman was very tall, nearly as tall as Vanderlinden and her eyes were the first thing everyone saw. They were large, perhaps half again as large as their own, in the deepest, darkest violet with specks of yellow-gold. Her hair cascaded over her shimmering translucent gown in great billowing clouds of gold and silver ending finally at the small of her thin waist. Her hands were long-fingered and refined as they folded together and her face was a glorious splendor. Beside her stood a man who was her antithesis. He stood a head above her, his skin dark, with pitch-black hair and eyes to match. He was also willowy and his golden garments shone with their own inward glow. He was so much like Joshan in face and manner it astounded Trenara.

Then, from behind them, another shimmer started, this time glowing whitely as the man and woman parted, letting it complete its course.

Great tears of joy erupted from Trenara's eyes and a brilliant smile flooded her face when she saw who stepped from that light. Joshan seemed small and frail next to the giants standing before him, with Ricilyn at his side and a small, timid child peeking out from behind her skirt—a child who tugged at Trenara's heart, he was so beautiful.

Joshan and Ricilyn seemed to be waking from a long sleep. They blinked first around themselves and then at the gods standing on the platform. Unbelieving, Joshan took Ricilyn into his arms. He lifted her up and kissed her face again and again. When he finally set her down, his eyes fell on the child. Seeing his son for the first time, Joshan fell to his knees and touched the boy's face in disbelief. The child was perhaps three with his father's deep, black eyes. His hair was the color of his mother's, rich earth brown that curled in gentle wisps around a perfect little face. He gathered both Ricilyn and the child into his arms and closed his eyes.

"How… how have you done this?" Trenara whispered, afraid to move forward, afraid to stand back. She wanted nothing more than to hold Joshan, Ricilyn, and the child; but she was afraid this was only a dream.

"We have not done this," the woman said gently. "You have." Trenara could only blink at her. "You know who we are."

The guider nodded. "You are Ethos… and Eraze."

"Yes. Do you know why we are here?"

"No." Trenara laughed, unable to stop the sound from escaping her lips.

When Ethos smiled back, a gasp went through every person present. "We have come to thank you," she replied to the guider. "To thank you all."

Van stepped to his wife and took her in his arms. "For what?"

Eraze stepped forward and took Ethos' arm. "For freeing our son—both our sons."

"Come," the goddess said, leading him down the bridge. "It is time for answers and to bring them peace. Joshan, Ricilyn, please come with us. I know you have many questions. I promise they will all be answered."

Without another word, she led the procession across the field and into the pavilion. All of them followed her without saying a word. When Joshan reached Trenara, she tentatively held out her hand, afraid he would not be there. She felt his warmth and threw her arms around his neck, sobbing uncontrollably.

Until they were all settled in the pavilion, Ethos would answer no questions. When they were finally all present, a hush fell on the crowd that filled the tent and the masses that surrounded it.

Joshan seemed immeasurably tired as he sat with his small family sheltering them in his arms.

"Trenara," the goddess said. "I must apologize to you as a feeble beginning. We have used you terribly and for this, we are sorry. It was necessary. Please..." She touched Trenara's hand softly and contentment filled the guider. "Please, ask us your questions. I will answer what I can."

Trenara looked at the god and goddess for a long time before saying anything. She was filled with a strange mixture of anger, confusion, and joy; her emotions a bright cacophony against the reality that surrounded her. She did not know how to feel—furious at their tricks, joyful at seeing Joshan and his family alive, humble before a being that she had never completely believed in—that she had convinced herself did not exist in the last few days. Trenara looked up into those brilliant violet eyes, but there was no worship in her own.

"The child," she finally said.

"Yes?"

"How did you save the child?"

"That was difficult," the goddess replied. "He was severely damaged by the sword. We had to..." Ethos tilted her head, searching for words, "...give him something special. Something to make him stronger. Then, we accelerated his growth in order to save him." Ethos stared at her a moment. "Just as we had to accelerate Joshan's growth—when the time came."

Trenara slowly shook her head. "Sirdar said..."

Ethos nodded. "I know. It is not for nothing Sirdar is known as the master of lies."

Trenara was not appeased and sat back scowling at the goddess.

Ethos smiled. "You do not trust us, do you, Trenara?"

"No," she said simply. "I do not trust you. You condemned Sirdar to begin with. Why should I trust you?"

Ethos lowered her chin and took a deep breath. "Because it was not us who imprisoned Sirdar. Trenara..." The goddess smiled sadly. "We are Sirdar's soldiers."

A stunned murmur ran through the crowd.

"If you will allow me," Ethos continued, "before you judge us, please listen to what I have to say. If in the end, you do not think what we did was wise, we will accept that condemnation. Just allow us to plead our case."

There was another faint murmur through the crowd, but it did not seep into Trenara's consciousness immediately as she looked at the gods. Although her instincts were shouting at her to trust them, to listen to what they had to say, the pain in her heart from so much abuse made her hesitate. "Why should we trust you?"

Golden tears appeared at the corner of the goddess' eyes and her chin quivered slightly. "I cannot think of a reason," Ethos replied honestly.

A faint smile dusted Trenara's lips and she nodded. "Good answer. I would love to hear what you have to say."

"Thank you," the goddess breathed, glancing at Eraze and squeezing his hand. As the night gathered around them, torches shone on her face like jewels.

CHAPTER THIRTY-EIGHT
ANSWERS

"What Sirdar told you was true," Ethos began earnestly. "He was a great man once. He fought hard for all of us and freed many before they caught him. In the end, he was betrayed by his wife and it almost cost us everything."

"His wife?" Trenara asked.

"Yes, his wife." The goddess searched Trenara's face. "You are so much like her. It does not surprise me that he developed an interest in you.

"She was captured and tortured until she betrayed her husband. That was the beginning of the end for Sirdar. Because of her betrayal, they captured him soon after. Tragically, when they allowed her to go home, she went mad. She killed his children in their sleep and then took her own life. Sirdar never forgave her for what she had done. He never forgave himself for neglecting her safety and the safety of his two sons. They were an early casualty in a very long war.

"During the long torture he endured at the hands of the bureaucrats, he would not give up the rest of us. Because of that, we were able to continue his work. Eventually, we won our war but we lost so much…" Her voice trailed off as a single tear fell untouched down her cheek. Taking a deep breath, she continued.

"Forgive me. I need to tell you something about our people and a bit about your own history to make this clear.

"We are not gods, not really. Actually, we are people very much like you, except we have a gift. Our civilization has been around for millions of seasons and we possess technologies and knowledge that are far above others. Contained in our make-up, is what I will call a spark, something residing in our life force that forms as crystals in our blood and skin. This growth allows us to control what you call the power and gives us a kind of immortality. Although we have innate abilities that make us capable of many wonderful things, the crystals themselves are not natural to us. You would think of this as a disease, which resides in our blood, but is not naturally activated. My people learned long ago in their research how to trigger this spark with machines— devices that stimulate its growth. We automatically condition newborns and activate this disease. When they reach adolescence, they will be as you see us now. All of us have had this done. It is what gives us our abilities, our strengths, and our longevity.

"However, on occasion, one in every billion of our kind is born with this spark already activated. This is what Sirdar had been trying to do for centuries."

"I do not understand…" Trenara began, terrified that perhaps she did.

"Sirdar needed a host to prolong his life—to amplify the catalyst he had discovered. Trenara, Sirdar, and Kerillian were not idle while they were here," Ethos replied slowly. "You must know that in the centuries they lived here they sired many children." Trenara's guider sense was screaming at her and she went a bit numb.

"In Sirdar's case, he knew that although these children would be quite capable, they would not have the crystals since he lacked the machines to spark them. His only hope lay in the chance that one of his progeny would be born with it naturally. That had always been his plan—to sire a child whose body he could possess using the power of the catalyst, so he could escape this world and seek his revenge. Ironically, it was these very children that would eventually destroy him."

"No, that is not possible," Trenara whispered.

Ethos looked down at her hands. "You must know where Assemblage came from, or at least suspected."

"No," she said. "It cannot be."

"Every member of Assemblage, to some extent, is a direct descendant of Sirdar or Kerillian, Trenara. They had many children through the seasons and you are products of these children. It is why you have such abilities, why you are able to control the Crystal as you do, why you can speak to the rest of us, even though the voice is very faint. Assemblage is a direct result of the seeds of our kind. You are our children. Just as the empirical line are also our children."

For the first time, Van spoke up. "What do you mean?"

She lifted her eyes and tilted her head. "Vorius, Kerillian was known as Cessas in those days. He started not only Assemblage, but the empire as well. Felos, the first emperor, was Kerillian's son. You are a direct descendant of Kerillian as have been all your forebears. As is the empress that Trenara now carries."

"If you knew all this," Trenara's tone was accusing, but she did not amend it, "why didn't you try to help us?"

Ethos' eyes became very sad and Eraze squeezed her hand. "We tried for a very long time to reach you," he continued for the goddess who sank her head and closed those violet eyes. "When Sirdar and Kerillian were taken, it galvanized our forces. Our numbers grew exponentially. Eventually we won against the tyranny of our own kind.

"However, when they were in the last throws of their rule, the regime burned everything. Plans, papers, witnesses, people, by the millions. All they could reach before we could reach them. When they were finally overthrown, no one left knew where Sirdar or Kerillian were. We have spent the last three thousand seasons searching for them.

"This planet is far away from our dominion and the crystal barrier shielded it from us. We could not detect it until recently, although we had tried. Because of Killian's diligence, you knew of our existence through your religion. You could even hear our voices, upon occasion. That kept us alive in your hearts. We could hear you, as well. We just could not answer.

"When we finally did find this place, the barrier could not be broken from the outside. It was nearly impenetrable. After all, this was a prison. They had used all their technology to keep it so.

"When we did find it, sixty seasons ago, we started our long plans for trying to salvage Sirdar, Kerillian, and their children.

"It was so frustrating to be able to see what was happening in your world through the eyes of our kind, but helpless to stop any of it. We watched as Sirdar nearly destroyed the world. If it had not been for the courage of Saminee and others like him, Sirdar would have gotten control over the crystal to bring down the barrier and escape, bringing his madness—and his new power—to the universe. Unfortunately, we made a mistake." His voice broke. Ethos touched his hand tenderly.

"We underestimated his abilities," Ethos continued apologetically. "We thought, as you did, that Sirdar was destroyed and so lifted our vigilance on your world to take care of more pressing matters in ours. Kerillian was still here, but his voice by then was so weak, we could not hear him and thought he was dead."

"Dead?" Trenara said. "I thought you were immortal."

"Only our crystals make us immortal. Kerillian's had been neutralized before he was sent here."

"Why weren't they scraped from him as were Sirdar's?"

"This was the culmination of their cruelty to Sirdar. He was given a choice; one of the two of them would be tortured and their crystals ripped from their flesh as painfully and as long as they could make it. Then they would take that prisoner to the edges of the universe with a daligon who would continue the torture until they died. Believe me, with their technology, they could make it last forever.

"Kerillian was Sirdar's brother. Sirdar loved him very much. Of course, he volunteered himself.

"When they were sent here, I doubt Sirdar even knew his brother was here. We think by the time he found out, the catalyst had already corrupted his mind. In any event, Kerillian was condemned to the frozen waste to the south and Sirdar the north.

"It was not until nearly two thousand seasons later that Kerillian was aware that his brother Lughati was even alive. When he tried to reach him, he realized that Sirdar was mad and could destroy everything they had fought to protect. When Sirdar forced the piece of crystal from the sky, Kerillian found it and used it to protect the people of this world. It was all he could do.

"By the time we were able to find them," she said bitterly, "it was far too late. The catalyst had already destroyed Sirdar and we could not break through the barrier to reach Kerillian.

"Then a miracle happened." She glanced at Joshan. "One of us made it through... and a child was conceived."

Trenara frowned at her. "I do not understand. I thought Sirdar was Joshan's..."

"No," Ethos replied simply. "Saldorian was already pregnant when Sirdar raped her. Not even he knew that."

Saldorian gasped. "What?"

"I wish I could have shared this knowledge with you sooner," Ethos said to her sadly. "I am so sorry for all the suffering it has caused you.

"We had to create a line, a heritage that Sirdar could not resist. You are a direct descendant from both brothers, Saldorian. Because of that, the chances of your producing an offspring who had the crystal naturally were greatly increased. All Sirdar had to do was impregnate you with his own catalyst enhanced seed to guarantee the results. We knew he could not resist the lure and it went as we planned. By the time he could reach you, we had already implanted another seed by—tampering with Jenhada's.

"The child had to be born, don't you see? If Joshan had not been born in exactly the way he was, Sirdar would now be ruling. He forced our hand when he planted Balinar with the royal family. We had to push up our plans by accelerating the boy's growth. If we did not, the mission would never succeed."

"I do not understand," Joshan's face twisted in pain. "I failed the mission. The knowledge you gave me is gone. I betrayed Trenara. I betrayed everyone. I succumbed to the catalyst and killed my wife and child."

Ethos stood up and crossed to Joshan to touch his face. "The test was never yours to succeed or fail, Joshan. The test was always hers." She lifted her sparkling arm and swept it toward Trenara.

"What?" she asked.

"Joshan was never meant to succeed. Quite the contrary; had he succeeded, we would just have a new horror to contend with. The test has always been yours, Trenara, yours and Ricilyn's. We had to know you would stand on your own feet no matter what the consequences; that you were worthy to continue the legacy we have given you."

Trenara stood slowly and confronted Ethos nearly eye to eye. "So you tortured this poor child to find out if we were worthy of your support?"

"Trenara," Van whispered, but she ignored him.

"You stole his childhood, you stood by as he was abused and tortured, you let him take the brunt of a madman's perverted desires, and you did nothing to help him? You left him alone, one of your own kind, to suffer as a test for our loyalty—just to see if we were worthy to worship you?"

The crowd gasped as Trenara's accusations smoldered in Ethos' eyes.

"Well," said a voice behind the goddess, "he was not exactly alone."

Trenara whirled around to confront Eraze. "Really? Who else did he have?"

"One of us was always with him, Trenara," Ethos said. Trenara held her tongue. "One of us made it through the barrier twenty seasons ago and has been with him since the day of his conception. Joshan carries his seed. His life force flows in Joshan's veins. And it is his throne that Joshan will one day inherit."

Joshan stood up slowly and looked at the goddess with his mouth open. "Who?"

"Begging your pardon, sir, but I think her ladyship means me."

Eraze shimmered like a lake of silver before them and turned at once into Haiden Bails, as alive and vibrant as he had ever been.

"Forgive me, lad, but I could not tell you, though I was sourly tempted to more than once. You see," he said in his own voice, the sound odd coming out of Haiden's face, "it was the only way we could free him. Sirdar had to give up the catalyst and the only way he would do that would be to give it to you. In the end, it was the only way we could release him from his torment. Lughati died a liberated being, Joshan, because of you. He found peace at last, because of you. For that, we are truly grateful."

"But I almost became him," Joshan replied angrily. "I almost destroyed everything. How could you know I would not?"

"Because of Trenara and Ricilyn," Ethos replied. "Ricilyn is truly gifted, Joshan. Her visions are unparalleled even by our standards. As we said, we see through the eyes of our own. I have always shared a special bond with Trenara, but on a night long ago, it was Ricilyn's visions I saw in the storm, just as she saw it. I knew then what we had to do."

Ethos took Haiden's hand. "I know you can probably never forgive us for what we have done, but please, understand, we did it to save our friends and their children. I misspoke earlier, Trenara; you have always been worthy of us. In fact, better than us, by far. You have taught us what courage truly is, what love and respect can do for a life. You have shown us greatness and real power. We will contemplate these things as we approach our new realm in the heavens and I promise you, we will not disappoint you.

"In the interim please accept this as my gift to you." Ethos lifted Trenara's chin and a beautiful light fell from her eyes. The guider's widened as the volumes of knowledge they all thought were lost flooded into her mind in an instant. She fell to her knees and Ethos would not release her grip until Trenara had it all. When it was done, the goddess released her to the embrace of Vanderlinden, who lifted her from the ground and held her tightly.

"I know you will use it wisely, Trenara."

"But, what about Joshan?" she stammered.

"That is up to him," Ethos said, looking at Joshan intently. "Will you come with us now, with your family to take your place at your father's side?"

Joshan sank slowly onto his seat and looked at the dirt under his feet with Ricilyn's arms wrapped around him. He did not speak immediately, as the crowd around them waited in anticipation.

"I do not think you need more gods in the heavens," he finally said quietly. "I think you have enough already." He shook his head. "Despite the spark you speak of, the seed you say is within me, this is where my family lives." He looked up at Trenara. "I did not want to be a messiah. I do not think I want to be a god." He stood up and crossed to Eraze. Taking him in his arms, he whispered, "I will miss you, Haiden, but I cannot come with you. Not now. Perhaps one day…"

Eraze's eyes glazed over. "I know, lad. I have known for quite some time now. I only wish I could stay with you, but I will be back from time to time to see my grandchild grow. I will miss you so much." Haiden held Joshan out at arm's length. "I am only a whisper away."

Joshan nodded quietly and embraced him.

A sad smile graced Ethos's lips. "Be well, Joshan. Be happy."

A soft warm breeze flowed swiftly through the pavilion, sweeping the tent cloth noisily as everyone watched. When they looked back, the gods were gone.

Joshan hugged his wife and then crossed quickly to take Trenara into his arms. He kissed her on the forehead and cradled her. "I am so sorry, Trenara," he whispered hoarsely into her ear. "My god, the things I did to you…"

She disentangled herself from his embrace and smiled up at him. "We both need to heal, Joshan. That will take time."

He nodded and then touched her belly with his open palm; he pressed hard. Trenara could feel a rush of heat from his hand. It sent pleasant warmth through her body and tranquility into her heart.

"She is going to be beautiful, Trenara." Joshan's black eyes glazed over with a deep opalescence in the darkened tent and his words echoed to every corner of the field, reverberating so that all ears could hear him. "She will be beautiful, intelligent, and powerful. Your child will bring a new prosperity to this world and her children's children will sing of the heroic deeds of their great-grandmother. Together, our children will one day unite the universe, and bring wisdom to the stars. The child that will come of this union will be more powerful than any other."

He lifted his hand off her belly quickly, blinking down at her as a flash of terror ran across his face. With an effort, he instantly smoothed his features and flashed her one last smile.

"Sorry, Trenara," he said quietly.

She scowled up at him and wondered what he had seen. But she had had enough of gods, prophesies, and magic for one day. Trenara patted her belly, took his and Vanderlinden's arms, and led them out of the tent.

"That is all right, lad. Come on. You owe me lunch. I am famished!"

APPENDIX A
GLOSSARY

Bullion Beast - A domestic animal bred for its meat and milk. The bullion is very large and docile, living mainly in the Palimar Plains where it roams freely. It looks similar to a giant, hairy tick with a large bloated body, small head, legs, and large feet. It is not very swift, but hardy and prolific as it delivers litters of several offspring two to three times a season. Bullions are "harvested" throughout the season from the plains.

Camamara - A small island to the far west of the provinces off the western shore of Selas.

Catalyst – The power source of Sirdar. Red stones similar to the Crystal of Healing.

Clurichaune - A small people living chiefly in the woods and on one or two islands. They have a charm about them, but are very rare since few females are born to the race. They tend to the trees and forests and are very reclusive.

Craistan Nuts – Similar to English chestnuts.

Crystal of Healing - A stone made of white crystal, which is the source of power for Assemblage. It is from this stone that the Starguider's via acquires the power. It rests in the secluded Sanctum on the Isle of Mathisma.

Da – A Tolan slang term for father.

Detachment - A serious depression that affects pre-guiders after first trial. In extreme cases, it can cause delusion, deep depression, and eventually madness. Suicide is very common with the disease. Some symptoms of the disease are manifested in all pre-guiders. This madness is rare in modern times, but was quite common in the beginnings of Assemblage. Guiders are rigorously trained to help the student avoid detachment.

Dispersion - Usually occurs in pre-guiders where they have sporadic control over the power, often causing some very unfortunate and often interesting "accidents" involving the power, but usually not fatally.

Driftlines – Used by the Trillone to travel through the limbs of the Signal Tree, these are living vines that allow the traveler to spring down and then up into the higher branches.

Eecha - An animal used for transportation, hauling, and pulling wagons (larger varieties). They are similar to the horse as they are hoofed with very long legs; however, they have some characteristics similar to camels as well. Eechas are bred to be very swift runners and have great endurance (about double that of a common horse). They have flat faces with wide nostrils, very long fine hair (usually two to four inches) that covers most of their body, long pointed ears, and short stubby tails. Their eyes are very large and are usually either very dark brown or green. Their night vision is excellent. They come in a variety of coats from very long (common) to some short hairs ranging in color from white to brown to black and a variety of coat patterns in many combinations of colors (again, depending on where they were bred). Though very hearty in most situations, they spook easily at danger (unless specifically bred otherwise. Mathismian eechas are bred for their intelligence and ability to suppress their startle reflexes).

Elite Guard - The emperor's personal guard. They see to the protection of the imperial family and the security of the Keep. They handle most of the duties for running the Keep on a daily basis. Only the most experienced guards are promoted to the Elite and only by the hand of the emperor.

Ethos, The Star - Largest star in the Imperium solar system. The belief is Ethos, the Goddess, inhabits this star and channels power down to the Crystal of Healing on the Isle of Mathisma in Sanctum.

Ethosian - Roughly December

Eventide - Roughly September

Figin Fruit - A yellow sweet fruit with a hard outer shell and mushy fruit inside.

Fireweed and Fratellas - A type of salad with red leafed fireweed that is very spicy and orange rinds of fratellas, a hard tuber root vegetable.

First Prince or Princess - First born of the emperor or empress and heir to the throne of the Imperium.

First Trial or Coming to Power - When novice Starguiders have their first confrontation with the power. When they can control it, they are capable of the first level of guidance. This is actually the most dangerous of all levels because of the unpredictable nature of the power. Young pre-guiders can easily die at first trial or go mad from the touch of the power.

First, Second, Third and Fourth Trial - The differing levels attained by the guider as he or she progresses through the training. Assemblage discovered the power had varying degrees of strength, and each was denoted by a differing color. White was the simplest and most common and came with first trial or the coming to power. Blue denoted the second trial or the coming to knowledge, which enables one to learn quickly. It is at this stage you begin to develop your sight. Green denotes the coming to nature and gives you power over trees, grass, wind, rain, etc., helping them to be—well, more than they are. There is also a fourth trial, but it is very rare and is thought to be a combination of the first three levels.

Fourth Trial – See First Trial

Goddesses – Ethos, Goddess of Ethics, Rule & Government, Leader of the Gods; Leuko, Goddess of Light and the moons; Krikos, Goddess of Life; Ventus, Goddess of the Air, Wind and Weather.

Gods - Eraze, God of the Earth; Pyra, God of Fire and the Sun; Hydor, God of Water, the Sea and the Rains; Noscere, God of Knowledge, Learning and Wisdom; Lughati, formerly, The God of Liberty, but became the God of Lies, Deceit, the Fallen One.

Guider or Starguider - A member of Assemblage whose duty it is to teach and guide a young student through First Trial and beyond as necessary.

Guider's Sense - Not exactly prescience, but rather a guider's ability to "feel" there is something wrong or when there is pending risk. They can sense when someone is in danger, hurt, or even alive, when there is doubt. They can usually also sense someone else's emotions, especially strong emotions like hate, fear, anxiety, or even love. Guider's Sense usually comes only after Second Trial and gets stronger as the guider does.

The Hold - The prison located in the lower three levels of the Keep on the eastern side toward the sea.

Imaka - A liquid medicinal that helps with pain and fatigue, usually administered by a Starguider. Made from water that is placed in the niche in the Holding Stone where the Crystal of Healing had been when it came to the Imperium.

Immunity Sanction – Security clearance.

Imperium - A number of provinces and the religious sanctuary of Mathisma, a large island to the east of the mainland provinces, both ruled by a combined supreme authority, the Empire on the one side and Assemblage on the other. Governance of the provinces and Mathisma is split into two ruling bodies. The provinces are chiefly run by the Emperor/Empress who oversees the Councils of Trade & Justice, which administer trade, security, and law. Mathisma is chiefly run by Assemblage, which governs religion, the arts, and education. The Northern Wastes and several smaller islands are not incorporated or protected by the Imperium.

Kerillian the Prophet - A man who traveled throughout the disperse tribes of humans scattered through the ancient provinces. He brought knowledge to those tribes he felt were deserving. "The Legend of Kerillian" is possibly the first written record of the Imperium history that covers his journeys and his prophecies of coming events. Many of his tenets are still strictly followed by the modern Assemblage. They used his writings as a basis for setting up the Imperium.

Knoshkin – A type of hard sweet pastry, usually toasted, made of whillen wheat.

Laminia – Creatures who live on the blood of the young and weak. They were associated with Sirdar during his first reign.

Last Defense - The trial of an accused criminal where he or she is allowed to offer their last defense against accusations and present evidence before sentence is carried out. Somewhat like our appeal process. Usually, before anyone is accused and brought before Last Defense; investigations, interviews, and evidence are meticulously gathered and evaluated by the Council of Justice. If someone is innocent, he or she is usually found so during this part of the process. If someone makes it to Last Defense, usually this is the last ditch effort to fight for their innocence.

League - The Imperium common unit of distance roughly one-half mile.

Locare - A very rare gift among guiders. Those who have mastered the art of locare can find people, things, and places using their vias and this sense. Some with this ability can even pick up an object and gain a very accurate insight into anyone who has held it, similar to psychic readers.

Low Season- Roughly winter

Makhia - A legendary trial by battle fought between the gods to settle matters of great importance. These were usually fought so wars could be avoided and usually ended when one would concede. There are legends that the makhia was also sometimes fought by ancient kings and to the death. The winner would usually inherit the lands of the loser.

Marshal of the Guard - Commander of the Elite, the Council, and the Gate Guards.

Mathisma, The Isle of - Home of Assemblage and the Crystal of Healing in the far east of the Ethosian Sea.

Mourna - A creature of Sirdar, a giant bird, similar to an eagle but much larger with black feathers and human eyes. Its voice sends out a sound that enchants a Starguider so he or she falls under its master's sway. The creature's voice, however, has no effect on non-Assemblage. Also called Assemblage Bane.

Meridian Season – Roughly Fall

Power - That energy which emanates through a series of three points, forming a rough triangle. The belief is it starts from the star Ethos, then through the Crystal of Healing on Mathisma and then into a via held by a Starguider. It is amplified by the resonance of musical notes sung by Starguiders trained to control the intensity, direction, and wavelength of the power. It is known to incinerate on contact anyone not trained in its use. It is strongest at night when Ethos is high in the sky.

Pre-Guider - A student who has gone through first trial, but has not been ordained as a Starguider yet. Many seasons of education and training are required before a pre-guider receives his or her via and are granted the rank of guider.

Prelacy – A group of Starguiders who advise the Provost headed by the Prelate.

Prelate - The Starguider who is the speaker of the prelacy. He or she officiates at meetings and acts as liaison to the Provost.

Provost - Leader of Assemblage, in essence the second most powerful leader in the world after the emperor. The Provost has almost limitless power and is aided by the prelacy, a committee of Starguiders who advise. The prelacy is chaired by the prelate who acts as liaison to the Provost.

Redwyn - A large red moon, largest of the two that orbit the planet. It rises first followed by Whilema about half an hour later.

Salminian - A large bass-like fish found throughout the provinces in fresh water streams and lakes.

Sanctum - The structure that houses the knowledge of mankind in a great library and the Crystal of Healing. It is located on a very small island bridged to Mathisma and is tended by the Provost and the Keeper of the Books.

Sea Scalards - Large bright blue and black sea birds, a common shore bird throughout the Imperium.

Season - A full rotation around the Imperium sun roughly approximating our earth year.

Second Trial – See First Trial.

See – See Vision.

Shoalfish - Largest fish in the Ethosian Sea. It is larger than our blue whales, but very timid and scarce. Despite its name, they usually only appear in the deep ocean.

Sight – See Vision.

Span - The Imperium common unit of measure - roughly six feet.

Springtide – Roughly Spring

Staking or The Stake - Brutal form of execution where the condemned are stripped and bound to a large stake, their hands, and necks stretched and tied to the top, and the ankles and legs stretched and tied to the bottom. The stake is lifted up and then quickly thrown into a hole where it is tapped down. When the stake hits the hole usually the prisoner's neck, shoulders, and hips come out of their sockets. If lucky, it will break the neck immediately and kill the person. If not, they will leave them there until the prisoner dies in excruciating pain the entire time.

Starguider or Guider - A member of Assemblage whose duty it is to teach and guide a young student through First Trial and beyond as necessary. All members of Assemblage are commonly called guiders.

Starmoths - Small points of light that are summoned by the power. They "dance" in the air merrily and let off a soft tinkling sound, like suspended glass in the wind, which to most, is quite enjoyable. Their main attribute is that they detect evil that lies in others. The latter can be seen by their reaction to the one being tested. Despite their airy countenance, they can be quite terrifying if aroused by evil thoughts or lies.

Tavelson - A Tolan acid used to clean rust from tools and dissolve iron.

Third Trial – See First Trial.

Via - An instrument of varying sizes and shapes, which contains a piece of crystal that allows a guider to channel the power. It is usually an object that can be held in the hand such as a scepter or staff. However, many guiders have vias in the shape of a ring or pendant. The original vias were made from the Crystal of Healing, however, another source of crystal was found in the Imperium that worked as well, thus causing a quick early expansion of Assemblage.

Vision or Sight - Precognition experienced by many guiders, usually occurring during one of the trials and sometimes in dreams. Occasionally guiders can experience a vision even when awake.

Vulcha - A very large predatory bird with black and red feathers, bare head, and neck. They can grow to be around ten feet tall.

Whilema - Smaller of two moons that circle the Imperium. It rises after the larger Redwyn.

Whillen – A staple grain of the Imperium. Grown and harvested everywhere in the provinces, it is used for most of their staple foods and their beer.

APPENDIX B
HIERARCHY OF EMPIRE
AND ASSEMBLAGE

The Imperium is broken down into two sections, the Emperor and his Councils and Assemblage. Below is a brief description of how each is broken into a chain of command:

EMPEROR/EMPRESS	ASSEMBLAGE
(Imperial Guards & Fleet*)	_____
Councils of Trade & Justice	Provost
Province Baron	Prelacy
Province Regent	Prelate
	Starguider - 1st, 2nd & 3rd Trial
	Pre-Guider

Both Councils have twelve members each. They can only over-rule the Emperor's decision by unanimous vote, and only as relates to rulings regarding their respective responsibilities (justice and trade). In contrast to this, the Provost can only over-rule the Prelacy in matters where they are deadlocked on a decision. The Prelate merely acts as an emissary between the Provost and the Prelacy, and has very little power beyond his or her status as a member of the Prelacy. The Prelacy has twelve members as well.

The Emperor/Empress or the Councils can only make decisions on laws governing secular matters; the Assemblage only on matters of religion, education, or ethics. Assemblage, by long standing law, did not get involved in the imperial wars or military actions, except as advisors. However, should an attack occur against the Assemblage itself, they would engage in retaliatory activities in conjunction with the emperor, such as the first war with Sirdar. *Note: The Imperial Fleet and the Guard are directly under the Emperor during times of war. At all other times they are technically under the Councils. However, both the fleet and the guard are fairly independent.

The hierarchy had remained as above for approximately 950 seasons until the Starsight reorganized the government during his reign.

APPENDIX C
SEASON/CALENDAR NOTES

COMMON SPEECH	*MATHISMIAN SEASONS*	*APPROX. ENGLISH*
Springtide	*Vernal*	*Spring*
High Season	*Estival*	*Summer*
Meridian	*Autumnal*	*Fall*
Low Season	*Gloaming*	*Winter*

COMMON SPEECH	CORRESPONDING SEASON	APPROX. ENGLISH
Prima	Springtide/Vernal	April
Seconda	Springtide/Vernal	May
Tertian	Springtide/Vernal	June
Cessian	High Season/Estival	July
Felon	High Season/Estival	August
Eventide	High Season/Estival	September
Gleaning	Meridian/Autumnal	October
Cordomber	Meridian/Autumnal	November
Ethosian	Meridian/Autumnal	December
Watembra	Low Season/Gloaming	January
Corma	Low Season/Gloaming	February
Equin	Low Season/Gloaming	March

*Unlike an English year, the Thrain calendar has only 360 days. The week is seven days long and there are thirty days to each month. The two times of equinox are rarely celebrated on the same day, but within five days of the dates given. Common speech is used most often for the names of the seasons, the Mathismian words only as needed for ceremony and by some diehards among Assemblage. The names of the months are the same in Mathismian and common speech.

APPENDIX D
HISTORY OF THE CRYSTAL
OF HEALING

As told by Trenara of Mathisma at a lecture for pre-guiders before the coming of Starsight:

"The origin—there are many differing ideas about that. The most popular and certainly the most enduring, is based on the old ballads that were handed down at the time. You have heard the story of Goddess Ethos descending from the heavens and entrusting the Crystal of Healing to us for safekeeping, until she returns to retrieve it and place it back in its rightful place among the stars. To be honest, I think that and all other embellishment of it are a lot of rot, though there are those who would ask my immediate expulsion for saying so. Personally, I am more of the opinion that the crystal did come from the heavens, but by a much more conventional route, simply falling from the sky when it came close to our world. Many of the scholars are now studying the heavens and have theorized that there are many such stones floating in the heavens. Not perhaps as the crystal is, nor radiating such force, but they have found other plainer stones in odd places that could only have gotten there in that way. But I will not pursue that. I have never had much interest in rocks from the heavens, except the crystal, so I cannot elaborate.

"But however the stone came here, the fathers found it and discovered its great power, though in rather a hard way. It is said that many people died from its touch the first few seasons it was here—thus the forming of Assemblage by the first Provost, Cessas, nearly a millennium ago. Unbelievably, the crystal was thought by most to be evil, a blight to the world. The first Assemblage guiders were considered demons or madmen. But Cessas had a great curiosity and many think he was a genius for his time.

"Of course, back then the world was quite barbaric, being for the most part several small countries that were in essence no larger than villages that bickered and warred among themselves. Cessas gathered what people he could and took the stone to where Thrain is now. There he began a methodical study of the crystal and its amazing properties.

"It is said that he discovered its healing powers quite by accident—his own, I am afraid. He had received a great injury and was laid in the same room with the stone. When his servants came to check on him the next morning, he was completely healed. He had gained a great measure of knowledge concerning the stone and Ethos after that. He taught its uses to his disciples and sent them out to find others that were special in the way they were; thus the custom of search each season. They grew in numbers rapidly, extending well beyond the borders of Thrain into the other provinces.

"Soon Ethos and the Crystal of Healing were thought of as gifts from the gods. Certainly, crops and people fared better when a Starguider was present with his or her via, which were made of the actual crystal in those days, rather than fabricated from other stones as they are now.

"The land had purpose and unity. Some seasons later, Thrain was looked on as the ruling province, and more and more the Assemblage was looked at as being the law. It is no small wonder Cessas in the last seasons of his life, conceived of the idea of the Imperium, a world governed by two bodies, the empire on the one hand to govern the provinces, and Assemblage on the other to promote the religion of Ethos and provide knowledge to the world. He had always wanted to study and learn, increasing his knowledge and that of Assemblage. He felt that was the purpose of the group. But more and more the people turned to Assemblage for leadership and the guiders became judges, administrators, and the like, until there was little time left for study.

"It was not until after Cessas' death that the Imperium began, when Felos was blessed as the first emperor. The empire ran the land, and Assemblage retired into study. However, Felos was killed soon into his reign, assassinated by the king of the north's guard. This sparked the Great Northern Wars, and the northerners attacked the still embryonic empire, nearly destroying everything Assemblage had built.

"That war lasted nearly sixty seasons, but finally Assemblage succeeded in driving the northerners back to their land on the other side of the mountains and dispersing them. Of course, the war continued for over six hundred seasons after that, but during this brief respite, they built the Keep to protect the young empire from attack, so they could find a more suitable place to continue their work. It is said that many of the corner stones in the Keep were placed there by the power, although I half wonder if that is not some fanciful tale spun by minstrels of the time. In any event, the Keep was built, much to the relief of the growing Assemblage. Once the empire could stand alone, they removed themselves to Mathisma, where they finally built their schools and temples. They took the Solemn Vow never to interfere in the affairs of the empire, except as advisors. The Imperium was at last complete."

APPENDIX E
STARSIGHT - VOLUME I
SYNOPSIS

Trenara's dream rapidly becomes a vision—a vision that will shatter the peace the empire won after six hundred seasons of war. Something is wrong and the aging Starguider cannot shake the feeling when she wakes to prepare for her morning lessons with Joshan. He is first prince, heir to the throne of the Imperium, not to mention an armful of ingenious mischief. The first member of the royal family to be selected for Assemblage, Joshan's skills frighten even the more acclimated warriors, sends children of his own tender age running in terror when he approaches, or giggling off into a noisy gaggle of girls. Trenara loves him more than life; in spite of the fact that the boy gives the Starguider wrinkles, frown lines, deep blackened circles under her eyes... and brilliant smiles. Joshan is a sparkling diamond to Trenara's rough.

Joshan and Haiden, the boy's life-long trainer and guard, have their good-natured brawling interrupted by the Emperor, Jenhada, once a strong and able leader, but now a thin, dark-eyed ghost of a man whose illness has left him cold, frail, and angry. He orders the brawling to stop and disappears with the skulking figure of Pravius trailing after him.

As Trenara and Joshan travel through the gates of the Keep, something is out of place. There is a scarcity of guards where once there were hundreds. These men are dark, rude... all of them strangers to her. Trenara shakes off the feelings and tells Joshan of the rise and fall of Sirdar thirty seasons before as they ride through the forests to the High Cliffs, the memory of how close this madman and his monsters came to ruling the world making her shudder.

When she runs Joshan through his lessons, Trenara is again amazed at the young boy's uncanny, almost genius abilities, his breathtaking voice and his unsurpassed control of the sung resonance notes that are used to control the power. With her voice and the beautiful crystal via called Andelian, Trenara shows him how the power works by calling up dancing starmoths. The boy is delighted.

Without warning, Joshan suddenly goes through the violent transition to first trial, and then, in almost the same instant, he reaches second, then third trial, something unheard of in the entire history of Assemblage. The power has never taken one so young.

As he reaches third trial, he has overwhelming visions that are so powerful they nearly drive him mad. Trenara has to use every skill she possesses to save the prince, and in the end, they both collapse.

Trenara wakes the next morning and Joshan is gone. She finds him high on the cliffs, but he has aged by ten seasons and she only recognizes him because of the imperial tattoo on his arm and a scar on his left arm. Her training takes over. She realizes he may well succumb to a type of dementia common among Assemblage children who cannot handle the pressures placed on them by the power, especially given these circumstances. She wakes him very slowly and skillfully brings him back from the edge of insanity.

On their way back to the Keep, they discover he has fine crystals on his palms made of the same stuff as Trenara's via.

When they arrive at the Keep Haiden stops and almost arrests them, but he recognizes Joshan and dismisses his guards. He tells them the consort Saldorian (Joshan's mother and the emperor's wife) was arrested for treason and that there is a warrant out for Trenara's arrest as well. They are accusing her of murdering Joshan.

When they attempt to reach the emperor, Pravius and his men surround them. He has them arrested, but not before he wounds Trenara with her own via, sending a bolt of painful power through her arm.

When the guards throw them into the Hold, power awakes in Joshan and he heals the guider's wounds. They manage to escape their cell, but Pravius' men recapture Trenara. Joshan and Haiden manage to escape.

Pravius tries to bribe Trenara into giving up where Joshan would go, but when she refuses, he orders her hung to the stake as bait to lure the prince back into the councilor's hands.

Joshan and Haiden make their way through the sewers of the Keep and escape into Keepton where they take up with Vanderlinden, the ex-captain of the imperial fleet, whom everyone thought had died two seasons before.

He helps them to escape to Foresons Inn. While there, a street crier reads an edict; Trenara will be executed the next morning. Vanderlinden relates what happened two seasons before, when Sirdar visited him. The demon cursed him and called up the winds to destroy his ship, killing all hands except Van. When he arrived on shore, Pravius' men arrested and tortured him. Condemned to banishment, they secured him in the back of a wagon and took him north. Van escaped and made his way to the Village where he later became the leader of The Scoundrels. He tried repeatedly to reach Trenara and the emperor, but Pravius blocked his attempts at every opportunity. Van tells them he now has an army of scoundrels and pledges them to Joshan to free the Keep and the emperor from Pravius, who Van is certain, may be someone else.

Van takes them to Pap's, a tavern where the scoundrels meet, and prepares men and women for war. Sark the Mercenary, the previous head of the scoundrels before Van bested him for the title, shows up and joins forces with the companions, bringing another three hundred men to help. He agrees to create a diversion so they can break into the castle.

Sark doubts Joshan and asks for proof of his identity. The power seizes Joshan and his laughter causes everyone there—and for many, many blocks in all directions—to break out laughing in joy. Sark bends his knee to the young man and presents him with his sword. This is the first time anyone has seen Sark pledge himself to any man.

When Vanderlinden, Haiden, and Joshan return to Wert's house to prepare for the fight, Wert betrays them. They find out Wert's daughter was taken by Pravius to secure his loyalty. Parvius' men arrest Van and Joshan and take them to the castle. Wert and Haiden are left for dead after Wert finds out his daughter has been killed by Pravius' guards.

Trenara stands before Last Defense and pleads for her life, stating that Joshan is not dead. She produces a witness who recognized him, but she is found guilty when Pravius produces evidence that she and Saldorian were working together to poison the emperor and replace Joshan with an imposter who would then run the Imperium. The story is so brilliantly contrived, the evidence so overwhelming, that Trenara has no defense. Pravius brings Vanderlinden and Joshan into the courtroom. The giant is under a spell and Joshan's appearance altered so that no one will recognize him. Van testifies that Joshan is an imposter.

As they are moving in to strip Trenara in preparation for staking, Joshan's power bursts from his palms. He melts his chains and attacks Pravius. After Joshan defeats him, he shows the people who Pravius really is; Sirdar's henchman, Balinar, the renegade Starguider who helped Sirdar rise more than thirty seasons before. Joshan's father comes out of his trance, but Balinar stirs and kills the emperor with a last bolt of red power before disappearing into smoke.

As they mourn Jenhada, they find out that Balinar beat and raped Joshan's mother. To make matters worse, something he said to her about Joshan put her into a coma that no one can break, even Trenara.

When Joshan finds out what happened to his mother, he appoints Trenara as Emperor's Regent and then goes into seclusion for several weeks, with only Haiden allowed to see him. Trenara tries repeatedly to see Joshan, but the emperor's elite guards politely, but firmly refuse her access, much to her irritation. She and Vanderlinden discover that Joshan has been experimenting with the power and that he has achieved a fourth trial, something so rare, no one has seen it in hundreds of seasons. When they arrive at his chambers to stop him, he has miraculously aged once more and is even more powerful. Frightened by Joshan's newfound strength and wondering where it will lead, Trenara is deeply concerned. To their amazement, Joshan tells them they are leaving for the Assemblage home, the Isle of Mathisma the next day.

Once on the ship, Joshan tells Trenara that he has seen many alternate futures, all leading into oblivion, that Sirdar is back and more powerful than ever, and that they are leaving the provinces to face a bloody war without them. When she asks why they are leaving when the provinces need them the most, he reveals that yet another of Sirdar's guiders has been on the isle with the rest of Assemblage for the last two seasons and will be appointed Provost if they do not stop him, giving him access to the Crystal of Healing.

Joshan asks Trenara to tell him about how she almost betrayed the Imperium thirty seasons before. Shocked that he would know her deepest secret, she relays how she met Vanderlinden and about their journey to the far southern Badain to investigate disturbing rumors. She tells him how Sirdar came to them in disguise in the wilderness. Sirdar fell in love with Trenara and she found herself surrendering to the persuasion of his voice, the seduction of his touch, and a terrible power he wielded… a power that was somehow twisted and wrong—the power of the catalyst. When he began to dominate her mind, there was only one escape; Trenara threw herself from a cliff rather than submitting to him. Only her power shield saved her life. Van found Trenara nearly dead and took her back to the Keep where she finally healed. Trenara vowed she would never love again. Joshan tells her that she turned her back on love when it would have filled her life, and for the first time she realizes that Vanderlinden had been in love with her for decades. Her pain blinded her to his devotion.

A giant sea creature attacks the ship. It is so large it could take the ship down with just one of its giant arms. Joshan and Trenara combine their power to stop the beast. As they are fighting, Vanderlinden sees love in Trenara's eyes for the first time. After the battle, he takes her in his arms overwhelmed with joy.

Joshan tells Haiden and Vanderlinden everything that has transpired and they pledge their loyalty, not to Joshan, but to the mission to stop Sirdar, no matter what the sacrifice.

At Joshan's insistence, Trenara reaches third trial (master of nature) and helps keep the winds blowing so they can get to Mathisma before Palarine becomes Provost. They discover that Ena, Trenara's aide, has power herself when she sees symbols on the guider's forehead. Joshan has a deep premonition about the girl that disturbs him, but shakes it off.

During a birthday celebration for Trenara, one of Sirdar's creatures, a deinos, takes Ena, thinking the heavily cloaked girl is Joshan. Haiden receives life-threatening wounds when he tries to stop the beast. Joshan is able to heal him, but just barely. To buy the girl time Joshan switches identities with her. They tell the people on the ship that Joshan is missing.

When they get to the isle, the Prelate (the body of governing guiders) greets them. To their dismay, they discover that Palarine has swayed almost all of the guiders. Assemblage will appoint Palarine to the post of Provost that night.

Unswayed yet by Palarine, Witen, the head of the Prelate, shows Joshan and Trenara the Gazing, an ancient mirror that reveals what is occurring in other places and times around the world. Ricilyn, the previous Provost's daughter, then bursts in and Joshan's heart stops; this woman has been in all of his visions. Ricilyn left Assemblage seasons before and only came to pay her respects to her father, but

Palarine's guards are keeping her giant bird captive. She demands Witen see to it they let them both go.

Van and Haiden in the meantime steal the key to Sanctum, the home of both the crystal of healing and the Assemblage library.

During the naming of the Provost, Trenara tells the Assemblage the story of Palarine. She relates how Sirdar deceived him and sent him to Mathisma to steal the crystal. Sirdar will rise again to power. With the Crystal of Healing, Sirdar will be indomitable. Trenara then reads an edict from Joshan appointing her to the post of Provost of Assemblage. Palarine challenges her to the trial by battle, which she accepts, feeling for the first time in many seasons, the touch of the goddess.

Van, Haiden, and Joshan enter Sanctum to allow Joshan to find answers directly from the crystal on how to destroy Sirdar. After escaping Sanctum's many traps, he enters the chamber of healing and finds out that he needs to take up the given sword, find a wise man the crystal calls the Obet, win him to his side, and bury the stones. Joshan discovers Vanderlinden. Joshan heals the giant's eye with the crystal's help, removing a sliver of the catalyst, implanted there by Balinar two seasons before. While Joshan is in the giant's mind, he discovers that Van is in reality the first prince of Thoringale, Jenhada's older brother, Joshan's uncle and the rightful heir to the throne of the Imperium.

Van relates the story of how, sixty seasons before, because of the war with the northerners, Thoringale left behind his beloved wife, pregnant with their child. For six long years, Ninia waited for her husband to return. When she could not stand it anymore, in secret, she let untrustworthy men take her north to find her husband. The northerners captured Ninia and the young Vanderlinden. In an attempt to force Thoringale from the safety of his fortress, the Northerners cut Ninia's throat at his gate. He watched from the parapet and did nothing. When imperial reinforcements arrived immediately after, in a rage, Thoringale gave the northerners no mercy and annihilated their people and their country. The remnants escaped with Van, thinking they could use him as a bargaining chip. Thoringale did not know about his son and would kill any northerner who approached. Van became a slave to the northern remnants and grew up to kill his master, escape into the woods, and then go in search of Thoringale. Van was convinced his father had allowed his mother to die, as Thoringale watched coldly from his safety on the parapet. When Van finally reaches Thrain, he chances upon Jenhada and saves his life. While Jen is recovering, Van finds it easy to tell him everything about his life, but Jenhada stays silent and tells him nothing of his own. When Jenhada has recovered, he divulges to Van the best way to get into the keep to kill Thoringale.

When Van finally creeps into his father's room, he finds an old sick man dying of grief. Jenhada emerges from the shadows to tell Van how his father had to watch his mother die. The Elite guard had tied him to the parapet and would not let him go to her. Thoringale returned to Thrain, married, produced an heir, and then locked himself in his rooms to die slowly from grief and insanity. When Thoringale finally died, Jenhada offered the emperor's crown to his half brother, but Van turned it down knowing Jenhada would make a better emperor than he ever would.

When Van finishes his tale, the crystal turns itself into a golden sword and tells Joshan to take it up to destroy Sirdar. It then grants him one wish. He wishes for the knowledge from the great Assemblage library and all of the knowledge from all of the books appeared instantly in his mind. Overwhelmed at the sudden influx of information, Joshan nearly passes out. The crystal says he will be the only one who can now use the power. The knowledge the crystal gives him will be his when he realizes his purpose. If he fails, the knowledge fails with him.

Trenara and Palarine fight the makhia, the trial by battle. She disarms him, sending him crumbling to the ground. Just as she is raising her weapon to strike him dead, a presence suddenly takes over her will. It is the goddess of the winds, Ventus. She stops the makhia. Through Trenara, the goddess tells them to prepare for the coming of the gods and then leaves Trenara helpless and so weak, she can barely rise from the ground. In that instant, Palarine throws a lump of the catalyst at her. She is too weak to stop it. A great wind comes up from the ground, whirls the catalyst back at Palarine, and kills him.

Just then, there are several explosions as Sirdar's northerners set charges on the Sanctum Bridge, shaking the assemblage home violently.

In the same instant, the guiders hear the cry of a Mourna flying above Sanctum to steal the crystal of healing. The warder, a giant bird that protects Sanctum, flies to destroy the Mourna. The Mourna's great claws open the belly of the old guardian. He dies in mid-air.

When the warder falls, it breaks the great vats of illiminium used to preserve the crystal and they catch the thousands of books in the great library on fire. Sanctum falls into ruins.

Out of the conflagration, great pieces of mortar and rocks fly at the gathered guiders. The ground shakes so violently, great rends open the earth beneath the luckless guiders, killing many and wounding more. The Assemblage buildings begin to tumble, killing hundreds of students and servants.

Hit by flying debris, Joshan falls before he can stop the devastation. Haiden stands protectively over him when he spots the Mourna diving for Joshan, charging out of the sky intent on death with Balinar clinging to his back.

Van shoots a long arrow through the bird's neck and it plummets over the cliff, leaving Balinar to hang precariously onto the edge.

When Joshan regains consciousness, he finds Van standing over a terrified Balinar. Joshan pleads with the giant not to kill him. Van just shakes his head and, with an apology to Joshan, kicks the man off the cliff.

Trenara is unconscious and will not wake until the next morning, so Joshan tries to help as many as he can. The power is as dead in him as it is in everyone else. Thousands have died including Witen, the old Prelate.

When Joshan comes out to speak with the guiders they only seem to be interested in what they will do without the power.

"Sire, what will we do? Without the Crystal, we are beaten."

"The Crystal?" he spat viciously. "Is that what you think is gone? By the gods!" Joshan tightened his fists until they paled. "You have no idea what you have lost." He reached into his belt and held the golden sword over his head. It caught the sunlight to dazzle in his hands. The guiders gazed in wonder and fell to their knees before him.

"Here is the Crystal. Here is your power, your magic! Gaze upon it. Relish it. Worship it. But hear me… all of you. It is because you listened to the voice of deceit that now a few brave souls must fight for our existence. The Crystal travels south with me, to undo what you have done. While we are gone, think hard about the blood that must be spilled, and the good people who have to die because of it. Think well! And, if any of you have a shade of honor left or a thought you can call your own, consider this while they are dying. It is the hands of heroes that shape the world. It is fools that tear it down!"

Joshan strode to the ship without another word.

VISIT STONEGARDEN.NET PUBLISHING ONLINE!

You can find us at: www.stonegarden.net.

News and Upcoming Titles

New titles and reader favorites are featured each month, along with information on our upcoming titles.

Author Info

Author bios, blogs and links to their personal websites.

Contests and Other Fun Stuff

Web forum to keep in touch with your favorite authors, autographed copies and more!

LaVergne, TN USA
17 November 2009
164444LV00009B/97/P